CHRISTOPHER COLUMBUS
AND THE LOST CITY OF ATLANTIS

E.J. ROBINSON

Christopher Columbus

And the Lost City of Atlantis

Copyright © 2018 *Erik J. Robinson*
http://erikjamesrobinson.com

All rights reserved, including the right to reproduce this book, or portions thereof, in any form.

This is a work of fiction. Names, characters, places, and incidents either are the product of the author's imagination or are used fictitiously. Any resemblance to actual persons, living or dead, events, or locales is entirely coincidental.

❋ Created with Vellum

(ILLUMINATI PRESS)

Edited by Jessica Holland
Cover design by Jordan Grimmer

ALSO BY E.J. ROBINSON

The New Chronicles of Robinson Crusoe

Robinson Crusoe 2244
Robinson Crusoe 2245
Robinson Crusoe 2246

For Ric

FOREWORD

Growing up in the latter days of the twentieth century, I was taught like so many generations before me that Christopher Columbus was a hero who had discovered America. Turns out neither of those things are true. The Americas had, of course, previously been visited by the Vikings, and possibly others. And it's tough to "discover" a place that's inhabited by a million or so indigenous people. It's also impossible to describe any actions as heroic when they include subjugation and genocide.

So why write a story with Columbus as the protagonist? Two reasons. First, Columbus was well on his way to earning that heroic title up until his second journey to the Americas. After all, he had risen from humble means to gain the audience of kings and queens of Europe. He had also earned the honor of being the first to traverse the mighty Atlantic, something no seafarer before him would have ever dared dream possible.

Secondly, as Columbus's audacious journey in 1492 brought European expansionism west, it also ushered in a wave of explorers that would fully map out the seven continents and, by extension, the rest of the known world. In less than a century, the globe would become much smaller place, and with it, the myths that had enter-

FOREWORD

tained and frightened mankind for centuries would slowly begin to ebb away.

Christopher Columbus and the Lost City of Atlantis is what might have happened had Columbus taken a left in his journey instead of a right. If fabled places like Atlantis had truly existed, Columbus was such a man who might have gone in search of them, for all men have wanderlust in their blood. They dream of finding new frontiers to explore and new secrets to uncover. And if Columbus had had more adventurer in his blood than explorer, he might have found that his ultimate legacy lay in the past as much as in the future.

For more information on Columbus and his journeys, I recommend reading *Admiral of the Sea: A Life of Christopher Columbus* by Samuel Eliot Morison, *The Last Voyage of Columbus: Being the Epic Tale of the Great Captain's Fourth Expedition, including Accounts of Swordfight, Mutiny, Shipwreck, Gold, War, Hurricane, and Discovery* by Martin Dugard, or consult your local library.

EJR
August, 2018
Minnesota, USA

PROLOGUE

A burgeoning contingent of Janissary guards closed in on the thief from the courtyard below. Hunkering down beneath a minaret, he paused to catch his breath as his heart clamored like a butter churner thick with fat. He wasn't sure how he'd gotten turned around, although that sometimes happened when a job went south and hordes of armed soldiers made it their personal mission to hunt you down and slice you chin to cock. He'd never considered himself a particularly greedy man, but the truth was he was partial to both as long as he could remember. He'd hate to lose them now.

Unfortunately, the thief could hear guards scaling the roof back near the palace kitchens. And more hustled by below, as they rushed to cut off any possible exodus in front of him. He was lost. His odds of escape were dwindling. Without a doubt, he was in serious trouble.

Most men in his position might have withered there or made some crucial mistake. But he knew he was at his best when things were at their worst. The thought emboldened him as he looked around. Finally, he saw it. Between the trees to his left—the steeple of the Justice Tower, the smell of honey and cypress carrying in from the Bosporus beyond. And to his right, the clanging of markers bobbing in the Marmara. Just outside the breakwater, his ship and crew waited.

Relief flooded him. His escape was all but assured.

With a grin, the thief bolted to his right, only to feel a moment of delayed surprise when he crashed into the stained-glass dome and a flicker of dread as he plummeted into the shadows below.

Glass showered the darkened room as the thief hurtled through a canopy and landed with surprise in a sea of pillows as shrill screams assaulted his ears. Someone moved quickly to light a hanging lamp. As his vision returned, he saw he was surrounded by a dozen near-naked figures swathed in silk, their perfume infusing the air.

Dread and excitement grew in unison as he realized where he was.

The Imperial Harem.

Among the scantily clad beauties, one particularly ferocious and exotic woman stepped toward him, hand on hip, eyes lit with fire. The thief recognized her. The *Efendi Kadin*, the sultan's favored wife.

"You…" she stuttered, eyes wild. "You…came back!" She rushed into the thief's arms. This drew a wave of giggles from the other consorts, who were obviously aware of the dalliance between the two —and the cost if they were caught. But, when in Rome…or Istanbul as the case was.

The *Efendi Kadin*'s kiss came with a whispering of sweet words into the thief's ear as his eyes flitted around for sign of an exit. Then he heard the door to the outer chamber thrown open, followed by the rumble of heavy footfalls.

The sultan appeared, surrounded by four armed eunuchs. To the thief, the sultan was a sight. His lustrous kaftan was rumpled. The aigrette of heron plumes of his colossal turban was askew. His voice was thick with sleep. He looked over the women as they *salaamed* in unison, touching hearts and foreheads before bowing.

"What was that noise?" the sultan asked, blind to the thief.

The consorts' gazes turned to the *Efendi Kadin*, who snatched an arrow off the marbled floor. "This broke the window above, my Padishah!"

The sultan took the arrow, looked up at the shattered dome, and heard the furor outside. "Assassins."

With that single word, the eunuchs drew their halberds, pausing only after the sultan raised a hand. He had noticed blood on the floor. "Someone is injured!"

"It is nothing, lord of life," the *Efendi Kadin* said nervously. "A nick from the glass." "Which of my doves has been hurt? Is it you? You?"

Each woman was asked in turn. Each shook their head and receded one by one, until only a single woman was left. She was much taller than the others, her silk garments stretched tight over her large torso. She looked down, noticing the trail led straight to *her*. She swallowed.

The sultan frowned. "I do not recognize you."

The *Efendi Kadin* stepped forward nervously. "A new *odalisque*. Taken at sea this month past. Very shy, heart of my heart. I will see to her injury. She is beneath your concern."

The sultan dismissed the thought with a wave. He eyed the tall girl and licked his lips, entranced by those gray eyes peering out between veils.

"Don't be frightened, child," he said. "You are in very good hands."

The sultan reached one of those hands out and the girl playfully slapped it away.

The sultan laughed, surprised. "Spirited."

He reached out again. She slapped his hand away again. The sultan frowned. He reached out a third time, and when his hand was slapped away again, he slapped the girl across the face. To his astonishment, the girl slapped him back. Everyone gasped. The sultan was stunned. He yanked down her veil, and his mouth fell open as he recognized the thief.

"Evening, sire," the thief said, "apologies for this."

The thief grabbed the sultan, taking him as a shield, as he set a golden, bejeweled sword to the sultan's throat. The eunuchs froze in their tracks.

"That sword," the sultan cried, more concerned with it than its present location. "You stole it from my treasury. Give it back!"

"Impossible, I'm afraid. I need it. But if it's any consolation, I left all your other valuables unmolested." The *Efendi Kadin* cleared her throat and raised an eyebrow. The thief shrugged, chagrined. "Materially speaking."

The sultan sneered. "I knew you were dishonorable the moment I set eyes on you. You're nothing but a common thief!"

"Actually, I'm an *exceptional* thief," the thief said. "Though I consider myself more of an adventurer really. Thievery is merely a welcome perk of my calling."

"Release me now or, Allah help you, my guards will strip your bones from your flesh."

"These fruitless four?" The thief laughed. "Hardly worth the effort."

The thief pushed the sultan aside, ready to fight when the eunuchs suddenly parted, revealing a giant of a man. Ebony skin, muscled physique, red turban, and the biggest *kilij* sword ever seen. *Ever*. This was the *Kizlar Agha*, the head black eunuch.

"You were saying?" the sultan taunted.

The thief swallowed, quickly requiring his sultan shield. Outside, he heard more voices.

Several shadows appeared through the broken dome. Things were going from bad to worse. "Your prospects grow dim," the sultan mocked.

"Indeed. Let's lighten things up."

The thief swatted a hanging lantern with his sword, sending a spray of oil and fire over the eunuchs. As smoke and screams filled the air, he ran across a short table and dove through the arabesque screen of a low window.

He landed hard with a splash. Wincing, he rubbed his backside, which was wet with water from the Bath of the Sultan and Queen Mother. "A pool," he muttered. "It was supposed to be a pool."

Approaching torches drove him from the bath, through the Courtyard of the Concubines and Queen Mother, past an empty sentry post, and through the Aviary Gate into the second courtyard. Back through the figs, toward the wall, where he could almost taste saltwater and his freedom. Nothing could stop him now.

Except the dozen guards atop the wall. And their crossbows. Funny how crossbows had that effect.

He was racing back toward the palace now. Guards behind him. Guards to the north. Guards to the south. The thief saw the shape of a building, its two doors cracked back. He ran inside, disappearing in the darkness as two Janissary slammed the doors, trapping him within.

The thief listened to the guards' cheer. The falcons cornered their quarry. They clamored over who would kill the man and earn the sultan's praise. Maybe one or two of them would even earn wives from his harem. Then one particularly observant Janissary among them called for silence before uttering an odd word. The thief knew little of their language, but he recognized that word. In part because he wrote it on his map. Also, because it was written above the doors he entered seconds before. *Armory.*

The doors were blown open by the horse-drawn cart, shocking the guards on the other side. A few dove out of the way, but more stood gaping at the sight of the thief standing high atop the cart, cracking the reins with one hand while the other lit the fuse of a grenade from a standing torch. He lobbed it over his shoulder. Janissary fled as the blast echoed through the courtyard, usurped only by the thief's rebellious cry. Now, he was adventuring!

A rumble to the east quickly tempered his spirits as something emerged from the trees. The sultan's cavalry! The thief gulped. Too much adventure.

Reins snapping, horse frothing, the thief tossed grenades as fast as he could pluck and light them. Just as he passed a pavilion, he heard a *thump,* and the horse cried. The thief looked up to find the *Kizlar Agha* standing on the animal's back, his *kilij* already hurtling down. The thief pivoted, narrowly avoided the blade as it split the seat. The thief kicked the man hard between the legs. The eunuch didn't even flinch. The thief shrugged. "Had to be sure."

As the *Kizlar Agha* tore his *kilij* free, the thief drew the bejeweled sword from its scabbard. Blades clashed as the horse galloped madly across the lumpy earth, both men fighting to keep their feet as well as their heads. The *Kizlar Agha* slashed with strength. The thief parried with dexterity. The cavalry closed in.

The horse bounded over a low rise, and both men fell. The *Kizlar Agha* landed on top of the thief. As his heavy hands wrapped around the thief's throat, he saw the torch was broken, the flames already warming the scores of fuses. When he reached to push it back, the thief jabbed a thumb into his eye. The *Kizlar Agha* howled, grabbing a hold of the thief again. When the torch fell a second time, the thief pushed it back. This routine continued between strikes, gouges, and a runaway horse hurtling madly through the night.

High above the fray, the thief heard the shouts of the Janissaries manning the Imperial Gate. Truth is, he would too if an out-of-control horse and cart was lumbering in his direction. On one hand, the guards knew they'd be executed if he escaped. On the other hand, the cart was full of ordinance that would kill them anyway, so he was optimistic they'd open the gate.

Inside the cart, the *Kizlar Agha* managed to wrap both hands around the thief's neck, squeezing until darkness started to close in. Then, the *Kizlar Agha* looked up to see the half-opened doors of the gate. He raised his arms, but it was too late. The violent crash splintered the doors, shaking the very foundation of the Imperial Gate. For the briefest moment, the *Kizlar Agha* loosened his grip on the thief's neck, allowing the thief to clobber him with a grenade to the head. As the *Kizlar Agha* fell unconscious, the thief pushed him off, grabbed the bejeweled sword, and leaped for the injured horse, slashing its remaining harness and rig before hastening away from the palace. With a final look over his shoulder, the thief saw the cavalry rein to a stop behind the debris and the aimless cart rolling slowly forward with the unconscious *Kizlar Agha* inside.

The thief and horse sped down the winding, cobbled pathway that cut back along the cliffside and down to the mouth of the long quay. At the very end was a gleaming Turkish galley, the finest ship in the sultan's fleet. A dozen more like it were berthed along the shore, running all the way to the horn. But as the thief slapped the horse away, he ran not for one of those ships, but for a dinghy tied off underneath. His ship was waiting in the dark near the breakwater, several hundred feet away. At least he hoped it was still there. With his crew, anything was possible.

As his fingers worked to untie his own knot, the thief finally let out a giggle. He couldn't believe he succeeded. Granted, the palace was on fire, and he was nearly killed by fall, by spear, by sword, by arrow, by explosive blast, and by the hands of the largest, fruitless Nubian he'd ever seen, but outside of that, things went pretty much according to plan. He stopped to offer a quick prayer. "In the name of our Lord Jesus Christ, I do offer my humblest gratitude for your continued support. And, Lord, while I know pride is a cardinal sin, I would like to point out that a reputation bolstered by such a night's endeavors could go a long way to furthering the success of my—uh, I mean, *our*—long-term ambitions. Goals. Aspirations. Anyway, just a suggestion. In your heavenly name I pray, Amen."

Pleased with himself, the thief was about to return to the knot when he heard a clatter back near the shore. Up the cobbled slope, the horseless cart appeared, winding its way down the road, bumping along the outer walls, before it settled atop the hill leading down to the quay, the upstanding torch flickering in the wind.

"Then again, I've always said, anonymity is highly underrated."

The cart crested the hill and picked up speed as it thundered for the quay.

The thief cried out as his fingers desperately worked the rope. As the horseless cart bounded on the quay, he cursed and dove into the water, swimming away as fast as he could. He was fifty yards out when he looked back to see the horseless cart slowing down as it approached the end of the quay and the sultan's prized galley. At the very edge, it came to a halt.

"Well," the thief sighed, "that was anticlimactic."

Suddenly, a dazed figure rose from the cart. The *Kizlar Agha*. He looked around, saw his predicament, and started to laugh. Then the torch fell over, and he opened his mouth to scream.

The night erupted like Vesuvius in Pompeii. The sultan's prized galley exploded into a fireball, sending gouts of flame over the next two ships. As they burned, their fiery masts slammed into the decks of the neighboring ships. One by one, they set to fire until the night was lit like day.

Near the breakwater, the thief was drawn from the water and dropped onto the deck of a caravel. A peg-legged man pushed through the hardened crew.

"Cap'n," the man bellowed. "Did you get it? Did you find the treasure?"

Christopher Columbus pulled the lone bejeweled sword out and looked it over. "No. But I now know where it is."

CHAPTER ONE

The carrack cut upriver at a languid pace.
Columbus knew the waters of the Guadalquivir well enough to navigate it in the dark, but he appreciated the waning moon that lit their path. He saw it as an omen that God approved of his plan—or at least he was invested in the outcome. After all, God had shared more than a few laughs at Columbus's expense over the years.

He was worried about the crew. Since entering the Bay of Cádiz, they had been sighted and approached by two ships from the Spanish Navy. Only the Red Cross of the Order of Christ on their mainsail and the Spanish flag protruding from the gaff allowed them to pass unmolested. The absence of all other vessels had only increased the crew's grumblings.

In the eight months since Columbus had taken on the forty-four hardscrabble sailors from the port city of Palos, he'd yet to deliver on his promise of quick riches—or any riches for that matter. Instead, he'd jaunted around the Mediterranean on several unexplained—and increasingly dangerous—excursions, the last of which saw them brave the Aegean to travel to Istanbul. Columbus was a gifted enough navigator to evade Ottoman warships and the corsairs of the Knights of

Rhodes, but his unwillingness to share mission details with anyone had left them all on edge. Now that they were returning to Spain, he feared some of the crew might jump ship; or worse, inform the monarch he wasn't where he'd been ordered to wait.

"The men are nervous," Fanucio, the first mate, said as he hobbled up to the poop deck. "They're askin' if you got a plan."

"Of course, I have a plan," Columbus said. "Have I ever not had a plan? Granted, not all plans have been *en totalis*. Some come about in the midst of things. They develop, like a fine wine."

"Or vinegar?"

Columbus shrugged. "Vinegar has its uses too."

"Oh, indeed. My mother used it for pickling. 'This is a fine pickle you got us into,' she used to say."

"She said that?"

"Possibly. She said a great deal of things when I weren't around."

Columbus smiled faintly. Fanucio had been his second-in-command for nearly two decades. The man had a face like spoiled pudding, but he could always be counted on to put things into perspective. Whether that perspective made good sense was another matter.

"Well, your mother's preservation methods notwithstanding, you and the crew should rest assured. A plan is in place."

"Excellent. Shall I share it with the men?"

"Not presently, no."

"Right." The first mate hesitated. "And why is that?"

"Because if they heard it, they'd likely leap over the gunwales and swim for shore."

"Ah, so it's a *regular* plan. Understood."

"Just do that thing where you laugh as if you've heard the best news."

Fanucio hesitated to gauge his seriousness before he erupted in laughter, punctuated by several cuffs to his captain's shoulder. Columbus thought he might have overdone it, but the ruse appeared to work. Tension on deck dissipated, and the crew returned to folding sails and securing the rigging.

Columbus walked to the rail and leaned against it, taking in the shadowed plains of Andalusia. "We're so close, my friend. If all goes well tonight, we should have everything we need to realize our dreams. Revelry, renown, and riches, the credo of adventurers everywhere."

Fanucio cleared his throat and looked away.

"What?" Columbus frowned. "No good?"

He'd been trying to come up with a catchphrase history might remember him by, but so far nothing had borne fruit.

"Oh, it's a fine saying, Cap'n. Only they all start with the same letter, don't they?"

"Yes. It's called an alliteration."

"Ah-ha. And ain't you the one always says being illiterate is bad?"

Columbus rubbed his temples. "You're right. A catchphrase needs to come about organically. I'll keep working on it."

At that very moment, a shout rang out from the top of the mizzenmast. The ship was banking around a peninsula, and the sprawling city of Córdoba came into view on the port side. The riverbanks were lined with ships as far as the eye could see, lit by the unnaturally bright glow of a city in celebration.

"So, the rumors are true," Columbus whispered. "The Reconquista was a success. The Moors have been vanquished."

"So, it's a party then?"

"One for the ages, I suspect."

"It's a party!" Fanucio shouted to the crew, who roared in response.

"But not for us," Columbus said.

"Party's been canceled!" Fanucio shouted. "Apologies."

The crew groaned.

Columbus dashed for his cabin, where he stripped off his clothes and used a clean rag to wash himself. The trademark *tha-clunk, tha-clunk* of Fanucio's peg leg preceded him.

"Um, Cap'n? Since we're here, might I run a quick errand?"

"What errand?"

"Hortencia," Fanucio stammered. "I'd like to see her."

"The whore? I thought she died."

"No. The doctor was able to save her. Most of her, anyway."

"This isn't a good time. I need you to arrange for provisions. We have a long journey ahead of us."

"Wee problem there. See, last time we was here, we left the harbor master under questionable terms."

"What terms were those?"

"We stiffed him."

Columbus winced. "Tell him he'll have his due and more, but I want the ship turned southwest and ready to depart immediately upon my return. And you can send for Hortencia if you have the time. Just clean up once you're done."

"Course. Might I ask why we'll be needing to leave so quickly?"

"Eager to get underway is all."

"So, you're *not* planning a visit with the queen?"

"I am definitely not planning a visit with the queen."

But, of course, they both knew he was lying.

FANUCIO WAS EXCHANGING insults with the harbor master when Columbus strolled over the dock's roughhewn planks, muscles bulging beneath a white doublet and gold-trimmed cape. He had chosen a red and blue striped cap with tassels to wear because it was fashionable, and it hid his identity. He could do nothing about his sword. The Galician driver eyed it as Columbus stepped into his carriage and said but two words: the Alcázar.

As the gray andalusians clopped over the dusty cobbling of the Roman Bridge, Columbus took in the festive Spaniards who packed the zigzagging streets six or seven deep. Eight hundred years they had suffered under the yoke of the Moors. Now, they were free. Many waved flags, banners, and kerchiefs while others held oil lamps, all intent on bidding welcome to the dukes and duchesses, barons and baronesses, who had helped fund Spain's victory.

The odor of the mob was palpable, but when mixed with the food of street vendors and Spanish wine, it smelled of victory. Tattered troupers waded through the crowd, some playing bawdy tunes while others played hymns. It all blended into one inharmonious cacophony.

As Columbus passed the Albolafia waterwheel that once raised the water to the caliph's palace, he wondered how much would change for Spain in the years to come. While this was no longer a city of alabaster mosques with minarets of burnished gold, they were still part of the country's heritage. Columbus hoped some of it would remain.

The carriage let out behind the Alcázar gardens, which were widely known for their Mudejar splendor. Columbus had strolled them many times before, usually under the arm of some beautiful court maiden. Tonight, his shadow glided over the still reflecting pools alone.

As he passed through the crowded entrance, the explorer found the castle bustling with Spain's elite, dressed in the colorful draping attire of the day. Guests sipped libations and ate from banquet tables laden with a bounty for the ages. Succulent cuts of meat and wild game left a dizzying aroma in the air, as did the endless pastries, pies, and rice dishes that had Columbus salivating.

When he had first arrived at court years before, he'd been viewed as an uneducated foreigner. It didn't matter that he spoke more languages or had seen more of the world than the host of gentry. He was not Spanish. He was not nobility. And he had an annoying habit of bedding anything with a dress and a smile.

As the years passed, he amassed some influential friends, but looking over the crowd, he knew without a doubt those days were past. Half the room wanted his head for failing to deliver on ventures they'd backed. The other half had daughters and wives, all of whom, not ironically, liked to wear dresses and smiles.

Nobility. He hated the word and all it represented with a passion. What right does any man under God have cause to mark another as his lesser by birthright or bloodline alone? None that Columbus could reckon. To him, deeds defined one far more acutely than familial, political, or financial capital. Inheretence, whether in name and title, might bequeath some degree of power, but too often it was fleeting.

The mark of true worth—of a life to be remembered—could only be christened by history. And history had a terrible appetite. Effort and desire could not feed it alone. One had to be bold. One had to be reckless. One had to have vision. And, a dash of crazy never hurt. Columbus had those in spades. He knew it. And one day the nobles of the world would too.

But today was not that day. Today, Columbus needed anonymity. So, he stuck to the shadows as he slunk through the room, head and eyes down. Mum's the word. He nearly made it to the great hall when someone stepped into his path. The man was slightly shorter than the Genoese, but broad through the shoulders with thick curly hair and a long, broken nose that lent his face a haughty petulance made worse when he smiled.

"Christopher Columbus," Amerigo Vespucci said, loud enough to draw the attention of those around him. "Late to the party, as usual. Tell us, what historical discovery accounts for your tardiness on this occasion?"

Columbus knew Vespucci was a favorite of the king, but he found the man self-serving and unctuous. "Nothing historic, Signore Vespucci. I've merely found yet another explorer living in my shadow."

Someone sniggered, and Vespucci flushed.

"But to his good fortune, God has granted him with an effete physique, so the occupation shouldn't cause too much discomfort."

This time, several laughed. Vespucci's face turned red. The man's hand drifted toward his sword, but the realities of such a blunder must have struck him quickly because he clenched his fists and stepped close instead.

"Your humor won't avail you when *el Gran Capitán* and Signore de Cárdenas learn of your arrival. Or perhaps you'd like to meet with Grand Inquisitor Torquemada instead? I'm certain he would be quite interested to hear of your extracurricular—"

Vespucci looked away for a moment. When he looked back, Columbus had vanished.

Columbus continued through the crowded galleries. Just as he was passing the chapel, he felt a strange presence, as if someone was watching him. As his heightened instincts had saved his life numerous times over the years, he slowed long enough for a backward glance. There, he locked eyes with a short, hooded figure at the end of the hall. Columbus craned his head as people passed, only to find the figure gone.

Under the vaulted ceiling of the audience chamber, Spain's highest courtiers waited patiently to congratulate the king and queen on their victory at Granada.

Ferdinand of Aragon was a dour figure—dark and brooding—but few underestimated his cunning and skill in battle. He wore a carmoisine velvet cloak lined with sable, and a golden crown fixed to his brow. He, too, was rumored to have quite an appetite for women, and yet he and the queen proved a perfect match to rule together.

Queen Isabella of Castile was a woman of prudence, piety, and grace. Despite that, few spoke of her without mentioning her beauty. Unlike most Spaniards, she was fair skinned, with the strawberry blonde hair and blue-gray eyes that bespoke her Visigoth heritage. She was dressed in a bejeweled gown shimmering with pearls and looked more radiant than Columbus could ever remember. When her gaze locked onto his, her breath caught, though no one else seemed to notice.

When Columbus reached the front of the line, the herald called, "Cristóbal Colón of Genoa!"

A murmur ran through the room. Columbus bowed deeply before the king.

"Ah, Columbus," King Ferdinand said. "How is our intrepid explorer? Still dreaming of traversing the world in pursuit of fortune and glory?"

"All my endeavors are undertaken for the glory of the crown, Highness."

King Ferdinand smiled perfunctorily. "No doubt. And the coin of our coffers. Should we assume by your presence here that your petition for a westward route to the Indies remains intact? Or do you have a more fantastical destination in mind?"

Columbus was bending to kiss Queen Isabella's ring and failed to hide his mischievous grin. "Well, there is one dark continent I'd like to revisit."

The queen inhaled nervously, but King Ferdinand was oblivious.

"We shall receive you in the coming days," he said. "Enjoy the festivities."

Columbus bowed again and broke away.

Near the back of the room was a small alcove that hid a special door. As carefully as Columbus could, he opened it and slipped inside. Only as the door was closing did Columbus glimpse that same hooded figure watching him.

A single torch cast the vacant hallway in a dusty glow of stone and mortar. A mosaic of Alfonso XI split the stairwell that led down to the Moorish baths in the basement and the royal bedchamber above. Columbus leaned back and waited.

Less than half an hour later, the door opened a second time, and Queen Isabella slipped inside. She looked calm and serene as she approached the explorer, which was ironic considering how hard she slapped him.

"I should have your head for such insolence!" she said.

Columbus grinned. "Then you would be depriving the world of my second greatest asset."

Isabella fell on him with a passionate kiss. He took her in his arms and spun her against the stones, feeling the heat of her body as he pressed against her.

"Two years I've waited," she whispered, voice dripping with hunger.

"Then I won't torture you any longer."

Columbus took her by the hand and led her up the stairs.

THEY LAY PANTING IN BED, their hunger fed but not yet sated. The sheets were strewn aside, and their bodies glistened with sweat. Even the cool air that crept in from the tower's star-shaped vents failed to relieve them.

"I swear," Isabella whispered. "Had I not sworn to expel the Nasrid Dynasty from our lands, I would have fled with you ten years ago. Though you likely would have cast me off at the first port."

"A man only gives his heart once," Columbus said.

"Yes. And you gave yours to the sea long ago."

She'd missed the mark, but not by much. Still, Columbus heard something in her voice he'd never heard before. Pain. She should have been elated. Her devotion to God and Spain was absolute. It was a great rarity to find those in life who were willing to sacrifice everything for what they believed in, but so often those who did found at the end that they'd left nothing for themselves.

"What is it?" Columbus asked.

Maybe it was the tone with which he asked, but even in those dark surroundings, Columbus saw the queen's eyes well.

"I never told you this, but when my father passed, my half-brother Henry ascended to the throne. He was supposed to look after us—my mother, brother, and me. Instead, he sent us away to a very remote and very grim castle in Arévalo. The conditions were dire. We rarely had heat. At times, we went days without food. I might have fallen into despair had our mother not insisted we focus on God and education. As we had no formal teachers, we turned to the Franciscan monastery nearby. The monks lent us many books. Among my favorite stories were Aesop's Fables and the legends of King Arthur. But only one book changed my life forever. *La Poncella de Francia*, the story of Joan of Arc. Imagine being a wispy child whose only view of the world was seen through bars of a gilded cage. To read of a simple farm girl who—under word from God—rose to the heights of power to challenge the order of men. It became the model for my life. In all the days since, all I've ever really wanted to be was her."

"Sounds like a spirited girl. Is she available?"

"She was burned at the stake before you were born."

"Well, I do like the smoldering types."

When she turned, he thought she might hit him, but she kissed him and laid her head on his chest instead. "You remind me of her. You, too, were born of common means, but look how far you've come.

Self-educated. Driven. Fearless in a way so few are. Most men look upon the world and cower at its vastness—its boundless mysteries. You seek to reveal and master them. I envy you."

"Me? Why?"

"You are destined for great things."

If only she knew how much those words both strengthened and terrified him.

"You seem to forget, Your Grace, that only a month ago you accomplished what no Spanish king could in eight hundred years."

"I haven't forgotten," she said softly. "But if history has taught me anything, it's that every feat comes at a cost. For every decision, a price to pay."

Columbus suspected she was talking about them now.

"If you're feeling guilty because of us, I can tell you stories about your husband."

"There's no need. I've heard them all. Toda de Larrea. Joana Nicolau. Did you know he brought Aldonza Roig de Ibarra to war with us? As if dressing her as a soldier fooled anyone. In my youth, I had seen what calamity a poor monarch could wreak. My brother nearly left Spain in ruin. I vowed never to marry a man with similar vices. But men are men. I knew Ferdinand had fathered two children before we met. And though he swore these were an aberration—the missteps of youth—I chose to believe him because his vision of the future mirrored my own. But now the future has arrived, and many of my countrymen will suffer for it."

Columbus thought he understood. He'd heard grumblings that the crown might expel all Muslims and Jews from their lands. He had a hard time believing it, though Grand Inquisitor Tomás de Torquemada had already subjected many to conversion. By expelling the rest, he could seize their assets. For all men knew of war, they often forgot the most damning costs came after it was lost or won.

"Enough maudlin talk," Isabella said. "Tell me of your most recent exploits. And spare me the claims you were at La Rábida as we bid you. I know the odor of brine when I smell it."

"It's ironic that you mentioned stories," Columbus said as he slipped on his pants and moved across the room. He approached an ornate bookshelf that held a library of old texts and velum manuscripts. He ran his finger across the spines, noting the works of the masters—Seneca, Prudentius, St. Augustine, Gregory, and Jerome.

"For they are where my tale begins. Eighteen months ago, I was in Egypt searching for a portal to the Field of Reeds when I stumbled upon an ancient ruin, recently plundered. But in the thieves' haste to escape, they overlooked a scroll that contained a tale of *Sekhet-Aaru*, but unlike any version I've ever heard described before. It spoke of an island civilization to the west, both ancient and advanced. An empire of great wealth and terrible power."

"You speak of Atlantis."

"Yes. You're familiar with it?"

"As I said, I enjoy myths."

"I, too, believed it a myth. Then I heard a story from a spice trader about a temple in India that had also been robbed of a petrified, sandalwood flute—centuries old—with carvings that told of the destruction of a similar city. The raiders were said to be foreigners and bore a striking resemblance to those seen in Egypt. I searched other libraries throughout my travels only to find that each place I looked, someone had beaten me to it. And then, at last, I found a detailed description of an artifact that was believed to contain a map to Atlantis. I traced it through numerous hands only to learn it had been looted by Ottoman sailors and taken to the sultan's palace in Constantinople."

"So much for that. Wait, you didn't—"

Isabella leaned forward, riveted. All the while, Columbus continued to peruse the library. Latin, Roman History, Catechism, heraldry, and philosophy.

"I made my way there under the guise of a Florentine trader and slipped into the palace in the dead of night. Yet when I finally reached the treasury, I discovered the artifact wasn't there. I questioned one of the guards. He told me it had been traded recently."

"Traded? To whom? For what?"

"For this," Columbus said, pulling a golden sword from under the folds of his robes. Isabella leaped from the bed and snatched it from his hands.

"This is my sword!" she cried. "It should be in the Royal Chapel of Granada. How did the Moors come by this? Who stole it?"

"No one, I'm afraid. You see, the thieves I spoke of—the ones who left clues wherever they traveled—they all bore the same symbol. Your husband's crest."

Queen Isabella reacted with a sharp intake of breath.

"I learned of other artifacts," Columbus continued, "both purchased and stolen, all shipped to Spain under the secrecy and security of the Crown."

"And, what? You believe this mystery ends with my husband?"

At last, Columbus smiled. He found the book he'd been searching for.

"No, Your Grace. I believe it ends where it first began—with Plato."

Columbus set a finger to the top of the spine of Plato's *Timaeus* and pulled. The fall of a tumbler echoed through the room. When the bookshelf retreated inward, Queen Isabella gasped.

CHAPTER TWO

The stairwell was dark and narrow, forcing Columbus to stoop as he wound upward. In his left hand, he carried a single candle, its flickering light laboring in the darkness.

With each step, Columbus felt his pulse quicken, the pounding in his ears fueled with nervous excitement. Would he find the map at last? He tried to temper his emotions. He had been disappointed so many times before, and yet something told him he was on the precipice of a genuine discovery, one that could radically change his life—possibly the world—forever.

Queen Isabella quietly kept pace behind him. The only sound being the pad of her naked feet and the rustle of the silken bedsheets with which she'd cocooned herself. It had been clear the moment Columbus revealed the secret door that she'd had no idea of its existence. For a woman who despised secrets, one in such proximity to her betrothal bed must have felt like a stinging betrayal. He almost told her to go back then and forget what she'd seen, to put it behind her and move on with her life. And yet he knew that was an impossibility. She needed to see what was behind the door as much as he did. Maybe more.

The top of the stairs spilled out onto a small landing that disappeared into the darkness. Columbus retrieved a lantern from a hook and lit it before passing it to Isabella. Then, he entered the room in search of others.

The windowless chamber came to life with a golden glow. When Columbus finally turned to take it all in, his breath seized in his chest. Feet rooted to the floor, the adventurer could only stare and marvel. *This is it*, he thought. *The haul I've been waiting a lifetime for.*

Columbus had seen his share of treasure rooms. Tombs loaded with gold and jewels. Fortified vaults full of plundered riches. This was different. It was more museum than repository, with objects representing vast swaths of lands, cultures, and epochs. There was no visible cohesion to the lot. The faded tapestry hung on the wall stood in stark contrast to the stone tools displayed atop a plinth. The cracked and broken vases that filled one wall of shelves appeared a thousand years older than the rusted spear tip nestled in a bed of silk.

Time stretched as Columbus took it all in. He startled when Isabella spoke, her eyes as round as saucers. He'd forgotten she was still there.

"All these years I never knew," she muttered.

Columbus was almost expecting her to thank him for the revelation. She slapped him a second time instead.

"That is for taking me under false pretenses."

Columbus rubbed his tender cheek and tipped his head. "If it makes you feel better, Highness, I have never taken a woman under any other."

Isabella simmered and turned to leave. Columbus caught her by the hand. He saw she was genuinely hurt. That hadn't been his intention.

"You know I could have come straight here instead of navigating that mess downstairs?"

"So, why didn't you?"

"I wanted to see you. And I thought you needed to know. To see this."

He let her anger subside before he walked deeper into the room. She followed, curiosity overweighing her anger. The collection *was* stunning, the pieces unlike either had seen. Queen Isabella paused when Columbus stopped in front of a brass bust of an older man.

"Plato was the first to write of Atlantis in *Timaeus* in 360 B.C. He said his father related stories of the island from others who had kept them for generations. Most of his peers scorned him for it, even suggesting he made it up, but he wasn't the type to believe in fancy."

Had Columbus days to peruse the room, he might have pored over each object in detail. Unfortunately, time was not on his side. The party downstairs remained in full swing, but for how long? There were too many guards on high alert, too many curious people lurking about. He had to find the map quickly. He moved through the room, scanning and dismissing items until he finally found what he was looking for.

The bronze disk was the size of a military shield and sat on a wooden pedestal. Raised letters of some indiscernible language were etched across its surface, swirling in toward the large crystal at its center. He was mesmerized.

"This is a most curious fashion," Isabella said.

Columbus turned. She was standing in front of a tattered skirt embroidered with stick figures.

"You have a keen eye, Highness. It's called a peplum. Created for the annual Panathenaea Festival in Athens to celebrate Athena's victory over Atlantis."

"Is that significant?"

"You remember I told you Plato was the first to write of Atlantis?"

"I hope so. It was minutes ago."

"The Panathenaea originated one hundred years before Plato was even born."

Isabella looked back at the skirt, stunned. If true, there wasn't a museum in the world that wouldn't have featured one of these pieces as their main attraction.

"One hundred and twenty-five, actually," a deep voice said behind them.

Columbus and Isabella whipped around. In the entrance stood a smug-looking Amerigo Vespucci next to a glowering King Ferdinand with several royal guards behind. Columbus cursed himself for not hearing their approach.

"You see, My King," Vespucci sneered, "even now the libertine seduces the queen for the treasures I have claimed for you."

King Ferdinand glanced at his wife dispassionately, suggesting he would deal with her later. Then he spoke to his guards. "Kill him but leave his head unblemished. I want to hear the lamentations of maidens ring throughout the night when I fix it to a spike on the Roman Bridge."

As the Royal Guards stepped forward, Columbus grabbed Isabella and pulled her in front of him. In his opposite hand, he held a small glass globe that appeared to be made of jade.

"I wouldn't do that if I were you," Columbus said.

"What is that?" Vespucci asked.

"A little something from the Orient. It may look benign, but I assure you it packs quite the punch."

As Vespucci hesitated, King Ferdinand stepped forward, incensed.

"You dare flaunt your baubles in my wife's face?"

"Wouldn't be the first time," Isabella muttered.

"I apologize, Your Grace," Columbus said. "But you leave me no choice. The queen will continue to be my captive unless we can come to an agreement."

"What agreement?" King Ferdinand snarled.

"We both believe Atlantis exists. You wish to claim it for yourself and your kingdom. I know for certain I'm the only person on Earth who can find it. I will agree to do that for you…in exchange for ten percent."

"Ten percent!" Ferdinand balked.

"And the title Viceroy of the Seas."

"Is that *all*?"

Columbus pursed his lips. "Admiral of the Spanish Fleet has a nice ring to it too."

"He promised the expedition to me!" Vespucci cried.

"Silence!" King Ferdinand shouted.

"Fine. As I find my current bargaining position tenuous, I'll amend my offer. All I ask is a single treasure of my choosing."

"And if I refuse?" Ferdinand asked.

"Not every empire has your scruples. Portugal, for example, does have a bigger fleet. And I am on first-name basis with King João."

"Did you bed his wife too?"

Columbus hesitated a moment. Isabella glared and then shook her head. "Your infantile insouciance is appalling."

"I don't know what that means, but thanks," Columbus said with a wink.

"He's bluffing," Vespucci said. "He would never harm the queen."

"I agree," King Ferdinand said before turning to his guards. "Kill him."

Queen Isabella gasped as Columbus's hand tightened around her waist. He whispered for her to close her eyes.

She did just as Columbus hurled one of the jade orbs at the king's feet. It exploded hot white phosphorous that momentarily blinded everyone. Columbus whipped his heavy robe off, grabbed the bronze disk from its pedestal, and slung it over his shoulder before sweeping Isabella into his arms. "Until next time, *mi amor.*"

The kiss was quick but electric. Isabella fell to the floor, breathless, as Columbus shouldered through the guards and ran down the stairs. King Ferdinand howled, "After him!"

THE CLAMOR of steel was hot on Columbus's heels as he burst into the audience chamber only to find it empty. The alarm had been raised, and he heard more soldiers approaching from the hall. Columbus dashed back into the servant's corridor just as Vespucci appeared, his shimmering blade biting into the wall where Columbus's head had been a moment before. Vespucci tore it free as Columbus fled down the hall.

The kitchen staff was busy cleaning when Columbus bounded into the room. As he swept pans and dishes off the tables to slow his pursuers, Vespucci was nimble enough to evade them, unlike the guards, who slipped on the wet tiles and went down in a heap.

Columbus burst into a narrow courtyard, making hastily for the rear gate. He was halfway across the yard when more guards appeared in front of him, crossbows rising. Columbus heard the bolts whistle overhead as he leaped onto a low fountain and vaulted up some empty wine casks before rolling over the lip of the roof.

Vespucci shouted orders from the yard as he kept pace with Columbus above. Columbus knew if he could reach the gardens, he could easily vanish in the crowd. From there, making it to the docks would be easy. But nothing was ever that easy. The top of a ladder appeared in front of him. He skidded to a halt a second before an arrow bounced off the tiles at his feet. He spun to see three guards atop the Tower of the Dove. One held a lantern, relaying Columbus's movements, while his two companions shot arrows at him. *The hat,* Columbus mused. *Only something so ridiculous could bring this kind of bad luck.*

Columbus serpentined across the roof and leaped through a narrow embrasure, landing on a long rampart that ran the length of the castle, right into the path of two spearmen. The first charged with a shout. Columbus knocked his spear tip into the ground and used the man's momentum to catapult him over the side of the rampart, screaming as he plunged into one of the pools below. The second spearman looked up as Columbus drew his sword and winked. The spearman turned and ran.

More arrows skipped off the stone battlements as Columbus took off again. He slung the bronze disk over his back moments before arrows clanged off it. Then, he drew two more jade globes and tossed them, creating just enough smoke to obscure himself. He was mere feet away from the rear stairwell door when it burst open and Vespucci appeared.

"Now, I have you," Vespucci growled.

He charged with a snarl, sword slashing wildly from left to right. Columbus backpedaled, finding it difficult to maneuver in the narrow rampart. There was little doubt Columbus was the better swordsman, but his style was predicated on craftiness—on outfoxing his opponents. The feints and tricks he was used to using would not work here. And with every second he spent engaged with Vespucci, it gave more time for the royal guards to close in behind him. He needed to do something quickly.

Columbus's eyes widened as he looked over Vespucci's shoulder and shouted, "Your Grace!"

Vespucci instinctively turned, and Columbus took two steps and buried his foot between Vespucci's legs. The sound that escaped his lips mirrored that of a baby bird falling from its nest. It was pitiful, and utterly hilarious. As the man curled into a fetal ball, Columbus leaned down to pat him on the cheek.

"I can't believe you fell for that," he chuckled.

He stepped toward the door but heard more guards hammering up the steps. When he turned, he found the second spearmen had returned, this time with reinforcements. He was trapped and took a moment to sigh. *Why can't it ever be easy?* He clambered atop the battlements and ran toward the soldiers, screaming. They froze just long enough for him to leap and latch onto the banner hanging over them. As he swung across the open courtyard, he felt that familiar thrill. *This is what it means to be alive!* Then, the banner ripped, and he thought, *This is what it means to fall.*

He hit the roof and slid to the edge, his fingernails cracking as he clawed himself to a stop. To his surprise, he saw someone had saddled a white Andalusian to a rail right beneath him.

"I guess fortune really does favor the bold," Columbus said as he leaped. The horse moved, and Columbus landed hard on his duff. "Oof. Apparently, horses do not."

Columbus scampered atop the horse and kicked for the open postern gate. He thought he was scot-free when the portcullis began grinding down. Columbus was about to yank the reins when a dagger sailed out of nowhere and skewered a rope to a post. The gate halted mid-descent, letting Columbus slip underneath it. He glanced back, wondering where the dagger had come from. All he saw was a small cowled figure disappearing into the shadows.

The back road wound down toward the marketplace and was still bustling with people when Columbus saw a blur to his left. He ducked as a second horse soared over a berm, its hooves scuttling across the cobbles as it landed.

The rider looked over and sneered.

Vespucci.

Columbus spurred his horse faster, but Vespucci fell in quickly behind him.

Drunken pedestrians shouted as the pair shot through the busy market, sending bodies scrambling and overturning food carts.

Vespucci pulled even with Columbus. "The king has offered a bounty for your head. One hundred thousand maravedis! And I plan to collect it."

His smile was short-lived. As Columbus's hand shot out with a blade, Vespucci clenched, as if expecting to feel its bite. Instead, Columbus's hand came away holding Vespucci's bulging purse.

"Then you won't be needing this!"

Vespucci howled. He pulled his sword and slashed out. Columbus muscled the bronze disk to his shoulder in defense. The horses collided and shrieked as the chase led down narrow streets, Columbus shouting to prevent people from getting trampled.

The bazaar emptied out at a stone staircase. Both men vaulted down it, colliding again and again. Their horses were wild-eyed and frothing at the mouth when they reached the main street and came into view of the river.

Vespucci knew Columbus would likely have men waiting at the Roman Bridge, so he slapped his horse's hindquarters with the sword until he pulled even with Columbus again. To his surprise, Columbus was smiling.

"What are you grinning at?" Vespucci shouted.

Columbus nodded ahead. Vespucci's head shot up to find a large cart straight in front of him. With no room to turn, he pulled the reins with all his might. The horse's hooves slid across the cobbles, and Vespucci flew ass over teakettle right into the cart's prodigious payload of manure.

Columbus wheeled to a stop as Vespucci shot up, repulsed; only the whites of his eyes were discernible through the cloak of dung.

"Poor Amerigo," Columbus tsked. "Once again I see your navigational skills have led you to shit."

Vespucci seethed as Columbus rode away, laughing.

Once across the Roman Bridge, Columbus saw soldiers gathered at the dock entrance. Unsure if they were from the castle, he headed for the hill above the river where a wooden crane held a net full of provisions over the Santa Maria. He was trying to formulate a plan when he was spotted. Soldiers ran in his direction.

Desperate, Columbus looked around and saw an old, rotting wooden catapult positioned toward the river.

"As you know, Lord, I love excitement, but I'm starting to wonder what kind of point you're trying to make."

A rifle shot buzzed over Columbus's head, providing all the motivation needed to leap into the catapult's bucket. Exhaling nervously, he made the sign of the cross, and cut the rope.

* * *

FANUCIO WAS PACING the deck when he heard a keening wail, followed by a grunt as something struck the cargo net overhead. He held up a lantern.

"Oh, evening, Cap'n. No carriage to be had?"

"No, no," Columbus squeaked, fingers desperately locked onto the net. "It's just such a blissful night, I thought I'd take in the stars."

Fanucio winced as Columbus lost his grip and fell hard to the deck.

"Take 'em in better down there, do ya?"

Columbus groaned. A second later, the cargo net snapped. Columbus rolled out of the way just before the provisions crashed down.

"Right," Columbus said, leaping to his feet. "About that quick launch..."

"There is the small matter of payment first," Fanucio said,

chocking a thumb toward the group of armed dockhands standing on the quay.

Columbus tossed Vespucci's purse. "I believe this should bring us current."

The harbormaster nodded, and his party walked away.

"Now, let's—" Columbus paused when he saw the crew. "Who are they?"

Fanucio looked at the men, most drunk or asleep.

"They're the new crew."

"What happened to the *old* crew?"

"Gone," he said before whispering, "Pay dispute."

"Ahh. And you dug up this lot where?"

"Lying about the docks."

"I'll bet. Well, beggars can't be choosers. Let's launch."

"Aye." Fanucio relayed the orders. The drunken crew stumbled to their feet, listlessly drawing lines and railing sails as Fanucio looked back down the quay. He hesitated when he thought he saw a small shadowed figure move aboard the back of the ship before dismissing it as nothing more than paranoia.

Just as Fanucio turned, a shout resounded from someone running down the dock.

"Oy!" Fanucio suddenly cried. "It's the visitor I've been waiting for."

Columbus turned, surprised to see only a balding old man hobbling toward them.

"I didn't think it was possible," Columbus said, "but Hortencia has gotten decidedly uglier since we were last here."

"That ain't Hortencia. *He*'s a cobbler, best in Spain. I paid him two years ago to craft me a new foot. Look, it's in his hand!"

The elderly man waved the wooden foot as he hobbled for them, unaware men on horseback were galloping hard across the Roman Bridge for the same destination.

"Push off, now!" Columbus shouted.

The new crew responded. Only Fanucio remained at the gunwale, shouting for the cobbler to throw his foot. The old man wound back, but before he could release it, he was hit by the first rider. The wooden foot sailed through the air. Fanucio lurched out to catch it, but the foot slipped through his fingers. He groaned pitifully as it splashed into the water below.

As the ship pulled away, Vespucci's horse skid to a halt at the end of the dock. His eyes simmered with fury. Something told Columbus he would see the man again.

"Where to, Captain?" asked a morose Fanucio, his peg leg rapping the deck as he sidled up beside him.

"South to the Mediterranean and then west through the Pillars of Hercules. We're heading west, my friend. Across the Atlantic."

"The Atlantic?" Fanucio gasped. "B-but no one's ever crossed it and lived."

Columbus held up the bronze disk, his fingers running over the raised lettering. "Then, we shall be the first."

"But, Cap'n," Fanucio whispered, "there be sea serpents out there. And the edge of the world."

"My friend, if we see a single sea serpent on this journey, I will not only buy you a new foot, but I'll have it crafted from gold."

The first mate sulked. "Lot of good it'll do me in some leviathan's belly." He looked back longingly over the glow of Córdoba. "Suppose we'll be back one day?"

Columbus shrugged. "Depends on the political climate."

Fanucio snorted. "Funny how every time we visit a country with a queen, I hear them same words. What's really waiting for us out there?"

Columbus turned hungrily toward the horizon. "Our destiny."

* * *

ON THE DOCK, Vespucci watched the *Santa Maria* depart down the Guadalquivir and slip away in the night. Behind him, one of Ferdinand's many generals appeared, stepping only as close as the smell of dung would allow him.

"Those ships," Vespucci said, pointing to two small caravels nearby. "Who do they belong to?"

"*La Niña* belongs to Juan Niño of Moguer," the General replied. "And *La Pinta* belongs to Cristóbal Quintero. Why?"

"I want them confiscated under orders from the king and prepared immediately for departure."

"Begging your pardon, Signore, but it will take days to man and provision them."

"Conscript the crew and appropriate everything else you need. I want to depart by dawn. First thing tomorrow we set sail, and I swear on my life, I will return with the head of Christopher Columbus or not at all."

CHAPTER THREE

The sun was stifling, and the waters becalmed from horizon to horizon. What few fibrous clouds were visible at dawn had abandoned the sky in favor of cooler climates, leaving behind an expanse of cerulean blue as beautiful and treacherous as the very sea it lorded over below.

Columbus wiped the sweat from his brow before he trudged over the withering deck to the bitácula to flip through the pages of the sunbaked Master's Log. Picking up quill and ink with his sweaty hands, he hastily scribbled:

Thursday, 24 September 1492. Skies clear. Ocean still. No wind.

It was the eighth such entry in a row.

They had been at sea fifty-two days, and only a handful of them hadn't made Columbus want to pull out his hair or drink himself into a stupor. The journey began inauspiciously enough when the ship's rudder came loose three days after they'd set sail, forcing Columbus to alter course south to the Canary Islands for repairs. Once docked, Columbus learned the rudder had been sabotaged. He shouldn't have been surprised. The 'misfortune' had come shortly after announcing his intention to cross the Atlantic.

Most sailors of the day called the Atlantic the 'ocean dark.' Legends said it had devoured a thousand ships since time immemorial and sent legions of men to their graves. What few men were foolish enough to speak of it claimed it was as fickle as a woman and as pitiless as a God. And though none would ever come close to grasping its vast mysteries or boundless reach, every seaman worth his salt knew a day or two on its waters without sight of land was enough to drive you mad.

Every seaman but one.

To Columbus, the Atlantic was no different than any of God's great wonders. Take one of the mountain ranges of Europe, for instance. The Alps or the Pyrenees. Imposing? Yes. Challenging? Of course. But they could be conquered if one had the proper tools, a capable plan, and the will to see the job through. Throw in a dash of luck and the deed was all but guaranteed. Or at least the odds slanted in your favor. It was difficult to balance the ledger when you'd been operating on the wrong side of the books for so long.

Unfortunately, luck had been in short supply since leaving Spain. First, the sabotage to the ship. Then, it was discovered the harbormaster had sold them spoiled provisions. If all that wasn't bad enough, the day they reached the Canaries, their damn mountain, the Tenerife, erupted in flames, spewing volcanic ash as far as the eye could see, Talk about ill omens. Seamen were a superstitious lot. When the crew culled these ominous events together, they decided they would be better to put off in Gomera and enjoy the local wine and whores until they could hire on with whatever ships were returning to Spain. At that point, any talk of gold, gems, spices, and pearls was fruitless. Columbus was at his wit's end.

Ultimately, it was Fanucio who saved the day. And it wasn't his usual verbal lashing that changed the crew's minds. Neither did he question their loyalty or bravery, but instead, he simply raised a tankard and gave a toast.

"To Columbus, who bedded the queen. May the king's call for his head—and ours—fall on deaf ears!"

As one might expect, this news didn't exactly endear Columbus to the men. In fact, more than a few thought Columbus's head—pinned to the bow of the ship—might have been a good show of contrition for those looking to return to the good graces of the monarchy. But, in truth, how could you not admire a man who seduced queens in every port? If the mighty Atlantic was to hold any sailor in its favor, why not one as daringly brave and as recklessly asinine as Christopher Columbus?

And so, it was decided.

Their departure from the Canaries began with a bang. Or several to be exact, as a cavalcade of cannonballs spotted the indigo waters all around the *Santa Maria* as she tucked tail and hastened away with yet another cache of ill-gotten provisions, including ten barrels of the finest African wine money could buy.

September sixth marked their final exodus from land on what would become their grand exploration oeuvre. For a week, the men were leaping from the rigging, so laced on wine and good cheer that they sang the Benedictine hymn "Salve Regina" until their voices ran hoarse and they fell to the deck for slumber, only to wake in the morning covered in piss and vomit, eager to do it all again.

They made good time, catching something Columbus called the trade winds. By mid-week, they were logging an average of twenty leagues a day. Once, over a twenty-four-hour period, they even did sixty. With only the occasional drizzle to wet the decks, the weather was as mild and pleasant as a seasoned Viennese whore. It reminded Columbus of Andalusia in April. Soon, the crew began calling out the sighting of birds—tunnies and wagtails. Everyone was certain land was near.

It wasn't until the ship came upon a fen of rockweed that the tenor of the men changed. The morass of sorrel kelp clung to the barnacles on the side of the ship, prompting more leaks in the hull from where shipworms had feasted. Almost simultaneously, the winds abated, and the supervening heat became so oppressive, no one dared to go below deck. The crew began grumbling. Optimism faded.

Then the wine had run out.

Columbus had been dead reckoning their course by the sun, leaving him nearly blind when he returned to his cabin each night.

There, he did his best to pour over his rutter, his secret maritime handbook in which he'd calculated the path to Atlantis using the bronze disk. He hadn't been able to decipher the words etched across it, though he had ferreted out a series of numerical values that he took as suggested longitude and latitude. When they finally arrived at the pre-determined location, Columbus ordered the sails lowered as he enthusiastically scanned the horizon for any sign of land. There was none.

Columbus decided to wait.

As the days passed, the grumblings grew louder. Then, the wind abandoned them completely. They were in the doldrums and the heat was rising, making it difficult for the men to sleep on deck and impossible to sleep below.

Fanucio kept the crew busy, but even he couldn't ease the tension that was brewing. On deck, the men deferred to Columbus as usual, but in private, they began questioning their commander's competence as a navigator. Realizing they had been sold a bill of goods without the goods, they debated locking him in chains and returning to Spain hat in hand. A few even suggested they toss Columbus overboard to let the sea sort him out.

Life aboard the *Santa Maria* was looking dour.

Columbus began to lose sleep. He doctored the logbook in hopes the men wouldn't think they'd come as far as they had. It didn't work. He scoured over the bronze disk day and night, mouthing his vespers as he did. He was desperate. He needed something to happen.

The rap of Fanucio's peg leg echoed across the deck as he made his way to the forecastle. He whistled as he walked, using a whittling knife to fashion a new foot from a piece of wood. Several of the carpenters had offered to do it for him, but he refused for fear of being indebted to someone. He should have reconsidered. The piece he'd been working on for a month looked like two sperm whales trying to copulate.

Fanucio cleared his throat. "A word, Cap'n?"

Columbus looked up from the bronze disk. His first mate had dark circles under his eyes. Columbus was sure his were worse.

"What is it?"

"Crew's getting antsy. Twenty-two days out, ya drop sail in the middle of nowhere. And now with the wind... We been here eight days."

"I can count."

"Aye, and so can they. Number of sleepless nights; meals ya missed. There's been talk."

"Talk?" Columbus heard something in his first mate's voice. "What about?"

"You. Your behavior; the way you stare at that dish day and night."

"This dish, as you call it, holds the key to the treasure of all treasures."

Fanucio fought the impulse to roll his eyes. "If you say so. It's not like we're low on rations or morale. Or need to worry over the Spanish Navy breathing down our necks."

"My neck is as cold and dry as yours."

The truth was both their necks were covered with sweat, but Fanucio knew what he meant.

"Sir, between you and me," Fanucio said, leaning in after glancing around, "they keep bringing up *the word*."

"The word?" Columbus frowned.

"The very one."

Columbus waited for him to elaborate. "Are we talking about the same word?"

"Is there more'n one frightens a sailor to his roots?"

"I can think of a few, actually."

Fanucio hooked his thumbs into his belt and tugged at it. "I been a sailor all my life. I know for a fact there's just the one. But for sake of transparency, maybe we should whisper 'em together like, to make sure we're on the same page."

"On a count of three?"

"Agreed. One. Two. Three—"

"Sodomy," Columbus blurted out alone.

Fanucio blanched as if quirt-lashed. "Oh. That is terrifying."

"What? You didn't say your word!" Columbus snapped. "We agreed on the count of three."

"I was on the cusp, but you beat me to it."

"How could I beat you to it? Counting to three is always the same. One. Two. Three. State your business."

"Begging your pardon, Cap'n, but where I come from, its one. Two. Three. *Pause*. Then comes the business."

"Pause? Pause?! I've never heard of any such thing. Why would anyone in their right mind pause before doing their business?"

Fanucio mulled the question. "Gas?"

Exasperated, Columbus said, "Tell me your word, damn it."

"Mutiny."

"Mutiny! Right. Of course. I was only joking about…" Suddenly, the gravity of that word hit him. *Mutiny*. His first mate was right. That was a terrifying proposition. Columbus felt like he'd been waiting his entire life for a race to get underway and here he was about to stumble within a few strides of the starting line. There was only one thing to do.

"Assemble the crew," Columbus ordered. "All hands on deck. We need to nip this in the bud here and now."

Fanucio relayed the orders. As the crew gathered, Columbus saw resentment in their eyes. He knew he would only get one chance at this. Thankfully, one man hoisted high atop the mast in a boatswain's chair was struggling to get down. It bought Columbus some much-needed time.

"So, what's the plan?" Fanucio whispered.

"I'm still working on it."

"'Haps some merriment?"

Not a bad idea, Columbus thought. "What do you suggest?"

Fanucio nodded to two diminutive figures emerging from below deck. They were dark-skinned foreigners called Pygmies. Columbus had won them in a game of chance, and yet they didn't crew or speak any of the common tongues.

"Your wee friends over there."

Columbus eyed the Pygmies, who were dressed in full African regalia and looking strangely carefree.

"Monday and Tuesday?"

Fanucio shook his head. "Never did savvy why you named 'em after days of the week."

"Because I captured them on Good Friday, but somehow naming a savage 'Friday' didn't sound right."

"Hmm. Maybe they could put on a show. Do they sing or dance?"

"Sing or dance? They're warrior chieftains."

This time, Fanucio snorted.

"All due respect, it's kind of hard to fear those big as children."

Columbus's eyebrow lifted. "Is this your new foot?"

Fanucio held the sculpted wood aloft with reverence. "Aye. It is almost done. Beautiful, isn't she?"

Columbus took the foot and looked it over. "It has four toes."

"Ahh. I knew a man of your ilk would 'preciate authenticity."

Columbus rolled his eyes before shouting to the Pygmies in a language full of clicks and grunts. Then, without hesitation, he tossed the foot high into the air. Faster than a viper, one of the Pygmies launched a short spear with incredible speed, pinning the wooden foot to the mast with a *thwang*.

Fanucio gaped, horrified.

The Pygmies laughed and chatted in their tongue.

"*Excellent toss,*" Monday said. "*The right mix of dexterity and fervor. Bravo.*"

Tuesday shrugged. "*You know how these savages like when we put on a good show.*"

As they tittered, Fanucio muttered, "I spent three weeks on that."

Columbus clapped a hand on his shoulder. "Fanucio, I did you a favor. That thing looks as if it would disintegrate at the first drop of rain. What did you craft it out of? Driftwood?"

"Mahogany, from the ship reserves."

"Oh. Well, I promised to replace it."

"In gold, if I'm not mistaken."

"Yes, but only if you spot a sea serpent. Have you seen one rise lately?"

"No, but another month without ladies, and I 'spect we'll see many."

Fanucio signaled one of the crew to retrieve the foot—what was left of it anyway. He was a youthful lad, lithe and lanky, who wore a turban around his head to stave off the heat. Columbus didn't recognize him.

"Who's the whelp?" Columbus asked.

"Don't go by a Christian name," Fanucio answered. "Crew calls him 'Boy.' Came on in the Canaries, I think."

"Looks feeble."

"To the eye, mayhaps. But he's no shirker. Scales the mast like a monkey and has the eyes of an eagle. I'll vouch for him."

Columbus suddenly had an idea. "Would you say he's faster than Pedro?"

"Half the crew's named Pedro, Cap'n."

"The quick one."

Fanucio suddenly understood. "Oh! I *wager* he is."

With a conspiratorial grin, Columbus slipped two fingers between his lips and whistled. The crew quieted and gathered around.

"Men, it's time for a little sport. Fanucio has issued a challenge. A race between Pedro…" Columbus looked around. "Where is he?"

Half the crew raised their hands.

"The quick one," Columbus clarified. A lean Spaniard, barely more than a lad himself, maneuvered to the front.

"And the boy. What's your name?"

The boy stepped forward, seemingly uncomfortable with the attention. Still, he managed to hold Columbus's gaze.

"Nyx," the boy said with a light voice.

"I like Boy better. Up for a show of skill?"

"Sure. What do I get if I win?"

Columbus was impressed by the kid's pluck. "Well, you don't look old enough for a ration of wine. How does one hundred soldos sound?"

"Promotion to boatswain sounds better."

Fanucio was about to cuff the boy when Columbus laughed.

"All right," he said. "Boatswain if you win. But if you lose, you'll be emptying my chamber pot for the remainder of this voyage."

Nyx shrugged. "I won't lose."

Columbus nodded. The only thing he admired more than confidence was bravado.

"Okay, lads," Fanucio said. "Give 'em some room."

As Nyx and Pedro readied themselves, the wagering began. Men shouted and waved money in their fists. The odds quickly slanted in Pedro's favor. The other boy followed the spectacle with amused detachment.

Above them, Monday and Tuesday took up position atop the poop deck rail.

"It appears there is to be some form of competition," Monday said. *"What shall we wager?"*

Tuesday considered. *"How about slaves when we finally wrest control of the ship?"*

Monday nodded with approval.

Down below, Columbus waited for the furor of betting to die down before pointing up to the crow's nest high atop the main mast. "The objective is simple. First crew member to scale the mast and retrieve the flag from the nest wins. To make things more interesting, I've asked Fanucio to slush it."

"Are there any rules?" Nyx asked.

"Three. Stay off the shrouds, don't fall, and don't lose."

The two youths eyed each other before glancing back at Columbus. "Well? Go."

Instantly, Pedro shoved Nyx backward before sprinting for the front of the ship, earning a hearty "Huzzah!" from the crew. Nyx recovered quickly, springing to his feet and scrambling across the deck just as Pedro leaped onto the forestay and began to cat crawl up toward the mainmast. Pedro was already a dozen feet in the air when Nyx pulled a dagger out of nowhere and slashed the forestay line. Pedro careened down and slammed into the deck.

Another cheer ran out, this time for Nyx, who was free climbing the foremast without a hint of fear.

"He does climb like a monkey," Columbus said.

The cheering grew more raucous and the betting fiercer. Pedro was running at full speed when he launched himself off the bowsprit and clamped onto Nyx's leg. Nyx lurched but managed to hold his position while using his other leg to kick at Pedro. Unfortunately for Nyx, Pedro had spent the last year and a half aboard the ship wrestling ropes, and his grip was like iron. Rather than let go, Pedro simply pulled himself higher until he could latch onto Nyx's waist and wrap his arms around him. Nyx managed to hold their collective weight for a few seconds before his grip gave and both boys tumbled down.

The crew groaned as the youths struck the deck. Somehow Nyx had gotten the worst of it. He swayed after gaining his feet. By that time, Pedro was again halfway across the ship. This time, he used the gunwale to boost himself high onto a lanyard, which he quickly began to scale toward the yardarm above.

When Columbus saw Nyx searching for his dagger, he knew the game was done. He was surprised to find himself disappointed. There was something about the lad that intrigued him, even if he couldn't put a finger on it.

Then, something odd happened. Nyx stood tall and did a quick appraisal of the ship. It took no more than a second, but in that one brief instant, Columbus felt a ray of hope for him. The boy's eyes were composed, the gears behind them churning.

In a flash, Nyx barreled his way through the crew, charged up the forecastle stairs and ran directly for the mizzenmast. The mizzen was the only sail that was lateen-rigged with a triangular arm that went from near the deck and shot forty-five degrees into the sky. He tugged free the cleat knot connected to the high end, wrapping it quickly around a small water keg on deck. Then he lifted the keg, put it on the gunwale, and rolled it toward the end of the boat.

"What in Hades' name is he doing?" Fanucio asked.

"Improvising." Columbus grinned.

Just as Pedro was reaching for the mainsail's yardarm, Nyx climbed atop the low end of the mizzenmast. The water keg fell, the line ran taut, and Nyx shot into the air.

The crew gasped as Nyx landed onto the mainsail boom two feet from Pedro, who was shocked. The small Spaniard was on the wrong side and knew he was beaten. Then he saw the slightest tug at the edge of Nyx's mouth and slammed one heavy foot down in fury. It shook violently. Both boys fought to maintain their balance. Pedro stomped again, but this time he lost his balance and pitched over the side, saved from certain death by seizing a reef line.

Nyx heard the flutter of the flag from the first breeze of the day. He could have easily turned for the nest to claim the win. Instead, he knelt and offered Pedro a hand. The boy was surprised but took it. As he climbed onto the boom, Nyx heard the crew sigh with relief. Nyx retrieved the flag before he slid down the slushed mast to cheers.

Columbus stepped to the boy, grim-faced. The cheers ceased.

"Boy, you cut my rigging, tore my aft-sail, and lost a keg of my best powder. You are rash, reckless, and lucky to be alive." Nyx swallowed. Then, Columbus clapped him on the shoulder and smiled, the boy's lost dagger extended in his hand. "You'll fit in perfectly."

Another cheer went up as Nyx took the dagger. Almost instantly, a sea of meaty hands latched onto him and began lobbing him in the air as they strolled around the deck singing an old bawdy Spanish song. Even Pedro—the small one—joined in. Nyx laughed, all the while shouting to be put down. The crew pitched him higher instead.

Columbus joined in the merriment. This was exactly what they needed. And when he himself felt a breeze on his sweaty pate, he knew their troubles were behind them. Then, Nyx was tossed even higher. Only this time, when he landed, his turban fell away. Someone gasped. Nyx fell to the deck in a huff.

The ship was silent. Columbus pushed his way through the stunned crew to see Nyx look up through long, stringy hair. For the first time, those eyes held fear. It was obvious why.

Nyx was a girl.

CHAPTER FOUR

"S-she's not a he," Fanucio stuttered. "He's not a her! It's a bleedin' girl!"

"I can see that," Columbus snapped.

"And, by God, she looks the spittin' image of—"

Columbus clapped Fanucio across the chest. "Don't you dare blaspheme on my ship!"

Columbus had also seen the resemblance but had no time to deal with the implications. The crew was already fuming, and he needed to take control of the situation before things boiled over and all the goodwill amassed over the last ten minutes proved irrevocably lost.

"What's the meaning of this deception?" Columbus barked as he pulled Nyx up by the scruff of her neck. "Speak quickly!"

Nyx wrested herself from his grip. "I knew I wouldn't be allowed within fifty feet of your ship if my gender was revealed, so I disguised myself."

"For what purpose?"

"Isn't it obvious? I wish to join your crew."

Half the sailors aboard laughed while the other half roared with disapproval.

"A crew with women is bad luck," Fanucio said. "Everyone knows that."

"And you're not even a woman," Columbus added. "You're barely a child."

"I'm no child," Nyx said as defiantly as a twelve-year-old girl on a ship full of hardened men could. "I've done everything asked of me, better than any at my post."

"And yet our voyage has been mired by setback after setback. No wonder the wind has abandoned us."

"A funny thing to hear from one whose hair is currently blowing in the breeze."

She was right. A breeze was stirring. Its effects could be seen twinkling across the surface of the ocean. Still, that truth failed to dissuade a crew whose blood was piqued.

"She's a harbinger of misfortune," someone growled.

"An affront to the Sea Gods," said another.

"Something must be done!" shouted a third.

"Aye. Put her in irons!"

"Keelhaul her!"

"Shave her head and dress her as a mermaid!"

Everyone turned to stare at that man.

"What?" he asked sheepishly. "I got a thing for mermaids."

"There'll be no foul play," Columbus said, "but something must be done. We can't afford bad fortune to plague this quest any longer." He stared at Nyx. "You'll have to leave the ship."

The crew was stunned silent. They hadn't expected Columbus to go that far. The girl was, after all, a mere child.

"Cap'n," Fanucio said. "You don't plan to just..." He motioned heaving her overboard.

"No, that would be cruel. We'll give her a dinghy and enough provisions for two weeks. After that, she's in God's hands. Take hold of her, men."

As several crewmen moved in, Nyx's dagger reappeared in her hand. "Any man comes at me will leave with more holes than a net."

The crew laughed. Then one of them reached for Nyx. Her blade flashed. The man's shirt and pantaloons hit the deck. The laughter ceased.

"Enough," Columbus said, snatching the dagger from Nyx's hand. "Don't make this harder than it already is."

"Please, Captain," The girl pleaded. "I can be an asset to you. I have skills. I'm clever and sneaky. I'm also loyal. I can watch your back and see trouble coming from a mile away."

"I can see my own trouble coming, Brommet. Heaven knows I have the experience."

"And where was that experience at the postern gate of the Alcázar?" Columbus pulled up, surprised. "You didn't mind my blade so much then."

"The portcullis?" Columbus said, incredulous. "That was you?"

"Aye."

"And inside the castle? You were following me then too, weren't you? Why?"

"I told you, I wish to join your crew."

"But why? The life of a seaman is brutal and lonely. Those lucky enough to survive the hostile seas are more likely to wind up destitute, crippled, and begging for crumbs in some godforsaken seaport than gaining any true wealth or prosperity." He glanced at the crew. "Present company excluded." He turned back to Nyx. "So, why would you want this life?"

"The same reason we all do. I come from nothing. And what awaits me there are a thousand shades of the same. At least out here, I can choose my own path."

Columbus hesitated. Those words resonated strongly with him. Nyx must have sensed this because she squared up and spoke her next words with even more passion.

"Give me adventure or give me death."

Fanucio whistled. "Now that is a catchphrase."

Annoyed, Columbus resumed the march toward the back of the ship. "I don't have time for this."

Atop the poop deck, Monday and Tuesday watched on.

"I believe he plans to set the girl adrift," Tuesday said.

Monday snorted. *"I wonder what the runner-up gets."*

"Perhaps we should reconsider, sir," Fanucio said. "She was right about the wind. Look."

High above, the sails began to flap, and the deck swayed. Relief came with each gust. Still, Columbus was undeterred.

"It only means I've chosen the proper course of action. And there's still no guarantee this will make up for the damaged rudder or spoiled provisions."

"But those weren't my doing!" Nyx shouted. "I wasn't even on the boat when the provisions were delivered. And it wasn't me who brought us here or cut sail to see for days on end. Has anyone asked why your nose is buried in that bronze dish day and night? Why don't you tell them why you're really here?"

The crew looked to Columbus, curious about that themselves.

"That's no concern of yours," he spat.

"But it is theirs," Nyx said as she lobbied the crew again. "Ask him. Ask him what riddle your captain seeks!"

"What about it, Captain?" one of the oldest crewmembers—and ironically, the oldest Pedro—asked. "What's she on about? What is the deal with that dish?"

Others repeated the question. Columbus felt his chest tighten. He briefly eyed the girl. *How had she put me on the defensive so quickly?*

"If you must know, this dish is a kind of ancient treasure map. It leads to an artifact so rare, so valuable that once recovered, none of us shall ever have need of money again."

"And where exactly is this treasure, Captain?" Nyx asked.

The crew awaited his answer. Grudgingly he said, "Very close by."

This time, the crew grumbled. They were used to his vague answers and didn't like it. Sensing this, Nyx pressed on.

"Don't be vague, Signore Colombo. This place has a name, doesn't it?"

Columbus forced a smile. "Indeed."

"Well, spare us all the suspense. What is the place you seek?"

The crew waited expectantly. Columbus mumbled the answer.

"Did he say, Johannes?" one of the crew asked.

"I heard praying mantis," another said.

"Appears they didn't quite hear you, Captain," Nyx said, now enjoying herself. "Maybe you should say it a little louder."

Finally, Columbus blurted out, "Atlantis."

A chorus of groans led very quickly to outright anger just as Columbus knew it would.

Fanucio leaned over and whispered, "Perhaps I should prepare the dinghy for two?"

Before things could escalate further, Columbus whistled loudly. The crew turned to see him holding a golden fish high above his head.

"This was found off the coast of Greece some three thousand years ago. It is solid gold through and through."

"Anyone can smelt gold," one of the crew shouted.

"Not like this. Where's Pedro?"

"The quick one or the old one?" Fanucio asked.

"The one with the axe."

Giant Pedro muscled his way forward, the axe in his hand. Columbus laid the golden fish at his feet and ordered him to halve it. Giant Pedro lifted the mighty axe into the air and brought it down with a thunderous strike. Columbus retrieved the two pieces and passed them around.

"Look inside and tell me what you see."

The crew huddled over the two pieces, their faces wracked with wonder.

"It's the guts and bones of the fish," Fanucio said, surprised. "They, too, is gold. Who could do such a thing?"

"No one," Columbus answered, looking over his captivated men. "There is an artifact in Atlantis as old as time. Legends say its pommel can turn anything it touches into gold. I believe this artifact is real. And should you follow me a little longer, I swear by the oceans blue, I will claim it as my own, and for your part, make us all rich as kings."

"What's this artifact called then?" someone asked.

"The Trident of Poseidon," Columbus answered.

The crew murmured again, but as the gold was passed around, Columbus's words became hard to deny. There was something about the sight of gold, the heft of it in your hands that spurred the heart and clouded the reason. It was the glimmer that widened the eye, the bulging purse that drew the breath and made all else pale in comparison.

"I say we support the captain," one of the crew shouted. "He's never steered us wrong yet."

"He's never steered us right neither!"

"True, but we're already out here, and I ain't headed back empty-handed."

"To Atlantis then?"

The crew murmured their agreement.

"To Atlantis!" Columbus shouted.

"To Atlantis!" the crew erupted.

And as if their fates were set by divine providence, the first heady wind blew across the bow, and then another louder cheer went up.

On the forecastle, Monday cheered too.

"What are you cheering for?" Tuesday asked. *"You don't even know what's being said."*

"I'm providing emotional support!" Monday answered.

Fanucio cleared his throat and nodded toward Nyx. "And the girl? Is it still...?" He motioned over the side of the boat.

Columbus had forgotten about the girl. She'd nearly cost him his head twice. Oddly, she was smiling.

"He can't," Nyx said eventually. "He needs me."

"Do I?" Columbus asked.

"The disk has taken you as far as it can. By my guess, you've correctly decoded the Greek numerals as coordinates, but you have no idea what to do next."

"And you do?"

Nyx shrugged. "Unless you have someone else aboard who can read ancient Athenian."

This time, Columbus couldn't contain his surprise. "Who are you?"

"I told you. My name is Nyx. And I am going to be the world's first female explorer."

Columbus glanced at Fanucio, and they both burst into laughter.

"A female explorer? There's no such thing."

"There is now," she smirked before setting the bronze disk on the deck to study it.

"Okay. Which way, *Captain* Nyx?" Columbus asked.

Nyx stood and looked over his shoulder, her smile vanished in an instant.

"West," she gulped. "As fast as you can."

"Speed is a requirement?"

"It is if we want to outrun them," she nodded behind him.

Columbus whirled to see two sails on the horizon, their red crosses visible even from afar.

"It's the *Niña* and *Pinta*!" Fanucio cried. "They musta been hidden in the sun."

Columbus cursed himself. Regardless of their eight-day idleness, he should have had his crew ready. And, now, his enemy had the wind-gauge. "All hands to the lines! Full sail!"

As the sails unfurled, a groan issued from the mast, and the slush of water rose.

The pursuing vessels were already moving at several knots. They were also lighter and faster. Barely midday, with no clouds on the horizon, their hope of escape looked bleak.

"Can we outrun them?" Nyx said, bluster gone.

"No," Columbus replied. "They're smaller, lighter, and carry much less draft. At best, we have an hour or two before they catch us."

"But you have weapons."

"Verso guns and breech-loaded lombards. Not enough to repel two ships. It'll be hand-to-hand fighting then. We have numbers, but I'm betting they have significantly more arms. Can you decipher that thing?"

Nyx eyed the disk, "I believe so."

"You believe so? Brommet, our lives are on the line. I need a better answer than that."

"Yes, though it's still just a map. Even if it leads us to a proper location, it'll be a miracle if we find something there to help us."

"Then you'd better get on with it. Because a miracle is exactly what we need."

As the girl returned to the disk, Columbus took up a spyglass and fixed it on the pursuing vessels. His fear was confirmed. It was the *Niña* and *Pinta*, two ships he'd seen docked in Córdoba, which meant they'd been pursuing him since his departure three weeks before. Eventually, he locked onto a figure at the bow of the *Niña*, a spyglass also in hand.

Vespucci.

Who else? Columbus had humiliated the man. If there was any good news, Columbus understood Vespucci's skills lay with politicking, not seamanship. If it came to a fight—and it appeared it would—Columbus would have the two best skills one could have in his position: experience and imagination.

"Wind's picking up astern," Fanucio said.

"It won't be enough."

"Not to worry, Cap'n. The men are itching for a fight. Even your two hairy pets appear to be game."

On the poop, the Pygmies sharpened their spears, undaunted. Columbus couldn't help but smile. Someone would board this ship thinking them easy targets. It would be their last mistake.

"Have the master-at-arms begin dispersing weapons. Send the youths to the pumps and prepare the coopers for patching holes."

"What about the girl?"

Nyx remained seated on the deck, staring intently at the disk, her quivering hand trailing over the raised letters.

"When the firing starts, send her below."

Fanucio took a slug from a flask. "At least it's a clear day for a fight."

Columbus took a slug himself. "Tomorrow's always better."

The first cannon blast came at midday only to fall a hundred yards short.

Columbus turned to his crew. "Maybe we should slow down and give them some hope before we send then to the depths, eh?"

The crew responded with an "huzzah!"

For their part, the *Niña* and *Pinta* had veered apart but maintained an equidistant approach as they closed in. The pincer move was obvious, but would it prove effective? Time would tell.

While Fanucio hobbled around the deck getting the crew armed and in position, Columbus stood stoutly at the wheel. To his surprise, the girl continued to ask questions. Where was the north star? How many leagues had they traveled since setting out from the Straits of Gibraltar? Could he tell her exactly when it was midday? With each answer, Nyx moved the disk alongside the ship's dry compass, watching it swing unpredictably on its gimbal, eyes flitting between the two as if their proximity might glean some answer.

Columbus nearly laughed. In his years of pursuing of Atlantis, he could have never imagined getting so desperate that he would turn to a know-it-all twelve-year-old girl. "Truth is stranger than fiction," Drakos, his first captain, used to say. Columbus hoped this might prove one of those occasions.

The second canon blast from the *Niña* splashed down just off the ship's stern. Columbus was about to order return fire when Nyx shouted, "South by southwest!" It was an extreme course correction and one that would immediately draw the pursuing caravels closer. Whether out of desperation or lunacy, Columbus complied.

As the gap closed, Columbus finally gave the order to fire. The blasts shook the deck and filled the air with smoke. Two more struck water, but the next made the unmistakable sound of hitting wood. A cry went up. First blood!

Barely a second passed before the *Niña* and *Pinta* returned fire. Hot lead whooshed overhead. Columbus was about to order Nyx below when she shouted another course change, two points west. He followed while noticing the strangest thing. The compass needle was spinning around, wildly changing direction.

"What's happening?" Columbus asked.

Nyx looked up, eyes wide. "I think we're close. Do you trust me?"

A cannonball struck the port side of the ship. Their pursuers were in range now.

"Hell no, I don't trust you!" he shouted over the din. Then one of the enemy volleys struck the forecastle balustrade, sending wood and debris flying in every direction. Desperate, he locked eyes with the girl again. *Has it really come to this?*

"Whatever you're going to do, do it quick!"

To his surprise, the girl stood, hefting the bronze disk up. "Remember you said that," she uttered. Then she heaved the disk over the side of the ship.

CHAPTER FIVE

"Are you mad?!" Columbus howled before turning the wheel to come around.

The sails tacked, the jib swung, and the ship shot aggressively windward. The move was so shocking it forced the captain of the *Pinta* to turn leeward to avoid crashing into the *Santa Maria*'s stern. At the same time, the *Niña* turned to portside. Columbus could hear Vespucci screaming over the din.

The move bought Columbus time. He turned to lay into the girl when he saw she stood at the starboard gunwale, looking down at the waves. Columbus figured the disk had settled to the bottom of the ocean.

"There!" Nyx shouted.

Columbus looked. The disk was floating in the water some two hundred yards away.

Columbus was flabbergasted. He had no clue why the girl had thrown the disk overboard in the first place. Now, she was pointing it out to him. Matters were made worse as he saw the *Niña* and *Pinta* also coming around, as if they were intent on reaching it first.

Columbus shouted for his weapons. A boy returned with Columbus's sword, which he quickly lashed around his waist along with the bandolier of jade explosives.

When the bronze disk was less than one hundred yards out, Columbus ordered the sails dropped. As their speed plummeted, the *Niña* closed in from behind.

Fanucio cried out to ready the men. A moment's silence was ripped apart as both ships exchanged cannon fire. The *Niña*'s sails dropped, and a dozen grappling hooks sailed through the air, latching onto the *Santa Maria*'s gunwale. Columbus ordered the lines cut, but several of the men were cut down by blunderbuss fire.

As the ships met, a gut-wrenching impact shook both decks and knocked many off their feet. Columbus was the first to meet the attackers as they swarmed the *Santa Maria*. A quick exchange of gunfire filled the afternoon air with smoke and blood. Then the battle turned to close quarters fighting.

A ruddy, armed Spaniard yelled as he charged Columbus, who parried the blade and buried his own in the man's chest. As he fell, three more took his place. Columbus quickly found himself on his heels. The largest attacker swung an axe with great arcing swings that threatened to take his head off. To his surprise, the man suddenly screamed out in pain as a crimson flower stained his jerkin. The man fell, revealing Nyx behind him, a sword in her hand.

"Get below deck!" he shouted. "This is no place for a child."

The girl gritted her teeth. "I told you, I'm no child!"

With unimaginable speed, Nyx ducked under an attack, her blade flying with adept precision as she cut one, two, three men down. She turned back with a smug sneer.

"Admit it," she said. "You need more sword."

"If that's true, I'm in worse shape than I thought."

Columbus shoved the girl as another blade nearly took off her head. She winced, guilty, as Columbus ran her attacker through and they both dove back into the fray.

On the deck of the *Niña*, Vespucci continued to shout orders. Then, he locked eyes with Columbus and sneered. There was no chance the man would leave the safety of his ship just yet. That didn't stop a group of Columbus's crewmen from preparing their own counterattack. Columbus saw it and waved them back. The crew looked confused but fell back.

The fight became centered over the gunwales. Fanucio shot off one of the versos and hot scraps of metal flew out, shredding flesh and anything in its way.

Through the wafting smoke, Columbus noticed the Pygmies still sitting atop the forecastle. They'd yet to join in the fight.

"Well?" he asked in the worst Pygmy this side of Africa. Or, any side, really. "*Are you going to spectate the entire battle?*"

Monday shrugged before pointing behind him. Columbus's head snapped around a second before the *Pinta* slammed into them.

"Aft side!" Columbus shouted.

His crew split in two. As the *Pinta*'s sailors charged the deck, the fighting intensified. Columbus's men were game but were mostly drunkards and criminals whereas those aboard the *Niña* and *Pinta* had fought against the Moors for years. The odds didn't look good.

Columbus heard Fanucio shout. A moment later, casks of burning oil crashed down from above, splitting on the decks of the *Niña*, forcing their sailors out of the fight. To their utter surprise, that was when two small Africans leaped across the Void and announced their presence with a foreign chant that sounded like a child's hymn. Many of the enemy laughed. Then, the Pygmies went to work.

They moved with uncanny precision; ducking, diving, slashing, and leaping like acrobats from a stage show. Enemy after enemy fell. The *Pinta*'s captain was forced to call back a group of men to counter the diminutive attackers. The plan backfired when the Pygmies leaped into the rigging and continued to slay from above.

For all the skills on display that day, however, none was as graceful or as deadly as Columbus. He moved with the speed and economy of one who had trained for this purpose all his life. His steps were light, his sorties precise. And any who saw him there—slashing, parrying, thrusting—would likely miss the most compelling aspect of all: the fire that burned in his eyes. *This was what he lived for.*

His one mistake came as a half-dozen men charged him simultaneously. He cut loose four barrels to take them out. The barrels mowed men down like bowling pins. One broke open, spilling the wine Fanucio had hidden for himself. His cry resembled the wail of a mother as her children were snatched away.

An axe blade narrowly missed his nose and struck the floor, cleaving his new wooden foot in two. Fanucio looked up. "You'll pay for that."

As the battle raged, Columbus was surprised to find himself looking after the girl. She meant nothing to him, of course. So, why was he so concerned with her? She moved easily through the swath of brute men. Someone had taught her well. He didn't recognize the style, but he could see it was effective. How was it that she showed so little fear for one her age? Who was this girl? He made a mental note to find out should they both survive.

Just then a shadow loomed over him. He looked up to see a towering dark-skinned Moor. The man had arms the size of porpoises, and the hammer in his hand was slick with blood. He eyed Columbus with a toothless grin.

"Hello, there," Columbus said. "Have you met Pedro?"

The Moor's brow furrowed. Then he turned to see Giant Pedro arcing his axe high into the air. The blade struck the Moor's head and split it in half. As the two halves fell and the body dropped, Pedro smiled. Then four men charged him and skewered him as he failed to pull his axe from the deck.

A few feet away, Fanucio waged his own fight, which Columbus had always called "the drunken fool." He swung a sword over his head, shrieking wildly. When a Spaniard charged him, Fanucio lifted his peg leg and rammed the split foot into his eye. As the man screamed, Fanucio winked at Columbus.

The fevered fight continued despite the casualties piling up. Then all at once a horn sounded. The fighting paused as Vespucci waved a white flag from atop the *Pinta*'s forecastle.

"Vespucci, you cur," Columbus growled, "are you surrendering?"

"Heavens, no, man. You're overrun. I'm giving you a chance to parlay."

"Parlay? Never was much good at that. Why don't you come down here and we'll have a proper discussion?"

"You've lost, Captain. You know it, and I know it. Stop here, and no more of your crew will be harmed. On behalf of the crown, I promise your men will face no charges. Only you."

"And I travel back in fetters? No thanks."

"I give you my word, you'll be treated like a gentleman. You can sleep and dine in my cabin."

Columbus pursed his lips. "So, it's to be torture, is it?"

Columbus's crew laughed.

"Is that your final answer?"

Was it? Over the course of his lifetime, Columbus had read many books on sea tactics. And almost every ship captain worth his salt said there were only two options when facing overwhelming odds: fight or run. The word surrender never came up because it most assuredly meant a life in chains. And to those hands used to the liberty of the sea, chains were a far worse fate than death. But here Vespucci stood offering something different. Freedom for his crew and a trial for Columbus. He had to consider it. Sure, he'd only taken on the crew a few weeks back and knew none of them. Yet they were still *his* crew. His responsibility. Were their lives worth his quest?

Columbus looked out over the water, considering how far they'd come—how far *he'd* come. To give up now, to push aside all his hopes and dreams was too much to bear. The girl claimed they were at the doorstep of Atlantis and he would be damned if he would hand it over for another man's glory. Live or die, succeed or fail, it would be by his own hand.

"You want an answer?" Columbus asked. "Here it is."

He hurled his sword at Vespucci. The blade narrowly missed him and stuck in the mast.

"Finish them!" Vespucci roared.

As the battle resumed, Fanucio noticed something off their stern. "Cap'n, look!"

At the back, Nyx had loaded herself into a dinghy and was lowering it into the water.

"Guess she preferred option one after all," Columbus said.

"Or maybe she's smarter than the rest of us."

As more enemies charged in, the men found themselves back-to-back.

Nyx paddled away from the *Santa Maria* as the clangor of battle echoed behind her. She felt guilty at slipping away, but she hadn't wanted the disk to escape her sight. Columbus had pinned all his hopes on it, and if she couldn't accomplish this task, the battle wouldn't matter.

When she finally reached the disk, she didn't reel it in. Instead, she turned it over so the protruding crystal faced downward. It shimmered momentarily before the *Niña*'s mast blocked out the sun. Using her paddle, she tried to push it back in the light. That's when she heard a voice.

"That is property of the king."

Vespucci stood in a dinghy of his own. He set a paddle down and withdrew his sword. Nyx suspected he thought it would intimidate her. She swung her paddle and clipped him upside the head instead.

"And this is the property of your face!"

As Vespucci sprawled back, Nyx once again paddled for the disk. She heard Vespucci roar with rage as he paddled after her.

Back on the *Santa Maria*, the odds were quickly turning against Columbus. The Pygmies had managed a string of casualties, but they, too, were falling back under superior numbers. Among the enemy, Columbus recognized the Pinzon brothers. They were good sailors and likely only acting under orders of the king. The idea of killing them—or being killed by them—didn't sit well with him.

Columbus charged the nearest Pinzon, his blade whirling. To no surprise, Pinzon maintained his focus and footing. The two men exchanged parries, challenging each other with skills well honed. Through it all, however, Columbus kept stealing glances at Nyx. As she neared the disk, Vespucci closed in on her. *Stupid and brave,*

Columbus thought. It wasn't hard to guess whom she reminded him of.

"Give me that disk, you retched creature!" Vespucci howled as he drew near. Nyx swung her oar again. This time, Vespucci caught it, ripped it from her hands, and flung it out to sea. To his amazement, the girl jumped into the water, continuing to push the disk toward the sunlight.

Back on the *Santa Maria*, Fanucio once again sidled up next to Columbus. "What the hell is she doing?"

"I don't know—" Columbus replied.

To their horror, Vespucci got close enough to grab Nyx by the hair. At that very instant, she shoved the disk with all her might and watched it coast into the sunlight.

A kaleidoscope of colors exploded across the water, and the crystal gem began to glow. Vespucci held his hand up to stave off the light. Nyx was frozen, entranced.

Almost immediately the swordplay on the ship came to a halt. Men turned in bewilderment as those lights cascaded over them.

"What devilry is this?" Vespucci asked.

As the sun continued to shine down on the disk, the crystal glowed brighter. A shimmering light seemed flowered above it, growing in intensity and coalescing into a kind of storm.

"What is that?" Fanucio gasped.

Columbus gave the only answer he could. "A miracle."

As the phenomenon continued to unfold, Nyx paddled away. Then, all at once, the colors fused in a blinding explosion. A powerful beam of light shot down into the depths of the ocean.

A beacon.

Everything grew still. The men had stopped fighting. Where a moment before they stood toe-to-toe, they now stood side by side, all eyes on the disk; all waiting in anticipation for what would happen next. They didn't have to wait long.

A bubble rose to the surface directly in front of Nyx. Two more appeared. When a torrent followed her, Nyx swam away as quickly as she could. Vespucci was frantically trying to paddle the dinghy away. Nyx grabbed the back and kicked with all she had.

Slowly, A dark shadow appeared from below, increasing in size as it rose. Before long, it had expanded beyond the boundary of the ship. An instant later, several giant tentacles exploded from the ocean and towered into the sky. The men recoiled in horror as the leviathan rose, its eyes black as pitch, its maw filled with razor-sharp teeth.

"You owe me a golden foot," Fanucio muttered.

The beast roared.

"Leviathan!" Columbus screamed as those giant tentacles swooped down and crushed the *Santa Maria*'s bow.

Men howled as they fled across the deck. Tentacles swooped down to snatch them up, tossing three into its roaring gullet while flinging the others a thousand feet away.

The largest tentacle latched onto the mast and ripped it free like an ingrown hair. It pitched it at the *Niña*, crushing the top half of the smaller vessel's deck and sending it reeling out to sea.

"Man the cannons!" Columbus screamed. "Fire everything!"

Aboard the *Santa Maria* and *Pinta*, men ran for the artillery. Cannonballs and lombards crackled as they fired at the leviathan. Splotches of black blood sprayed the air, but it only enraged the creature. Some men were reduced to slashing at the tentacles with their swords, only to be rewarded by crushing blows or worse, a mouth full of teeth.

DOWN IN THE WATER, Nyx tried desperately to climb aboard Vespucci's dinghy.

"Go away!" he shouted.

"I can help row, you idiot," she said.

A tentacle whipped overhead, nearly upending them both.

"Yes," Vespucci cried. "Get in. In!"

As they rowed away, Columbus dodged another tentacle as it slammed down, cracking the spine of his ship. Water flooded around his feet.

"Should we abandon ship?" Fanucio shouted.

Columbus shook his head. In the water, they were sitting ducks. At least here, they could scramble around and give themselves time to come up with a plan. What they needed was to identify a weakness in their enemy. Then it came to him. "The eye! Concentrate your attack on the eye!"

The remaining seamen began firing their weapons at the leviathan's eye. When one finally struck, the creature roared.

Fanucio spied the last versos gun up near the front of the ship. He hobbled as quickly as he could, ducking under a tentacle as it gathered up more men before shoveling them into its maw. Fanucio swung the gun in the creature's direction and took careful aim before pulling the trigger. The blast was defeating. It hit true. The monstrosity shrieked.

"I got 'im, Cap'n!" Fanucio cheered. "I—"

A second, much larger eye rose up in front of him.

"It was him," Fanucio pointed to one of the Spaniards.

The first mate was thrown from his feet as the entire ship began to rise. Tentacles wrapped around it as the remaining crewmen leaped overboard.

Columbus watched with dread as the leviathan lifted his vessel high into the air, fixing it over its giant maw. *That breath is horrendous.*

Looking around quickly, Columbus saw Giant Pedro's axe still planted in the deck. He wrenched it free and climbed atop the railing.

"Just my luck," he grumbled. "A death for the ages and no one around to see it."

As the ship canted down, Columbus jumped. The leviathan's remaining eye opened wide as the mariner buried the axe deep into its ocular orb. A defining roar echoed across the sea as the creature thrashed in the water.

All at once, the ship hurtled toward the water. It struck the surface and continued downward. Columbus locked onto the mast and tried to hold firm as the water rushed over him. The other tentacles continued thrashing, wrapping around anything they could find until they, too, were plummeting into the cold, dark depths.

Columbus felt his lungs burning and his head threatening to explode from the pressure. He released the mast and kicked for the surface, but the light had grown too dim. He tried to follow the rise of bubbles, but black stars flooded his vision as he continued down toward a watery death.

CHAPTER SIX

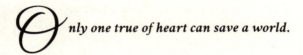*nly one true of heart can save a world.*

THE VOICE WAS DEEP, disembodied. It filled every corner of Columbus's mind, piercing the veil that marked the boundary between the living and the dead. For, surely, he was dead, wasn't he? What else could lie beyond the vast depths he'd traveled? The endless fathoms he'd plunged? The crippling pressure that had risen with each second, setting his blood afire, until at last it seemed the only relief might be that endless slumber that awaited us all. Had he taunted it too long? What else but death could feel so cold and infinite?

With a gasp, Columbus opened his eyes. Instantly, his chest seized, and a stream of seawater exploded from his lungs. He retched again and again until a few short breaths managed to pilfer air between the convulsions. Spittle ran over his trembling lips. It tasted coppery—of blood. *Is it mine?* If so, it meant he was alive. But how? Where?

At first, the darkness was all-encompassing. Then, slowly, shadows began to appear. Somewhere in the distance he thought he saw a light. No, not a light. A *torch*, flickering from a craggy cavern wall. There were a few of them peppered around, spaced too far apart to illuminate much.

Columbus tried to sit up. His wet hand slipped, and he cut it on some rocks. He was drenched, shivering. He smelled dank earth and something else. Something rancid that drew tears to his eyes. He clenched his gut and buried his head in the crook of his arm to avoid retching again. It was death. He'd never smelled it so strong.

Another voice called from far off. This one different than before. *Did I dream it?* He wasn't sure. All he knew for certain was that he was colder than he'd ever been in his life. And he was lucky to be alive.

The new voice came again, hurried and hushed. Something about it sounded familiar. Columbus wasn't sure why. He tried to turn. The rocks clattered beneath him and he slipped again. He looked down. The rocks were ochre, oddly shaped, both smooth and jagged. He blinked several times. When they came into focus, the horrifying truth hit him. He wasn't lying on rocks. He was lying on bones. A bed of bones filled the cavern floor.

"Cap'n!" the whisper sounded, clearer this time.

Columbus turned, muscles cramping. Several bulky shapes hovered in the air a few yards away. Bodies hanging on gibbets. Others in cages. *Did one of them just move?*

"Cap'n, can you hear me?" the whisper asked again.

"Fanucio?" Columbus replied, teeth chattering.

Several of the caged prisoners shushed him at once.

"You have to free us before they return," another voice said, panic torqueing the pitch higher. Columbus blinked, finding Amerigo Vespucci. He was in a cage with the girl who deciphered the bronze disk. *What is her name again?*

"Who?" Columbus asked.

"The creatures," Fanucio hissed. "They pulled us from the water, feasting on half the men before hauling the rest of us in here. They went back to look for more. Once they see we're the last—"

He never finished the sentence. A thrashing noise echoed down one of the subterranean passageways, followed by a ghastly scream. That scream chilled Columbus to the bone.

A shadow filled the passage as something approached. Its movements were fluid—more sashay than steps. When it neared the cavern entrance, Columbus realized it was dragging a flailing man behind it. The sailor moaned pitifully.

"Down," the girl hissed. "Lie down!"

Columbus's face settled among the bones, the odor of death taking root in his nostrils. He pleaded with God to quell his stomach for fear he'd vomit again.

The creature entered the room, crunching over the bones on the ground. Columbus cracked an eye to take it in. It was humanoid, taller than a man, but with sagging breasts draped with mottled skin. Its beak-like snout was wet with blood, its legs like chicken feet. But what stood out most were two malformed protrusions on its back, spindly bones with torn webbing and snatches of feathers. If they were wings, they had never known flight.

The man wailed as he was thrown to the floor. Two wet strikes and he went silent. Columbus hadn't seen the man, hopeful he wasn't one of his own.

The creature shuffled forward, crunching more bones underfoot. Columbus held his breath as it neared. Then, the sailor shouted. His incapacitation had been a ploy. He drew a hidden blade and charged the thing, screaming. The blade moved too quickly to follow. The creature retreated a step to avoid the strikes before its long arms lashed out in response. Even in the dark, Columbus could see its razor-sharp talons tear through the sailor's shirt and flesh beneath. The man cried out, falling to his haunches. Desperate, he looked to charge his attacker again when the creature suddenly lifted its head, opened its mouth, and released a melodious note that froze the sailor in his path.

Columbus had never heard anything so beautiful and abhorrent at the same time. It seized him in a crushing grip. He tried to turn away —to cover his ears—but he was frozen. Spittle ran from his lips, and he felt a longing in his loins that was both agony and ecstasy. When the note changed it felt like a small mercy, until he realized his desire was now compelling him to stand. He fought it with every fiber of his being, though it was a losing effort. Those notes burrowed into the deep recesses of his brain, activating some animal instinct that would not be denied.

The sailor rose first. With each step, he lumbered toward the creature, powerless to deny its call. His head shook as he mumbled a prayer, the whites of his eyes growing bigger with each step. As its prey neared, the creature opened its craw, revealing two sets of piercing, blackened teeth.

All at once, the note ended. The creature sprang. The song turned to one of screams.

Columbus saw the man's flesh rupture, gouts of arterial blood spraying across the bone-laden floor. The creature shrieked with delight as it struck again and again. Finally, the sailor mercifully stopped moving.

Released from the song, Columbus turned away, praying the thing couldn't hear the pounding of his heart. For all he knew, he would be next. His eyes darted around. The sailor's blade lay in the center of the cavern, too far to retrieve. He even saw his bandolier of jade globes, but they were also out of reach. Eventually, he saw what appeared to be a broken femur protruding from the pile of bones, its jagged edge fit enough for a weapon. His trembling hand crept toward it. Then he heard a hiss and looked up and locked eyes with a woman.

He had never seen anything like her before. Ghostly pale eyes, skin so fair it almost glowed. She wore a strange bodysuit of reflective material sparsely covered with netting, though its worn appearance suggested she had also put up a fight against her captors. Even hunkered down, Columbus could see she had an athletic frame. And most curious of all was the swoop of tiny, colored gems that marked one side of her face. In a word, she was breathtaking.

The woman eyed the creature before tipping her head to Columbus. His brow furrowed. He had no idea what she was saying.

Carefully, the woman reached through the bars and pointed behind him. Columbus looked to see a silver trinket in the shape of a globe protruding from the bones. He glanced back at the woman, confused.

A rustle sounded behind Columbus. One of the men—maybe Fanucio—whispered a warning. Nyx—*that's her name*—drew a sharp intake of breath.

The woman nodded again, insistent. Her eyes bouncing between him and the thing that was clearly closing in behind him. Columbus heard the crunch of feet, the opening of its bloody snout. His eyes bounced between the broken femur and the silver globe. He needed to choose.

As a shadow fell over him, Columbus's trembling hand inched forward, expecting to hear that agonizing note at any moment.

Then Nyx shouted from her cage. Columbus heard the creature spin. His hand shot toward the globe, delving deep into the bones. He had no idea what he was reaching for when his hand wrapped around a hilt. His eyes went wide, flashing back to the foreign woman in the cage. She yelled something he didn't understand. He pulled the sword out as quickly as he could and spun.

The blade struck bone and flesh, jolting Columbus's arm. The sword had cut through its shoulder and deep into its chest. Its mouth opened with a spray of blood, followed by a horrible screech. Columbus whirled to his feet, ripped the sword out, and hacked at the thing until it ceased moving. Only when Fanucio called his name did Columbus stumble back, chest heaving.

"Thank God," Nyx called out with relief.

"Quickly, Columbus," Vespucci said, "free us before the others return."

Columbus didn't hesitate. He used the sword's silver globe pommel to break the locks of the cages, releasing the others.

"How many are there?" he asked, his voice raw and hoarse.

"Too many to count," Fanucio replied. "Even if I could count. Likely, they're scouring the cove for more men, but once they realize we're it, they'll be back."

"Where are we? What happened?"

Vespucci coughed as he pulled a handkerchief from his pocket and held it over his mouth and nose. "You don't recognize hell when you see it?"

Fanucio scavenged two more blades from the debris, slapping the hilt of one against Vespucci's arm. "You would know."

"Don't you dare touch me, you filthy—"

Nyx muscled her way between them. She put the dead sailor's dagger in her waistband and tossed Columbus his bandolier of jade globes.

"The leviathan drew us down," she said. "After a time, we passed through a barrier of some kind and the pressure relented. It left us on an underground shore before it retreated. It was dark. There were many dead and more injured. We were pulling the wounded from the water when we saw torches approaching. Those things," she nodded toward the dead creature, "attacked us without provocation. Some of us tried to fight, but in the end, it was a slaughter. Only those who surrendered were taken."

"You did the right thing. We're still alive and that's all that matters."

"*Still*," Vespucci repeated, "a designation that shall change rapidly if we do not find a way out of here."

To everyone's surprise, the caged woman spoke next.

"*Anak-Ta Eleece?*" she asked.

Columbus turned back to the woman. He'd almost forgotten she was there.

"Who is she?" Vespucci asked.

"I have no clue."

The woman rattled her cage, unleashing a torrent of words they did not understand.

"What language is that?" Fanucio asked. "Greek?"

"Not like any Greek I ever heard," Columbus replied, crossing to the woman. "Who are you? What are those things?"

The woman rattled the bars but would say no more.

"Tell her we'll set her free if she helps us," Vespucci said.

Columbus glared at Vespucci, holding up the sword in his hand. "She already has."

He brought the pommel down on the cage lock. The door broke open. The woman leaped down and began sifting through the bones for weapons.

"I wasn't being serious, you fool," Vespucci spat. "For all we know she's in league with those demons."

"Vespucci, how is it a man of your learned capabilities can be so ignorant when it comes to women?"

"Now, see here—"

A shriek echoed from the lit tunnel. A second followed a split second later, closer.

"They're coming," Vespucci stuttered.

The tension grew exponentially. Columbus grabbed a torch off the wall and looked around. Three tunnels led in opposite directions. "We go this way," Columbus said, turning for the central tunnel. He stopped when the foreign woman called out.

"Exfugio?" she whispered.

"Isn't that—?" Fanucio asked, amazed.

"Latin," Nyx said. "It means escape."

Columbus nodded to the woman. "Escape, yes. Do you know which way?"

She motioned for the sword. Columbus shook his head. The woman hesitated a moment before hobbling for the rear tunnel. Vespucci and Fanucio grabbed torches and followed.

The tunnel was cramped and wound through jutting rocks that drew blood when met with bare skin. Several times the group was forced to stoop low or sidestep areas too narrow to maneuver. They had barely gotten going when a chorus of piercing screeches echoed behind them. The dead creature had been found. Its brethren would be coming for revenge.

The woman moved with surprising speed despite her obvious fatigue. She also appeared to know where she was going. She was so quick Columbus feared they might be left behind. But every time they reached a fork, she paused before choosing a path. Columbus prayed it was more than guesswork.

Vespucci stayed on the woman's heels with Nyx right behind. Columbus brought up the flank, driving his first mate hard despite his peg leg sinking into mud or scudding over rocks. Occasionally, the globe-pommeled sword would clang against those rocks, and the shrieks would grow louder behind them. Initially, it sounded like they were being pursued by one or two creatures, but the farther they went, the louder sounds of movement and hissing grew.

All at once, the tunnel opened and a set of steps carved from rock rose to a stone archway of some ancient design. As they passed through it, Columbus saw many graven images of terrifying faces and strange symbols. Immediately, the smell of fresh air hit them, and the torches flickered, buoying the strange woman and making it difficult for the others to keep up.

Only when they reached a long, stone corridor did Columbus glance back. He knew instantly it was a mistake. A handful of those wretched things were hot on his heels. The foremost one locked eyes with Columbus and raised its head, releasing its own chilling note. It sounded vastly different than the one before, though the effect was the same. Columbus, Fanucio, and Vespucci all stumbled to a halt, eyes glazing over, free will ripped from them.

Nyx appeared unaffected by the song. She raced back to the men, doing her best to break them from the trance, pleading with them to push on. It did no good. Columbus could see her lips moving but heard nothing.

As more creatures flooded the corridor, each opened its mouth to add its own discordant note to the hypnotic cacophony. Nyx looked panic-stricken as those horrid things stalked forward, eyes burning, talons lashing out, crooning in the near dark. She was backpedaling when something slammed into her from behind. She hit the dirt hard as the strange woman pushed past her and twisted the sword from Columbus's grip. She swung it with such speed and ferocity the lead creature never had time to shriek. The blade split its skull in two.

The spell broken, the men woke from their thrall. Columbus looked up, stunned to see the woman wielding the blade, her skill and fearlessness beyond impressive.

Vespucci had already resumed running, urging the others on though he had no idea where he was going. Fanucio grabbed Nyx and pulled her to her feet, pushing her on as Columbus followed.

Columbus heard more screeches. With the woman already being

pushed back, they would soon be overrun. It was clear there was only one thing to do. Columbus peeled the bandolier of jade balls over his head and threw the entire thing down the hall. It exploded in a blinding light. The creatures shrieked, but the woman was also blinded. Columbus grabbed her by the arm and resumed their flight.

The corridor spilled into an even larger one with ornate stones on all sides. It gave Columbus a scintilla of hope. *Men built this.* It had to lead somewhere. As the screeches behind resumed at a more furious pitch, Columbus led the women down a final corridor and finally saw an oval doorway at its end, sunlight pouring in. Vespucci bounded through without hesitation, followed by Fanucio and Nyx. Hisses flooded the room, and a gasp of air was followed by the first utterance of a note. Columbus covered his ears just as the woman pulled ahead. At the last second, she grabbed Columbus, and they both jumped through the doorway to whatever waited beyond.

They tumbled down a steep hill, rolling through sparse stalks of grass until they landed hard at the foot of a beach. Gasping, blinded, and utterly exhausted, Columbus looked up with relief only to find himself surrounded by a new group of foes. Men and women with fair skin, dressed in the same uniforms and facial gems as the woman. As soon as they saw the sword in his hand, a shout went up, and several golden staves rose to attack.

CHAPTER SEVEN

"I do believe we are overdressed for this occasion," Columbus quipped as the stave-wielding party in scarlet bodysuits filled in around them.

"I vote we retire to find better attire," Fanucio said.

"Excellent idea. Let's do that."

As soon as Columbus moved, more staves were shoved in his face. He wanted to tell the holders where they could put it, but they looked like a serious lot. Grim-jawed, each bearing a multitude of scars, their stout forms obvious under the thin, reflective material. Alert, well-spaced out. No question. These were warriors, but which country did they represent?

The situation remained tense until the woman stood and began issuing orders in her foreign tongue. The others seemed shocked but relieved to see her. On her command, they lowered their staves, but only slightly. As Columbus's eyes continued to adjust to the light, he got his first real look at the woman. Her hair was the red of deep fire, of embers kissed by a lover's breath. A line of freckles danced among those small gems. Even covered in grime and guts, she was truly beautiful. And for half a second, Columbus forgot where he was. Then the woman barked orders at a male and female warrior—clearly twins.

They peeled off to cover their flank. Nyx gasped when she looked back and saw that aperture was the mouth of a giant stone face cut into a mountain several hundred feet high.

The woman continued issuing orders until she heard others approach from the beach. Over a dune, the biggest man Columbus had ever seen appeared. He had to have been over seven feet tall with legs like powder kegs and a chest thick as a mast. Around his heavy-set eyes glittered those same patterned gems, only he bore more than any. The man must have been mute because when he stopped in front of the woman, his hands spoke for him.

The woman watched, then shook her head adamantly. She pointed to Columbus, using the same phrase she'd uttered inside the cavern, "*Anak-Ta Eleece.*"

The giant sneered, his meaty fingers snapping crisply. Columbus and his crew waited. At last, the woman turned.

"*Vester gladias,*" she said to Columbus.

Latin again. It sounded so formal coming from her.

She repeated the phrase. The giant and others stood firm behind her.

"I believe she wants our weapons," Nyx said.

"I know what she wants," Columbus snapped. "I'm not certain I want to give them to her."

At Columbus's hesitation, the giant stepped forward, a golden stave appearing in his hand. With a single twitch, the weapon began to hum like a hive of angry bees. Columbus didn't want to see what happened next. He gave the order to drop their weapons but added, "I'll be wanting those back."

Once the weapons were collected, the woman motioned for them to follow. They headed through the dunes toward the sound of surf. As Columbus passed the giant, the man gave him a withering stare.

The bigger they are the harder they hit, Columbus thought.

The dunes gave way to a vast sea of crystal blue waters peppered with a handful of islands in all directions. Some were massive with arching mountain ranges, densely forested. Others were flat and barren as deserts. Columbus and their crew were in awe.

"Look." Fanucio gaped.

He was looking skyward. Columbus looked up and his mouth fell open. The sky was the color of sapphire with only a smattering of clouds that appeared almost opaque. Even odder, an intermittent shimmer raced across it like quartz lines in some mountain stream.

"Where are we?" Columbus asked.

"Don't you know?" Vespucci replied. "You've found your buried kingdom, Columbus. Congratulations. I suspect the shimmer we see is the barrier we passed through earlier, holding all of this in place."

For a moment, Columbus couldn't breathe. *Had he truly found it?* If so, it was nothing like what he expected. He turned to the woman who was still watching him. "Is this...Atlantis?"

To his disappointment, she shook her head, which only prompted Vespucci to laugh.

"You're asking her? These *people* are barbarians. Look at their clothes, their rudimentary weapons. Face it. The stories of an advanced civilization might have originated here, but they're a far cry from the truth. As I've always said, Atlantis is a myth. One you bought hook, line, and sinker. I hope it was worth the lives lost getting you here."

Columbus turned to hit the man, but held off. He knew those words stung for a reason. Most of his crew had died following his orders. And while that was part and parcel of being a seaman, few had signed up knowing Columbus's true intention. *Would they have come with me if they'd known the truth?* He didn't want to think about it. Guilt was an achor with an impossibly long chain. Let it run too deep and it will drown you quicker than the heaviest swell.

The moment was interrupted when a discordant note echoed from the mountain. Columbus, Vespucci, and Fanucio all winced and covered their ears. Surprisingly, none of the warrior men reacted.

The woman issued more orders, directing them to the water.

"Imagine," Vespucci scoffed. "A woman in charge."

Nyx smirked as she passed. "Maybe this is an advanced civilization after all."

Vespucci grabbed Columbus and pulled him close. "I see an opportunity here. Tread carefully and you might be able to repair your relationship with the monarchy."

"You speak for Spain now?"

"If not I, then who?"

Columbus jogged forward to draw even with the foreign woman. He asked her a question in Latin. She responded curtly before the giant drew her away.

"What's that about?" Fanucio asked.

"I asked if the big one was her husband or if she was single."

"You didn't!"

"I find—with many primitive types—sex is always the best diplomacy."

Fanucio groaned until Nyx spoke.

"He asked about our safety," she said.

Columbus eyed the girl. *She speaks Latin too? Who is she?*

"She said the sirens rarely venture out during the day but admits they're unpredictable when riled," Nyx continued.

"Sirens!" Fanucio said. "So, it was their song that bewitched us. We're fortunate. I heard many a tale of sailors falling prey to—"

A clamor from within the mountain silenced him. Columbus heard more screeches, followed by something else. The foreign woman shouted. Her warriors fanned out, aiming their golden staves toward that giant stone mouth as Columbus and his crew hunkered down.

A cry spilled from the mountain, followed by a stream of hisses. An instant later, two small forms shot out, rolled down the hill, and crashed onto the beach. First, one popped up, shaking off sand, followed by the second. Both burst into laughter.

"Those vile singing creatures nearly killed us!" Monday said.

"I know!" shouted Tuesday gaily. *"What a grand adventure!"*

Columbus sighed with relief as the Pygmies helped each other to their feet. When they turned and took in the scene, however, their smiles died.

"Either the sunlight deceives me," Monday said. *"Or these new fellows are holding our slaves hostage."*

"*Hmm,*" Tuesday replied. "*We can't have that. We have a reputation to consider.*"

Columbus recognized the looks on those cherubic faces. "Monday, Tuesday," he warned in terrible Pygmy. "These people were welcoming us to their homeland. Remain calm and let me handle this."

The Pygmies attacked instead.

"Damn," Columbus muttered. "I really must brush up on my Pygmy."

The ferocity of the Pygmy attack surprised the warriors. First, the small foes used their spears to catapult inside the warrior ring. Then they followed up with some dizzying strikes to knees and heads. When Tuesday lowered his spear to run one warrior down, the man depressed a button on his golden stave, and a reddish barrier repelled the African's weapon.

A female warrior also raised her stave, releasing a blast of energy that sent a cloud of sand exploding into the air at Monday's feet. Before she could get off a second blast, Columbus grabbed her, flipped her on her back, and ripped the stave from her hands. Nyx leaped onto the back of a third warrior as Fanucio planted a peg leg between his thighs with devastating effect. Vespucci winced but raised his hands when confronted. He wanted no part of this fight.

Columbus swung the stave, clocking one warrior across the cheek before he spun toward another. The woman shouted to quell the fight. Columbus's stave started to lower. That's when the giant blasted him. The shot struck Columbus in the chest and catapulted him ten feet backward. His torso was a smoking mass of carnage. He couldn't breathe.

Nyx screamed, followed by Fanucio. "You didn't have to kill him!"

Columbus gasped. The pain was worse than anything he'd ever experienced.

The giant was moving forward to finish him off when the woman shoved him aside. She dropped to Columbus's side, horrified by the extent of his wounds. She shouted at the giant, using that phrase again, *Anak-Ta Eleece*. It seemed to finally register. The other warriors shared glances of confusion and dismay. Only the giant appeared unrepentant. Then the woman held out her hand. The giant shook his head without emotion. The woman shouted again. This time, a young female warrior with short, curly hair, dashed over, ripping a lanyard from around her neck before handing it to the woman. A young male warrior—clearly her twin—tried to dissuade her to no avail.

Columbus's gasps came more frequent now, each breath harder to take in. Blood filled his mouth and lungs. It felt like he was drowning.

The woman loomed over him, whispering words he didn't understand. She held the lanyard by the crystal that hung at its end. No. It wasn't a crystal. It was a vial filled with dark fluid. The woman cracked it in half before pouring the fluid over Columbus's wounds.

For the second time, Columbus felt like he had been set ablaze. He howled, working his crew into a new fury. As smoke hissed from his wounds, he felt dizzy and nauseous. He reached for his chest, desperate to wipe it clean, but the woman grasped his hands.

"*Curare*," she said. "*Quievi.*"

Her eyes were filled with compassion and worry. Columbus felt himself ease. The instant he did, the pain began to ebb. The fiery sensation faded, replaced by what felt like a thousand needles tickling his body. Soon, they itched. He tried to scratch, but the woman stopped him again.

Columbus heard Nyx sob, but his breath was growing longer, the drowning feeling fading away.

"I don't believe it!" Fanucio exclaimed. "His wounds are healing."

Vespucci leaned in for a closer look, riveted. Even the Pygmies stopped struggling against their captors.

Finally, Columbus sat up. He looked at the faces around him. His crew was stunned, but not the warriors. Their faces betrayed only some odd sadness. *Or was it resentment?*

The woman sat back and sighed with relief. Columbus pulled his torn tunic open and looked down at his chest. The wounds were *gone*.

"What did you do to me?" Columbus asked.

The woman shook her head, beyond exhausted. She struggled to her feet and stalked toward the beach. Columbus and his crew were set free.

"*Consequi*," the woman said to him, signaling Columbus to follow. He looked to the mountain and then to the giant who held their weapons. He nodded.

When they reached the surf, one of the warriors raised a thin whistle to his mouth and blew a single, high-pitched note and waited. Columbus touched his chest again. Amazing. Even his old scars were gone. When he looked up, he saw the woman was watching him.

"I guess this makes us even," he said. She tilted her head. "*Aequare*. I saved you, you saved me."

The woman said nothing, turned back to the sea. Columbus reached out and touched her arm. She looked at his hand, then him.

"*Gratias tibi ago. Mihi nomen est Columbus.*"

"Elara," she responded.

"Elara," Columbus repeated before a smile cracked his face. "A beautiful name for a beautiful woman."

Nyx rolled her eyes as Fanucio muttered, "Here we go again."

Columbus held Elara's gaze until she looked away. *Had she blushed?* Columbus thought so. Then he saw the giant glaring at him.

"*Quod nomen est ejus?*" Columbus asked Elara.

"Dion."

"Big guy, Dion. Think he and I will be friends?"

The woman scoffed.

A second whistle rang out. This time, the call was answered when several dark shapes approached beneath the surf.

"*Equi Oceanus*," Elara said.

"Water horses," Columbus translated.

"*Eldocks*," Elara clarified.

Seven strange mammals surfaced. They were the size of baby whales and looked like a hybrid of walruses and horses. Each bore a saddle and a thin, golden bridle that ran over their brows. One chittered excitedly when it saw Elara. She walked into the water and ran a hand over its hide. The two obviously shared a bond.

A feeling of wonderment tickled Columbus's senses. *Now this is the kind of thing I was expecting.*

Fanucio sidled up to Columbus and whispered, "Are we meant to ride atop these beasts?"

"Better atop than within," Columbus replied.

The remaining warriors walked into the surf to mount their eldocks. It was obvious Columbus's crew was expected to follow.

"Well?" Nyx asked. "Are we going with them?"

"Even if we were in a position to refuse, which we are not," Vespucci said, "I, for one, would like very much to get off this island before any more of those things appear."

"He's right," Columbus said. "At least, about this."

Vespucci strode into the water and mounted an eldock behind the male twin warrior. As Nyx and Fanucio followed, Columbus turned to the Pygmies. "Are you coming?"

The Pygmies stood, arms crossed, pouting. Columbus groaned. "I wasn't the one that attacked them without provocation. If you wish to get your spears back, you'll have to ask them. I would suggest doing it nicely this time. Unless you'd rather stay here until dark and reunite with our singing friends."

Monday and Tuesday grudgingly followed.

Columbus avoided Dion's eyes as he climbed up and nestled in against Elara. "Bucked as a child. I'm sure you understand."

The curl of Elara's mouth suggested she understood perfectly. She called out and the pack turned in unison, cantering out to sea.

On the back of the rearmost eldock, Monday signaled Tuesday.

"*Intriguing motion*," he said. "*Reminds me of the first hippo I ever mastered.*"

Monday snorted. "*Reminds me of my first wife.*"

The water was surprisingly warm, the temperature fair. After a short spell, the party slipped into a current and moved deeper out to sea. Though the eldocks moved at a brisk pace, Columbus suspected they could go much faster. He reached down and ran a hand over the creature's hide. It was thick and clammy, firm muscles moving beneath.

Elara rode her eldock without reins. She used her knees and balance to dictate direction and speed. Even if Columbus hadn't seen their greeting on the beach, he'd be able to identify the obvious bond between animal and master. *Do the others share similar relationships with their eldocks?* Columbus couldn't tell. *Did Elara's know she'd been held captive? How long was she imprisoned there?*

Columbus knew he should have been more concerned about where they were headed, but he was too astonished by the sights around him. Everywhere he looked there were islands. Some were sprawling with verdant meadows, teeming with life. Others bore singular trees that jutted high into the sky.

Wildlife was everywhere. Some of it was recognizable—deer and elk, squirrels chittering in trees. Others were astonishingly unique. Howler monkeys that changed colors. Eels that scuttled between water and shore. Exotic birds with plumage in unbelievable colors.

With a shout, Nyx broke Columbus from his reverie. She pointed beneath them. Far below the surface, a team of eldock riders in familiar uniforms appeared to be harvesting plankton while stave-bearing warriors patrolled the area.

"How do they breathe?" Columbus asked.

Elara tapped a mask hanging from her saddle. Each rider had one. Columbus saw Vespucci's envious eyes take them in. *He wants one.* Truth told, so did Columbus, but for different reasons. He had sailed atop the waves his entire life. To explore beneath the surface—to see the world as no man had before—would have been a revelation.

Out of nowhere, Dion surged his eldock forward, his golden stave in his heavy hand. Columbus heard the buzz build moments before a large shadow appeared to their left. The biggest sea turtle Columbus had ever seen breached, rows of trumpet-like protrusions on its translucent shell.

Fanucio whooped. "It's like Soupy, me ol' pet! Think it'll mind if a give 'er a nuzzle?"

The giant turtle opened its mouth for a huge breath. As it exhaled, dozens of minuscule coral projectiles shot out, caroming off Dion's magical shield, which he'd activated a second before. He fired his stave into the water and the turtle quickly submerged and swam off.

"Nuzzle away," Columbus laughed. "Maybe you'll earn a new nickname."

Fanucio paled.

A few moments later, Nyx's eldock drew alongside Columbus, and she caught his eye.

"Is this what you expected?" Nyx asked.

Was it? He'd read accounts of Atlantis from a score of different cultures. Few had anything in common beyond the sinking of a powerful island nation. He was disappointed Plato's city was nowhere to be seen—with its concentric rings and glimmering towers—but this was equally unique.

"No," he said eventually. "Though I daresay we've barely scratched the surface. Perhaps more awaits in some unseen corner of this world."

He heard Vespucci scoff. Columbus didn't care. All his claims had been validated. His hard work paid off. Now he only needed to find the treasure. It was out there somewhere. He was certain of it.

As the ride continued, the strange sun poured down heat. Columbus felt beads of sweat dotting his hairline.

Passing a long peninsula, Elara turned. *"Postquam autem interrogavit Atlantis?"*

"Yes," Columbus answered.

She smiled and nodded ahead as they rounded the peninsula. *"Ibi est Atlantis. Regnum et domum suam."*

The crew gasped.

Like a mirage, it emerged from around the bend. On a low, circular island in the distance sat a city of glimmering towers that shone brilliantly in red and gold. The spires that rose like translucent blades of grass seemed to both reflect light and absorb it. Even from afar, Columbus could see elevated walkways devoid of buttresses and sprawling domes that defied gravity. It was a feat of engineering beyond anything known to man. Even the great Plato's description failed to do it justice.

"It's how I always imagined heaven would look," Nyx whispered.

Columbus looked at the girl. It was as if she had taken the words right out of his mouth. This was a city of enlightenment. The city of *his* dreams. He had nearly lost his life in pursuit of it a hundred times. The years he'd spent searching, the crew members lost, his blessed ship sunk—all led up to this. *It was all worth it,* he decided. *A thousand times over.*

"It could be heaven, or it could be hell," Columbus said. "That's the true allure of the adventuring life, Brommet. In this realm or any other, no man—*or woman*—knows fully what wonders await."

"Or how they shall be received," Vespucci added.

Columbus refused to let Vespucci ruin the moment. "Given our previous actions, I'd say with a hero's welcome."

Elara's head tilted slightly. *Can she understand us?* Not likely. But their awe was apparent. Still, she seemed to take no joy in it. That surprised Columbus. As did the fact that the nearer they drew, the darker her features grew. It was almost as if they emanated not from eagerness but from trepidation.

Columbus soon found his initial excitement tempered on approach. A bevy of glass-like projections ran from the city, out over the water to different isles. But many of these were cracked or broken; some laying in ruin, abandoned long ago.

Even more perplexing were the signs of wear. The spires that shined so brightly from afar lost their luster on approach. The highest had been shorn near its pinnacle. Fissures wound through stone edifices. Gilded statues had grown dull. Even now, a crew of workers sat perched along the side of one tower, working hastily on repairs. This was not Elysium.

This was a city in *decay*.

The reason quickly became evident. Behind and above the city brooded a dark mass of clouds. It was as if a storm of unparalleled size was preparing to feast on Atlantis. Maybe it had already begun. Only when they passed into the city's shadows did Columbus realize it wasn't a storm at all. It was the invisible barrier that protected the underwater kingdom. And it was pulsing as if it were alive.

CHAPTER EIGHT

The cry that went up from the watchtowers set in motion a flurry of activity as Elara's name echoed across the burnished ramparts with joyful reactions. It reaffirmed Columbus's belief that Elara was a person of real importance. Hopefully the part they played in liberating her would play in their favor.

The party drew to a halt fifty yards from the city wall. No clear entrance could be seen. Elara and Dion conferred briefly before Dion signaled the watchtower above. A moment passed before a jolt shook the city walls, the sounds of rusty gears preceding the rise of a large circular plate near the water's entrance, revealing a tunnel half-filled with water.

As the group entered, dust and debris wafted down from above. Columbus suspected it was because this path was rarely used.

The tunnel carried on for a spell, eventually emptying out into a cavernous stone bay with scores of gated water pens. Within lanterns affixed to the walls were red alchemical lights that burned with an otherworldly glow.

A man waited on a stone quay. He was older, with a plaited beard and scarlet frock coat that suggested he was someone of importance. He, too, wore one of those healing crystals around his neck. Other than Dion's, Columbus hadn't seen another. Were they rare and valuable? If so, Elara might get into trouble for using one on him.

As the group arrived, the older man signaled a group of youths, who quickly corralled the eldocks and helped their riders off.

When Elara stood, the older man embraced her warmly, relief evident as they spoke. Fanucio whispered to Columbus, asking if he thought the man was her father. Columbus didn't think so.

The quay shook when Dion climbed onto it. Whereas the other warriors helped the charges to their feet, the giant merely stepped back to supervise the proceedings.

The older man glanced briefly at the strangers, his gaze darkening. Elara shook her head and spoke that odd phrase again.

"What do you suppose it means?" Nyx asked. *"Anak-Ta Eleece?"*

Columbus had no idea, so he shushed her instead.

Once the party was dismounted, the young workers ushered the eldocks into individual pens, locking them behind steel gates that sunk beneath the surface. Elara's eldock was the last. She knelt by the quay and rubbed the creature's head. It chittered once again. Then the older man directed it to the nearest pen with a long wooden pole. When the gate closed, the old man looked at the youths. Each stood in front of a pen. With a single nod, they all bent down, reached inside the cage and removed the golden bridle covering the eldocks' heads. Instantly, the eldocks started thrashing in their cages and screeching so loud that Columbus and his crew had to cover their ears. It was a striking change from the passive animals they'd ridden for the past hour.

The crew was escorted down a long stone hallway into a moderate-sized room lined with partitions bearing more scarlet uniforms. The room smelled of salt and sweat.

At the room's center was a raised, circular platform with the edifice of a mouth carved in the ceiling directly above. Dion pointed to Columbus and then the platform.

Columbus shook his head. "I'm good, thanks."

Dion gestured with his hands, and several of his warriors laughed. Elara spoke one word and the laughter died. She nodded toward the female twin, whom she called *Thetra*. To the surprise of Columbus's crew, Thetra stripped off her clothes and stepped onto the platform. Dion struck a red plate on the wall, and a shower of water sprayed from the ceiling's mouth. A rush of hot air dried her an instant later, and the woman walked to a partition to put on a lighter set of clothes. Her twin brother, *Sareen*, followed.

"No way in hell I'm doing that," Nyx said, looking pale.

The giant sneered, waiting to see what Columbus would do next. He peeled off his torn shirt and trousers.

"No one cares for your giblets, girl. Unless you're afraid we'll see you're a boy after all?"

Nyx looked away, mortified and angry.

Having stripped bare, Columbus stepped onto the platform. He glanced at Elara, but she was busy removing her torn uniform. He smiled, thinking she was trying hard not to look his way.

Dion struck the red plate again, but this time only a trickle came out.

Columbus snickered. "Weak stream?"

Glowering, Dion punched the plate twice more before the water finally began to pour, blessedly hot. The relief it brought was instantaneous. Columbus felt half his tension ebb away. When he was done, he glanced at the red plate again. It was the same sanguine material that made up part of the city's towers. He remembered Plato spoke of a similar, precious metal, known only to the Atlanteans. *Orichalcum*. It was said to be a mixture of rare metals, possibly gold. Was it plentiful here? Columbus made a point to find out.

Freshly showered, the group was given threadbare robes before they were escorted into an adjacent room. Columbus looked back as Elara stepped under the shower, locking eyes with her just before the door closed.

Hours passed, during which they were provided what appeared to be dried seaweed and water. Nyx asked after a latrine and was shown to a closet with even more orichalcum plates. The others weren't privy to what happened inside, but when Nyx reappeared, her face was flush, and she refused to utter a word. The Pygmies went off to see the closet for themselves and didn't return.

Through a cracked rear door, Columbus watched as four grim-faced men and one woman questioned Elara. They wore robes similar to the eldock wrangler, but they had serious faces, reeking of self-importance and faux concern. Columbus knew their type well. Elara answered their questions before they shuffled off, leaving her looking troubled. She glanced at his door once before signaling Thetra and whispering in her ear. Trepidation briefly lit her features before she hustled off. Columbus hustled back to his seat a moment before Elara walked through.

She spoke in Latin again, trying not to let her fatigue show. Her tone was serious, escalating the tension in the room.

"Wot goin' on?" Fanucio asked.

Nyx hushed him before pulling close. "She said we've been summoned to something called the Nave. I think it must be the city's center."

"Who summoned us? Her leaders?"

"No, the *king*. Now, be still."

After Elara had spoken, Columbus and Vespucci both asked her questions. There was some fumbling—her Latin was far more archaic than theirs. Finally, she left the room.

"What?" Fanucio asked. "Somethin' wrong, isn't it?"

Columbus leaned forward, chin in hand.

"Apparently, we've come at a bad time. There's trouble in paradise, though she wouldn't elaborate. Also, they appear to hold some pretty hard feelings toward us."

"*Us*? Us who?"

"Man," Vespucci said. "Presumably she means the Athenians."

"It's almost as if they see themselves differently. As a species, I mean. What was that phrase she used?"

Vespucci repeated it in Latin.

"Wot's it mean?" Fanucio asked.

"Really, Fanucio," Nyx snapped, "didn't you study Latin when you were young?"

"Latin? Ha! I was born in a fishing village, lass. We had stars for a roof and mud for a floor. The only letters I studied were them on our eviction notice. Where did you learn it?"

The others curiously looked to the girl.

"At school," she answered vaguely.

Columbus knew she was hiding something, but he didn't have the time or inclination to figure out what. There were far more important things to worry about.

Vespucci cleared his throat. "She said, 'Though eons have passed, the strife between our races has not been forgotten.' Doesn't bode well for us, does it?"

Columbus heard heavy footfalls approaching. "We're about to find out."

The door opened, and four warriors signaled them to follow. One of them noticed the Pygmies had disappeared and asked Columbus about them.

"Haven't a clue, friend," Columbus said.

Their escorts led them through the daunting city, down circular tunnels that fed to hubs, each branching off into four or five different directions. Those strange alchemical lamps burned at each intersection, bathing everything in a dull red glow.

At one of the larger hubs, Columbus noticed a series of vacant tubes that ran from high atop the tower to somewhere far below them. At first, he assumed they were for ventilation. Then, a rushing sound shook the tube as it filled with liquid. An instant later, two people rose from below and stepped through an invisible door, dry as could be. Columbus and his crew could only marvel at this remarkable form of transportation.

More citizens emerged as they walked on—men, women, and children. They wore pale-colored garb of unusual fabric, unadorned but for the occasional belt or necklace. Like the warriors before, all were fair-skinned with light or reddish hair. A few of the men had beards, but most were clean-shaven. One constant, however, were the gems that graced a single side of every face. The patterns and colors seemed to signify something, though Columbus couldn't guess what. Children had fewer than the adults. Still, none came close to the warriors. Theirs ran from just above the brow, around the eye, and down to the jawline. *Are these marks of honor? Or do they indicate one's name or trade?* Columbus made a mental note to ask Elara later.

The crowd's gazes weren't overtly hostile, but they were tinged with suspicion. A few children laughed and tried to get close, only to be drawn away and scolded by their parents. Word of the newcomers' arrival must have spread through the city, so no one was surprised by their presence. Still, there was an intensity to the crowd, as if they were all eager to see what happened next.

The final ramp descended to a large archway, from which the murmur of a larger crowd could be heard. A nervous tick began to beat inside Columbus's chest. He pushed the feeling down. He had no idea what awaited them in this Nave. He would need to be ready for anything.

At last they entered a great hall and froze. Across a ringed plaza was a grand amphitheater crafted of stone. It was gilded in orichalcum that shone despite its wear and age. Two stories of superimposed arcades were filled with marble statues of athletic figures in various modes of combat. Some of these statues were broken or outright removed. Still, there was enough of them to paint a picture of what might have once—and possibly still—transpired inside. Rome's colosseum came to Columbus's mind. But he had to wonder if they were to be the guests or the entertainment.

The escorts drew them to the side as the Atlanteans continued to filter into the amphitheater.

"This is the Nave?" Nyx asked, her mouth still hanging open.

"It sure isn't the bathhouse," Columbus replied.

"I smell sulfur," Vespucci said.

Columbus nodded. He'd smelled it too. "Might be we're above some volcanic artery."

"Or maybe you have delivered us to hell after all."

"If that's the case," Columbus said, cuffing Vespucci on the shoulder, "you can make the introductions."

As the plaza continued to empty, Columbus and his crew

wondered what they were waiting for. Then, Elara appeared. She crossed to them hurriedly and asked a question in Latin.

Nyx leaned toward Fanucio. "She's asking about Monday and Tuesday."

Columbus played dumb, though the truth was he rarely knew where those two were or what they were up to. With a frown, Elara sent off two of the guards to find them.

"Good luck," Fanucio snorted. "Bloodhounds couldn't find them two when they're on the hunt. Speaking of which, she say anything about food?"

Nyx hushed him as Elara spoke on, translating afterward. "She says there are a few rules before we go inside. First, don't speak to the king unless he addresses you first."

"Speak to a king? Wouldn't know what to say. Hello, Your Worship. Nice place you got here—"

"And, second, do not approach him for any reason. Failure to obey these rules will result in..." She swallowed.

Fanucio didn't need a translator for that. "Why I never learned Latin."

Just then, Thetra returned, winded, as if she'd run a long way. In her hand, she carried a dusty jar of black glass. She handed it to Elara, who nodded. Thetra rushed into the Nave.

Elara turned to the strangers and spoke again in Latin. Nyx translated.

"She said the jar is very old. And few people know of its existence. It's said to contain—I'm not sure about this part—slivers of the tongue of Mnemosyne?"

"What's a Mnemosyne?"

"Not what, you buffoon. *Who*. Mnemosyne was the Greek Goddess of memory, remembrance, and time."

"Your school teach you that too?"

"I had a very *thorough* teacher."

Columbus watched as Elara struggled to open the jar. Once the lid came free, he looked at the murky liquid within.

"Appreciate the offer," Columbus said, "but I'm trying to cut down."

Near the Nave, a robed man emerged and called out. Elara nodded before turning back, her eyes intense.

"Columbus," she said. "*Faveo. Juvo.*"

She touched her heart as she said it. Columbus sighed, realizing she was making some sort of promise.

"Fine," he said, reaching for the jar. "One sip, but that's it."

She pulled the jar back and shook her head before pointing to his ear. "*Audio.*"

"Usually pillow talk comes after the deed is done."

Elara raised the jar to his ear and waited. With a sigh, Columbus lowered his head to the jar. He heard nothing. Then, a warm feeling coursed through him. He picked up his head.

"Am I supposed to hear—"

Nyx screamed. Fanucio grabbed Columbus. "Cap'n, it's in your ear!"

Columbus staggered back, his fingers grasping something eel-like before it wormed its way into his ear and disappeared. He fell, groaning in pain.

Fanucio took a step toward Elara, asking, "What have you done?"

Her guards grabbed him. Elara held up a hand, "*Patientia.*"

Columbus's pain finally eased. Fanucio and Nyx helped him to his feet.

"What did you do to me?" he asked.

The others gasped in surprise.

Elara looked relieved. "I have empowered you with a gift of the Titans."

"Y-you spoke her language," Fanucio said, amazed.

"Do you truly understand her?" Vespucci asked.

Columbus nodded, stunned. "It was like she spoke Spanish. Or Ligurian."

"It was definitely neither of those," Nyx added.

Elara nodded to the jar in her hands. "Not since the fall of Babel and the conflict between Enmerkar and the Lord of Aratta has man been free of the 'confusion of tongues.' Use this gift wisely."

"Does this mean you can speak multiple languages? *Pouvez-vous parler français?*"

Columbus shrugged. "*Qui. Bien sûr.*"

"*Und Deutsch?*" Vespucci asked.

"*Die Sprache fließt durch meinen Geist, als wäre es mein eigener.*"

"Incredible. There isn't a ruler the world over that wouldn't give his kingdom for such a gift."

Elara interrupted again. "We must hurry. If the others want to share in this, it must be done quickly."

Vespucci and Nyx volunteered first. Only Fanucio refused, and no talk of lashings or demotions could convince him otherwise. In the end, one thing did the trick. Columbus threatened to ban rum from all their future journeys.

"Now, reading," the first mate grumbled as he rubbed his sore ear, "that's where I draw the line. I ain't putting nothing in me eye. Or any other orifice for that matter. You even ask and—"

He gaped as they entered the Nave.

If the exterior had been a shock, the interior was a revelation. Several thousand Atlanteans were gathered in the amphitheater's seats, surrounded by giant columns in the shape of men and women, their raised arms acting as buttresses to hold up an immense ceiling of glass. High above, the blue sky shone down, only the fringes of the storm beyond visible.

Columbus felt a momentary thrill when he saw that the red banners around the room featured golden tridents, suggesting this truly was the kingdom of Poseidon. But how to find the real trident?

The crowd hushed as Columbus and crew were escorted to the center of the amphitheater. The floor was strangely cobbled, misshapen stone, three feet in diameter at its center. Next to the newcomers, it was the only thing that looked out of place.

A hush fell over the room, the current more hostile than before.

"A hero's welcome, eh?" Vespucci said.

Columbus ignored him. He was looking around for this king when a thunderous pounding of drums reigned down from the upper echelons. It shook the banners and spurred the crowd to their feet.

"Why must it always be drums?" Columbus groaned.

From a tunnel midway up the seating area, a flock of bannermen appeared, followed by a half-dozen imposing guards dressed in scarlet armor. Dion was among them, his cursed golden stave dangling from his belt. Immediately, the giant locked eyes with Columbus, his sneer flashing like a blade.

The drums beat to a frenzy before going silent as a lumbering shadow filled the tunnel. The crowd took to knee in unison, heads dipping as their regent arrived.

"All kneel for King Atlas," Elara said as she took a knee.

Columbus and the others followed suit.

King Atlas was a towering figure. While not quite as large as Dion, he was imposing nonetheless. Barrel-chested and thick-necked, he wore shimmering orichalcum armor and was the only man with a sword at his hip. It looked like the one Columbus had found in the caves. He also wore one of those vials around his neck, though again, Columbus didn't see many others.

King Atlas also had red hair interspersed with gray and a surfeit of gems surrounding both sides of his eyes. His brow thick, his countenance severe, the man was the very definition of imperious. He used a large bejeweled stave to walk down to a stone throne near the stage floor. As he fell into it, the people sat. A youthful lad ushered forward with a golden chalice for the king. He took a hearty drink. When he wiped his mouth, he spoke, his deep voice echoing throughout the auditorium.

"Frailty permeates the air!" he bellowed. "*Man* is in our midst again."

A chuckle ran through the amphitheater, swallowed quickly by the tension.

"Is there one among who speaks for the rest?"

Columbus moved to stand, but felt a hand press him down as Vespucci marshaled past.

"I do, great King," Vespucci said.

The crowd gasped. King Atlas leaned forward, brow furrowed.

"You speak our tongue? How—" His eyes snapped to Elara, who

looked down.

Undaunted, Vespucci pressed on. "It is a great honor to stand before you and to be welcomed into your glorious city. My name is Amerigo Vespucci, and I humbly submit myself to your service."

Vespucci bowed deep.

Bored, the king took another gulp from his chalice. "Eloquent," he said before belching. "Though you have neither been welcomed nor your service requested, humble or otherwise."

Vespucci blinked. "Pardon me, Your Grace. I did not presume to speak on your behalf."

"And who's behalf do you speak on?" the king replied.

"Spain's, sir. The Monarchy of Spain."

"Ah. *Iberia*. I remember this land from my teachings. A lazy people, if memory serves. Would this make you their king and my equal?"

"No—"

"A prince, then? Or some lesser sovereign?"

"I am merely a nobleman, sire, who finds himself unwittingly cast in the role of ambassador between our peoples. It is my sincere hope that we might establish relations."

King Atlas leaned forward, a dark smile creasing his face. Columbus recognized that look for what it was. One of power looking at one without it.

"You wish to have *relations* with me?" King Atlas asked.

Vespucci nearly shit himself. "N-no. I—"

Already the man was floundering. Elara looked to Columbus.

"Help him," Nyx whispered.

"Why?" Columbus asked. "He's doing so well on his own."

HIGH ABOVE THE PROCEEDINGS, two diminutive figures stole through the shadows, eventually settling into a pair of seats at the top of the Nave. In their hands, a stolen bottle of grog that they passed back and forth.

"*Excellent seats!*" exclaimed Monday.

Tuesday balked. "*I can see nothing from here.*"

"But we are the tallest in the room!"

Tuesday nodded to an Atlantean man a few seats away. "Except him."

Monday's eyes narrowed as he pulled a hidden dagger. Tuesday caught his kinsman before he could make a scene.

DOWN ON THE FLOOR, Vespucci realized things were not going to plan. "Forgive me if I have offended you, sire. I have not spoken in court in ages."

"Unprepared as well as stupid," the king belched. "If these are the traits of a kingdom's ambassador, one can only surmise their ruler's prowess."

Sniggers ran through the crowd. The king ate them up. When he took another gulp from his cup, liquid splashed his chest. He didn't even notice. Only then did Columbus realize the truth: *the good king was drunk.*

When Vespucci tried to speak again, the king raised a hand.

"Enough," he grumbled, his smile gone in an instant. "You come into my city with no tribute and attempt to court me with your silken tongue. Is the art of diplomacy forgotten to your people, or do you think me beneath common courtesy?"

The amphitheater was silent. Vespucci was visibly shaken. What he didn't understand—what Columbus knew from the moment they had walked into the room—was that the king had been itching for a fight from the start. The question was why? Columbus was content to let Vespucci fumble along and suffer his ignominy until the truth was revealed, but by then it could be too late.

"M-my Grace," Vespucci stuttered. "Perhaps if we spoke in private—"

Elara called out a warning as Vespucci took a step forward. It was too late. One of the guards struck him across the back of the legs with his stave. Vespucci cried out as he fell to the ground.

King Atlas chuckled. "That was for approaching me without permission."

Vespucci tried to stand. The guard hit him a second time.

"And that was for trying to stand without it."

Vespucci clutched his legs and moaned in pain. King Atlas tsked and shook his head.

"Look at this craven man. Is this *all* the upper realm has to offer me? Cowardice without an iota of courage or strength?"

Vespucci tried to speak again. The guard raised his stave a third time, but it was caught by Columbus.

"I think he's had enough," Columbus said.

The guard looked to the king, who waved him away, his attention fully focused on this new man.

"You are the true leader of this rabble," King Atlas said. "Why the deception?"

Columbus snapped his finger and Fanucio rushed to pick up Vespucci. "Sometimes a dog must be kicked to know its place."

A smile cracked King Atlas's face. "And to give its master the lay of land. Now, you have it…?"

"Columbus. Christopher Columbus."

"Columbus does not sound like a name of Iberia. Are you an *ambassador* for Spain as well?"

"No. I was born in Genoa to the east, but these days I make my home upon the sea. My kingdom begins with the deck of my ship and ranges as far and wide as the ocean will carry me."

"A mariner," King Atlas said.

Columbus smiled. "Some say sailor, others privateer. I prefer adventurer."

At this, King Atlas laughed. "Well, *adventurer*, welcome to *my* kingdom. In Atlantis you will find adventure in no short supply. If you live that long. Now that pleasantries are out of the way, why don't you tell me why you've come to my city."

"Interesting story that. You see, there was a storm. Something between a squall and a tempest. And in the chaos that ensued, the mast of my ship was damaged. When I cut the sail to repair it, a serpent rose from the depths and dragged us asunder."

King Atlas's eyebrow rose. "A serpent rose from the depths and dragged you asunder?"

Columbus nodded. King Atlas looked around and began to chuckle. The chuckling turned quickly to laughter.

"Man has not set foot in my kingdom for two thousand years. And when they do finally return, it's not aboard an armada of warships, but as the unwitting passengers of a sea serpent."

The laughter grew until it filled the entire amphitheater. Then the building shook with an unexpected jolt, sending dust falling from above. The laughter died in an instant. The king's smile vanished. Only when the quake subsided did the king signal Columbus forward.

"Come closer, mariner," he said. "I have a question for you."

Columbus took a deep breath before striding forward. He kept his head high, his eyes locked on the king. He didn't want to betray any weakness. He stopped a few feet away. The king beckoned him closer. When he was within reach, the king's hand shot out and grabbed him by the throat.

"Do you take me for a fool?" he snarled. "Who really sent you? Was it the Athenians? What forces align against us?"

"None," Columbus croaked.

"Lies! I am descended from the Gods themselves! I know a threat to my throne when I see one."

"Only if you share it with a queen," Fanucio muttered.

"Father, please!" Elara cried.

Columbus's head snapped around. *Did she just call him father?*

Fanucio grumbled. "A *princess*. I spoke too soon."

King Atlas pulled Columbus closer, his face turning purple. "You saved my daughter's life. If not for that, you would already be dead. But I cannot allow interlopers to run free in my kingdom. I will give you one final chance. Tell me why you are here!"

Columbus shook his head in defiance as a cascade of black stars blotted his view.

Suddenly, Nyx bounded forward, blurting out a single word, "Treasure!"

King Atlas's gaze shifted to her. *"Treasure?"* he repeated.

Columbus shook his head, but when Nyx saw his eyes flutter, she continued.

"Columbus—our captain and leader—found a disk, great king. A bronze disk whose map led us across the ocean above, to this very place."

"A map, you say? To what reward?"

"Gems. Gold. Precious objects. In return for joining his crew, we were offered whatever we could carry."

"He even promised me a golden foot!" Fanucio yelled, his peg leg raised in the air.

King Atlas shook his head. "For ages we've feared the footfalls of man, and when they finally return they are not warriors or spies, but thieves."

He heaved Columbus to the floor before falling back in his throne. He reached for his chalice only to find it empty. He growled before turning to the strangers once again.

"No shortage of gold and gems will you find here, child, little good they will do you. All of it is useless in this accursed place."

Color returning, Columbus stumbled back to the others. The king continued.

"The disks you speak of were created long ago by the First Tribe, yet they are more than a map. They are also a vessel to bridge the depths between our worlds. We once sent emissaries above to protect our interests, but few returned. The disks were thought to be lost."

"Is it possible, your Highness, that the leviathan was part of this mechanism?" Columbus said, his voice raspy.

"Possible?" The king mused. "Anything is possible. Our ancestors had many boons at their disposal, among them a knowledge of how to communicate with the beasts of the world. Only our way with the eldocks remain. Do you have it still, this disk?"

Columbus shook his head. "It was lost in our descent."

"Pity," King Atlas said. "Now, you are imprisoned here just as we are."

Just then another tremor shook the city, and those strange alchemical lights fluttered on the walls. It ended quickly but had a lasting effect on the mood in the room.

"As you see, our kingdom has lost much of its wonder. The magic used to craft this realm is waning. Each day the Void that protects us grows smaller and weaker. We have done our best to halt it but have little grasp of the science of our elders. I fear the end of Atlantis draws nigh."

"But he is the *Anak-Ta Eleece*, Father!" Elara pleaded. "I have seen it!"

King Atlas shook his head. "'Tis folly, daughter. The old ways left after the Gods abandoned us. No one can save us now."

"But the prophecy!"

"Blasphemy. The lies of the slaves offer no succor."

Elara opened her mouth to speak again, but no words came out. She looked desperately to Columbus, hoping he might say something, do something. But he was as silent as the others. He was surprised to feel a kernel of pity for the king. Moments ago, he raged like a storm. Now he looked weary. Impotent. "I long imagined the day our races would meet again and wondered what the outcome would be of such a reunion. Would we find ourselves once again at war? Or would we become allies, brothers? The answer matters little now. The days ahead of us are dark and dire, and we have no time for uncertainties. Guards. Take these *people* and cast them into the Void."

As the guards moved, Elara rushed toward the king. "Please, Father. I beg of you. Do not do this! He is the *Anak-Ta Eleece*! If you kill him, you doom us all!"

The king sighed and signaled for his cup to be refilled. "Doom, child, is all we have left."

As Columbus was being pulled from the room, he managed a parting salvo. "Don't forget self-pity."

The king looked up, snarling. "What did you say?"

The guards hesitated, unsure what they were supposed to do.

Columbus seized the moment. "You spoke of strength when we first entered, but I've seen none on display here. Only self-pity and weakness. In our culture—as with most cultures of our world—a condemned man is offered an opportunity to prove his worth."

"You wish to *fight* for your freedom?" King Atlas asked, amused. "I remember tale of these ways. And though the thought of such barbarism appeals to me, you are no match for an Atlantean."

"Join me and prove it."

King Atlas bellowed again, and his men laughed nervously with him. "Did you hear nothing I said? I am a descendant of the Gods. In my lifetime, no man has come close to challenging me. Still, the thought of returning to battle after so many years gives new rise to my blood." He nodded. "Yes. I would take you up on your offer, but for one minor thing. Were you—by some miracle—to prevail, the future of my kingdom would fall into the hands of my daughter. And that is a danger I cannot risk."

If Elara was hurt by that sentiment, she did her best to hide it.

"But laws be damned!" the king shouted. "You have courage, adventurer. I will give you your match and allow one to fight in my stead."

Surprised, Columbus said, "I don't suppose I get to pick?"

King Atlas chuckled before looking to his right. "Dion shall be my champion."

For the first time, the giant smiled. Columbus felt his stomach drop. Still, it was a chance.

Fanucio pulled close. "I'll bet he ain't as tough as he looks, Cap'n."

Nyx smirked. "I'd take that bet."

Pounding drums filled the auditorium again. Elara pulled Columbus to the center of the room, nodding to the others to get back. She pulled the golden stave from her belt. "This is a sonstave. It has two functions. Depress this colored jewel and it sends out a blast of sonic energy. You remember its sting. This second jewel provides a barrier—like a shield to protect you, though it only lasts a second or two."

Columbus glanced at Dion. The giant had stripped off his armor and was getting himself loose. He moved fast, athletic. This was not going to be easy.

"Any rules?" Columbus asked.

"Yes," Elara answered. "If you're hit, you die. Avoid getting hit."

"She's got jokes," Columbus smirked.

"And whatever you do, don't let go of your sonstave. Here, it is considered the same as a forfeit."

"Understood."

The drums surged as the trial was about to begin. Dion had worked up a sweat and was ready. Elara faced Columbus, her back to her father. "He likes to use his shield as a battering ram. Watch for a feint first."

Columbus nodded as Elara slipped away. Columbus took another heavy breath and wiped the sweat from his hands.

"Are the combatants ready?" King Atlas asked. "Begin!"

Dion fired an immediate blast from his sonstave. Only Columbus's lightning-fast reflexes allowed him to activate the shield barrier to parry it.

At the side of the room, Columbus's team shouted support.

"Come on, Captain! You can do this!" Fanucio said.

"Teach this fish lover something," Nyx howled.

Vespucci stayed silent.

Columbus traced a circle around the outside of the room, firing off a blast that Dion easily defended.

Dion paced the opposite direction, forcing Columbus back to his left. Columbus was a natural counterpuncher. The giant seemed to sense this, only firing a probe when Columbus broke eye contact.

He's fast, Columbus thought. *And careful. He's looking for weaknesses.*

All at once, the giant fired off three blasts in quick succession. The first two struck Columbus's shield, but the third was aimed at his feet. Columbus spun away as the energy skipped off the cobbles where he'd been standing. He lost his footing and went down, rolling to avoid Dion's fourth and fifth shot.

HIGH ABOVE THE FRAY, the Pygmies watched on.

"*Our prisoner appears to be at a disadvantage? Shall we step in?*" Monday said.

"*Let him fight,*" Tuesday replied. "*Our bottle's still half-full.*"

. . .

As Columbus regained his footing, Dion charged him. Columbus fired, hitting the giant's shield. He shrugged it off and grinned. Dion fired the next blast, but it sailed overhead. Columbus was relieved until he realized the behemoth had only fired to edge closer. Once he was near enough, Dion barreled into Columbus with his shield just as Elara had warned. A quartet of brutal punches followed, spilling air from Columbus's lungs. Columbus spun away, firing to aid his retreat.

The giant grinned. Columbus swallowed. Things were about to get serious.

While Columbus's crew members continued to encourage their captain, Elara noticed her father sat grim and silent on his throne. His fists were clenched, his blood up. He was invested in the outcome.

The crowd *oohed* and *ahhed* as the competition continued, but surprisingly they cheered neither contestant. To them, a fight to the death was a sacred thing, and each combatant deserved respect. Still, there was no question where their hearts truly were.

Columbus was gasping, falling harder on his heels. The room was sweltering and sweat trickled into his eyes. He wiped it away, taking deep breaths between each blast that struck his shield—each like a hammer to the chest. He wasn't sure how long he could take it.

All at once, Dion stopped to reposition his feet and feinted like he was about to fire. Then he charged. This time, Columbus was ready. Rather than retreat, he stepped toward his opponent just as Dion activated his shield and lowered his shoulder behind it. To his surprise, Columbus didn't set himself to defend it. Instead, he fell back, letting his opponent come over top of him. Just as the giant's weight was poised to crush him, Columbus wedged the butt of his sonstave between the cobbles of the floor and fired. The blast catapulted Dion ten feet into the air. He hit the ground with tremendous force, his sonstave slipping from his hand.

Fanucio and Nyx cheered as Columbus limped toward the beleaguered giant. He was reaching down to take his sonstave when Dion turned over rapidly, his sonstave already back in his hand. He fired off a surprise blast. Columbus managed to raise his shield in time, but he was too close. The blast propelled him backward. When he landed, his sonstave rolled across the stone floor.

The match was over.

"Bad play!" Fanucio shouted.

"He cheated!" Nyx screamed. "He lost his weapon first!"

"His body never lost contact," King Atlas said. "My champion has triumphed."

The crowd applauded as Dion struggled to his feet. Despite being crowned the victor, he looked anything but pleased. He was even more incensed when Elara went to aid Columbus.

"He fought valiantly, Father," she said to the king.

To her surprise, the king nodded, somber. She thought he would have been celebrating.

"Yes. But the law is the law, in my kingdom or any other. This man has failed. The bargain is kept. Take them to the Void."

"No!" Elara shouted as the guards pulled Columbus to his feet. "This is wrong! We can have peace!"

King Atlas rose wearily and turned for the tunnel. "There can be no peace while Atlantis withers. The Void awaits us all."

Elara shouted again, but it was no use. The guards had taken hold of the entire crew and were in the process of escorting them away when a gasp ran through the room, followed by many others. King Atlas turned at the sound. When he saw what they were looking at, his face grew pale.

Just inside the front entrance stood a stooped figure in a woolen cowl, a gnarled walking stick clutched in her hand.

Whispers filled the room. For the first time, King Atlas looked ill at ease.

"What is it, Crone?" he asked with obvious disdain. "What brings your wrinkled old face from its hovel?"

The figure looked up, revealing an ancient, frail woman with milky white eyes. She pointed a shaky finger at Columbus, speaking only one word.

"Him."

CHAPTER NINE

The crone padded slowly down the hallway, silver hair a-tangle under her earthen cowl. Her walking stick echoed with each strike on the floor, slower and more foreboding than Fanucio's peg leg, like a pronouncement of doom.

Columbus had left his first mate and the others in the care of Elara's guard. She had promised no harm would come to them until after he'd met with the old woman. Columbus had no idea what such a meeting entailed, but by the foreboding look of every citizen they passed, it couldn't be good.

Even Dion appeared wary of the old woman. He had protested briefly with the king. In the end, it did no good. King Atlas might be ruler of Atlantis, but this stooped woman had some other authority that he feared. If only Columbus could find a way to use that in their favor.

Guards were posted at various intervals along their path. Columbus wasn't sure if this was normal or if they'd been tasked with protecting the princess while she was in the stranger's company. What struck Columbus, however, was how each guard went rigid as the old woman passed. He recalled the princess's reaction upon first seeing this *crone*. At first, there was relief, followed quickly by reverence before finally succumbing to fear. He'd seen that kind of woeful mix in primitive cultures where mysticism flourished. He never imagined seeing it in a place like this. What power could such a frail old woman yield over a kingdom that her mere appearance unnerved everyone who looked upon her?

Columbus knew he should have been more afraid, but he was still reeling from the events that unfolded before her arrival. He'd had his share of close calls over the years, but the battle in the Nave topped the list. How had things here turned so badly so quickly?

Vespucci.

That bootlicker had tried to bluster his way into the king's good graces. While that might work in a court full of toadies, anyone with the sense of a scullery maid could see Atlantis's leader's hunger for confrontation. The question was why? Elara had warned them about the king, but more was left unsaid than spoken. The man was a tyrant, blithely willing to send five strangers to their deaths, and yet Columbus sensed some turmoil in the man. Then again, he had ordered they be sent...where was it again? Oh, yes. The Void.

Columbus inquired about it.

"It is the barrier that surrounds and protects Atlantis from the realm above," Elara replied.

"It can be penetrated easily?"

"All one has to do is simply walk through. And there, you will be greeted by the weight of ten thousand leagues and crushed in an instant."

"Have you ever seen it happen?"

"I have seen many pass into the Void. What happens on the other side is obscured by the barrier itself. If you get close enough, you can hear it, though."

"What?"

"Its power," she answered hesitantly, as if even talking about it brought her pain. "It's like a storm pounding at a door desperate to get in. Here, it serves as our harshest punishment. In my lifetime, I have witnessed twenty or so condemned to pass through. But I have never seen anyone come from the other side...until you. What was it like?"

"It's sort of a blur, really. There was a battle raging between my ship and two others. I was wounded and dazed. Then the leviathan appeared, rising so high I feared it might blot out the sun. My crew fought valiantly, but in the end, we were no match for it. It destroyed my ship with ease and drew those it did not kill asunder. I recall plummeting fast, past the corpses of my men, until the light of the world faded away and there was nothing left but the cold and dark. Something strange happened then, though it's possible I imagined it. A voice spoke to me."

Elara searched his face, troubled. "A voice? What did it say?"

Columbus noticed the crone had stopped walking, her head turned as if awaiting his response. He caught a glimpse of those milky blind eyes and felt his chest tighten. Something told him he'd said too much.

"'Hurry, there's a fair maiden here that needs rescuing,'" he answered. Elara rolled her eyes and continued walking. "How did you get there anyway?"

"I was taken captive by the sirens while on a mission. For two days I hung in Gaia's Craw. I'm not sure why they spared me. We have been at war with them for centuries and still understand so little about them."

Up ahead, the crone had reached a stone staircase that seemed incongruous in a city made of glass. As they headed downward, Columbus caught the smell of moisture. They were descending below the waterline.

At last they came to a long stone corridor, lit with those same alchemical globes, only burning blue instead of red. This part of the city felt much older than the one above. As the old woman continued to lead them, Columbus felt his throat tighten and his breath come faster.

"Who is she?" he whispered.

"She is the Seer," Elara answered. "I know of no other name for her. Some say she is the last descendant of the slaves, but that is impossible."

"Why?"

"Their line ended a thousand years ago."

"She looks good for her age."

Surprisingly, Elara smiled. "Why does it not surprise me that you enjoy older women?"

"Who doesn't value experience?"

"My father says she has not aged since he was a child. His father's father once called upon her for council. Now, she lives down here, alone."

"In a dungeon?"

Elara elbowed him. "Once there were even lower levels than this. The slaves' quarters. But they flooded after the last rebellion four hundred years ago. Even *she* dares not go there."

"Why do you say *she*?"

"Sometimes at night, the guards see her walking about the city like a ghost. It unnerves our people. Moons pass, and we think she's finally gone, but then she appears again. No one knows her purpose."

As the Seer walked by an alchemical lamp, it flickered intermittently.

"Does she have magic?"

Elara shrugged. "My mother used to say magic was lore beyond our understanding. Would your people see our marvels and call them magic?"

"Witchcraft, more likely."

Elara stopped. Up ahead, the Seer was closing in on an old wooden door. It was the first wood save the Seer's walking stick that he'd seen since he'd entered the city. Elara spoke with urgency then. "She leads you to the Chamber of Fates. There, you will see the past, present, and future of your choosing. In the last hundred years only one other has received this blessing."

"Let me guess. The king."

"No. *Me*."

Curious. Elara glanced at the Seer again and swallowed. She was afraid. But of what?

"My vision revealed that I would find the *Anak-Ta Eleece*."

"That phrase doesn't translate. What does it mean?"

"It's the language of the slaves. Crafted by their God, not our own. It means, 'Rider of the Stars.'"

"Rider of the Stars. Hmm. I like it. It has panache. 'Hear ye, hear ye. Here stands Christopher Columbus, Admiral of the Seas, Rider of the Stars!' I wonder if I could turn that into a catchphrase?"

Elara looked at him askew. "You avail yourself of this humor often?"

"It's one of my best skills."

She sighed. "Then we are in more trouble than I thought."

Down the hall, the wooden door creaked open, and the Seer entered. She left the door cracked as a light flickered to life within.

Elara grew even more intense.

"Listen. My quest to find the Star Rider is why I went to the sirens' lair alone. It is why I was captured. But the Fates are tricky and cruel. They reveal glimpses, but not everything. Columbus, this is important. You must pose your questions carefully, leaving no room for interpretation. Of the past and present, I ask of you nothing. Any wisdom or treasure you seek is yours for the naming. But of the future, I beg of you, ask this and this alone: *How might Atlantis be saved?* The survival of my people depends upon it."

"Sure," he answered.

It wasn't enough. Elara gripped him harder. "I would have your word."

He saw how important this was to her and how vulnerable that made her. He suspected this was a woman who never showed such emotions, which if he was being completely honest, excited him. "All right, Princess. I promise."

Her relief was evident in the smile that split her face; it was like a sunbeam that shed light even in those dreary confines.

She pulled close. "I knew when I first saw you in the cavern that you were the one. Now, go. It is unwise to keep the Seer waiting."

She pushed him toward the door. Columbus knocked, and a scratchy old voice told him to enter. With one last glance at Elara, he entered and closed the door behind him.

The room was long and narrow with an arched ceiling that

sprawled upward. The Seer had lit several candles, which cast shadows on the stone floor and walls. Old wooden shelves lined the walls with dusty relics and glass containers filled with indistinguishable kinds of matter. Some of it twisted Columbus's stomach, and he refused to let his gaze stay on anything too long.

In the center of the room was a long table, upon which numerous dusty tomes sat splayed open, the vellum pages brittle and aged.

At the far end of the room was a window that took up the entire wall, revealing the depths of the sea outside.

"We are beneath the ocean," Columbus noted.

"He's wise, this one," the Seer said, dryly. "Let the city rejoice. Our savior has come!"

She cackled as she said it and a swell of nerves roiled Columbus's belly.

He stood silent as the old woman stepped onto a stool and set a black jar on a dusty perch. It was the same jar that had given him the power of languages.

She was blind, but she had set the jar in the only vacant space without touching anything else around it.

Once she stepped down, the Seer peeled off her cowl and hung it on a hook next to her walking stick.

"That's better," she sighed. "I dislike wearing that thing, but I have an image to maintain."

Columbus nearly laughed but wasn't sure if she was making a joke. "Is the staff where you derive your power?"

"My *power?*" she repeated, amused.

"Your magic."

"Yes. The staff gives me the power to walk and the robe the power to stay warm."

She cackled again and shook her head.

Columbus was confused. "Elara—the princess—says you're old. Very old."

"Any fool with eyes can see that."

"And you're saying you have no magic?"

"*Magic,*" the old woman scoffed. "Magic is a conjurer's word. And conjurers are performers, agents of illusion. Man has no real magic—or none that is inherent to him. But some can gain access to magical things."

"I don't understand."

The Seer sighed. "Pretty, but dim."

She made her way to a large wooden chair and sat. Her eyes closed. Columbus waited, but she didn't move.

"I'm sorry, but what are you doing?" he asked.

One of the Seer's eyes opened. "Resting. What does it look like? The Nave is a long walk for someone as *old* as me."

Once again, Columbus wasn't sure if he should laugh or keep his mouth shut. Thankfully, the Seer took pity on him.

"Since man first crawled from the muck, we believed the earth was ours and ours alone. But it has always belonged to the Gods. Atlantis—and the realm above—is their playground, and we are but their playthings. It is an ugly truth, I know. But it is truth nonetheless. Once, the Gods saw us as children. We entertained them, delighted them, enraged them. They competed for our affections, reveling in our adulation and unleashing terrible fury upon us when we chose another's favor. But when at last they grew bored—as all Gods do—we were abandoned, and they moved onto new lands and new pleasures. They left us to forge our way alone. Yet, in their heedlessness, a few special remnants remained. These are the relics men like you have sought for ages. Tokens of power. Of real *magic*."

Columbus felt his breath quickening. The trident came to mind.

"And how does one find these tokens?"

She cackled again, but those milky eyes never blinked. "Freshly plucked from the arms of death, yet so eager to return."

"Right. About that, I never properly thanked you for saving my life and the lives of my crew."

"Don't. The Void is an easy passing. Yours will not be so painless."

Columbus felt his mouth go dry. "You speak of the prophecy?"

"Call it intuition. Reckless men always die recklessly."

"True, but some do it with a smile."

He was disappointed she didn't laugh. Instead, the Seer's hand latched out and grabbed his wrist. She pulled him close, as if those milky eyes could see into his soul.

"You have strength and courage, and you have lived much to this point, but there is a darkness inside of you—a hunger—that will not be sated. A time will come—perhaps soon—when you will be forced to choose between those you care for and what you desire most. I fear you will make the wrong choice."

"I...I don't know what to say to that."

"Say nothing then. Silence is a gift few men are blessed with." She stood with great effort and pointed to something on a high shelf. "Hand me that basket."

Columbus retrieved a basket with a rolled-up rug in it. The Seer took it and ambled toward the wall of glass that illuminated the sea beyond.

"You spoke of the prophecy. It was written by the Athenians who were bonded into slavery after Atlantis fell. That was their penance for dooming this island nation beneath the sea. They knew they would never escape this realm, but they hoped its inhabitants might one day find peace. The prophecy says one will come from above —*The Anak-Ta Eleece*."

"The Star Rider," Columbus whispered.

"Only he can unlock the riddle of the slaves and return Atlantis to greatness."

"Am I the one?"

The Seer pulled the rolled rug from the basket and flung it open. It unfurled on the stones, stopping a few inches short of the sea window. "Let us find out."

The rug was aged, torn and fraying, but Columbus found something mesmerizing in its patterns. It seemed to pulse as if it had a life of its own. He had a hard time looking away.

"Crafted by the three sisters of the Moirae before time immemorial. Thread from Clotho's spindle, measured by Lachesis's rod, and cut by Atropos's shears." The candles dimmed as the Seer's voice grew strong. "Christopher Columbus, kneel upon the mat as Zeus once did and let the Threads of Fate reveal your destiny."

"Now?" Columbus swallowed.

The Seer shrugged. "Unless you have somewhere else to be."

With a deep breath, Columbus stripped off his boots and knelt on the rug. He rubbed his sweaty hands together before he closed his eyes and said a short prayer.

The moment stretched. He opened one eye. "Bit anticlimactic, isn't it?"

The glass window exploded with a deafening roar and the ocean waters surged in. They thundered around him, swallowing him on all sides as candles were snuffed out and tables overturned. The bookshelves were pulled from their moorings, disappearing as the stones behind were stripped away by the rising waters until all that was left was Columbus, the carpet, and the fathomless sea.

Columbus sat rooted to that carpet, his mouth filled with cold sea water. He couldn't breathe, couldn't see. The familiar convulsion in his chest told him he was drowning all over again.

And then, a breath. It filled him with air more pure and sweet than he had ever known before. He hadn't even realized his eyes were closed until he opened them and saw he was no longer in the Seer's room or even under the sea. He was high atop a mountain in an acropolis of columns and mist.

A woman's laugh echoed there, short and sweet. It sounded like music. A shadow flit by in the mist. Columbus called out, but no one answered. Then, another giggle behind him. More forms with shapely curves. He felt a stirring in his loins. The tittering continued.

"W-who are you?" he managed, breathless.

A chorus of laughter. Then, three female voices spoke in unison.

"We are the Fates," the voices answered.

Dry mouthed, chest heaving, Columbus felt lightheaded, as if he might swoon from pleasure. Then, a memory. *The questions!* Just as the first reached his tongue, one of those melodic voices broke through the mist.

"Ask thy questions, numbered three; heed the answers, if you're to see. One of past, one of present, and one of thy future you hope will be."

Columbus struggled to concentrate. Those damn naked nymphs kept distracting him. He gritted his teeth, opened his mouth. It took everything in him to expel the words.

"Three questions. Right. In order, then. First, the past. Show me—"

Lightning flashed, and his body lit with electric fire. The voices laughed, feeding on his pain.

"Answers only for questions posed," the second of the Fates tittered. "To err again is to taste thy woes."

Columbus cursed himself. He needed to pose his queries in question form. Quickly, he gathered himself and asked his first. "What is the true history of Atlantis?"

The mist began to swirl and coalesce. All at once, the clouds dissipated, and Columbus found himself in a free fall. The wind roared over him as he tumbled down. Hot tears streaked his cheeks. He clenched his fists, expecting to strike earth at any moment. Then he turned and saw the glorious sun-lit sea below. As he neared the water, his direction changed in defiance of gravity until he found himself hurtling across the surface of the water, cool spray wetting his face, his feet quickly finding purchase on the hull of a mighty ship.

The third of the Fates spoke next, her voice, wispy and sonorous. It rose above the sound of the waves smashing against the hull.

"Once there was an island kingdom," the voice said. "Gifted by the God of Sea and Wrath. Powerful beyond measure. Home to a city of exiles, the wisest of all men."

As the island neared, it became more sprawling and radiant than Columbus could have ever imagined. The glistening towers and long-reaching tendrils that fed to smaller islands harkened of something beyond Columbus's understanding. He was awed by its magnificence. *Now, this is heaven*, he thought.

Almost instantaneously, the skies darkened, and the voice of the Fates returned.

"But another God grew jealous, and war was waged."

Columbus's point of view changed as he flew forward and spun around. He wasn't aboard *his* ship, but the attacking army's. Black hulled, with green trimmed sails, more formidable than anything seen upon the sea before or since. And there were thousands of them—so thick they blotted out the very blue of the ocean waters beneath them.

"Man's future hung in the balance."

A barrage of drums accompanied the shouts of one hundred thousand men. They stood at the rim of their ships in golden armor, weapons poised. They were lean, hardened, fierce. Spittle flew from their mouths as bloodlust overtook them. Each in turn, knowing in their heart: *This is the moment I was born for.*

At the bow of the foremost ship, their commander roared, "Athenians! To war!"

The army answered. Their cries once again filled the air, deafening.

The battle of the ages had begun.

"From a high hill atop a distant isle, the old God watched as his beloved children answered the call."

The silhouette of a powerful figure twisted in the swaying grass, his feet sandaled, his muscles robust. But it was the tip of the golden staff hovering a few inches above the earth that set Columbus's heart churning.

"Though the Athenian forces were superior, the exiles of Atlantis had mastered crafts far beyond their foe's imagination. Chief among these was the power to call upon the creatures of the sea."

From high towers, men and women in flowing red robes blew mighty horns. From beneath the waves, their call was answered. Some were recognizable. Whales and sharks of impossible size. Others were creatures of lore. Leviathans like the one that attacked Columbus's ship. Krakens awoken from slumber far below the earth's crust. They met the Athenian armada head on, rolling their ships, crushing their spines, and tearing them apart until the sea ran red with blood.

"Atlantis might have survived then had its fate been left up to men, but their enemy had also been armed with weapons not of their making."

Another horn blasted—this one from the Athenians. Their front vanguard gave way for ships with black-trimmed sails. These bore enormous, orichalcum guns that dominated their hull. The lead ship fired, imploding in the process, but not before it unleashed a magical sphere of green fire that sailed across the distance and struck the towers of Atlantis with unfathomable destruction. Successive shots decimated the city, leaving its citizens to flee in terror or die in waves of green fire.

"The God was enraged. He had been deceived, but he wouldn't accept defeat so easily."

The sandaled figure bellowed. From across the sea, the Athenian captain watched in horror as the God grew and grew until his form filled the sky. He held his mighty scepter aloft and lightning lit the heavens. With a deafening roar, the earth rumbled, and the seas fell. A tsunami of epic proportions appeared, speeding toward the enemy ships...and Atlantis.

"Only after unleashing his fury did the God of Sea realize he had doomed his own people too. Calling forth all his power, he did the only thing he could to ensure their survival."

The God stabbed his trident into the earth—three prongs into stone. A barrier rose around the city, the churning waters capsizing any ships close to land. The Void solidified moments before the tsunami descended. As the waves settled, the Void disappeared into the fathoms, lost forever beneath the sea.

Amid the cries came a light—the manufactured sun. The firmament turned blue as the underwater kingdom was born.

The citizens of Atlantis rejoiced.

"Life began anew," the Fates said, "separate from the realm above. Populated with man, beasts, and creatures of the sea; all meant to shape a new kingdom together."

Mountains, forests, meadows, and deserts appeared. Ordinary creatures turned into magical ones. From the whales and dolphins came the eldocks. From the birds of the sea, winged women sang hauntingly beautiful songs.

The Atlanteans rejoiced. Paradise had come again.

"But much time passed," the Fates continued, "and allies born of a common bond became foes."

A war broke out between men and the winged women. Aided by

the Athenian slaves, the Atlanteans ripped their enemies from the sky and sheared their wings. They scrambled for the safety of underground caves. Eldocks were captured as Atlantis became a war machine.

"As the old God's children grew asunder, his once powerful kingdom aged. They had rebuked his gift, and in return, he abandoned them."

The Void began to shrink, eating land, darkening the sky until it hovered over the very heart of Atlantis, leaving the fragile, decadent city of today.

"And a civilization borne of the noblest of ideals…"

Columbus once again found himself rushing over the surface of the water, the sun about to set on the horizon. There, at last, he came upon a small island with that golden trident perched alone in a familiar stone.

"…was lost with a god's favor."

The trident disappeared. Only the rock remained. Then, the mists swirled in and claimed him again.

"The first is answered," the Fates said. "Answered and past. The second is present, yours to ask."

Columbus was still dazed by all he'd seen. "The present? Right. How can I see the trident today?"

A golden light appeared out of the darkness, revealing the trident lying atop a velvet dais in a chamber full of jewels.

"No!" Columbus shouted. "Not the room! Where? The structure. How to get there."

But the Fates only laughed. They had tricked him!

Elara's warning came to mind….*the Fates are tricky and cruel. You most pose your queries carefully…*

Columbus grit his teeth. The mist was starting to fade. Time was running out.

"One final question," the first of the Fates tittered.

"Third of three," the second added.

"Of the future," the final teased. "Ask wisely to see."

"Wisely," Columbus repeated. "Fine. How—?"

Elara's words reached out to him again.

...of the future, I beg of you, ask this and this alone: How might Atlantis be saved?

Columbus struggled. "How can I...?"

"The final question," the Fates said in unison.

"I'm thinking!"

Elara's voice again. *I would have your word.*

"I..."

The kingdom of my people depends upon it.

"The future," the Fates whispered as their shadows faded.

Columbus gnashed his teeth before he looked up with pure clarity and asked the only question his heart would allow.

"How can I obtain the Trident of Poseidon?"

From the mist, a pair of giant underwater gates appeared. The Fates' voices rose above them.

"The Trident of Poseidon rests in his temple, protected by his Immortal Guard."

Two rows of six mammoth golden warriors stood frozen in a great hall.

"To enter the temple," the Fates continued, "three keys bearing three marks are needed."

Three images appeared in the mist. The first was of a book. The second of a snake biting what looked to be an apple. The third of an egg.

"Only one who proves worthy of uniting the *three* can gain the keys and the trident."

As those images faded, so did the whispered laughter.

"Wait!" Columbus shouted. "How do I find the keys?"

A moment of darkness. Then, Columbus opened his eyes. He was back in the Chamber of Fates, the Seer by his side.

"The Fates have spoken," the Seer said.

Columbus dropped his head.

ELARA WAITED PATIENTLY OUTSIDE the Seer's door. She wanted nothing more desperately than to be inside that room, to hear what Columbus heard. She had been given her turn before the Fates, but her questions failed to provide the answers she needed. The Fates had tricked her. She hoped with every fabric of her being that Columbus had not made the same mistake.

An eternity passed.

At last, the door creaked open and the mariner appeared. His eyes were downcast, his face troubled. Elara felt her heart sink. Then he looked up and nodded. With that single gesture, relief flooded her, and she felt her heart fill with something she had not known since she was a child. Pure joy.

CHAPTER TEN

The Garden of the Blest was situated at the rear of the city. It boasted mossy plots of grass, a few slender trees, smatterings of wildflowers, and a dry creek bed filled with colorful rocks that twinkled with dewy sunlight. The biggest draw, however, had to be the trellis bridge, which extended over the creek, but only by half. Its latter half couldn't be seen, as it disappeared into the Void.

The Atlanteans who escorted Columbus and his crew out there the next morning couldn't explain why the bridge hadn't collapsed in the years since the Void had encroached upon it. They only said the garden had once extended far beyond that point, and somewhere in the city there were paintings to prove it.

"I'll bet it was beautiful here once," Nyx remarked once they'd been seated at a stone table near the creek's edge. It was still wet with dew and made for uncomfortable sitting.

"I don't like it," Fanucio grumbled.

"The garden?"

"All of it. This city. These people. First, they threaten to kill us. Then, they lock us in that room. And now, they send us out here to admire the sunrise and that bloody curtain of death behind it. No subtle message there, I say."

"You're being paranoid," Columbus said.

"Never met a sea dog worth his salt that wasn't."

The Pygmies were at the end of the table. Monday sat head-in-hands, eyes drooping, which was marginally more respectful than Tuesday, who lay face down, snoring.

"And where'd you two go to last night?" Fanucio asked.

Monday mumbled something, but in all the clicks and grunts, Fanucio still couldn't understand the half of it. Columbus grinned like a proud father.

"What'd he say?" Fanucio asked.

"He said they went in search of a privy."

"Twelve hours looking for a shitter? Bah. Them savages wouldn't know what to do with one if they found it. Probably went hunting for whores. Or food. Which reminds me, my stomach's grumblin' like that damned mountain in the Canaries. When are we going to eat?"

"I'm hungry too," Nyx added.

"We'll eat soon enough," Columbus said.

"So," Nyx said, the edge of her mouth curling into a smile. "You were gone some time with the princess. How'd that go?"

How to answer? If Columbus explained his visit to the fates in detail, it would require admitting that he had been deceived. And while the others might not blame him for falling victim to those treacherous gods of old, the same couldn't be said of himself. Those witches had blinded him with smoke and artifice; turned his greatest weapon—his sexuality—against him. Even now the memory both enraged and excited him. At least he'd gleaned enough clues to set him on the next stage of his journey.

As for the princess, she'd gotten what she wanted too. So far as she believed. He'd told her their purposes were aligned though nothing could be further from the truth. Yes, he made a promise to help her, but he broke promises to women all the time. Such was the nature of being a man. He knew he couldn't find the trident without her just as he knew her kingdom could not be saved. That would require a true hero of old. And as much as Columbus hated to admit it, those fellows existed only in stories.

"Well enough," Columbus said finally.

Nyx and Fanucio shared a smile.

"She sure was beaming when she returned. And to think, you were only gone an hour."

"Fifty-eight minutes longer than it normally takes him," Fanucio said. He and the girl burst into laughter.

"Suppose he pleased the old one too?" Nyx teased.

"A good Cap'n should always be willing to take one for the team."

"Ha, ha," Columbus said, looking straight at Nyx. "Did they teach you to talk about such things at that school of yours?"

"Oh, relax," Nyx answered. "It was just a joke. I thought that's how the crew was supposed to talk."

"Oh, they do. But you're not crew, remember?"

Nyx sulked. Columbus felt a pang of guilt before Vespucci exited the city door.

"Peacock ain't struttin' now, is he?" Fanucio asked. "Almost feel sorry for the smarmy bastard. Think he's learned his lesson?"

"Yes," Columbus said, "and that's what troubles me. Go get him."

"Aye, Cap'n," Fanucio said before limping off.

Columbus focused on the *tha-clunk* of his first mate's receding steps before he noticed the girl watching him. Keen blue eyes. So familiar. Was it possible? No, it couldn't be.

"Have you ever considered working with the man rather than against him?" Nyx asked at last. "I mean, I know it would probably bruise both your egos, but the two of you aren't all that different. You're both explorers hailing from the same region. And he's intelligent enough."

"One doesn't work with someone like Vespucci. It isn't in his nature. Oh, he can play along well enough at court, even bend the knee for a monarch or two, but it's all in pursuit of one thing—the only thing that interests him."

"Power," Nyx said.

Columbus was surprised by her answer. "Yes. And anyone who can't help him realize that power is, at best, insignificant, and at worse, in the way."

"Mansa says power is an illusion. That it only leads to self-destruction."

"Tell that to the victims of the Romans. Or the Mongols. They'll tell you their suffering was quite real."

"Mansa also says the enemy of my enemy is my friend."

Columbus smiled. "He knows his history, this Mansa. Who is he? I'd like to meet him."

A look came upon Nyx again, as if she'd said too much.

"He was my teacher."

"Hmm. A skilled fighter, capable linguist, and wise to boot. Where did you grow up again?"

Nyx hesitated. Fortunately, she was spared when the other arrived. Fanucio beamed as he sat, chocking a thumb at Vespucci.

"Our friend here tells me breakfast is on the way. Let's hope they can cook pork."

* * *

HIGH ABOVE THE GARDEN, King Atlas watched the interlopers from a narrow balcony. Word had gotten back to him quickly after the mariner, Columbus, emerged from the Seer's lair to confirm his daughter's beliefs that he was the *Anak-Ta Eleece*. The fact that there was no evidence to support his claim didn't dissuade her one bit, which was troubling. What was even more so was that it had gotten the citizens talking.

Hope.

On its own merits, hope was a good thing, provided its goal was achievable and didn't run counter to the king's agenda. Hope inspired people, gave them something to believe in. Under the right conditions, hope could unite a people.

But there was also a point where hope overtook logic and reason. In desperate times—times such as these—hope could be a dangerous substitute for purpose, for it took the responsibility of finding a solution out of the people's hands and put it somewhere else.

In this case, a man. A man of the old world. The world that had once attempted to annihilate them. The reasons didn't matter. Only that the outcome of that attack had led them here—imprisoned in a godforsaken realm on its death knell.

Even worse, the one claiming to be their savior was a self-described 'adventurer;' his singular objective—the pursuit of wealth and riches. What a fool. He should have had them all executed the moment he first set eyes on them. Damn his daughter. Damn the Seer and his people. Mostly, damn the slaves and their old lore. Of all their senseless acts, the only one he approved of was their self-chosen end, which ironically enough took place on the bridge below.

"Father?" a voice beckoned. "You wished to see me?"

King Atlas nodded and made room for Elara on the balcony.

"Look at them down there. No doubt conspiring our ruin, thanks to you."

Elara swallowed. "The Fates revealed our salvation to him."

"So he says."

"He recalled events no man from the upper realm could have known."

King Atlas grunted. "Even if that were true, seeing a path and walking it are two separate things. In the Nave, you told him about Dion's weakness, didn't you?"

She couldn't lie to her father. She nodded.

"Why?"

"I wanted to even the odds."

The king shook his head. "You have always been an impetuous child, far too curious for your own good. Your mother used to say that you see the best in people, but you never see what lies beneath. At least your brother understood that to rule one must first be feared before they can be loved."

"But Atreal was never loved."

"*I* loved him," the king seethed.

"As did I, Father. I only meant…the people saw him differently. He was a great warrior, the best I ever saw with sonstave or blade, but it was not the security of Atlantis that seeded his heart."

"*You* knew his heart? What was it then?"

"His love for you."

King Atlas sighed heavily. "Even your flattery wounds me. Tell me of the mariner. What's he like?"

"Cavalier. Arrogant. Rude. What you've always told us of man. But a fire burns within him. A thirst for life that cannot be quenched. Should he keep his footing, he might one day achieve great things."

King Atlas shot her a glance. "You fancy him."

"Never," she said, mortified. "I only meant—"

"Can he be trusted?"

"You taught me to never trust anyone."

"Aye. And it was the wisest thing I ever did. *Trust* is a fool's bargain, offered by the strong and accepted by the weak. Do not forget what this man is."

"And what is he?"

"Were you not listening? He and the child told us themselves. Fortune hunters. Privateers. They live upon the sea and to the sea they'll return. But not before commanding their price."

"Then perhaps we should set the terms. Offer him all the gold and jewels he can carry in exchange for seeing the prophecy through. I am certain he would jump at the chance."

"Aye. Which is why *you* will strike this bargain."

There it was. He had set a trap, and she'd walked into it freely. Would she ever learn?

"After all, it was your actions that precipitated this. You broke my law and traveled to the caverns alone. It is your defiance that has the city stirring, so it should be you that bears the cost when he fails."

"*If* he fails."

"He will. Men always do. It's why the Gods have cast them from paradise again and again. Not that I can blame them. From on high, it's easy to recognize a lost cause when you see one."

* * *

DOWN BELOW, Fanucio continued to grumble until he saw two Atlanteans with trays headed in their direction.

"Finally!" he shouted. "Breakfast be served. Haha! I can only imagine the delicacies they eat. No more porridge and salt tack I tell you. I want meat!"

As the servers set the trays on the table, Fanucio's smile faded.

"What's this?"

"Morning meal," the Atlantean woman answered. "It is what all citizens of Atlantis eat."

"Raw fish and seaweed? This is supposed to be blasted paradise! Where's the cod slathered in butter? The lamb with saffron and pepper?"

"In Atlantis, we value sustenance over taste."

"But this couldn't sustenate a canary!"

Everyone at the table laughed. Even Vespucci cracked a smile. Monday and Tuesday were too busy eating to join in. Columbus thanked the servers, who bowed and left.

"Poor Fanucio," Nyx teased. "You look like someone just nipped the last of your rum."

"Laugh it up, *cabin boy*. At least I have provisions in store." He patted his prodigious belly. "You ain't savvy enough to know, but these gill lovers are starving us. I seen it before. Starve us, and when the time comes we won't have the energy to fight back. Then, it won't be fish on this dish. It'll be *you*."

"Please," Nyx laughed. "There's no such thing as cannibals."

Monday and Tuesday froze before looking away sheepishly.

"No?" Fanucio asked. "So how do you think I come by this?" He plopped his peg leg down on the table. Nyx's eyes ballooned.

Columbus locked eyes with his first mate, who winked. The mariner had to turn away to keep from laughing.

AN HOUR LATER, Columbus and crew were escorted to Atlantis's military command chamber, already bustling with a bevy of warriors, including Dion. The giant could barely contain his ire for the newcomers, especially Columbus. When he wasn't scowling at him, he was ordering his own people about, crisp fingers flying in lieu of words. Columbus made a mental note to ask Elara more about him.

The room was located high atop the city's westward tower. Bookended by two batteries, it faced the sea with a wall of windows that afforded a view of the realm's many islands. More curious, however, were the interior sheets of muted glass, which were positioned here and there, but with no discernible use. It wasn't until Columbus saw a few intermittent flashes of lights on one that he realized they were part of some advanced technology—or, more accurately, ancient technology—that largely went ignored. This—like so many other aspects of Atlantis—created an overwhelming sense of awe in Columbus, and not for the first time did he wonder if he was both figuratively and literately out of his depth.

Then, Elara walked in.

She wore a white silken bodysuit, adorned with a single belt made of orichalcum. Her scarlet hair was plaited in the back, clean and lustrous, ceding rule to her rich green eyes, which only shined brighter in their halo of gems. The room fell silent in an instant. Columbus guessed those gathered weren't used to seeing their princess in such refinement, which boded well for him.

"You clean up well, Princess," Columbus said, meeting her mid-room. "I'm impressed."

He thought he saw her color, though it could have been the light.

"I see a good night's sleep has done little to diminish your crude ways," she responded coolly, which only made him laugh.

He leaned in as she drew past. "Oh, I doubt either of us slept well last night."

She frowned before making a show of ignoring him. She strode to a large, elevated table that looked like a sandbox. With a nod, Dion and the others gathered around. Then, Elara touched a control panel and the nodal "sand" came to life, rising in patterns that Columbus eventually recognized as the terrain and topography of this kingdom. *It's a living model*, Columbus thought.

"Atlantis, as it was in the beginning," Elara said. "But over the course of the last century, our realm has been reduced by the condensing of the Void."

Another swipe saw the land mass diminish, as a black circle representing the circumference of the Void closed in from all sides until more than half the map's area was gone, excising even a portion of the city itself.

"The quakes you've felt precede these reductions. We're not sure why. Some have theorized the Void's power comes from the volcanic core beneath the city and that it is waning. Others have suggested the Void is itself a sphere and in shrinking, it compresses the crust below, forcing mass upward. What we do know for certain is that the frequency of these events is accelerating and that it will soon reach a critical stage—if it hasn't already."

She turned to Columbus. "Yesterday you visited the Fates. They spoke to you and showed you a way Atlantis might be saved."

"That's right," Columbus said, holding her gaze.

"I would like you to share with us how."

Columbus looked around the table and swallowed. He knew a tough crowd when he saw one. The Atlanteans stood mostly grim-faced, willing to listen only because they'd been ordered to do so. Especially, Dion. The man clearly suspected Columbus was full of shit. More reason he was glad he'd invited his crew along. They *knew* he was full of shit, but at least they'd had practice pretending like he wasn't.

"As you forewarned, Princess, the Fates were cunning. They used their sorcery and female wiles to beguile me and to cheat me of our right to the truth. I wholly rebuked them."

Fanucio cleared his throat loudly, drawing the eyes of the others. He tapped his neck and said, "Seaweed."

"In doing so," Columbus continued, "our task was revealed. To save your city and all the inhabitants of Atlantis, we must recover three magical keys from three separate locations. I have no doubt this will prove challenging, but I believe *together* we are up to the task."

"I recall a story my mother told me as a child," Elara said. "It, too, spoke of magical keys, though the details elude me. It was, however, slave lore, so it's possible it is the same."

"Do you have access to this lore?" Columbus asked.

"No. Several generations back, there was a rebellion. Fanatics seeking to 'free us from our reliance on the old ways.' They were quelled after a time, and dispatched through the Void, but not before destroying many of the advances our ancestors had created. It's why these mechanisms you see around us no longer work. They called it 'the purge.'"

"Shame," someone said at the back of the room.

All eyes turned to find Vespucci. He, like many in the room, looked surprised he'd spoken. But he refused to rebuke the attention. "I imagine just a few of these tools might have aided your quest spectacularly."

"Indeed," Elara said before turning back to Columbus. "Did the Fates reveal where these keys were kept?"

"Not exactly," Columbus replied. "But they did offer clues to their whereabouts by attaching a symbol to each. The first looked like this."

Columbus stepped unnervingly close to Elara and used his finger to draw something with the table's controls. A symbol emerged in the nodal ocean before them.

"It's a book," one of the Atlanteans said.

"An open book," Fanucio clarified, not that he'd ever bothered to read one.

Dion grunted, and Elara looked up. He gestured something with his hands and she nodded.

"We know this symbol. It means library. This one is carved into the relief above the entrance to the Tower of Illumination."

Several of the Atlanteans murmured.

"Is that bad?" Fanucio asked.

Elara touched Columbus's arm to move him from the controls. His smile. His touch had once again unnerved her.

"The Isle of Light is to the east," she said.

Her fingers swiped again across the control screen, and the surface of the nodal map changed, zooming in on an island with a tall tower upon it.

"On it, you see the Tower of Illumination, where once all our knowledge was stored. See its proximity to the larger land mass to the north? That's where you first entered our realm and where the sirens call home."

"That's close," Columbus said. "Do they ever visit this isle?"

Elara nodded grimly. "It has become their hunting ground. They are overbred and have depleted most of the resources on their own island. It's one of the reasons our people no longer go here."

"Have you ever tried to reason with them?" Nyx asked. "I mean, I saw a few things down there that suggested they're more than just animals."

The idea was met with derision among the Atlanteans. Nyx glanced at Columbus and saw him shake his head.

"They are savage creatures, Nyx," Elara said, not so quick to condemn her. "Once, they captured a family of fishermen close to their shore. They feasted on them—man, women, and children. They even left behind the catch of fish as a warning. There can be no peace between us. The good news is that the sirens don't venture out in the day. Not often, anyway. If we're cautious, I believe we could land a party on the southern part of the isle, make our way to the tower, retrieve the key, and be gone before our enemies are any wiser."

"There's one problem with that," Columbus said. "There's no guarantee the key's still there. You say your people frequented this tower after the slaves left. Why didn't any of them find it? Or maybe someone did?"

"Unlike men, we Atlanteans hold little value in treasure. Had such a key been found, we would know. And, besides, they weren't searching for it. We are."

"Welp," Fanucio said. "It's decided then. What's for lunch?"

"We'll need to keep the landing party small. No more than eight. Dion will accompany me along with Saren and Thetra."

"Cap'n and I make five," Fanucio said. "That leaves two."

Columbus rolled his eyes at his first mate's bad math.

"I'm coming," Nyx said.

"Not so quick," Columbus said. "If there's even the possibility of a fight, I want Monday and Tuesday there."

"Those two?" Nyx pointed at the Pygmies, asleep at the back of the room. "You'll be dead before they draw their spears! Captain, you must take me. You know I can handle myself."

"I do, but this isn't a game. I need fighters, not children."

"I am *not* a child," Nyx spat.

"I've made my decision. Speak out against my orders again and I'll have you locked away until our departure."

Silence filled the room. Nyx looked around, chin trembling. Only Fanucio returned her stare, but it was one of pity.

Elara laid a comforting hand on Nyx's shoulder. "I can have one of my valets escort you about the city, Nyx. There is much to see. Much you will—"

Nyx sprinted from the room. Columbus sighed and turned back to the map. "Now, where were we? Ah, yes. Battle. I assume we'll all carry weapons?"

At this, Dion gesticulated firmly.

Columbus snickered. "By all means, man. Speak up if you have concerns." Dion's hand went instinctually to his sonstave. Columbus smiled even brighter. "We all saw how that turned out last time."

Enraged, Dion came around the table and Columbus rose to meet him. Elara stepped between them.

"Enough. Both of you!" she shouted. "This stops now. We cannot assail the isle with a retinue half-armed," she snarled at Dion before facing Columbus. "And you can't recover the keys if you're dead. We are in this together, so whatever enmity exists between you, it ends *here*. Do you understand?"

A simmering Dion gave a curt nod. Elara looked to Columbus, who maintained his carefree demeanor.

"Happy to oblige, Princess."

"I'll see to the preparations," Elara said. "We leave at first light tomorrow."

The Atlanteans saluted and exited the room. Elara turned to Fanucio and Vespucci. "I would speak to your captain alone. Now."

Fanucio looked to Columbus, who nodded. He and Vespucci left, leaving only the sleeping Pygmies.

"Even if they understood your language," Columbus said. "They sleep like the dead."

"You are a fool, Columbus. Of all the warriors in our kingdom, you taunt the one best capable of providing your protection and crushing your skull with his bare hands."

"He's a bully. I don't like bullies. Nor people who take themselves too seriously."

"He has reason to take himself seriously. He has pledged his life to protect me and all those in our kingdom. Would you do the same for yours?"

"Doubtful. Then again, none of my crew has your..." He looked down at that silken suit again. "Vitality?"

Elara shook her head. "You are insufferable."

"Thanks." Columbus grinned. "What's his deal, anyway? Dion? Has he always been mute?"

Elara sighed and looked out over the sea. "He took a vow of silence many years ago."

"Caught masturbating? I've heard some cultures look down on that."

Elara looked at him with disgust. "No. He was tasked with protecting someone and failed."

Columbus could see the memory was painful for her. Was there something between them? It didn't appear so, at least from her end, but he'd have to tread carefully until he had a better read on the situation. "I'm surprised he's ever failed at anything in his life."

Some of the tension ebbed from Elara's shoulders. She appeared grateful for the chance to move on. "Tell me of the girl. Nyx. Is she yours?"

"As in my daughter? No. Definitely no."

"She looks like you."

"It's the hair color. Nothing more."

"She's stubborn, unyielding, and brash. Three of your most defining traits."

"And here I thought you were going to say, handsome, roguish, and irresistible."

He smiled again. Despite herself, Elara smiled softly too. She had a nice smile. Columbus found himself wanting to see it more often.

"You joke often. I see it is your way. But you are strangers to us. The only stories we know of man—of you—are ones of greed, jealousy, and war. Can you not tell me something real?"

This time, it was Columbus that looked out toward the sea. Even from on high, he could see the white caps rising and falling, reflecting the light of the faux sun. Did it matter that magic powered the waves? They looked identical to the ones he'd known all his life. In that moment, he longed to be back aboard a ship, sails fat with wind, spray wetting his face, and the future running before him.

"I have two sons," he said at last. "Back in Spain. Good lads. Very *unlike* me."

"And their mother?"

Columbus hesitated before crossing himself. "Dead. God rest her soul."

"I'm sorry. You loved her?"

The question unnerved him. It'd been a long time since someone asked him something so personal. And even longer since he spoke the truth.

"I loved…once."

The vagueness of the answer seemed to pique Elara's curiosity, but it was clear he'd say no more.

"Perhaps we should move on to other matters, such as your compensation."

The trident. It was all he wanted.

It was everything.

"Whatever you suggest is fine," Columbus said. "Though if you'd like to sweeten the deal…"

He ran a finger over her arm, goosebumps rising in its wake. She pulled her arm back quickly.

"Some things are beyond price," she said, indignant. It only made Columbus smile brighter.

"I totally agree," he said. "But in the spirit of diplomacy, I'm willing to cut my rate."

She fought it, but in the end, Elara couldn't help but smile. It was a small victory. One Columbus would have normally seized on, but this time he left it alone.

* * *

NYX HOVERED NEAR THE DOORWAY, listening to the voices inside. A throat cleared. She turned to find Vespucci.

"You have a penchant for appearing in the most unusual places, little bird."

"I could say the same of you. What do you want?"

"What I've always wanted. To represent the interests of Spain." She started to turn. "And myself."

"At least you're being honest now."

"If only the same could be said of others."

Nyx simmered, still smarting over what happened inside. "I don't have time for games, Signore Vespucci. If you have something to say, say it."

"Fine. Our dear captain is an enigmatic fellow. And it's easy to see why people follow him. He is larger than the stars. But do you know why a man his age is still helming a carrack of mercenaries and not leading, say, His Majesty's fleet? Because he is unreliable. He is *selfish*. He has always put himself first. Before God. Before country. Even before his own *family*. All those who follow him eventually realize this. Most realize it too late. Don't be one of them, Nyx."

"If you're asking me to betray him—"

"No. Columbus's interests are his own. Oh, I suppose there is an allure to an artifact that can transmute gold, but this city has far more intriguing advances to offer. Diseases could be eradicated. Wars ended. You and I could help usher in a new age of peace. Think of the possibilities, Nyx. A *woman* with your talent could revolutionize the world."

Nyx hesitated. She saw his logic, but she'd met men like Vespucci before. They always wanted more. Despite this, she didn't walk away.

"All I'm asking is to keep your eyes and options open. Your captain would encourage no less."

CHAPTER ELEVEN

They gathered the next morning at the eldock pens. The red-frocked stable master had eight eldocks separated and was in the process of having them saddled. Four were distinctly outfitted for Elara and her warriors, whom Columbus learned were called the Gadeir. Another four had been chosen for Columbus's party.

For their undertaking, Columbus and Fanucio had donned new scarlet bodysuits the same as the Atlanteans, which gave Dion another reason to scowl. The suits were said to repel water and retain body heat, though Fanucio thought it was the most uncomfortable thing he'd ever worn. Columbus nearly laughed when his first mate tried to slip the thing on.

"Problem?"

"Aye," Fanucio grumbled. "I think they gave me a girl's suit."

"Probably difficult to find one that fits your *dimensions*."

"I'd settle for one that cupped my turtle eggs. This one's so tight I might never bastard a whelp again."

The only ones who refused to don the suits were Monday and Tuesday, and only because they'd learned the ones set aside for them belonged to children. So, they shed their clothes instead and wore only loincloths. They drew a lot of stares.

"The young one fancies me," Tuesday said of Thetra, who peered at him again and again. *"She shall be my first wife here."*

"Given the food and lack of battle, I'm not certain I want to stay that long."

"Then I better find the other three quickly."

The men were also given things to put in their ears to repel the sirens' song. Columbus tucked his away for later.

ONCE EVERYONE WAS READY, the stable master rallied the newcomers. "I am told you speak our language. Good. Listen carefully and you may survive long enough to make it outside these walls. What happens after that, I am absolved of responsibility. At sea, eldocks are solitary creatures—they swim, they hunt, they eat alone. But under Atlantean control, they congregate in a pod. We do not know why. Neither do we understand how their hierarchy is established. But the pod will always follow its leader until the lead rider chooses otherwise. Note what I said there: it is the will of the *rider* that dictates course, direction, elevation, and speed." He leaned down to touch the nearest eldock, which chittered in response. "Some would tell you this is because they are highly instinctual mammals, acutely sensitive to both movement and energy. I say it is more than that. I believe when a rider spends enough time with an eldock of equal temperament, a bond is formed. A bond that transcends the normal modes of communication. It is almost as if rider and eldock become of a single mind."

Fanucio snorted, only to fall under the stable master's withering glare.

"You doubt me?"

"Begging your pardon, but I rode this one yesterday. I didn't feel no connection. I saw a man give orders and an animal obey. Same as back home."

"Your honor, then," the stable master waved toward the eldock. Columbus opened his mouth to interject, but Fanucio was already slipping a leg over the creature's back.

"Seems easy enough," Fanucio said. "First, ya mount—"

The instant Fanucio settled onto the eldock, the creature screeched and began bucking furiously. Fanucio's eyes ballooned as he tried to hold on, but he was thrown to the deck where he landed hard enough to make everyone wince. Dazed, he looked up to see the eldock charging him, its teeth focused on his one good leg. Fanucio screamed but was saved when several Gadeir grabbed him and pulled him away.

Laughter filled the grotto and eased much of the tension. Columbus helped Fanucio up and patted him on the shoulder. "Nearly earned a new nickname."

His point made, the stable master continued. "Even if a bond has been established, an eldock will still not allow a rider on it unless it has one of these." He held up a golden bridle. "It pacifies them, though we do not know why. It is yet another mystery our ancestors left us."

Columbus whispered to Elara. "Apparently, your ancestors were good at leaving everything but directions."

Elara patted her eldock once it was saddled and reined, leaving Columbus and Dion alone. The giant eyed him a moment before offering an orichalcum belt with a sonstave.

"Why, Dion. You shouldn't have."

Dion wrapped the belt around Columbus's waist and cinched it so hard Columbus groaned.

"Tight," Columbus squeaked, "just the way I like it."

As the others mounted their eldocks, Columbus knelt by his, sitting passively in the water. The creature looked hearty enough and quite tame. It chittered, showing no signs of agitation. Columbus reached out to pat it as Elara had, but his hand froze as a strange sensation coursed through him. It was almost like one feels in a lightning storm. Was this the bond the stable master spoke of?

He was about to dismiss it when that voice he'd heard in the caves returned.

Only one true of heart...

The eldock bucked and Columbus reared back, looking to see if anyone else had heard it. It didn't appear so. It unnerved him.

Nearby, Fanucio also mounted his eldock, but much slower this time around.

Easy, girl," he said. "Easy." The eldock jolted several times. "I don't think this one likes me either."

The stable master looked down his nose. "Perhaps because you called *him* a girl."

Fanucio craned his head over the side. "Huh. Thought that was a fin."

Finally, the stable hands came around to dispense masks. Columbus asked about them.

"We'll be approaching the isle from beneath the surface," Elara said. "These allow us to breath air through a mechanism at the hood's end."

An awestruck Columbus shook his head. "Breathing under water. Will wonders never cease?"

Behind him, Columbus heard a cheer. He turned to see the Pygmies had been given back their spears and were spinning them around in the air, much to the chagrin of the Atlanteans.

Once everyone was ready, the stable master nodded, his lone smile saved for Elara.

"Be safe, my princess," he replied. "And this time come back in due fashion."

Elara nodded before giving the signal to descend. One by one, the eldocks sank beneath the waterline and disappeared through an underwater tunnel.

On the dock, the stable master's scowl returned.

"Well?" he said to the stable hands. "What are you standing around for? See to your duties. I want the rest of the brood fed before third hour. And these eight pens need to be cleaned before the party's return. I shouldn't have to—"

He paused. Odd. There weren't eight gates open, but nine. Behind him he heard a trickle of water, but when he turned, there was nothing to see.

. . .

DOWN THE TUNNEL, the party glided, passing the red alchemical globes that somehow also burned underwater. They hesitated briefly as a portcullis lifted, then they were off.

Entering the sea, Columbus was still astonished by the mask, which clung to his face by way of some unknown pressure. There was a light that shone within, allowing him to identify the other riders. Elara took the lead, the others falling into formation behind her. Columbus and his crew settled in at the rear.

A short distance outside the city, the coral shelf fell away, revealing a vast seabed brimming with life. Some species were recognizable—dolphins, rays, octopi, and eels. Others were variants of the upper realm—triple-finned sharks, dual-sided squid, bioluminescent jellyfish. But the third group were true anomalies—sabretooth seals, whales with wings, and schools that swam apart only to coalesce into one mighty form when predators drew near.

"Beautiful," Columbus whispered.

He thought he saw Elara turn her head, though there was no way she could have heard him.

As the pod entered a larger canyon, Columbus was surprised to feel the water grow warmer until the chill disappeared completely. He felt as comfortable there as he was on land. Had they entered some new current or did the volcanic activity below the surface play some part? More mysteries he would likely never know.

Only then did he allow himself to think of the world above. Was it day or night? Were the waters of the Atlantic calm or swelling with storms? Were the *Niña* and *Pinta* still up there, making repairs, searching for survivors? Or had they been scuttled in battle or felled by the leviathan?

Columbus decided to push those thoughts away for now. He knew he would have to find a way back to the surface, but first he needed to concentrate on the task at hand: the retrieval of the keys. The Fates had shown him much, but those keys took the entirety of his focus now. Three keys to enter to Poseidon's Temple. Three keys to net him the ultimate prize. Three keys and Christopher Columbus's legacy would be secured forever.

One-two-three, Columbus is key! Nope. That was a terrible catchphrase. Where were all the great poets when you needed one?

* * *

As Vespucci moved through the city, he felt the eyes of every citizen fall upon him only to look away with indifference or outright disdain as he passed. After what happened in the Nave, he had been labeled persona non-grata. *Weak.* He almost laughed. The depiction itself didn't bother him because he knew the opposite was true. He was not weak. He was strong. Only his strength—the bulk of it anyway—came from within. In the annals of history, no sword wielder ever achieved true greatness. It was the man who commanded the army—who moved the pieces into place—that the people remembered.

Amerigo Vespucci was just such a man.

He had never expected to find Atlantis. While pursuing Ferdinand's secret passion, his objective had always been to curry the monarch's favor, never once suspecting the myth of all myths might actually prove true. Yet, when he first saw this glorious, decadent city appearing from around the bend, everything changed, and he devised a new plan. He would learn all he could of Atlantis. He would steal all her secrets. And once she was mined for all her worth, only then would he return to the true realm of men where it would be his favor that was curried. And not just by kings, but emperors, countries, even the Pope himself. It was a vision he could see clear as day. The question was how to realize it?

With the mad king, obviously. The man had humiliated him upon their first meeting. Vespucci knew why. He needed to make a point. Not to this party of strangers—he had no intention of even entertaining them. No, Atlas had acted solely to reinforce his position with his people. Vespucci understood that, however shortsighted it was. If Atlantis truly was dying, nothing mattered more than its leader maintaining his aura of strength, even if that strength was a fabrication. For Vespucci to achieve his goal, he would need the king to see him as a person of value as Columbus had done.

Columbus.

The very thought of the man stoked a flame in Vespucci's belly that threatened to immolate him from within. How could a man of such little intelligence, such poor breeding, come out on top again and again? Blind luck. There was no other answer. Columbus claimed to be pious, but he was a womanizer and a thief. Could God truly support such a scoundrel? Of course not. If anything, Columbus was an affront to His name. Which meant all the Genoan's successes were simply stepping stones leading him up the side of a very large mountain. One false step and he would take his tumble at long last. Vespucci's one regret was that the world wouldn't be there to witness it.

He promised himself that he would be there in their stead.

And like a candle put to flame, an idea came to him. How he might achieve both goals. And, as fate would have it, he was afforded the opportunity that very afternoon when he saw the king enter the Nave alone. This was his chance. He waited an appropriate amount of time before making his entrance.

He looked like a man deeply troubled, chin in hand, slumped over his throne, staring into space. Vespucci spared the king a single glance before crossing toward the center of the amphitheater and halting to examine the rock he'd noticed in the center of the floor.

A rock with three holes.

Vespucci suddenly looked up, a show of fright lighting his features.

"Your Grace, forgive my intrusion. I didn't think anyone would be here." He waited for the king to respond, but the man simply glowered instead. "I saw this yesterday and for some reason it struck me. I'm not sure why."

The moment stretched. Vespucci thought he might have erred again when King Atlas finally spoke.

"Legend says it is real," the king grumbled. "That the earth turned to stone when Poseidon thrust his trident into it."

Vespucci's eyes widened. "You mean this is..."

"I have always had my doubts. Through the years, stories get turned around, making it hard to know what to believe."

Vespucci took a small step toward him, praying it wouldn't result in a repeat of the previous day's events. "If I might inquire, sire. There is an odor in the air."

"Sulfur. From a volcanic artery beneath your very feet."

"I see. Fascinating."

"Tell me again what nation you speak for?"

Vespucci realized the king had forgotten, probably because he was no longer drunk. He took another small step toward the monarch. "Spain, Your Grace. Iberia as you know her."

King Atlas nodded. "She is powerful, Iberia?"

"Very. They recently expelled invaders that had plagued their country for over eight hundred years."

King Atlas scoffed. "If they are so powerful, why did it take them so long?"

"A fair question," Vespucci chuckled, moving closer again. "The real answer I believe is that there is profit in war. The longer the war..."

"The greater the profits. And Athens? Are they still a force to be reckoned with?"

"I'm afraid not, sire. Many nations have risen and fallen since your kingdom slipped under the veil of sea. Athens—or Greece as it is now known—is a lesser player on today's stage."

The king deflated as if he was disappointed his old enemy was no longer there to challenge.

"But there are others," Vespucci continued. "France. Prussia. The Mongols. The heathens of the Far East." He stepped to the bannister to whisper. "It is said they use black magic and can set fire to the sky."

"Black magic?" King Atlas repeated, skeptical.

"Oh, nothing that could challenge Atlantis. As far as I know."

King Atlas murmured again. Vespucci let the man think. "This ruler you serve, he sends out emissaries like you and Columbus often?"

"Oh, yes, sire. King Ferdinand has trading partners the world over who have come to count on his kinship and sound judgement. I should point out, however, that Columbus—as he himself stated last night—is but a ship's captain and nothing more. Surely, he is a capable man of action, but I would be remiss if I didn't warn his Highness to keep a close eye on him. Especially around your *daughter."*

"My daughter?" the king growled.

"Undoubtedly a formidable woman in her own right. But the young are so impressionable. So apt to making mistakes. I hate to even mention it but forewarned is forearmed."

In the ensuing silence, Vespucci thought he might have pushed things too far. Then, the king spoke.

"This Ferdinand of Iberia. He welcomes new allies?"

Vespucci fought hard to hide his smile. "Yes, sire. Allow me to tell you how."

* * *

"Columbus?" Elara's voice rang in Columbus's head. He was so shocked he nearly fell off his eldock. He looked up to see the princess staring back at him. She spoke again. "Touch the circular orb on the belt near your waist."

"This?" He said, his own voice amplified in his mask. He thought he heard Elara laugh.

"Yes. We can communicate now."

"By the holy trinities, how…?"

"Yet another wonder of my people. Only a handful still work, and only I can activate them—one on one or all at once. I wanted to ask you something in private. You don't have to answer."

"By all means, Princess. I have no secrets."

And by none, I mean plenty.

"What did you ask the Fates of the past and present?"

Columbus had been relieved that she didn't ask when he first stepped from the room. During the night, he'd had time to fashion his answer.

"Of the present, I must admit with great shame, I was duped. You warned me, but those lasses are cunning, indeed."

"I know it well."

"But of the past, I asked after the history of Atlantis. And I saw how all this was made."

"And?"

"And what can one say after witnessing Genesis? It was amazing, horrifying, grander than anything I've heard of save the flood itself."

"You said horrifying."

"Yes. I saw what Atlantis represented before the Gods clashed, before your city fell. All shine and promise, like an apple in the tree. If those memories are true, then these gifts were but a paltry smattering of what your ancestors possessed, or what they dreamed possible. Imagine had they continued unmolested. What might Atlantis have been? What might it be today?"

"Some believe it was for this reason the Gods waged war. Not over Athens or petty jealousies, but for fear we might one day grow strong enough to challenge Elysium itself. I know, it is blasphemous to speak—"

"But it could be true. Zeus and his siblings challenged the Titans after all. And won."

"Yes, the Gods won. But we are not Gods. Though it is in our nature to reach for the heavens, it is also in our nature to stumble when the prize is within our grasp. For some, success can be as daunting as failure."

That, Columbus understood. "For some, indeed."

"But not for you?"

"I tasted enough failure in my youth to last a lifetime. These days, I always keep my eyes on the prize."

He saw her glance at him and imagined her wondering if he meant her. To his surprise, she didn't seem displeased. That's when he noticed another one of those red vials hanging around her neck. He asked about it.

"We call them the *second heart*. As you've seen, they can heal most wounds short of death. Long ago, every citizen possessed one. Now, there are only a handful left. They are usually reserved for the king's line."

"And you used yours to save me? I'm flattered."

"I used mine to save the *Anak-Ta Eleece*. Actually, the sirens took mine when they captured me. That one belonged to my mother."

She looked down. Columbus decided not to press her.

Just then, Columbus felt a flutter in his chest. It was the same feeling he'd experienced in the caves when the voice spoke to him. He was so focused on it, he failed to hear Elara call his name. When he finally answered her, she pointed off into the distance. "Look. Gadeir capture an eldock. It is a rare sight. Would you like to see?"

"Do we have time?"

"We'll make time for this."

She touched her belt to communicate with the others before leading the pod off to a long plateau where six Atlanteans were wrestling with a very large eldock in a net.

"Poseidon's Crown," Elara gasped. "he must be old as the sea. I have never seen one his size."

The creature was indeed massive, almost as big as a whale. It was spotted with blue and gray, making it difficult to distinguish through the rustling net. When one of the Gadeir lost their grip on the net, Columbus saw Elara turn to Dion, presumably to issue an order. Dion spurred his eldock forward. That's when all hell broke loose.

The spotted eldock bayed. The sound was so loud and piercing, most of the party had to cover their ears. Then the spotted eldock flipped sideways, using its massive tail to shed the net while ripping the Gadeir from their saddles.

Rather than flee, the spotted eldock charged. Columbus was aghast to see it headed straight for Elara. She fumbled for her sonstave but had no time to extricate it and she braced for impact. That's when a blur shot in from her right and Columbus reined his eldock to a stop straight in the behemoth's path. With unfathomable power, the spotted eldock drew to a halt, the water rushing over Columbus, carrying with it that same flutter that he'd felt before, only this time with the power of a tempest.

When he came to his senses, he saw the spotted eldock was only a few feet away. Columbus stared into those inky gray eyes and felt a strange connection. A sense of peace came over him. Life and death seemed trivial. And then all at once, the beast turned and swam away.

For a moment, Columbus couldn't move, the only sound: the pounding of blood in his ears. And then Elara's voice rang through.

"How did you stop him?" she asked.

"I didn't. I—" He had no answer. He patted his eldock instead. "I think it was this one."

Even underwater, Columbus could tell she was dubious.

"Regardless, twice you have saved my life. These debts I will repay."

The moment was still too raw for Columbus to joke.

"Where did it go?"

"Not west. That way lies the Gaia's Craw. To the south, Atlantis. It must have headed east to the eldock dens, though adults rarely return there past breeding age."

"Not north?" Columbus asked.

"There's nothing to the north but…"

"But what?"

"The Temple of Poseidon. But it is beyond the border of the Void now and out of our reach."

Columbus heard someone suck in their breath. It took him a moment to realize it was him. He'd hoped Elara hadn't heard it. He prayed she was wrong.

When Columbus looked up, Dion was next to Elara, worry apparent. This was more than duty, Columbus realized. The man loved her. It explained a lot, though to him, it was just another complication. When the princess pointed toward Columbus, the giant surprisingly didn't glower. He returned to formation instead.

"We've stayed here too long," Elara said. She reined her eldock around and resumed course.

It was just past midday when the group reached the Isle of Illumination's beach and ran for the first line of trees. Once they were in position, Sareen whistled and the eldocks swam away.

"So, where's this tower?" Columbus asked.

Elara peeled back some palm fronds. Columbus whistled.

The tower was made of smooth stone that glistened like pearl. It had arched columns that alternated in height as it rose, giving the appearance that it had no floors but grew from the earth like a vine, twisting and turning as it rose. Stained-glass windows reflected colors from the sun while a wooden waterwheel at least three stories high stood motionless at the tower's side. The most stunning sight, however, was the tower's apex, which had been shorn off by the Void above. Even now, Columbus could see that roiling darkness crowning the tower's zenith.

Elara saw only the tower. "I have seen paintings that revealed a beacon at the pinnacle of the tower, lighting the path for citizens at night. As you can see, it was lost when the Void descended."

"It's stunning. Bigger and grander than I could have imagined."

Columbus had seen the Tower of Pisa in his travels. Even it, with its famous lean, couldn't compare to this. He recalled another famous tower—the Tower of Babel, which was said to have existed in the land of Shinar in Mesopotamia. Biblical scholars claimed that tower offended God, so he smote it and took away the speech of its builders, so they would never again threaten his domain. Was this the tower they spoke of? Had word of it also been bastardized over the ages? There were other versions—Christian, Babylonian, Sumerian. Could they all be traced back to this?

The thought was interrupted when Sareen suddenly appeared out of the brush.

"My Lady," Sareen whispered. "Stay low. Make no quick movements."

"What is it?" Elara asked.

"We are being watched."

CHAPTER TWELVE

"How many?" Elara whispered, lying behind the sandbank, sonstave in hand.

"It appears only one," Sareen answered. "Twenty paces ahead. Dion spotted fresh tracks near the beach. Thetra is attempting to draw its attention while Dion works to its flank."

"Is it a siren?" Elara asked.

Sareen wasn't sure, so the trio sat tight and waited. They didn't wait long. A minute or two later, a shout rang through the trees. The trio rushed out as Dion emerged from the brush holding a thrashing figure in the air by one leg.

"Let me down!" Nyx shouted.

"Looks like someone caught a fish," Fanucio howled.

"I said let me down, damn you!"

With a nod from Elara, Dion dropped Nyx. She hit the sand with a thud. She was on her feet instantly, hitting Dion with punches and kicks that might have felled a normal man. The giant never flinched.

"Well, well. What do we have here?" Columbus said as Nyx turned to meet his stony gaze. "You followed us from the city?"

"That's right," Nyx said defiantly. "And I'm not sorry I did it either."

"How did you get out?" Elara asked.

"I borrowed an eldock. How else?"

"You mean you *stole* an eldock from under Master Leopole's nose? Wait until news of this spreads. He'll never live it down. I take it you also slipped past our position when we stopped to watch the hunters?" Nyx nodded. "You are resourceful, Nyx. I am impressed. But what did you plan to do next?"

The girl's cockiness faded. "Next?"

"Hadn't thought that far ahead? In making your choice, you now force me to make one too. I can send you back, losing one of my people in the process, or we can take you along and pray you cause us no further trouble. Do you see the position you've put me in?"

Nyx's gaze shifted between Columbus and Elara. Then her lip started to tremble. Elara softened.

"Every decision comes with consequences. You defied my wishes, the wishes of your captain, and you will be punished for it. Later. For now, you may come with us, but only if you promise to do as you're told."

Nyx gave a curt nod. Anything else might let loose the tears brimming in her eyes, which would have been humiliating. Still, it wasn't enough for Elara.

"To an Atlantean, a promise is the greatest gift we can offer another. It means we place our name, our worth, and our belief in another's hands. Do you understand?"

This time Nyx verbally agreed. Satisfied, Elara told her team to continue. Nyx sulked along behind them.

"Apologies, Princess," Columbus said. "I don't know what she was thinking."

"Isn't it obvious? She seeks your approval."

"*My* approval? The girl doesn't care what I think. She's hardheaded and believes she has an answer for everything."

Elara smiled. "Remind you of anyone?"

It was a ridiculous comparison. Yes, the girl was brash, but in a clumsy, uncalculated way. If she did indeed seek Columbus's attention, it only underscored how different they were. He had never needed anyone's approval. Since the day he left his father's house, Columbus had one goal in mind: assuring his own legacy. And you couldn't do that if you were worried about stepping on toes or feelings. Currying favor was just another way of following rules and Columbus made his own rules. Still, he could see the princess had taken a liking to Nyx. Perhaps she'd even invite her to stay once Columbus had secured the trident and departed. At the very least the girl might prove a capable distraction. So why did her presence bother him so?

They moved quietly over a grassy berm, through another thatch of trees before following an old stone path overgrown with weeds. At last, they came out at the rear of the cyclopean tower, which loomed even larger up close. The massive blocks that made up the base were nearly as large as a man and riddled with cracks.

Through the brush to their right, Dion returned. Thetra translated his gestures.

"Path is clear," she reported. "No sirens visible, but there are some tracks two hundred yards to the north that look like they were made this morning."

Elara nodded. "Set up a perimeter. Dion and Thetra will take the northern quadrant near the siren tunnels. Sareen, you have the west. Fanucio... Where's Fanucio?"

"Here!" Fanucio shouted, limping through some brush, out of breath. "Sorry. Had a wee bit of trouble, what with the sand and all, but look what I found!"

He'd tied something to the bottom of his peg leg.

"Is that...a coconut shell?" Columbus asked.

"A half a one, yeah," Fanucio beamed. Someone sniggered, which quickly led to laughter. Fanucio frowned. "I know it ain't much to look at, but it works good on sand. Plus, it smells nice."

More laughter followed. Even Dion's features lightened briefly. Then, Elara held up a hand.

"Enough. Fanucio, you'll stay here." She looked around. "Where are the little ones?"

Columbus scanned the area, but they were nowhere in sight. "I'm sure they seized the initiative and are out on a patrol of their own."

Elara looked dubious. "Don't worry, Princess. If a battle breaks out, those two will be the first to answer the call."

"Hope it's for our side," Fanucio muttered.

"Columbus and Nyx are with me," Elara said. "The rest of you—"

Just then, a tremor rattled the ground. Something fell from the tower. Everyone waited nervously until it stopped.

"You said the Void only shrinks following a tremor, right?" Nyx asked. "Is there any way to distinguish those from the regular ones?"

Elara shook her head. Nyx looked to the top of the tower again, noting the Void was already touching it.

Columbus chuckled. "You wanted adventure, Brommet. Let's get to it."

Nyx sighed and followed Columbus and Elara as they hustled across the open expanse toward the front of the tower.

Up a wide set of steps and flanked by two dry fountains was the biggest set of stone doors Columbus had ever seen. They were ornately carved with thousands of stars and scores of constellations. Some he recognized from reading the work of Ptolemy. Cassiopeia. Orion. Ursa Major and Minor. Others he didn't know at all. He was aware the Babylonians and Sumerians had also studied the stars, but images that looked like goat-fish and ziggurats were alien to him.

"We mustn't stay in the open long," Elara said. "Is that the symbol the Fates revealed?"

Columbus looked to the relief over the doors and saw the symbol of the open book inlayed in gold. It shimmered in the light.

"Yes," Columbus replied.

Elara put her shoulder to the door. It didn't budge. Columbus and Nyx tried to help her, but that proved fruitless as well.

"Is there a mechanism to unlock it?" Columbus asked, scanning the area.

"Actually," Nyx called from the windowed ledge she'd scaled. "I can see a beam blocking it from the inside. Boost me through here and I'll see if I can move it."

A few moments passed once Nyx slipped inside. Then, the sounds of a beam striking the ground was followed by the giant doors grating open.

"You are going to love this." Nyx grinned.

The entranceway smelled of dust and mildew. Columbus saw the beam Nyx cast aside had come from a collapsed archway above. They worked their way carefully through the debris and into the main body of the tower. There, they froze in stunned silence at what they found.

The room was over two hundred feet in diameter, and every inch of the walls was crammed with books, parchments, cartography maps, and pictures of such impossible clarity their very existence defied reason. The shelves that lined the walls were irregular with no conceivable pattern. One section was as small as a cubby hole; the next, thirty feet tall and a dozen feet wide. The only spaces that weren't covered were the stained windows that let light steal through tableaus of the Gods at play. They were all there. Zeus with his lightning bolt. Aphrodite hypnotizing mortal men. Charon the Ferryman with a coin in his hand. Pan the Satyr playing his pipes. And, of course, Poseidon, trident in hand, watching over them all.

Mesmerized, Columbus walked across the room until the light of the golden trident lit half his face. Then, Nyx sneezed, and Columbus turned.

"Dust," she said, eyes cast down in shame.

Nearby, Elara was clearing dirt from the ground, revealing a wood floor inlayed with intricate geometric patterns. How had any of this survived the scourge of time? Mildew alone should have reduced the wood and books to rubble.

Another small tremor shook the tower. Dust rained onto Columbus. He looked up to see other wooden floors above them, pie-shaped sections in staggering intervals that resembled a staircase only a Titan could scale.

"It must be bigger than the Library at Alexandria," Columbus whispered in awe. "How many books do you suppose there are?"

"I have no idea," Elara answered.

"This is a treasury unlike any other. And to think your people let the sirens keep you from it."

"It wasn't the sirens alone. Atlantis was created by men and women who believed acquiring knowledge could lead to a higher state of being. So, they pursued it with an unrivaled furor. But too much knowledge can be as dangerous as none."

"The Bible warns of the same."

"Bible?"

"A book of my religion, handed down from God to men. The first man and woman, Adam and Eve, bit an apple from the Tree of Knowledge and in doing so were cast from Garden of Paradise forever."

Elara nodded. "Much like Pandora. Our allegories may differ, but the meaning is the same. Knowledge without wisdom is a poison. And wisdom can only come from experience."

"My father had a saying he used every time I fell or scuffed a knee. He said 'God created scars for a reason. It reminds us everything comes for a price.'"

"This is why Atlantis gave up the written word. And, for a time, they were better for it."

"But you read. I've seen it."

"I'm a princess," she said, almost embarrassed. "The royal family has a small library of their own, though we don't speak of it."

Across the room, Nyx called out. They made their way to her. She'd found a small doorway that housed a lift tube that resembled those from the city. It rose all the way to the top where the open sky broke through. Unfortunately, the tube was broken in several sections and probably hadn't worked in centuries.

"*That* would have made our job a lot easier," Elara said. "As it is, we'll have to take the stairs. It will go quicker if we separate. Each of us takes a level, leapfrogging as they're cleared. Agreed?"

Nyx nodded. "What are we looking for?"

"Anything that appears out of the ordinary."

"Well, that's not vague in the least," she quipped.

Columbus searched the first level while the girls headed up the stairs. From time to time, he heard the creak of footsteps overhead, but little else. He rifled through shelves and books, looked under tables and desks. He pored over vellum parchments that disintegrated in his hands. He studied the stained-glass imagery until he thought his eyes might bleed. Up, down, and all around he looked—and found nothing.

It felt like hours had passed when Elara called out from above. Columbus and Nyx rushed to find her on the fifth landing.

"I hadn't noticed it before because of the dust on the floor," she said, "but there are symbols marking the subject matter of each section. See here? This one shows the image of a pyramid."

"And these titles all seem to reference building," Columbus added, enthusiasm growing. "It's an index." He shuffled off to the next section, clearing the dust with his boot until a second symbol appeared, followed by a third. A rock for minerals. A sun above a head for philosophy. A ship for ship building. They continued.

"Quickly," he said, "look for one with a key."

They spread out, clearing symbols as they went. Columbus returned to the lower floors while Elara and Nyx headed upward. It wasn't long before another shout rang through the tower, this one from Nyx. She was on the eleventh floor.

"I found something," she said, unsure. "It may be nothing, but you should see for yourselves."

She led them to a small niche just out of reach of the sun's rays. There, on the floor, was the symbol of a half-circle.

"It could be a dome, right?" she asked.

Columbus leaned down. "Possibly. Or a setting sun."

"This is it," Elara said.

"How can you be so certain?"

"The others are inlayed with orichalcum, but this one is cast in gold. And there's something else. Look." She knelt and blew the dust away to reveal very fine lettering.

"Writing," Columbus said. "What does it say?"

"It's the language of the slaves," Elara answered. "I cannot read it."

"I can," Nyx said, casting a smug grin at Columbus. With a roll of his eyes, he moved aside.

"To seek the riddle of Cyclops's crown, scour beneath the papryus bound. But to avoid Icarus's fate, one must learn to fly before the wind abates."

"What does it mean?" Elara asked.

"It means your slaves were tricky," Columbus answered. "Either they enjoyed playing games, or they wanted to ensure the right people found what they had hidden."

"There's something else," Nyx said. "Greek numerals marked around the outside, like one would find on a coin."

"This could take ages," Elara said. "The light is already falling."

"We just have to break it down," said Columbus. "One stanza at a time. First, *To seek the riddle of Cyclops's crown*. What is a riddle?"

"A puzzle," Nyx said. "And to unlock a puzzle you need all the pieces."

"Or a key," Columbus said. *"To seek the key of Cyclops's crown...* What do we know of Cyclops?"

"He was from the race of giants," Elara said. "With a single eye in his forehead. They were builders, the cyclops. They built the walls of Tiryns and a labyrinth so large they called it cyclopean."

Columbus felt his pulse quicken. "Like this tower. And what sits atop a tower?"

"Its crown," Nyx exclaimed.

"Second stanza. Repeat it."

"To seek the key of Cyclops's crown...scour beneath the papuros bound. Papuros is Greek for papyrus, isn't it? The first form of paper. And books are *bound*."

"She's good at this," Elara said. Nyx beamed. "But we can't be expected to look under each book. It would take an age itself."

"No, the answer's here," Columbus said. "Read the rest again."

"But to avoid Icarus's fate, one must learn to fly before the wind abates."

"Well, we know Icarus fell for getting too close to the sun." Columbus's eyes narrowed. He stood and crossed to the old lift tube that serviced the tower, noting once again how sunlight filtered in near the top where the stones had crumbled away.

"Elara, when we first saw the tower, what was the one thing you noticed?"

"That its apex pressed against the Void. Why?"

"This transport tube never fed all the way to the crown."

She immediately understood. "There's another section!"

"And another entrance."

"What of the final stanzas?"

"Maybe the numbers have something to do with it," Nyx said from across the room. Columbus was about to dismiss her when something struck him.

"Tell me the numbers," he said.

Nyx read them. *"Pena-iota. Deka-penta-iota-iota. Iota-iota.* Six, fourteen, and two."

Columbus wracked his brain for any hint of a clue. Then he remembered he'd seen a few numbers etched into the stacks here and there, but he dismissed them for being too small. Suddenly, the truth hit him.

"It's an index," he said.

Nyx's smile widened. "Section, row, and number!"

She leaped up and began to scan the stacks again. Columbus waited patiently, praying they were right. After a few moments, Nyx cried out, "I think I found it."

Near the top of the stack, wedged in between two larger folios, was a small vellum-bound book with no discernible title on the spine. But at the very bottom, in gold inlay, was the faint image of a trident.

"Careful," Elara warned as Nyx reached for it.

Once retrieved, Nyx slowly peeled back the cover, only to find the pages inside were barren.

"It's blank," Nyx said confused. "Do you think it faded?"

"No. Look underneath," Columbus said.

Nyx turned the book over and her mouth fell open once again. She held it up, but all Elara could see were many tiny dots.

"Is it code?" Elara asked.

"Another riddle," Columbus said. He gnashed his teeth in frustration. This was taking way too long.

. . .

OUTSIDE, Elara's team was patrolling the perimeter as ordered, completely unaware that Fanucio had wandered off on his own.

His stomach had been growling like an alley cat ever since the Atlanteans had thrust their *sustenance* in front of him. What kind of a word was that anyway? The worst kind. Offering a shipwrecked sailor seaweed and uncooked fish was like giving a cup of piss to a man dying of thirst. Sure, he'd drink it down, but it would taste like *piss* and only make him desperate for more.

As Fanucio stumbled through brush, he thought of Rosa, the portly innkeeper in Palos who served him watered wine every morning with a bowl of eggs, pork, leeks, and *queso manchego*. And on those rare occasions when she was feeling particularly generous, she'd give it to him half off, if he graced her with a good drubbing in the back room where the staff couldn't hear her cries. Not that it mattered. The only thing louder than Rosa's screams was her snoring, which was why he never stayed in Palos more than a few days. Still, the thought of it made his mouth water.

Then he saw the plumage of a bird bobbing in a thicket nearby. "Ooh! A squab! I promise me two teeth won't hurt a bit!"

He slowly extracted the sonstave the Atlanteans had given him, pushing the red gem up to soften the blast. *It was up, wasn't it? He was almost sure of it.*

Mouthwatering, Fanucio took aim, giggling to himself. "Time for some white meat."

With a press of the gem, Fanucio was catapulted back on his hindquarters. The bird's plumage exploded, followed by the shriek of something much larger. The thicket burst apart as a large bull-like animal—its bald tail smoking—charged. Fanucio screamed and tried to fire another salvo, but his fat fingers couldn't find the right gem. Just as the monster closed in, he shut his eyes and said a prayer. That's when two other blasts rang out, and the beast slid to its feet, dead.

Fanucio opened his eyes, ecstatic to be alive. Then, he saw Dion and Thetra glowering at him from the trees. Fanucio forced a smile, which promptly died away when a familiar note echoed in the distance.

A siren had been roused.

BACK IN THE TOWER, Columbus and the others were too busy looking for the hidden entrance to the apex to hear the commotion outside. They had reached the top floor of the library but couldn't find a hatchway or set of stairs. The wooden ceiling above was solid, save the four large wooden trusses that held it aloft.

"I don't understand," Elara said. "There has to be a way inside."

"We could shoot a hole in it," Columbus suggested.

"And risk the entire structure collapsing? No. I'd rather—"

Before she could finish her sentence, a tremor shook the tower. It was slow at first, rolling like a wave. It soon grew increasingly violent.

"Hold onto something," Columbus warned. "It's a big one!"

A series of jarring jolts ripped through the tower. Stone and mortar fell from the walls, and the ceiling splintered above. The nearest stained-glass window shattered, sending glass across the floor. Nyx curled into a ball, covering her ears as the rending of stone reverberated throughout the room. Columbus grabbed her and Elara, and they hunkered down together.

Eventually, the quake abated, leaving only the sound of rusty lamps swinging on the walls to vie with the trio's panicked breathing.

"Is it over?" Nyx asked.

No one answered. She was set to ask the question again when Elara shushed her. Then, the sound of a deep thrumming filled the air. Terror filled Elara's face.

"That is the sound the Void makes before a contraction! We have to hurry."

Columbus bolted for the lift tube. "If I climb up through here, maybe I can find a path inside."

"Look!" Nyx gasped.

The others turned to see what she saw. One of the large wooden trusses had cracked during the quake, revealing rusty steps hidden inside.

"Poseidon favors our quest," Elara said.

"Or he wants to tease us before we die," Columbus quipped as he ran to the base of the truss and kicked it. The facade crumbled, revealing the rising ladder. Moving as quickly as possible, the trio scaled upward, unlocking a hidden hatch. One by one, they crawled through.

The tower's apex was circular, unadorned save decorative stones jutting from the walls. At opposite ends of the room were two bureaus from which a multitude of metal pipes ran over the walls, each inexplicably disappearing at odd intervals. Columbus was approaching one of those bureaus when Elara gasped. He followed her eyes skyward.

One hundred feet high, suspended in air at the tower's apex, was the first gem-encrusted key. And it was glowing.

The trio was dumbstruck by the sight.

"Look, beyond the key," Elara finally managed. "Do you see it?"

The Void. Its dark surface roiled ten or twenty feet above their prize.

"I see it," Columbus said. Then he noticed several stone steps jutting out of the wall. They ran in a pattern that wound all the way to the top of the tower. The problem was the distance between them. It was at least eight feet.

"I could traverse these if they weren't so far apart. Maybe If I climbed—"

Another tremor rocked the tower, followed by a warbling thrum. Everyone covered their ears and looked skyward only to see the Void collapse several feet, instantly devouring more tower and edging ever closer to the key.

"There isn't enough time," Elara said once the thrum had stopped. "We need a plan now."

"I'm working on one, Princess," Columbus said, unable to keep the edge from his voice. "Maybe less ordering and more thinking might help."

Elara was about to retort when a trumpet-like blast filled the room, sending hundreds of streams of dust and mortar into the air. As it cleared, both Columbus and Elara turned to see a sheepish Nyx stepping away from the bureau she'd accidentally bumped into.

"Damnit, Nyx!" Columbus shouted. "Watch what you're doing!"

"Don't shout at her," Elara snapped.

"Why not? She shouldn't even be here."

"I got it," Nyx said softly.

"Got what?" Columbus snarled.

"The second stanza."

Columbus grunted, ready to rail her again when Elara spoke his name. The clarity of her voice silenced him. She turned back to Nyx, gently. "Go ahead, Nyx."

"*To seek the riddle of Cyclops's crown, scour beneath the papuros bound.* What did we find on the bottom of the book?"

"Codes," Columbus offered. "Gibberish."

Nyx shook her head. "*Notes.* Do you see these?" She pointed to the bureaus at opposite ends of the tower. "They're organs. And these pipes feed the blowholes in the wall. *...to avoid Icarus's fate, one must learn to fly before the wind abates.*"

Columbus looked. Could she be right?

"Try it," Elara said.

Nyx sat and wiped the dust from her organ's keyboard. Then she depressed a single key. Nothing happened.

"I don't understand," Nyx said, confused. "It should work."

"I told you this was foolish," Columbus said.

"No," Nyx snapped. "I know I'm right. And I need you to believe me."

Columbus stared at her and gritted his teeth. If she'd been a man, he would have trounced her. Then, he heard the Void warble again, and his senses returned. As did the realization that he could not do this on his own. Finally, he gave a curt nod for her to go on.

"Organs emit sound by air. The air comes from these bellows. But to fill them would require enormous pressure. Where could that kind of power come from?"

Columbus considered the question before turning for the nearest window. Far down below he saw the static waterwheel. And to his left, an orichalcum wheel. He tried to turn it, but it wouldn't move. "Give me a hand."

Elara turned for him, but Nyx called out, "Wait!" She turned back to Columbus.

"We need to hear you say it," she said.

"Say what?"

Nyx tipped her head and crossed her arms. "The magic word."

Elara snorted and rolled her eyes.

Columbus's face went as red as a strawberry. "Unless you wish to fly, *get over here*."

"Good enough for me," Nyx gulped as she and Elara joined him at the wheel.

"Why must all the women in my life be so cheeky?" Columbus bemoaned.

"Because you wouldn't notice them otherwise," Elara replied.

With their combined strength, the wheel began to turn. First it groaned, and then it snapped free. A great grinding noise echoed through the tower as the waterwheel down below began to turn.

"That's sure to draw the sirens," Elara said.

"I think we're beyond that point," Columbus said. "To the organs."

Nyx rushed to her organ and depressed the keys again. This time, air fed the pipes and more dust exploded from the tower's blowholes.

"Do you know how to read music?" Nyx asked Elara. The princess shook her head. "Come on, then. I'll teach you."

As Elara joined Nyx, Columbus made his way to the lowest stone step.

"Another skill," Columbus remarked. "That teacher of yours sure was prolific."

"For your information, Mansa only knew how to play the drums. This I learned from my mother."

Columbus was surprised to find he wanted to know more. Though the girl was a nuisance, she'd obviously led an interesting life to date. And despite the weeks they'd travelled together, it came as something of a shock to realize he knew so little about her. For a man that took pride in reading people in an instant, her secrets unsettled him.

"See how the blowholes alternate?" Nyx asked Elara. "That's because we need to play in unison, alternating one note at a time. These are your seven." She played them twice until Elara nodded. "Go." Elara ran to the opposite organ. Nyx rapped on the organ to establish their rhythm. "Together. One, two, three, and…"

The notes trumpeted out of the organ, sending more dust into the air, but this time Columbus saw the pattern emerge.

Stairs made of air!

As if the Void had somehow sensed their progress, it warbled again. Only this time the pitch was so low it shook the building and plummeted another few feet.

"It's nearing the key!" Elara shouted. "We have to hurry!"

Columbus mumbled something about time. When he was in position, he nodded, and Nyx counted her lead-in once again. As the first note sounded, Columbus stepped onto the stone step before stepping onto air. It was a terrifying sensation, and he leaped for the third stone. He hesitated, let out a loud curse, and shouted for the others. "Start again!"

This time, the women were ready. One after another, those fourteen notes rang out in time. It took everything Columbus had to trust in them, but with each step, that trust was rewarded. And then Elara fumbled a note, and Columbus fell eight feet and hit the floor like a stone.

Nyx shouted, but Columbus waved her back, rubbing his tender backside and groaning. "It's only my third greatest asset. Begin again. And no matter what happens this time, don't stop."

Elara offered a sheepish smile. Columbus took several deep breaths as Nyx counted out the time again. Then the notes rang, and he ascended.

* * *

OUTSIDE THE TOWER, the notes carried across the isle and far out to sea. The music was so loud, Dion imagined even those in the city could hear it. His attention quickly turned to the wooded area north of them when movement flickered within the tunnels between the two islands. The sirens were coming.

Prepare yourself, Dion signaled the others. Thetra and Sareen signaled that they were ready. The ones called Pygmies had already prepared their weapons.

* * *

NEAR THE TOWER, Fanucio watched on with a growing sense of dread. He held the sonstave in his sweaty hand, doubting it would do much good against those things. Maybe the giant was wrong. Maybe the sirens hadn't heard the music. Well, of course they heard it, but maybe they didn't care. That was possible, wasn't it?

The question was answered when a flood of sirens erupted from the tunnels and the defenders opened fire.

* * *

COLUMBUS'S CHEST heaved as he continued his march upward. He was just getting used to the difference between the real stepping stones and the fabricated ones when he glanced upward and saw the key, clearer now even in the haze of dust. Another dozen steps and it would be within his reach.

Then the Void warbled again.

"Faster," he shouted, his thighs burning as those notes came one on top of each other now, the three-way dance as dangerous and precarious as anything he'd ever done before. It took immense focus, pushing everything else but the timing and notes from his mind. The organs sung, the tower trembled, but Columbus continued to rise.

Three quarters up the tower, Columbus braved another glance at that glowing key. His sweat-stained shirt clung to his back, his heart pumping in time with the melody. Each step was a balancing act between life and death. *Air, step, air, step!* Then one of the stones crumbled beneath his feet. His hand flailed out, fingers gouging stone, but he managed to catch the next gust of air. Twenty steps left. Then fifteen. He was nearing the apex of the tower.

But with every step he drew closer, so too did the Void. The diaphanous veil of corruption pulsed harder, longer, winnowing its way into every cell of Columbus's body until he thought the very nature of it might drive him mad.

At last, he reached the final stepping stone, shouting as he drew even with the key. There was only one problem. *He had no clue how he was supposed to get down.*

Columbus shouted, but the women couldn't hear him. The warbling had grown too loud. Cracks spread across the tower's wall. More stone steps crumbled and fell. Columbus covered his ears but couldn't keep out that sound. It was like the Void knew he was there to stop it, and it wanted to stop him first.

At that moment, Columbus closed his eyes and tried to clear everything from his mind. He knew the chances of his survival were thin, but should he succeed? A feat like this could put him right up there with champions like Hector or Sampson. Champion? Hell, he could become a *legend*. He liked the sound of that.

"Where others run, I leap!" he said aloud. Then he nearly slipped off his rock. "Okay, okay. I'll keep working on it."

Columbus jumped.

The key was much farther than Columbus anticipated, but when his hand locked around the key and it came away with a tug, he gave a silent cheer. And then he fell. Nyx cried out. Elara shouted something unintelligible as he tumbled down the tower, limbs flailing, muscles tightening for the fateful impact. But just as the floor rushed up to meet him, Elara and Nyx turned back for their organs again, slapping their hands across the keyboards just before the air assaulted Columbus from every direction. The organs shrieked in unison as Columbus hit the ground hard, but very much alive.

"Huh." He looked up at their shocked faces. "I do believe I've developed a new appreciation for chamber music."

The women rushed to embrace him, and a strange joy filled his heart. He was surprised how good their smiles made him feel. Then, the Void fell, swallowing ten feet of tower, sending more debris tumbling down, smashing the wood at their feet.

"We need to get out of here," Nyx shouted.

It was the understatement of the millennia.

As the wall began to crumble, the wood trusses splintered with ear-piercing cracks that left no doubt that the tower was coming down. Columbus stuffed the key in his trousers as they raced for the hidden ladder. Bookshelves toppled, and floors crumbled. They made it fifteen levels down before one side of the tower split open and fell away. Columbus knew they'd never make it the rest of the way in time. He spun around until he had determined which way was south. Then he turned his sonstave toward the wall.

"Take cover," he said before blasting a hole in the wall. The trio raced to it and looked out. The waterwheel was below and to their left. Directly underneath them was the flowing river.

"You can't be serious," Nyx said.

Columbus smirked. "You wanted adventure."

Without hesitating, Columbus shoved Nyx out. She screamed expletives all the way down. She hit the water and emerged a moment later. Columbus turned to Elara.

"I am a princess," she warned. "The last of my line from the kings of—"

"Oh, shut up," he said before grabbing her arm and pulling her in for a kiss. Stunned, she didn't utter another word as he wrapped his arm around her and jumped.

They hit the river like stones, the water's crisp chill washing over them as they struck the muddy bottom and pushed off for the surface. As they burst above the surface, the rest of their party arrived, firing salvos as the host of sirens stormed in their direction.

"Captain!" Fanucio exclaimed gleefully. "You're alive!" Then an arrow sailed past his head. "Don't suppose you can lend a hand?"

A groan of astonishing proportions shook the earth. As the tower's base broke, everyone looked up and saw it was teetering in their direction. They ran screaming and shouting as the shadow hurtled toward them. The tower struck the ground with such force that everyone was thrown from their feet. Through the dust, they saw the tower had cut off the sirens from their path.

One by one, they crawled from the dust, coughing, but alive. Only Fanucio sat immovable in the rubble. Columbus rushed to his side.

"Fanucio?" he said. "What's wrong? Are you hurt?"

"No," the first mate grumbled. "Just hungry."

Columbus clapped his friend on the shoulder and laughed.

CHAPTER THIRTEEN

Word of their success had somehow preceded them back to the city.

As the sore and weary eight-man party drew near the rocky breakers, they were met with rousing cheers from the Atlanteans gathered on the walls and balconies, waving flags and banners while chanting some melodic battle cry that to Columbus sounded more like a funeral dirge than anything. Still, it raised his spirits, especially when he saw all the children tossing flowers in the water only to laugh when a league of exotic waterfowl swooped in over the shoals to claim them.

It wasn't until the transit tubes spit them out at the central colonnade that the true enormity of their accomplishment set in. The halls were lined with the citizens of Atlantis, jockeying from the balconies by the hundreds with smiling faces, tossing gossamer petals and streams of silk.

Now this is a hero's welcome, Columbus thought.

Elara and her Gadeir betrayed no reaction, though there was no denying their chests were a little fuller, their chins a little higher. This they could *feel*. They marched on until they reached the lobby of the Nave where King Atlas stoically stood waiting. Even he appeared to be standing a little taller, his eyes a little sharper. It was the first time Columbus had seen the man look like he didn't want to kill someone.

"Daughter," the king said once the din died, "on behalf of Atlantis, I congratulate you and your fellow Gadeir on your successful mission."

Another rousing cheer ensued. Elara gave a curt nod, embarrassment mixing with pride.

"You have the key?" King Atlas asked.

Elara turned to Columbus. He drew the key from his waistband, hesitating a moment before he handed it over. Elara gave it to the king. To the delight of the crowd, he lifted it triumphantly into the air, and the crowd roared. Even Columbus's crew weren't immune to the gaiety. Nyx's teeth shone bright and full, and when her cheeks flushed she looked every bit her age. Fanucio also basked in the adulation and combed his hair back several times, his tooth-gapped mouth on display for all to see. Even the Pygmies got in on the action, singling out a few female admirers who tittered at their attention.

After passing the key to an attendant, King Atlas addressed the group once more. "There will be a celebration tonight at evening bell." For the first time, he acknowledged Columbus. "You will be my guests."

Columbus bowed, low and fitting for a king, but he couldn't let the moment pass without a *coup de grace* of his own. "I'll see if I can fit it into my schedule, Your Highness."

Elara's eyes ballooned. Even the king froze a moment before he burst into laughter. He cuffed Columbus hard on the shoulder before he turned and walked away. Once out of eyesight, Columbus groaned and rubbed his shoulder.

"You enjoy playing with fire, don't you?" Elara admonished.

"Sometimes it's the only way to *heat things up*," Columbus replied.

She shook her head but did not look away. Instead, she held his gaze in a way all men wanted women to look at them. But where he should have felt joy, he felt only trepidation. Soon, she would learn it was all for naught. Even with this victory, the writing was on the wall. Time was their enemy and it was marching steadily closer. Yes, he was developing feelings for the princess, but such admissions did him no good. Nor would ruminating on the promise he made her or how she'd feel when she discovered his betrayal. He had a job to do. He needed to keep all his attention on the prize.

Just then Dion cleared his throat and Elara said, "Until evening bell."

Columbus bowed again as Elara turned and melded into the crowd. At the same time, Vespucci approached.

"Congratulations, Columbus," he said. "You're the first man in history to lay siege to a library and be praised for it."

Columbus nodded, unwilling to let the man spoil the moment. "Worry not, my friend. Nyx saved you a book before the haul was lost. It even has pictures."

Nyx laughed, but Vespucci took the insult in stride. Behind him, a very attractive female attendant approached. "Your new rooms are this way, mariner."

"New rooms," Columbus boasted to his companions. "We're moving up in the world."

As they headed off, Columbus and the attendant exchanged smiles, prompting Nyx to make a gagging gesture with her hand.

* * *

THE SUITE of rooms was high atop the central tower with a view of the ocean and islands beyond. After a thorough bathing in a golden basin, Columbus retired for a much-needed rest. When he finally awoke, he found Nyx alone on the balcony watching the sun set.

"There are parcels in the foyer," he said.

"Garments, I was told," Nyx answered. "I guess they want us to look our best for tonight."

Columbus plopped down in a chair, rubbing cheeks that were smooth for the first time in a long time. "Or maybe they're giving us the apple before the spit."

"Why do you do that?"

"Do what?"

"Always look first to the darker side of things."

"When you live as long as I have, Brommet, and see what I've seen, you will too. Beyond ship and sea, mighty perils await."

He said it theatrically, but she refused to laugh.

"You joke too often."

"And you too little. Humorless women make terrible companions. It gives them lines on their face. In fact, I see one forming now."

He reached out to touch her forehead, and she slapped his hand away. He repeated it several times until she laughed. Then he got that feeling again. The one that told him the girl would bring him nothing but pain.

"Have you seen Vespucci?" he asked.

"He came in while you were sleeping but left shortly after."

Columbus's forehead creased. "And he said nothing?"

"'These will do,'" she repeated in a nasally tone. "I figured he was talking about the lodgings."

"The man cares not one whit for the rooms. He's up to something."

Columbus stood, crossed to the bevy of packages, and retrieved the one with his name on it. He was headed for his room when Nyx called out.

"Captain?" Nyx said. "It's not bad here, is it? I mean, when we're not being shot at or threatened with death. What I'm saying is, I like it. I like *her*. Can we help them?"

Columbus hesitated. He didn't want to admit he liked the princess too. But he also didn't want to give Nyx false hope. For better or worse, she was part of his crew and he might need her to make some hard choices. At the same time, he needed everyone to keep up appearances. As Nyx was unable to keep her emotions in check, he decided the best thing to do was allow her to enjoy the evening. He could always rein her in later.

Columbus held up his hands and grinned. "In a realm made of magic, anything is possible."

As he disappeared, Nyx looked worriedly back out to the sea and the storm raging above.

* * *

CHRISTOPHER COLUMBUS

THE GRAND BALLROOM was another marvel of Atlantean architecture. Rising several stories into the air, its ceiling and walls were made entirely of glass, revealing the interior of the city and the Garden of the Blest beyond. Alchemical chandeliers floated magically throughout the room, changing colors in time with the globes on the walls. But the most awesome site was the golden fountain at the room's center, which featured a dozen golden mermaids holding tridents. Water would spray from those fountains only to coalesce in the air—taking on the forms of animals or symbols—only to slowly evaporate back to water, filling the fountain's pool to repeat again.

As Columbus passed through the entryway, the party was already in full swing. Discordant but pleasing music filled the room, though he saw no sign of musicians. Still, it set a mood Columbus had not experienced up until that moment. Warm. Peaceful. Almost happy. It made him look anew at the garments he'd been given. Black pantaloons, black silken shirt, and a red vest brimming with tassels that he suspected were meant to connect in some fashion. He'd given up after aligning three or four for risk he'd never get the damn thing off again. Now, he regretted not taking the time to do it right.

As Columbus walked down a short set of stairs, he was struck by the aroma of the banquet tables that aligned the eastern wall. The diversity and artistry of those many dishes made his mouth water. The citizens must have found the same true as they stood in long lines before returning to the bevy of scarlet-covered tables spread about the room.

Columbus scanned the room for Elara but couldn't find her. He did spot King Atlas, however, seated on a golden throne in a broad mezzanine. He was wearing a navy cloak with sable epaulets and a thin golden crown on his brow. He was surrounded by a coterie of elitists, who stood poised, laughing at his every word, blissfully oblivious to the fact that their monarch clearly wished he was anywhere else. Still, Columbus spied no goblet within the king's reach, which was a welcome surprise.

A shout beckoned from the center of the room. It was Fanucio trying to get his attention. As Columbus made his way to him, he saw his first mate had taken refuge behind a table laden with serving plates. Half were brimming with food while the other half looked as if they'd been licked clean. He, too, wore Atlantean attire, though it looked as if his had been put together by a child. The charcoal coat fell to the floor, covering the ill-fitting white fabric beneath.

"Captain!" Fanucio shouted. "By my word, join in! Look," he waved his hand across the table with a flourish. "Food. And it's edible!"

Columbus looked over the spread, settled on what looked like a turkey leg, and sat down.

"Delicious, ain't it?" Fanucio said. "Now, ask me what animal it comes from."

"I'd rather not," Columbus said.

"That's the thing! I couldn't name it if I wanted to!"

Columbus looked at his first mate askew. "Have you been drinking?"

"Aye! They do things with grapes here that'll pop your cork." Then he winked at a nearby Atlantean woman. "Big'uns and little'uns too."

"Have you seen the princess?"

"Not yet. I don't see her as the type who likes making a grand entrance. Your ruffian pal's behind you though."

Sure enough, Dion sat two tables away. He ate from a plate overflowing with food. He was surrounded by his fellow Gadeir, all looking as serious and backlogged as him.

"And the crew?"

"Eh? Oh. The wee ones stopped by for some grub before disappearin' again. And I saw Vespucci skulking 'round. Man's got a gift for bending ears, I'll give 'im that. Hey! There's the lass!"

On a crowded dance floor, Columbus spotted Nyx among a group of Atlantean youths. Someone had done her hair up and even applied coloring around her eyes to mock the appearance of gems. She wore a red gown that glistened as she twirled and a matching necklet that made her look older than her years. With every spin she laughed, long arms moving gracefully to the music as if she was having the grandest time. Columbus smiled a moment before his brow furrowed.

"I'll call her over," Fanucio said.

Before Columbus could stop him, Fanucio whistled loud enough to draw the attention of the entire room. Nyx waved in response before excusing herself and heading over.

"Phew," Nyx gasped as she plopped down at the table. "These fish boys might be poor dancers, but they learn quick. I was just showing them a tordion."

"What's that?" Fanucio asked, his mouth full.

"It's a five-step dance similar to the galliard. It's very big in the courts of France."

"And how do you know what's big in the courts of France?" Columbus asked.

Nyx shrugged. "I've been around."

The answer troubled Columbus again. The girl was an enigma. Highly educated, well spoken, not to mention trained in a variety of skills. Why on earth had she sought him out? It certainly wasn't to join his crew. What was she really after?

"Our li'le boatswain cleans up right nice, don't she?" Fanucio asked, tipping cups with her before they both belted them back. She must have noticed Columbus's stare because she changed the subject quickly.

"I spoke to Thetra earlier," she said.

"Who?" Columbus asked.

"Thetra? Gods, Columbus. She went to the isle with us. The twin? Sister to Sareen? She said the king is going to honor her with a gemshard. The tiny gems that decorate their faces? Apparently, it's like an award or something. She said I could probably get one if the king gets crocked enough tonight."

"And that idea appeals to you?"

She shrugged. "I don't know. Some of them look all right."

Columbus shook his head, his irritation increasingly visible. "Brommet, in our line of work we travel to a great number of places and encounter a broad range of cultures, most of them primitive. I would think a wise person might consider some discretion when it comes to partaking in the customs and rituals of heathens. Not that your appearance wouldn't benefit from a chicken bone through the nose or tribal tattoos covering every inch of your skin."

"Captain," Fanucio chided, "she's just having fun."

"*Fun?*" Columbus hissed. "We're not here to have *fun*. We're here to recover the damn trident!"

His outburst drew the attention of several, including Dion. Columbus sat back, waiting until the moment had passed before leaning in again.

"That's what the keys are for. I didn't say anything earlier because I didn't want to spend the next several days looking at your sour faces. We need to face facts. Atlantis is dying. And all *this*," he waved his hand with a flourish, "will only distract us from the task at hand."

"But Atlantis has survived thousands of years—more," Nyx said.

"Aye, and it's just our bad luck to arrive for its final act. Look out there. Go on. Look, and tell me what you see." He pointed beyond the windows—beyond the garden—to the Void itself. "That *thing* is the will of their Gods. Gods far more powerful than you or me. This kingdom with all its power and all its creations has been unable to stop it. Now we're expected to? Two sailors, two Pygmies, and *you?* Nyx, this isn't our home, and we're certainly not its heroes. *I* am no hero. And the sooner you get that through your thick little skull the better off you'll be. You said you wanted adventure. Well, lass, this is it. But adventure is born of risk and great peril and the only way to survive it is to harden your heart. Do that and with some fortune, you might escape with your life and a little treasure for your troubles before the towers and voids of the world come crashing down around you. Don't, and you are as doomed as they are."

Nyx had paled. Even Fanucio had stopped eating. But Columbus wasn't finished. "Atlantis and her people are lost. Growing close to them now will only cause you more pain in the end."

"But you care for Elara," Nyx said, her eyes welling. "I can see it."

"No. I pity her. There's a difference. She refuses to accept the reality of her plight. As do you. When you first spoke your desire on the ship, I laughed. And then I saw you in the tower and thought, why not? But now I think my original assessment was true. You have the skill to be a privateer, perhaps even the heart. Unfortunately, you lack the stomach. What I can't decide is if it's the woman in you or the child."

With a sob, Nyx stood up and ran away. Fanucio stared at his captain.

"That was mighty cold, sir," he said.

Columbus grabbed a cup of Atlantean wine and sucked half of it down.

"I did her a favor, and we both know it. The sting will wear off soon enough."

Fanucio sighed and pushed his plate away. "Me mum said something once. How when people speak with venom, it's most often directed at those they love."

"Love?" Columbus laughed. "Fanucio, please tell me you're not going soft on me too. I don't love that girl. I don't even know her."

"Aye. But I remember you loving someone like her once. Full of spit and fire, she was. With more adventure in her heart than any man I'd met before. *Or since.*"

"You overstep, my friend," Columbus warned.

"Apologies, Cap'n. Sometimes I can't help it, what being a man with one foot and all."

Fanucio stood, tipped his hat, and limped away. Columbus listened to the sound of that *click-thump* recede before rising.

THE NIGHT WAS warm and pleasant with a cool breeze that filtered in from the east that almost made this world worth dying for.

Columbus stood on the balcony, nursing his cup of wine. He knew he'd crossed the line with the girl, but in the end, he'd be proven right. This was no place for one like her. No place for feelings. The sooner she was gone, the sooner he could get back to being himself. That was what he wanted, right?

As he looked out over the gardens, his gaze kept returning to that truncated bridge that spawned from wavering grass to the abyss. It was a visual metaphor for something he wasn't sure he wanted to understand. *The Void*. It terrified him. And yet he found himself drawn to it for reasons he couldn't fathom. Maybe it was its inexplicable power. Or the totality of its indifference. In a way, it was the manifestation of the end we all had waiting for us. Only this one you could see coming and couldn't do a damn thing about.

"Enjoying your evening?" a voice said.

Columbus turned to find Elara standing in the doorway. She was wearing a light blue dress made of silk that flowed like the waters of the sea. Her arms were bare. Her hair tied up, with the thinnest string of sapphires running across her brow. She looked radiant.

"It's just gotten a whole lot better," Columbus said.

Elara smiled and stepped out onto the balcony.

"My grandmother used to come here some evenings. She loved the way the gardens looked in the moonlight. Is yours very different?"

"Clearer perhaps, but not nearly as romantic."

Elara blushed.

"Do you have stars? I haven't seen any."

"No. We've heard of them, of course. And I have seen paintings that attempt to capture their essence, but I imagine few do them real justice."

She glanced at his vest and covered her mouth. "You've done this all wrong. Here." She stepped close and began connecting the tassels of his vest, making a pattern. It was an intimate gesture. One that drew Columbus closer.

"Sometimes when we're at sea at night and there's no fear of attack or storm, I take the wheel as my crew sleeps so I can feel the waves beneath my feet as they pass. On especially clear nights, the stars fill the heavens, though none are as beautiful as the ones that dance upon the surface of the sea."

"So, you're a Star Rider in your world *and* in mine. I would like to see them."

He reached up and pushed an errant string of hair from her eyes. "Maybe one day I'll show you."

When their eyes met, it felt like they were destined to kiss. Then, a cheer went up, and Elara stepped back, awkward. "My people needed this."

"Any victory is well earned."

"It's not the victory they celebrate. It's the promise of what it brings. *Hope*. You gave them this." Elara watched his smile fade. "Does that trouble you?"

"I've never been good at meeting the expectations of others. They tend to weigh on people. Just ask your father. He wears the crown."

Elara looked inside to see the king observing the festivities but not taking part.

"I don't have to. I feel it too."

* * *

FANUCIO HOBBLED THROUGH AN EXTERIOR CORRIDOR, opening the first door he came upon. "Oh! My apologies." He went to shut the door, but added, "I admire your flexibility."

As he closed the door, a sob resounded nearby. Fanucio saw Nyx on a bench near an atrium. She was crying into her arm. He limped over and sat beside her.

"Go away, Fanucio," she said.

"Knew it was me, did you? It's this damn soap. I'll never be rid of the smell."

When she looked up, her cheeks were wet with tears, but she smiled. Then she laid her head against his shoulder.

"Why does he hate me?"

"He doesn't hate you, girl. At worst, he fears what you represent."

"What's that?"

"Responsibility maybe? Manners. Duty. All the sh...stuff he swore off when he stepped aboard his first ship."

"Have you known him long?"

"Aye. Since he was a wee lad in Genoa. See, his father was a wool carder and tavern owner and all Columbus knew of life was cleaning up the piss and muck of others. Then, one day, Lorenzo de' Medici came to town and there was a parade. Lorenzo the Magnificent he was called. Patron of the arts, protector of the people. Ah, lass. He was a sight. One look at that grand peacock—and how the people loved him—and Columbus knew his destiny was elsewhere.

"He hung about the docks then, learnin' the tongues of the merchantmen, their skills. One day a caravel put into port. I still recall her name. *Flor de Inverno.*"

"Flower of Winter," Nyx translated.

Fanucio smiled and nodded. "She was owned by a Portuguese trader. Ugliest bastard you ever did see. And mean to boot. Men used to joke he ate iron for breakfast and shat out nails for supper. I knew that weren't true cuz I was his cabin boy. Not that it made the job easier. Still, he took Columbus on. And went on to torment him for the better part of a year."

"Why? Was Columbus bad at his job?"

"The cap'n? He done every job he was given quicker'n a maid-in-waiting loses her britches. Fast, I mean. There was a hitch though. You see, the captain had a daughter."

"Ah," Nyx said, suddenly understanding.

"She was a flower too. One he hoped to marry off for a price. She went everywhere with us, set up in a posh cabin like a princess, though she was no dandelion. Truth was she could handle steel or wheel better'n any man aboard. Then Columbus come along. One look at the two of 'em together and even the hardest sea dog had to admit true love was real."

Fanucio smiled fondly at the memories. Then his smile faded.

"Near a year later, we come under attack by pirates. Our crew fought valiantly, but we was outnumbered and heavy with provisions. When the ship caught fire, Columbus tried to find her, but there was no time. When he and I made it to shore, we found we was the only survivors."

"So that's why he refused to take me on? He can't bear the thought of losing another woman on his watch?"

"No, lass. It's more than that. You see, you are the spitting image of her. Had I not seen it with my own eyes, I wouldn'ta believed it."

Nyx's eyes widened, and she turned to face him.

"Fanucio, I have something to tell you. I never knew my father. I was raised on an island by my mother. Last spring, she came to me and told me she had to go away, but that she would be back by the end of the summer. When summer came, and she hadn't returned, I went crazy with worry. She'd never broken her word to me before. I knew something must have happened to her, so I went to my teacher, Mansa, for help. Fanucio, this is the most fearless man I've ever known. But something about my mother's disappearance frightened him. He refused to go after her. Instead, he said I needed to seek out Christopher Columbus, someone I'd never heard of before. You don't think…?"

"That Columbus is your da? No, I don't."

"How do you know?"

"Because the woman I speak of died ten years before you were born."

He watched the girl deflate, and it took a small part of him with it. "Oh, I suppose it's possible he sired you by some other. He's had his share. But I got trouble believing any God would be so cruel as to give you the bearing of his one true love. I'm sorry."

Nyx wiped another tear. "What was her name?"

Fanucio hesitated. He hadn't spoken it aloud in many, many years. "Lizete," he said at last. "It means, 'consecrated to God.'"

"My mother's name is Horacia."

"A pretty name. She's still missing, is she?"

"Yes," Nyx said with a sigh.

* * *

"THE SIREN ATTACK TODAY," Columbus said, eager to bridge the silence that had come between him and Elara. "You said it's rare for them to go out in daylight, and yet there were so many."

Elara nodded. "Even a squadron of Gadeir trespassing into their territory wouldn't normally draw those numbers."

"Is it possible they were compelled by something else?"

"Such as?"

"The music perhaps? I know this might sound foolish, but when you and Nyx were playing the organs, I felt something. Like a force guiding me, as if I was a part of something bigger than myself. It sounds crazy."

Elara didn't look as if it sounded so crazy. "We have always considered the sirens feral creatures—barely more than beasts—but our history says they were beautiful once. I find this very hard to believe. And yet if men can be enchanted by their song, is it so outlandish to say they can be enchanted by another?"

Columbus nodded faintly, her words had grown thin. A familiar tickle fluttered in his chest and his eyes kept returning to the Void. When he looked back at Elara, he realized she'd said something.

"I'm sorry?" Columbus said.

She shook her head. "You're tired and have had a long day. Tomorrow bodes to be even longer. I should let you rest."

As she turned, he reached out for her hand.

"Wait. Don't leave. Not yet. Tell me something else. Tell me...about that bridge. It's strange, isn't it? How it stands there in defiance of gravity. In defiance of the Void."

Elara looked uneasily in its direction.

"The Garden of the Blest used to extend several leagues to the south. It is said its beauty once rivaled Eden itself. To reach it, you had but to cross that bridge, a right that was reserved for only the most prominent citizens of Atlantis." She paused, lost in a memory herself.

"You know of the Athenians. How they were captured and enslaved after Atlantis fell. What you don't know is the cruelty they suffered in bondage. For a thousand years, my people forced them to build everything you see around us. They built our towers, grew our crops, served our whims, all while living in the most insufferable of conditions. To their credit, they never rebelled nor complained. They considered their punishment just, for we both lost everything in that war.

"But where we flourished—mostly on the fruits of their labors—they suffered, and no one asked if it came at a cost. When the quakes began, and the Void started to shrink, we refused to consider it was punishment for our actions. All the while, the slaves were secretly at work, building their prophecy, creating an endgame by which we might be saved. Only when they were done did they finally ask for their release. Our king, my ancestor, laughed at them and told them the only thing that would free them was death.

"So, one day, with all the city watching, they crossed that bridge, and they entered the gardens for the first and only time. They did not stop to drink from the rivers. Nor did they stop to taste the grapes blooming on the vine. They did not stop until they walked one by one into the Void and whatever awaited beyond."

"You almost make it sound like you were there."

"I was. This is the past I asked the Fates to show me."

He knew she must have been affected by that vision because he'd experienced the same thing. Seeing the history of Atlantis—the catastrophe it and his people had suffered—made him question how he could succeed in the fate of such overwhelming odds. Was he mad to believe he could waltz in here and do what no one else in history could do? The idea daunted him, and that was not a feeling he liked.

"And the present?"

"How we might make amends. I believe that is why the bridge still stands. Not in defiance of gravity or the Void, but in defiance of us. I am young, but I know this of life at least. To have a future one must first be free of the past. Are you free of yours?"

Columbus looked down, unwilling or unable to answer.

CHAPTER FOURTEEN

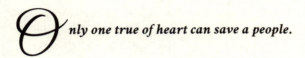*nly one true of heart can save a people.*

COLUMBUS BOLTED AWAKE to find the walls rattling. He heard Nyx shriek from the adjoining room. He leaped from bed, banging his knee as he pushed through her door and found her clutching her sheets tightly, her face rife with worry.

"What's happening?" she asked.

"Another earthquake," Columbus answered. "It should subside soon."

He was right. A moment or two later, the shaking stopped, though Nyx didn't look any more relieved. Columbus's instinct was to go to her and comfort her, but he dismissed the notion as Vespucci and Fanucio appeared.

"Oh, my bleeding head," the first mate cried. "All the 'vances these idiots got, you think they'd be able to fix a head dry o' drink."

"Go back and sleep it off," Columbus said.

"Not without you seeing this first."

They moved out onto the balcony to see a dozen cones of black smoke broiling up from the sea.

"A fissure opened up last night," Vespucci said. "Teams of soldiers have been coming and going all night."

The smoke trailed in their direction, marring the rising sun.

"It's getting worse, isn't it?" Nyx asked.

Columbus nodded grimly.

"Captain," Fanucio said, "even with this key business, how do we get home? We got no ship."

Columbus looked to Vespucci. "The *Pinta* and *Niña* were still seaworthy when we went down. Let's assume at least one of them survived. Any chance they would stick around?"

Vespucci shrugged. "The crew was given strict orders to wait four days should I or Juan Niño take leave of the ship. This was assuming we disembarked on land, not dragged to the depths by a monster that could return at any time. Were I in their position, I would have set back for Spain with all haste."

Of course, you would, Columbus thought.

"That said, I believe the *Pinta* suffered at least moderate damage in the fight. It's not inconceivable to think they stayed to make repairs."

"In your estimation, how long would those repairs take?"

"I'm not a carpenter, but factoring in damages, as well as losses to the crew, I'd give it the same four days."

"Which leaves us two days to find the trident and a way out of here. That's assuming we can all work together."

He locked eyes with Vespucci.

"You needn't worry about me, Columbus. I want leave of here as badly as you do."

"And afterward?"

"Back to Spain, of course. Given the manner of your exodus, I understand your reticence to return, yet I suspect Ferdinand would look quite favorably on the man who discovered Atlantis."

Vespucci didn't say who that man would be, something Columbus took note of.

"Someone's coming," Fanucio said.

A moment later, a bell sounded, and the door opened. Elara entered. She was back in her Gadeir uniform with her back straight, her hair plaited. Gone was all trace of the woman he'd been with the night before.

"You've seen the smoke?" she asked.

Columbus nodded. "We assume the tremors opened a volcanic rent in the seafloor?"

"The largest one on record. My people have been working all night to contain it. They'll need a few hours more. In the meantime, our meeting to discuss the retrieval of the second key has been postponed."

"How long?" Fanucio said.

"An hour or two, no more. Your people can have morning meal in the garden, or I can have it sent up here."

"Here would be fine," Columbus said. "If yesterday's mission is any indication of things to come, we could use all the rest we can get."

"Actually, I need to borrow you briefly."

Columbus traded glances with the others. "I'll be back in a few."

* * *

"So, where are we headed?" Columbus asked as they strode down an empty corridor.

"My chambers," she answered. "And before your primitive upper-world brain begins to conjure any lewd or distasteful fantasies, let me assure you nothing is going to happen. This is purely a research outing."

"You wish to research me. Got it. I am your willing subject."

"Columbus," she groaned, as if scolding a child.

"And just to let you know, if nudity is required, I am more than willing to suffer through my shame again in the name of Atlantean science."

"Of that I am certain," she said, hitching a thumb toward the transport tube.

"Ah, your water chutes. I must admit, I'm still confused how these work."

"Simple enough," she said, stepping inside and on a round platform before she signaled Columbus to follow. "Step inside, enter your coordinates..." She tapped out a series of symbols on the hub surface. "And you're off."

Liquid appeared at their feet and quickly began to rise.

"And no one's ever gotten hurt in one of these?"

"Only those without gills," she said with a wink.

Columbus's eyes widened as the water spilled over them and they shot upward with a *whoosh*.

* * *

THEY ARRIVED at the southeastern most tower, the liquid sloughing off like quicksilver, leaving them completely dry. Columbus stepped out into an ornately decorated hallway with three grand sets of doors.

"What a ride!" he whooped.

Elara shushed him and pulled him forward.

"Wake the king," she said, "and your next one will be far less fun."

"These are the royal quarters? Why are there no guards?"

"They are helping with the rift," she hissed. "Now, be quiet."

She crept toward the left set of doors.

"You know, most palaces have secret doors for just these occasions."

"I'm not sure what occasions you're referring too."

"Sneaking boys into your room."

"I am not...I have never—"

"You mean I'm your first?" Columbus said loudly. Elara shushed him, which only made Columbus snicker. "Relax, Princess. I understand this is purely a *research outing*."

"That won't stop my father from killing you if he finds you here."

"Which is why I live by the philosophy that it's better to ask forgiveness than permission."

"Hard to ask for either when your tongue's been removed."

"You do that here?"

"What do you think you had for breakfast?"

Columbus swallowed as Elara pulled him into her chambers and closed the door.

* * *

ONLY A FEW SECONDS LATER, another whooshing sound filled the antechamber before two small figures plopped out on the floor.

"*Exceptional!*" chuckled Monday. "*We must have a set of these for our village.*"

"*But our village is only seven huts,*" said Tuesday.

"*Should cut down our construction time.*" He looked around. "*Hmm. Three doors. Want to flip for it?*"

"*Yes.*"

They grabbed each other by the shoulders and began to wrestle until one of them was flipped toward the central set of doors.

Light spilled across the marbled floor of the darkened king's chambers as the Pygmies padded through the foyer, shoving each other as they bumped into ancient vases. They mocked a powerful sculpture of the king holding the world on top of his shoulders.

The corridor fed into a grand sitting room full of strange artifacts and timeworn antiquities. Stepping in front of a mirror, Tuesday was stunned to see his form change into that of a chiseled Titan with a giant sword and a bevy of scars. Monday shoved him out of the way only to see himself become a pregnant female Pygmy. Tuesday laughed, and Monday pummeled him.

On the floor sat a sleek box with a single button. Like a curious child, Monday depressed the button and shrieked when he was encircled by insubstantial, ghostlike figures of himself. He stomped on the box until it fizzled, and his doppelgangers vanished.

Tuesday called out at the same time, holding up a skull made of crystal. The two began tossing it, leaping off furniture, and sliding across the floor. Then, it skipped off Tuesday's fingers and hit the ground with a large crack, rolling through an open doorway at the far end of the room.

Monday picked up the skull's broken jawbone and went to retrieve the skull. He signaled Tuesday when he heard heavy snoring inside.

There, in a bed of incredible size was King Atlas, shirtless, mouth open under silken sheets. Monday pointed at his prodigious belly and giggled. But Tuesday's attention had been drawn to something else.

High above the bed was a disk made of bronze. Tuesday recognized it as the one their sailor captain had lost. He thought it might be a nice gesture to give him another one. He was destined to be eaten in their village after all, and happy meat always tasted better than the alternative.

Tuesday went to the king's bedside and climbed onto its gilded headboard. He straddled his way to the center and reached for the disk. He came up short. Monday giggled down below. Tuesday went up on tip toes, craning, when his feet began to slip.

* * *

KING ATLAS SAT UP, blurry-eyed, bed shaking. *Another damn quake no doubt.* His Gadeir had informed him of the new rift hours before, but they had pleaded with him to get some sleep.

As his legs fell over the side of the bed, he had an eerie feeling he was not alone. He looked around but saw no one. With a sigh, he rose, completely unaware one stranger was hanging from the chandelier over his bed while another was hiding under it.

The king padded to a water closet, his feet stopping in front of a water cistern. Soon, a heavy stream echoed through the room, punctuated by a robust fart that had Monday and Tuesday covering their mouths to keep from laughing.

A few moments later, the king was reentering his room when he stepped on something and let out a shout. He bent over and picked up a glass crystal jaw. What the hell was that doing there? Confused, he looked around. That's when he heard what sounded like giggling children and the closing of a door. Must have been the wind, he decided, as he scratched his backside and returned to bed.

* * *

IN THE ADJOINING SUITE, Columbus followed Elara into her chambers. The decor was minimalist. A sitting area. A table with a basin. A bed. On the floor were a large number of weapons and a few discarded uniforms.

"Not as clean as I would have expected," Columbus said.

"I don't spend much time here."

Columbus looked at the bed and was about to make yet another remark when Elara said, "There are weapons within reach."

"Point taken," Columbus said. "Metaphorically speaking."

Elara led him toward the back of the room where a large portrait hung. In it, a young, vibrant man in uniform stood regally with his hand on the shoulder of a severe but beautiful woman seated in a chair. The woman wore a crown atop her auburn hair and looked very familiar.

"My mother and brother," Elara said. "Atreal was killed while raiding a stronghold with his vanguard. His death devastated our parents and our people. My father used his sacrifice to rally the kingdom to him, but my mother never got over it. She died when I was five."

"She was beautiful," Columbus said.

"Many that knew her say so. The memories I have of her are vague and not particularly endearing. What I wanted to show you is through here."

She triggered a secret lever, and a doorway behind the portrait swung open.

The hidden library was paltry when compared to the Tower of Illumination, but it was impressive nonetheless. The walls were lined floor-to-ceiling with tomes. Oddly, each glimmered with a high polished sheen as if they'd only been recently bound. Odder still, there was no smell of decay, no dust motes in the air. *Were the Atlanteans craftsmen at every trade?*

Light spilled in from two rectangular windows high atop the far wall, illuminating a single chair and a square table. Stacks of books lined the table along with rings of wax from an untold number of candles.

"So, this is where you spend your free time," Columbus said.

"People think the life of a princess is glamorous, but as a child, I was most often told I was in the way. This became my refuge. They call it the King's Library, though I doubt any king has looked upon it in a century or two—my father included. Here, I learned of Atlantis— the true city state—by those who lived it. A thousand years' worth of history at my fingertips. What curious child could ask for more?"

"Why not use this to rebuild? Elara, the mechanisms alone—"

"Led my people to generations of apathy and indolence. I would not have us return to that path. It's only in the last century that we've begun to emerge from those dark ages to learn that the true value of this life comes from overcoming its hardships, its struggles. Your people knew this." She touched a scar on his shoulder, reminding him of their earlier conversation. "Mine must learn it again."

She ran her hand over the books, emitting a subtle trill that sounded like rain. "Medicine, mathematics, language, the arts—these are the foundation upon which every civilization is built. To survive, we must do more than uncover our past. We must define our own reason for existence."

"But surely there's something in here that can help you stop the Void from collapsing?"

"I have searched and searched. But you must remember, the Void is not a geographical phenomenon. It is a construct of a God. To undo magic, one must first possess magic, and nothing within these walls offers that."

Elara's desperation was clear. Columbus swallowed and asked the obvious question.

"Why reveal this to me?"

"Because I need your help. I need someone to look through these with a fresh pair of eyes. To tell me if I'm missing something. The lore of the slaves is fragmented. We are to blame. My people mocked it, only realizing its importance long after it was gone. And in a few hours' time, we are supposed to go in front of my father and tell him the location of the second key and how to retrieve it. If we cannot do that..."

Columbus understood. "Tell me what you have so far."

The tension in Elara's shoulders eased. She turned to the two stacks of books on the table.

"These are the only volumes that reference the slaves and their lore. The first stack was written by my ancestors. I've looked through them for anything that mentions keys, the Void, its creation, or the symbols the Fates showed you, but I've found nothing that resembles a snake biting an apple from the Tree of Knowledge. The second stack was written by the Athenians. As you know, I do not read or speak their language."

"Let's have a look."

Elara offered to bring another chair in, but Columbus deferred. He thought better on his feet. Because he couldn't read her language, she sat at the table and read for him, detailing titles, subject matter, sectional headings. If something struck him as interesting, he asked her to expound upon it. While she read, he walked the small room, running his hands over the leather-bound volumes and occasionally looking out the window.

Elara had read for the better part of an hour when something she said struck Columbus. "Stop. Go back."

"To which part? The description of Sheria?"

"Before that. You said something about a pilgrimage and nomads."

Elara turned several pages to find it. *During the eighth span of Agenor, Emperor _____ (blessed is his wisdom and forbearance) did on this occasion, the third of his reign, approve a pilgrimage to the foremost southern continent in hopes of fostering a new haven for his people. By sea, two vessels and one military escort born two hundred and sixteen souls east one full moon save six and return west by four, encountering calm seas and no hostile forces, where after they arrived at an arid land, the location a confluence of* many rivers. While the terrain was bare, and the soil desiccated, water was plentiful, and the region remote enough to prove tactical advantage by both land and sea. A nomadic race of hunter-gatherers inhabited the land but were deemed too primitive to provide opposition or support. But before their sacrifice could be struck, their chief, an aged man of _____ years, strode toward the adjunct, showing neither fear nor resolution, where he placed both forefingers to thumbs in lemniscate form and spake the words in his tongue to say, "One is the All." So, stunned was the adjunct by this display that the people were spared and made custodians of the river haven for an age to come. From the tail, the eater is reborn."

"Incredible," Columbus said. "If my suspicions are true, I believe we've just uncovered the founding of Egypt."

"Egypt? But they are a sworn enemy of Atlantis."

"It tracks, though. The 'foremost southern continent' is surely Africa. And this expedition headed west only to turn back east, which suggests entry through the Nile. The land there is arid, and there are several rivers."

"But Egypt has been a dynasty for thousands of years. Surely their civilization dates back further?"

"In Greece, I read an account of a geographer, Siculus was his name. He said as late as 3,100 B.C., the Nile was sparsely populated, with rudimentary people living in thatched huts as they had for ten thousand years. And then, almost overnight, the valley was transformed. Great temples were erected. Irrigated agriculture was introduced. Metallurgy. Shipbuilding. Government. Medicine. Music. Religion. Art. It was as if a great pre-existing culture had brought with it all their knowledge and wisdom and supplanted it there. No one could ever explain it before."

"If this is true, how did these people go from custodians to our enemies?"

"A thousand years passed. Maybe two. During which they developed their own identity. Their own nation. Maybe they figured their time serving others was done. Or maybe something happened to ease their fears. It's not an uncommon story. It's said Egypt defeated the Atlanteans in war twice. This would make sense in the Antediluvian age. The survivors of Atlantis would've been without access to its weapons and advances. It's sadly ironic if you think about it. The haven they built became both the means and site of their destruction."

"Ironic and interesting, but how does it help our hunt for the serpent and the apple?"

"Read the last sentence again."

"From the tail, the eater is reborn."

Columbus shook his head. "God in heaven, how could I not see it?"

"See what?" Elara said, excited by Columbus's enthusiasm.

"The Greek word for 'tail' is 'oura,' and the one for 'eating' is 'boros.' *Ouroboros*. The image I saw in the dark wasn't a serpent eating an apple. It was a serpent eating its own tail."

"I'm afraid you've lost me."

"Ouroboros is one of the oldest symbols in the world. It represents infinity or the cyclical nature of the universe. Just as the snake represents rebirth because it sheds its skin, Ouroboros represents the cycle of life and death. Creation from destruction. *One is the All.* Plato, the philosopher I spoke of, wrote of Ouroboros in the same dialogue in which he mentioned Atlantis, an account his father heard from the Athenian statesman Solon after he visited Egypt. *Egypt.* And what's another symbol for infinity?"

Columbus made two circles by putting forefinger to thumb and then brought them together in a number eight, just as the Egyptian was said to have done.

"Your ancestors recognized it and understood a deeper connection was at hand. So did the Athenians since they've included it in their lore. The layers here are staggering."

"I still don't understand how this helps us," Elara said.

"Somehow the slaves foresaw the end of Atlantis. They realized the only way to save your people was to go back to the beginning."

"The beginning of what? These islands were here long before us, long before Poseidon chose it as his kingdom. Are we supposed to return to the sea?"

"I don't know. Maybe the answer is more literal. Maybe we have to find a serpent."

Elara snorted. "There are many serpents here, but I know of none that eat their own tail."

"The leviathan that brought us from the surface makes an interesting candidate. Especially if he's meant to be the means of our escape. That would be cyclical, indeed."

"And convenient. Though I must remind you we have no shield to draw this leviathan from...wherever it waits."

Columbus nodded.

"But it does make me think of something," Elara said.

Columbus stopped listening. He had seen something on the table next to her. A book near the bottom of the second pile. It was bound in red leather with lettering in gold. He couldn't read the title clearly, only the last few letters. "—DON." Something about the ornate scrawl surrounding it made him curious.

"Columbus?" Elara said.

"Hmm?"

"Are you listening?"

"No. I was just imagining what your father would do to us if we're late."

"I was recalling a nursery rhyme from my youth."

"A nursery rhyme? We're discussing life, death, and the vagaries of infinity here, and you're talking about nursery rhymes?"

"Wisdom takes many forms," she chided. "And comes from many conduits, often those least expected. You are a prime example of that."

He looked around, trying to do anything but look at that damn book.

"Do you want to hear this or not?" she asked.

"By all means, Princess," he said, inching closer.

"Now, I can't promise the mnemonic value will come across clearly given the manner of your translation—" Columbus feigned a yawn. "All right. Fine. But don't say you weren't warned."

She took a breath before she spoke.

"Gentle waters carry me to the west, north, and south,
But stay my sails from wind that bear near to Ophidian's Mouth.
Swallowed whole are many there, lost to light of day.

Deep in labyrinth's belly, where floe and flame await."
"Ophidian's Mouth?"

"It's the name of the caves to the east where the eldocks breed. The rhyme was devised to keep children away from it."

"Why? I mean, I understand caves are dangerous, but how?"

Her faced turned wan with some memory. "For starters, the entrance way is surrounded by razor-sharp coral. Enter when the tide is high and you're likely to get scalped. Go when it's too low, and the fish will be feasting on you for months to come. But that's not why my people avoid it." She hesitated. He wondered why this was so hard for her. "What do you know of the eldocks?"

"You mean other than what I've seen? You capture and ride them, much like we do horses."

"The eldocks appeared shortly after Atlantis fell. History makes no mention of them before—in your world or mine. It is believed Poseidon created them to ease our burden. And for a time, the bond between us was strong. But as our populous grew, our relationship changed. Maybe it was their conscription into our war with the sirens. Or perhaps—like your Egyptians—they simply grew tired of serving others. When at last they rebelled, we turned to hunting them, mostly at sea. Only later when their numbers began to wane did our hunters seek the caves. Many Gadeir were sent in. Few returned. Those that did were changed."

A strange sensation washed over Columbus. "Changed?"

"It was as if their minds had been broken. Their words were jumbled and made little sense. Mostly they spoke of caverns and fire and ice. And 'the one that sits at the hearth of the world.' Whatever that means. They called it the seraphim."

"You're saying an angel lives there?"

"Some Hebrew scriptures refer to seraphim as angels. But more often it translates to 'the fiery one' or 'serpent.' There's another word for serpent. *Ophidian.*"

Columbus felt the hairs on the back of his neck stand up. "So, something is in there, we just don't know what."

Elara nodded. "Entry to the caves was forbidden for many generations, but after the slaves left, our people began to return. Like before, most died, but those who survived told tale of a labyrinth with a great treasure hidden inside. Foolishly, my people began to see it as a test of bravery. Recover the treasure and be blessed by the Gods." She shook her head. "They called it the Trial of Seraph."

"And you think the second key might be the treasure?"

"I can't say for certain. I only bring it up because you said the place you saw this Ouroboros was wet and dark, and that's how I've always imagined the caves."

"And no one ever mentioned this labyrinth before the slaves left?"

Elara shook her head.

"These guys are their puzzles."

"There is one last thing. I hesitate to even bring it up because frankly I never believed it to be true."

"This should be good."

"From the beginning, the slaves were charged with the eldocks' care. They fed them, bred them, and even rode them on occasion."

"Why is that so hard to believe?"

"Because until the day they left, the slaves needed no bridle."

"And the wheel turns," Columbus mumbled. "We should share this with dear ol' Dad. Hopefully we can convince him to send a larger party this time."

"That may be easier said than done."

"Why's that?"

"I told you our people participated in the Trial of Seraph? The last time was twenty-two years ago."

Columbus saw the pain on her face and understood. "Your brother."

Elara nodded.

"We have a saying up above. I wonder if you've ever heard of it. *Don't kill the messenger?*"

"No."

"And that's why you go first."

Despite herself, Elara smiled. She rose and strode for the door. Columbus followed her, only to stop in the doorway.

"Oh, almost forgot," he said.

He returned to the table to blow out the candle. And just before his breath passed his lips, he nudged the books on the table to reveal the title of the red bound book on the bottom.

The candle flickered and went dark, but not before Columbus saw the golden letters spelling *Poseidon* and the golden trident running through them.

CHAPTER FIFTEEN

The mood in the command room was subdued, a far cry from the festive atmosphere of the previous evening. These were Gadeir—the best Atlantis had to offer. Their strange red suits of amorphous armor were notched and scratched, their faces battle hardened. All displayed the gem shards that denoted their rank and accomplishments. Only Dion, Thetra, and Sareen bore new ones. Red as rubies that glinted with the afternoon sun. Had Elara been too busy to receive hers? Or had the king deemed his daughter's actions at the tower unworthy? Columbus couldn't imagine that being the case.

Of the fifteen warriors present, five were women, though Columbus noted there was no disparity of treatment between the sexes. Instead, they worked as a cohesive unit, blending rank and role. When a woman spoke, her word carried the same gravity as a man's. When tasks were assigned, all were distributed equally. It was an odd thing to witness. Like most men of the modern world, Columbus had always believed the fairer sex had no place in battle. For one thing, they lacked the strength and ferocity to match their male counterparts. For another, women were nurturers by nature, their instinct to create countering man's instinct to destroy. Columbus considered himself progressive too. To his mind, Isabella was a far better ruler than most of her male counterparts because she had fewer vices and her ego never got in the way. And yet the Atlantean army chose to embrace their women because of their differences rather than exclude them because of it. It gave them more options and different points of view. Columbus was surprised to find that he approved. At the same time, the situation reminded him of Nyx. And his resentment of the girl continued to trouble him.

When the king entered, he walked with a pronounced limp. One of the Atlantean asked him if something was wrong with his foot.

"Nothing stuffing it up someone's backside wouldn't improve," King Atlas said.

Columbus laughed out loud, drawing stares from the gathered. Even King Atlas regarded him a moment, though he said nothing. Columbus had a sense the king liked him despite their initial meeting. Men of their ilk—the kind who knew the feel of dirt and blood beneath their fingertips—often did. That wouldn't prevent the king from gutting Columbus like a fish if he failed him or his kingdom. Another thing Columbus had to push from his mind.

"So, this hunt for keys continues?" King Atlas said once he'd finally settled at the table.

"Yes, my lord," Elara said. "Though this part should prove considerably more difficult."

"Because the tower was such a cakewalk," Columbus interjected.

Elara cast him an irritated glance before continuing. "Columbus's visit to the Fates produced three images. The first was the book, which we correctly interpreted as the tower. The second was of this."

She slid an illustration of the second symbol to the king.

"Is that a snake eating its own tail?"

"It's a true delicacy, your Highness," Columbus quipped. "Comes around once in a lifetime."

Someone in the room groaned. Dion glowered at him.

Elara spent the next five minutes detailing the image of Ouroboros and what she and Columbus had uncovered in the King's Library.

Columbus watched the king's complexion grow wan as the conversation turned to the eldocks' den and to Ophidian's Mouth.

"No," the king said once Elara was finished.

"Father—"

"I forbid it. I will not subject my people to the horrors of that place. It cannot be done."

"But it *has* been done," Columbus added. "Several times, the princess said."

"A handful among the legions lost. Would you risk your life on such odds?"

"I have, and I am."

"Yes. While the dead of your crew feed the carrion above. You may care little for your charges, *adventurer*, but I take my responsibilities more seriously."

"Inaction leads to the grave as surely as defeat, my Grace. The suffering just lasts a little longer."

The king grit his teeth angrily. "Don't speak to me of suffering, boy. You have no idea what we've suffered through."

"This is true. Which is why I find it odd that when given an opportunity to change your people's fortune, you seem more intent on preserving your own skin."

"What did you say?" King Atlas shouted, enraged.

"Columbus," Elara warned.

"What?" Columbus said. "I'm the one risking life and limb here. You think the man could show a little more gratitude."

"I'll show you gratitude!" the king roared as he pulled his sword from its scabbard and leaped from his chair.

"Stop!" Elara shouted, raising her hands between them. "Stop this, both of you!"

The room went quiet. None of those gathered had ever heard Elara raise her voice with such ferocity. Even her father was taken aback. "You quibble over words while the sea bleeds beneath us and the sky tumbles overhead. And for what? Pride? Fear?" She turned to Columbus. "You. You are a guest in this kingdom and ignorant of our ways, but this man is our king and my father. If you ever speak to him in that manner again, I swear on my life I will kill you myself!" She turned to her father. "And you, Father. No one knows how much you have lost more than me. But Columbus is right. The time for waiting out storms is done. The end has come, and if we don't stand and face it together, there won't be a tomorrow for any of us. A moon ago I visited the Seer, and the Fates revealed to me that Atlantis could be saved. They said I would meet the Star Rider in Gaia's Craw and I did. The same Fates showed him where we could recover the first key and we did. I beg of you, let us seek the second one. The Gods have put their faith in us. Now, we must put our faith in them."

The room fell silent. All eyes went from Elara to the king. Eventually, he spoke.

"You move me, daughter. Perhaps some part of your mother lives in you yet."

Columbus suspected this was a rare compliment and one Elara had probably waited a lifetime for. Still, when he looked at her, her face hadn't changed. She was too focused on the goal to revel in personal moments. For a brief moment, Columbus did it for her.

When King Atlas walked toward the window, the eyes of the room remained rooted to him. None of them noticed his limp had disappeared, but everyone could see a change had occurred.

"Keys," King Atlas muttered as he looked out over the sea. "It is a fitting token the slaves chose for this quest. I imagine it gave them a moment of wry amusement before the end. If such a moment could be had." He glanced back at Columbus. "You see, in Atlantis, keys are an outlawed thing, for our ancestors saw them for what they truly were—devices forged of mistrust and deceit. Keys are the closed gate, the high fence, and the drawn shutter that tempts and seduces our curious nature. They are the glimpse we cannot turn away from. The apple we cannot wait to taste. What one man finds worthy of hiding, another cannot help but covet. The slaves knew this. I suspect you know it too."

Columbus fought hard to hold his gaze. Thankfully, King Atlas spared him by looking back out to sea.

"You might also be surprised to learn in all the days the slaves toiled here, they never saw the inside of a cage. We set no bars to hold them, crafted no irons to stay their feet. Instead, we gave them free rein to do our bidding because...where were they going to go? It's only recently that I've come to understand that even freedom can be a kind of prison if the sacrifices made achieving it are forgotten. This, the slaves also knew. Each day they paid its price. We on the other hand..." He shook his head before looking to Elara. "Now, I am asked to trust in visions I cannot see, foreigners I do not know, the slaves who had every right to hate us, and the Gods I have cursed since the day I first drew breath. If I say yes, I send my people to the dark heart of the world, a place that has haunted my nightmares for longer than I care to remember. And if I say no, it may be my hand that draws the veil over this realm for good. Poseidon, why must I bear these costs?"

"No one can answer that, Father," Elara said. "But please know you do not have to bear them alone."

King Atlas took a heavy, measured breath before he turned to survey the room.

"I cannot trust what is foreign to my heart, but I can trust those in this room. If salvation is to be had, *you* are the key. I will let you decide."

The silence didn't stand long. A chair scraped across the floor as a familiar woman stood.

"I will go, My King," Thetra said.

Elara smiled in approval. A second later, Sareen also stood.

"As will I," Sareen said.

A gruff warrior shuffled to his feet. "My sonstave is yours, sire."

"And mine!" another bellowed.

"And mine!" shouted another.

In a rush, the Gadeir stood, committing themselves to the task. King Atlas physically swelled with pride as every man and woman in the room stood ready and waiting.

"Now, all we need is someone to lead," Columbus said.

"I will lead them," Elara said.

A chair slid back as Dion stood. He raised a fist to his chest and bowed his head. None of the others bothered to challenge him.

"You honor me, sons and daughters. But Atlantis is still my kingdom and I have sat idly on its shores far too long. If we are to secure our freedom, it will be me that leads the charge." He raised his sonstave into the air. "For our people!"

The Gadeir cheered.

"For the Gods!"

The Gadeir cheered louder.

"For Atlantis!"

The Gadeir roared until the room was deafening.

King Atlas growled, "Let's go kill something."

* * *

THE GADEIR SPILLED from the room with a roar, the king within their ranks. As they stormed down the corridor, Columbus and Fanucio appeared behind them. Nyx took in her captain's smile, his swollen chest, and felt a flicker of pride. Then he saw her and his smile disappeared.

"He enters alone and leaves with a king's escort," Nyx said. "Well played."

"Is there anywhere you can't eavesdrop?" Columbus asked. When Nyx shrugged, he turned to Fanucio. "Find Monday and Tuesday. I have a feeling their size will come in handy. Meet us down at the holding pens."

"Aye, Cap'n," Fanucio said before limping away.

Columbus turned back to Nyx.

"I know, I know," she said. "This is where you tell me I can't come with you."

"Actually, I need your services in a different way."

Columbus paused and looked down the hall. Nyx thought she saw movement there but couldn't be sure. To be safe, Columbus drew her aside and whispered his plan into her ear.

* * *

THE VANGUARD BROKE the surface of the sea like a pod of dolphins, shimmering in the sun as they galloped across the water. Sixty Gadeir accompanied the king, tapering out in skein formation with Elara on his left and Dion on his right. Columbus rode next to Elara with Fanucio and the Pygmies behind them.

With each mighty thrust of his eldock's fluke, the cool seawater sluiced over Columbus's legs, chilling him while heightening his awareness. Even then, he understood he was making a mistake. He was breaking every cardinal rule he'd ever learned about warfare. Never go into a fight unless you know what you are up against. Never attack an enemy on his own ground unless you're sure you could win. And his personal favorite, never pursue a cause that doesn't also advance your own. Columbus could have sat this battle out or hung back on the fringes until the tide turned in one side's favor, but in that moment as the group thundered across the sea, Columbus felt a kinship with the Atlanteans. A camaraderie that said it was more than a bond of shared needs. It was the feeling of being a part of something bigger than yourself. He suspected this was what all soldiers felt as they rushed toward the enemy, knowing death was the most likely outcome. Later, he would go back to compartmentalizing his feelings. For now, however, he let himself enjoy the thrill.

Elara rode gracefully in her saddle, chin held high, forearms taught. She looked truly regal in that moment, every bit the princess one might imagine of a fantasy realm. Even the king looked spryer and haler as he rode point, his red-gray hair whipping in the wind, skin lit with spray. *This is what he was born to do*, Columbus thought. *Could I ever look this majestic?*

Of all the riders, one looked more in his element than any other. Dion sat high in his seat, powerful legs gripping his eldock. His face was stern, as if carved from granite. His eyes were narrow, and there was an intensity that smoldered like a fire awaiting the first gust of wind. If this was to be his moment of redemption, Columbus had little doubt he would either succeed at his task or die. He made a note to ask Elara about Dion's story again should they survive.

As they pushed past mountainous islands, more monuments of Atlantis's Golden Age were revealed. A crumbled stone figure holding a bronze shield. Carved effigies of the Greek Gods. A grand harbor rusted over with ruin. A series of empty bronze hands that once carried transport tubes across the sea. Columbus could only imagine what it all must have looked like in its glory days. It reminded him that all empires, no matter how great or small, all eventually succumbed to time. It is the one extricable force that even the Gods could not defeat.

At last they arrived at the Isle of Lethe, the Isle of Oblivion. Its granite peak, dark and foreboding, rose high into the air. A small bay wrapped around to the north. When they entered it, the sun fell from view, casting them all in shadow. To the west, Columbus finally saw a low, hooded cave entrance fifty-feet wide. Ophidian's Mouth. The name was perfect. It loomed like a half-opened mouth, poised to swallow them whole. Columbus felt a chill run up his spine. The animal part of his brain told him to avoid that place at all costs. The poise of the others allowed him to push that feeling back.

As the king reined his eldock to a stop, the others fell in around him, halting when his mighty hand rose into the sky. Only the ripple of the water coursing away made any sound. Then, the eldocks grew restless. Columbus mentioned it to Elara.

"Do you think they sense more of their kind inside?"

"They sense *something*," Elara answered grimly.

Columbus swallowed, his mouth suddenly dry. He felt a familiar fluttering in his chest. His hand instinctively rose as if he could wipe it away, but he knew the true source lay elsewhere.

King Atlas noticed his discomfort. "Are you frightened, adventurer? Surely you've never looked upon a place so bleak."

"Once," Columbus answered. "The queen of England's boudoir."

The king's eyebrow lifted. "For what purpose?"

"To end the War of the Roses."

"Did it work?"

"Only after three days of hell. Personally, I don't think the peace was worth the sacrifice."

King Atlas bellowed with approval. "With queens, it never is!"

Columbus smiled, but it was perfunctory. His eyes kept returning to the cave entrance. In his heart, he knew something evil lived in there.

And it was waiting for him.

* * *

NYX HAD BEEN LYING in bed pretending to sleep for the better part of an hour. She had been waiting for Vespucci to leave, but unlike every other hour since they'd arrived, he appeared intent on staying where he was. Finally, she grew tired of waiting and headed for the door.

"Nyx," Vespucci called, his voice smooth and grating at the same time. "I see the grown-ups have left you behind again."

"I don't see what concern that is of yours, signore."

"My concern is for you, dear girl. You have proven your value time and time again, and yet Columbus continues to treat you like one of his servants. Were you under my command, I would have given you a rank and duties worthy of your talents."

"Your generosity knows no bounds."

She turned for the door again.

"Headed somewhere?" Vespucci asked.

"If you must know, I was going for a walk around the garden. I need some fresh air after being cooped up in here all morning."

"Well, enjoy yourself. I'm sure your friends will be back in no time with even more tales of grand adventures that you took no part in."

Nyx smirked, then left.

Outside, Nyx walked to the end of the hall and dashed around the corner, only stopping when she reached the transportation tubes. Vespucci's last comment gnawed at her, even though she knew that was his intention. It was true enough that Columbus treated her poorly, but all captains did this. Young crewmembers always needed to pay their dues, and sometimes those dues included uncomfortable tasks. Nyx had hoped the job she'd been given might prove her loyalty and her ability to follow orders. What was important to him was important to her.

Still, the manipulations seemed to have no end. Both Columbus and Vespucci treated her like she was vital one moment and nothing the next. She felt like a piece in that game Mansa taught her—chess. Pawns were the lowest piece on the board and almost always sacrificed, and yet they were key to the game as well. Sure, the other pieces could fly about the board with ease, but at the end of the day it was the pawns that sealed the deal. And on rare occasions, if the pawn moved deftly beyond the attention of her enemies, they could reach the other side and be crowned queen.

Nyx depressed the button that opened the transportation tube. While Fanucio and the others had complained about using them, Nyx found them to be a marvel. Sure, they were frightening, the rushing water bubbling up from your feet, threatening to swallow you whole. But once it drew still and the second button was pressed, it became a wild ride. With a smile, Nyx depressed the sequence Columbus had given her, and she was whisked away.

Nyx stepped out in front of the royal suites. As Columbus had promised, there were no guards in sight. The most important Gadeir had accompanied the king to the Isle of Oblivion. Nyx was relieved. She had concocted a story about getting lost just in case she stumbled upon some errant citizen. Part of her was disappointed she wouldn't get to use it.

At that moment, the water of the tube began to fill again. Fearing someone would see her, she rushed for the door on the left, just as Columbus had instructed her. She entered and closed the door quickly behind her. Placing an ear to the door, she heard the opening of the transport tube outside, but no footsteps followed. Odd, she thought.

Moving quickly, she sped through Elara's room. At the sight of the princess's bed and personal belongings, she felt a moment of guilt at this act of betrayal. Then she remembered she wasn't there to hurt the Atlanteans but help find a way to save them all.

It took her a few minutes to find the hidden mechanism that opened the door behind the painting. Once inside the library, she lit a candle, and retrieved the book on Poseidon. It was right where Columbus had told her it would be. Knowing the others wouldn't be back for some time, she sat down to read. She soon discovered the things the slaves had written about Poseidon's kingdom was far more troubling than she ever imagined.

CHAPTER SIXTEEN

King Atlas used the bay as a secondary staging area. He had given orders to his unit commanders in the city, and they now relayed those orders to the Gadeir squadrons. They knew they had a daunting task in front of them, but every single man and woman appeared ready. Fear, it seemed, was not a commodity the Atlanteans trucked in. Theirs was a life filled with extraordinary battles and unspeakable dangers. Death in the line of duty was more than a possibility—it was the most likely outcome. Therefore, they devoted all their energy to preparing for each individual task as if it would be their last. The fact that the king would be riding with them only heightened their sense of duty. To die in his service *and* his presence would be the highest honor.

Over the centuries, many details had been amassed about the caves, though they were largely fragments—and often, tales from minds warped by what they'd seen inside. It must have been difficult separating fact from fantasy. Still, enough verifiable intel had been culled and distilled to put together a rough map of their initial pathway. King Atlas didn't try to gloss over the dangers. Instead, he reminded them of the prevailing tenants of warfare. *Remember your training. Stay in tight formation. Keep your eye on the prize.*

Despite himself, Columbus found himself getting caught up in the excitement. It was thrill that preceded battle, a condition only those who had faced battle understood. At the same time, Columbus knew that rush often led men to make mistakes. And in warfare, one mistake was usually your last. He decided his best plan of action would be to remain near the back of the column. Should things get too hairy, he could always flee. It's a narrow pass between bravery and cowardice and only a wise man knows when to step aside and when to keep going.

Once the plan had been relayed, Columbus was handed a sonstave and a breathing mask. He was told it would contain a few hours of air and how to monitor its use. Amazing things. He hoped when he finally left Atlantis—*if* he left Atlantis—he'd be able to take one with him.

Once the weapons were dispensed and the saddles drawn tight, the King spoke again. "Bring forth the pyre worms!"

Two men at the rear of the column spurred forward. They drew two heavy bags from the water and opened them, withdrawing a handful of what looked to be gray mush.

Columbus leaned over to Elara. "Pyre worms?"

She whispered back. "Parasites that glow in the dark. When we travel to dark waters, we attach them on our uniforms to illuminate the area around us."

Sure enough, the two Gadeir began distributing the gray mush onto the armor of the others. The small masses wriggled. Columbus winced in disgust.

"They're alive," he said.

Elara nodded. "Yes. And very rare. They live near the vents of volcanic arteries. Normally, gathering so many in such a short amount of time would have been impossible, but the Gods favored us with the rift this morning."

"I suppose that's one way to look at it."

Fanucio watched a Gadeir place the wriggling grubs on his shoulders, arms, chest, and legs.

"Look like leeches, these," Fanucio said. He blew onto one on his chest and smiled as it bucked up.

"It would be wise not to touch them," Elara said. "Their secretions are poisonus and will kill if it comes into contact with human skin."

Fanucio gulped and tipped his head back. Way back.

"Won't these make us more visible to whatever's in there?" Columbus asked when the worms were placed on him.

"The creatures that inhabit this place can see in the dark. This will—how do you say—even the odds?"

Columbus didn't look relieved.

A light moment came when the Gadeir tried to array Monday and Tuesday with the squirming parasites. The Pygmies shook their heads and raised their spears before the king waved his men away.

Once the group was ready, the king spurred his eldock a few yards forward before turning back to face the party. There would be no lengthy speeches this time.

"The way in is narrow," he said. "We travel in threes, in tight formation."

With a nod, he turned for the cave and Dion fell in beside him. A second Gadeir of similar size and disposition took up the opposite side.

Slowly, the vanguard funneled through the mouth of the cave. Columbus and Fanucio joined Elara in the middle.

"Whatever happens, we should stay close," Elara said.

"Don't fret, Princess," Columbus said with a wink. "I won't let anything happen to you."

Elara grunted. "It's not *my* safety that concerns me."

Once inside the cave, darkness descended, revealing a narrow chasm of black water that wound its way deeper into the mountain. A few sparse rays of light broke in from small fissures overhead, but one by one, the Gadeir were forced to turn their sonstaves upside down and activate the light source there.

The chasm filled with a golden glow, casting a slew of shadows across the crags of narrow coral that closed in around them. The column moved slowly, three wide. At one point, Columbus saw the Gadeir in front of him lean away from an outcropping only to see her exposed arm brushed up against it. A trickle of blood immediately appeared. The woman didn't seem to notice.

Columbus felt his heart thumping in his chest and heard Fanucio take in several deep breaths.

A light breeze slipped in from somewhere, filling the cavern with the smell of brine and little else. The only sounds were the water moving in their path and the occasional passing of bats overhead.

As they delved deeper into the mountain, the light disappeared entirely, and the water turned black as night. *How easy it would be for something to come up below them*, Columbus thought. It was the only direction the vanguard couldn't cover.

They wound their way through several more chasms, some so narrow it forced them to pass single file. It took longer than expected. From the sharp looks and gestures, it appeared nerves were already fraying. Columbus took his own deep breath to settle himself.

Once through the bottleneck, the group continued, the rocks above closing in until the slightest movement echoed like thunder. Only then did one of the eldocks mewl. Something moved underwater. A half-dozen sonstaves whined, ready to kill, but no enemy appeared. King Atlas nodded for the group to continue.

It seemed like they'd been in the cave for hours when they came to a dead end in a round grotto. Dion pointed to something on the far wall. It was the symbol of Ouroboros. *A snake eating its tail.*

"This is the place," King Atlas said grimly. "From here, we descend."

Everyone slipped on their breathing masks. Several of the eldocks mewled this time. A few bucked, agitated. They didn't want to be here, but the bridles compelled them against every instinct. Columbus saw the inherent wrongness in this. Elara did too. She patted her eldock to calm him.

Once ready, King Atlas nodded again, and the riders disappeared beneath the water. Elara nodded to Columbus and he returned the gesture, but to his surprise, his eldock resisted his command. He nudged it with his legs. The eldock resisted him again.

As the last several Gadeir vanished beneath the waters, Columbus found himself alone in the grotto, the only light stemming from the pyre worms on his armor.

Then he heard the voice again.

A CHILD SHALL LEAD *to the heart.*

COLUMBUS'S CHEST SEIZED, the flutter stronger than ever before. His head whipped around. There, in the water behind him was a large form. He could barely make it out in the dark, but he thought he saw spots.

"Who are you?" Columbus's voice echoed over the rocks. "What do you want from me?"

The answer never came. The large creature sank beneath the water and disappeared.

Columbus nudged his eldock again. This time, the creature descended. Columbus pulled his breather over his face as the water enveloped him.

The cavern beneath the surface was deeper than Columbus had expected. He saw the faint glow of the king's party up ahead. Columbus spurred his eldock forward to catch up, imagining the serpents of the dark seeing him alone, like a cub left behind for slaughter.

"Columbus?" Elara's voice rang in his head as he reached the group.

He almost started, having forgotten about the damn communication device. It was like having her in his mind. She called again.

"I'm here," he said, though he thought his voice wavered a bit.

"Is anything wrong?" she asked.

"No. My breather was loose, but I've got it now."

He heard her sigh. *Was it out of disappointment? Relief?* He hoped it was the latter.

Through the scrim of exhalation bubbles, Columbus found his way back to Elara's side. Fanucio gave him a nervous nod. The

Pygmies remained close. Even they recognized the seriousness of the situation.

"Stay close," Elara said. "We should be coming to the eldock dens soon."

"Any clues on what to expect?"

"There are many conflicting accounts. A network of tunnels is our best guess."

"But your father has a map to get us through, right?"

"He has a map," was all she said.

Columbus swallowed again.

They continued another few hundred yards before the Gadeir started to branch out. Columbus felt a stream of warm water roll over him as they reached another breach. When they passed through, Columbus exhaled.

The cavern was enormous, rising a hundred feet above them and several hundred below. There were a dizzying number of tunnels stacked like a honeycomb. Some were small enough for a dolphin while the largest could fit the *Santa Maria*, sails and all.

One of the Gadeir shouted as he spotted an unfettered eldock peering out from one of the tunnels. Sonstaves turned in its direction. Elara shouted for them to hold.

"We mustn't harm the eldocks," she said. "The serpents live beyond the dens."

King Atlas glanced back at his daughter but didn't countermand her order. Instead, he ordered his troops to spread out and investigate. As they did, Columbus signaled Fanucio to wait with him just inside the cavern's entrance. If they had to flee, they would be the first out.

One of the Pygmies swam near the eldock tunnels and was using the party's lights to make hulking shadows. When one of the Gadeir startled, he turned and fired a blast from his sonstave, making the Pygmies roar with delight. The rest of the vanguard wasn't so amused, especially Dion who fixed Columbus with a withering stare.

Eventually, someone found the honeycomb entrance marked with a second symbol of Ouroboros.

The Gadeir entered two at a time behind Dion and the other hulking guard. King Atlas fell in behind with Elara, Columbus, Fanucio and the Pygmies in the middle.

The tunnel was shrouded in darkness. Thick algae coated the walls, its span filling the water like soup. At every turn, the party found more offshoots heading in a myriad of directions. Down some of those blackened corridors, Columbus saw sleek shapes hiding just out of sight. Eldocks. Wild ones. Their presence was enough to induce the tamed eldocks to mewl. The Gadeir sat poised for an attack.

The formation moved slower in those narrow confines. At various points, Columbus noticed someone ahead had rubbed the muck near the tunnel entrances, only turning down those that bore the Ouroboros symbol. Eventually, the column stalled. Columbus asked what was wrong.

"They've lost the path," Elara answered.

Up ahead, Columbus saw the king and a few others looking over the map, protected in a waterproof slip. Columbus felt a surge of panic. The thought of getting lost down here, hundreds of feet below sea level with a limited amount of air terrified him. He could only imagine the lot of them, fumbling around, increasingly desperate and unable to find their way out.

With a deep breath, Columbus relaxed. He understood the nature of fear, how it could plunder the very soul of men. Sitting patiently, listening to the sound of his own breathing, Columbus felt a subtle tug beneath his hips. He ignored it until his eldock moved a second time. He looked down and saw the creature's head canted to the left. He turned his sonstave light toward the tunnel and saw movement within. It was an eldock, the smallest he'd ever seen.

Just then, the voice in his head spoke again.

A CHILD SHALL LEAD THEM.

THE SMALL ELDOCK *was the child.*

A wave of goosebumps rolled over Columbus's flesh. He signaled Elara. "I think we're supposed to go this way."

"What makes you say that?"

Columbus looked back down the tunnel only to find it empty. "Call it a hunch."

To her credit, Elara didn't dismiss him. Instead, she touched her arm and spoke, presumably to the king. He and others looked back at them.

"My father wants to know if you're certain."

Columbus nearly laughed. Was he certain? How could anyone be certain of anything down here? But something in his gut told him this was the right thing to do. He had begun to suspect the eldocks played a bigger hand in his quest than anyone suspected. He had to trust his instincts.

"Yes," he said.

Elara relayed the answer before turning back to him. "You are to lead."

Columbus saw surprise on Fanucio's face as he directed his eldock into the tunnel. Elara followed right behind him. Inside the tunnel, the darkness grew more oppressive. The sonstave lamp and the glow worms lit a halo of space around him, making it difficult to track the small eldock ahead. It swam through more winding tunnels, but each time Columbus feared he'd lost the creature, he'd find it waiting just ahead.

At last, they came to another opening where the temperature of the water dropped to just above frigid. A final symbol of Ouroboros confirmed this was the place. Spilling through that final opening, Columbus saw the whelping eldock heading for a different tunnel that led back into the dens. When it hesitated, Columbus raised a hand. The creature turned and disappeared.

One by one, the vanguard exited the eldock dens into a long underwater channel. Columbus's eldock moved uneasily. Elara's must have too because she said, "We must be getting close."

"Holy Mary, Mother of God," Fanucio gasped. "Look!"

At the far end of the cavern beyond two crumbling columns, the facade of several buildings loomed. Stairs lay broken and crumbled on the cavern floor while windows and doorways beckoned like foreboding mouths of doom. *This must be where the slaves once lived*, Columbus thought. The king must have thought so too. His voice rang in Columbus's head.

"We draw near," King Atlas said. "Be ready, my Gadeir. The labyrinth awaits beyond."

The vanguard pushed forward again, each Gadeir's head on a swivel, each sonstave charged and ready. The path continued to narrow. Dion lifted two fingers. The column splintered into two groups, one above the other. As the walls closed in around them, Columbus understood this would be where they were most vulnerable.

The silence was deafening, punctuated only by Columbus's breathing, which he could no longer regulate. With each exhalation, the mask he wore clouded over, only to dissipate a moment later. Fanucio must have been feeling the same thing. He rode just in front of Columbus, the bubbles rising from his mask continuous now. Columbus wanted to push ahead, move through this corridor as fast as possible, but he knew that would only cause chaos. All war columns were vulnerable, but it was always those that broke the line that were the first to die.

The attack came without warning. Something black as pitch burst from one of the vacant windows, its spindly arms latching onto a Gadeir before vaulting with him to the other side. A burst of sonstave fire lit up the channel. When it stopped, there was no sign of the rider.

King Atlas was shouting orders when a second shadow exploded down from above and enveloped a female Gadeir in a crushing embrace. Even underwater, her screams could be heard, followed by the blinding release of more sonstave fire. This time, the creature was hit, black blood filling the water and sending shockwaves through the column.

"Ride!" King Atlas howled.

All at once, the eldocks burst forward, moving in haste for the end of the cavern. The enemy's response was immediate as a tidal wave of stygian hell spilled from the doorways and windows in swarms of black death that maneuvered as fast as the eye could see. Those slender limbs tore at the Gadeir armor, slicing through them with ease and searing the flesh beneath. In response, sonstaves erupted at will, turning the cavern from night to day.

Black blood mixed with red as the pitched screams of both sides rang through Columbus's mask. He stayed close to Elara, firing his sonstave as quickly as he could. He hit one, then another, before a third evaded him. Elara proved even more adept, spinning and pivoting her eldock to fire behind, below, and above them.

Fanucio screamed out as one of the serpent creatures wrapped its appendages around his eldock and flung him from his saddle. As Columbus swooped in to grab him, Monday and Tuesday charged forward, their spears sinking into the enemy with deadly precision.

Gripping his first mate, Columbus saw the column rising in front of them. They'd cleared the channel, but the cavern had come to a dead end. He broke the surface of the water just as the king's party was leaping off their eldocks to make for solid ground. He ran next to Elara, both firing blasts as the serpents shot from the water.

The cavern was filled with shouts, screams, and the pitched whine of sonstave fire as the Gadeir drew a line at the water's edge. Elara ripped off her mask. "Send the eldocks back into the dens!"

A piercing whistle echoed through the cavern and one by one, the riderless eldocks sank and swam away.

The sonstaves fell silent. The serpents had either given up the hunt or pursued the eldocks back toward the dens, leaving only the laments of the wounded or dying. King Atlas and Dion had taken up position near a large rock formation with tooth-like projections overhead.

"A-are the serpents gone?" Fanucio asked shaking from fear and cold.

A rustling sound echoed through the cavern. Water splashed beyond their light. Rocks crumbled behind them.

"No," King Atlas said. "The real battle starts here. Atlanteans! Defensive formations!"

The vanguard divided into several clusters, Gadeir standing back-to-back. Columbus found himself in a different cluster than Elara and his friends. The serpents attacked again with blinding speed, using the stalactites and stalagmites to spring toward their victims. Even in the low light of the cavern, Columbus could see the fiends better, marking the long flexible limbs aligned with scores of razor-sharp talons and several mouths that hissed in unison as they descended.

If they were looking for easy prey, they'd come to the wrong place. The ranks of Gadeir split in two, the foremost warriors activating shields to form a barrier while the hindmost group alternated blasts. The first wave of serpents was rent apart, quickly replaced by a second, which upon seeing their fallen brethren, altered their attacks, moving through the rocks in spurts, their spindly appendages whipping forward to sling jagged barbs that mostly bounced off the shields. Those that did get through, must have been poisoned though, for the victim's skin quickly began to smoke and sizzle, and they collapsed in convulsions, dying within seconds.

The battle was pitched and brutal, but the Gadeir did not flounder. They stood strong together, working in unison as they had so many times before. There was a beauty to their method, an art beyond ken. Even the king was lost in the rhythms, his mighty sword felling creatures again and again. His great booming laugh galvanized the others and galvanized Columbus in turn. No wonder the Atlanteans followed this man. He was born for this.

Though casualties piled up on both sides, the battle soon turned toward the Atlanteans. The serpent forces grew fewer and more harried until the sonstave fire was no longer constant and the ranks had a chance to breathe again. The smell of ozone and gore filled the air, but when the cavern finally went silent, Columbus looked to ensure his friends were still there. Fanucio's chest rose and fell heavily, and his ill-fitting armor was torn, but when he locked eyes with Columbus and offered a half-hearted smile, he knew the man was all right.

Monday and Tuesday had moved toward the water and were using their spears to finish off the wounded creatures that remained behind. Columbus didn't see Elara until she touched him on the shoulder, seemingly grateful he was alive. He'd seen her during battle, firing her sonstave with a fury devoid of fear. If she was an example of what women could do in battle, then he'd been wrong about them all along.

King Atlas ordered the wounded and dead to be gathered while the remaining Gadeir stood poised for a second attack. Columbus wasn't surprised to see Dion among the living nor the shroud of enemy blood that covered him. When he caught Columbus's eye, the mariner expected to see him smirk or jeer, but to his surprise, the giant nodded instead.

The king sat to gather his breath, taking water from a skin offered him. When the twins approached with the final tally, the king nodded grimly. *Thirty-one dead. Twelve wounded. Eleven still alive.* The numbers were horrific, though not a single Atlantean dropped their head or cried.

"May Poseidon honor their sacrifice and greet them at the gates of Elysium," King Atlas said, standing over the body of his dead bodyguard. "Fine Gadeir, all."

The remaining warriors shouted in unison. It chilled Columbus, and for a moment, he regretted not joining in.

"Over here," Elara said.

She'd found a stone path that led through the rocks. King Atlas and Dion trailed after her, followed by Columbus and his crew. They arrived at a wall made of stone, ancient writing barely discernible on its surface. Still, something was missing.

"This is the place the old books spoke of," Elara said. "But it appears little more than a tomb."

"A tomb with no doors," Columbus added.

"There are always doors," King Atlas said. "Some just need the proper key." He walked up to the writing, shining his sonstave light over the words. "Can you read the language of the slaves, seafarer?"

"I have some knowledge of Koine, Your Highness."

"To think of all the useless languages I learned instead of the slaves'. English for one. There's a tongue that will never catch on."

"What do you make of it?" Elara asked.

The truth was Columbus couldn't read Athenian or Mycenaean but noted some similarities with Proto-Greek.

"These symbols here," Columbus said. "This is man. Or, more likely, Atlantean. And these, subjugated, in chains? I would presume they are the Athenian slaves themselves. These are obviously eldocks."

"And these?" Sareen asked.

Columbus looked closely at the image and saw a creature with breasts and wings.

"I'm not sure," he said, but something else had captured his attention. He thought he saw a glimmer of something underneath the dust. He wiped it away, revealing a golden image of a snake eating its tail. It was the same image from his dreams.

"There you are," he whispered.

As he ran his fingers over it, Elara shouted out a warning. Columbus turned his head, but too late. The gilded image glowed brightly a second before the stones beneath his feet gave way and he tumbled into the darkness.

CHAPTER SEVENTEEN

Nyx was eight years old when a stranger moved into the island's abandoned monastery. According to her mother, no one from the village had gone within a thousand feet of it since its previous occupants—a religious cult of some nominal order—were found dead from a mass suicide after their bacchanal love fest went bad. It shouldn't have come as a surprise. Reportedly, the group's primary tenets were hallucinogenics and abstinence.

For seventy years, the derelict structure had sat vacant high atop the sheer cliffs of the eastern side of the island, far removed from the motley crew that populated the opposite end. And then one night, out of the blue, someone noticed a flicker glow in the northernmost window and a shadow moving within.

The villagers were understandably upset. They performed a headcount. No one was missing. Nyx sat atop the old psaltery at the back of the room, watching with guilty amusement as the gathered debated the situation.

"It's a ghost," said Esmerelda, the voluptuous tavern owner. "No one can stomach living up there alone. Remember old Jahar? He went for a walk up there one day and never returned."

"I thought Jahar was stung to death by wasps," someone said.

"These were no mere stings," Esmerelda scoffed. "He was covered in bleeding ulcers, like something unholy was inside him trying to get out."

The villagers murmured grimly. Nyx was entranced.

Giuseppe, a short, balding Italian who was rumored to have escaped a hundred prisons stood up from the bar. "I volunteer to look. All I need are provisions for me and eight wenches. It shouldn't take more than a week."

Half the villagers laughed while the other half jeered.

"A week with any of these harlots and you'll be dead," someone said.

"Aye, but what a glorious death it will be."

More laughter. Esmerelda pounded a serving tankard on the table until the tavern went quiet.

"This is nothing to make light of!" she hissed. "We need to act before this apparition gathers strength and comes for us. Now, who's seen the priest?"

Everyone looked around until they saw a man of the cloth passed out over a rear table.

"I see him," someone said. "Pickled like pigs' feet."

"And as a reformed Christian, I, for one, vote we follow in his Godly example," a slender drunkard said.

Arguments commenced and didn't stop until the front door opened and Nyx's mother walked through. One look from her and the entire room went silent.

"What's going on here?" Horacia asked. She scanned the faces and found her daughter. "Nyx? Why aren't you outside doing your chores?"

"A village meeting was called, Mother," Nyx answered. "Since you were at the docks, I thought I would attend in your stead."

"How thoughtful of you. Why was I not summoned?"

Although the island had no official leader, Nyx's mother kept the island running and was the person most of them went to when there was trouble. Now, it seemed they might have found it on their own.

"This meeting was too important to shuck off," Esmerelda said. "Not with that *thing* hovering above our heads."

Nyx's mother wasn't sure what she meant by *thing*.

Nyx clarified it for her. "They think a ghost has moved into the monastery."

"A ghost?" Nyx's mother asked. "Really?"

"How else do you explain someone slipping past our scouts?" Esmerelda plied. "Jacque and his lot can spot a sail at twenty leagues. And with no wreckage washed ashore and no footprints leading up there, a specter of devilish intent is the only reasonable answer."

"There is no ghost," Nyx's mother said.

"How can you be so sure?"

"Because this island has seen more death than the Hundred Years' War. Throughout history, it has served as garrisons for the Phoenicians, the Romans, and the Moors. During the black death, the Genoese built a colony here to house their dying. Religious orders have fled persecution here. Pirates have operated from its shores. And in all that time, no one has ever mentioned ghosts. Plus, whoever's up there cooks his meals over a fire each morning. You've all seen the smoke."

They had. The energy in the room dissipated. Nyx noted her mother had a way of doing that. It was why the island had functioned as long as it had.

"Well, he's still a trespasser," Esmerelda said. "Shouldn't we at least go up there and see what he's about?"

"Why? He's no threat to us. He had an opportunity to strike us unaware and chose not to. This has always been an island of orphans —a refuge for those who have no other home. If this man wishes to join our ranks, even if it's a solitary place among the clouds, who are we to deny him?"

"So, we do nothing?" Giuseppe asked.

"Go about your lives. Leave the man in peace. If he comes down, he comes down. If he doesn't, it's no skin off our backs. Agreed?"

A few murmurs ran through the room. Nyx's mother asked again. This time everyone agreed. Even Nyx spoke the word when she saw her mother looking right at her, though it was much harder than the eight-year-old expected.

That promise lasted three days. Each morning as Nyx rose to do her chores and schooling, she saw the cone of smoke stemming from the temple above. And each night before she went to bed, she was mesmerized by the haunting glow of candlelight filling the window in the clouds.

On the fourth day, her resolution broke. Just after lunch, she found herself wandering near the path that ascended the mountain. She told herself she was just hunting berries, but before she knew it, she was moving through the trees that bordered the monastery, looking for a glimpse of anything inside.

A collapsed wall afforded her a view of the courtyard where a small fire crackled. On a spit over the coals was a bird. By the smell, Nyx thought it might be a quail. She looked around, but no one was visible. She did see a thin bedroll splayed out by the fire. Next to the fire was a pack with a weapon protruding from the flap. *One person*, she thought. *And, he—or she—is unarmed*. If she could get a good look at that weapon, Palo the Deserter might be able to tell them where the stranger haled from.

Nyx found a narrow inlet covered by ivy nearby. She slipped through as quietly as she could, wincing every time a twig or needles snapped under her feet. She looked right and left as she tiptoed toward the pack. As she drew near, she saw the weapon was a short staff made of black, dappled wood with gold rings a third of the way down the handle. She was reaching for it when a deep, accented voice spoke behind her.

"Careful, thief. The coals are hot. I wouldn't want you to burn yourself."

Nyx spun to see a tall African man in dirty, colorful robes standing behind her. His face was stern, though he didn't appear angry.

"I-I'm not a thief," Nyx said. She couldn't believe this man had snuck up behind her. Where had he come from? She needed to extricate herself quickly and glanced to the doorway behind the man. "I was walking the hills when I smelled food."

"Then you've come to steal my meal and not my possessions? I should feel comforted."

He took a step toward her, and she stepped back.

"I have friends nearby. They'll hear if I scream."

The man smiled softly. "You are as bad at lying as you are at sneaking around, Nyx. That is something we shall have to rectify."

Nyx froze as the man strode to the fire and stoked it with a long stick, ignoring the girl as if she didn't matter.

"Who are you?"

"I am Mansa. I've been expecting you."

* * *

"What did you say?" Nyx gaped.

The Seer parted her door wider.

"I said, I've been expecting you. Now, are you going to stand there gaping, or are you going to come in? There's a draft in the hall."

Nyx entered, passing by the Seer, still confused over how she'd found her way to this place. For the lesser part of an hour, she'd wandered the city, debating what to do about what she'd discovered. She never expected to run into anyone, much less the Seer, and much less arrive at her door. And to hear her speak the same words Mansa had spoken at their first meeting all those years before? It unnerved her.

"How did you know I would be here? I didn't even know I would be here."

The Seer chuckled. "One of the great secrets of the universe is that we are all made up of stardust. It flows in us and around us, everywhere. People are a force all unto themselves, bumbling into things, causing confusion and chaos. But sometimes a mind can be so consumed with a thought that it sends energy out into the world, directly into the path of what it wants to connect with most. And, when I am that thought, I hear it like a small voice in my head."

"What does it sound like?" Nyx asked.

"Like a worm rooting around in my brain. But I wanted to frame it nice for you because of what's to come."

Nyx shuddered. "What is to come?"

"Why, your visit to the Fates, of course. It will be different for you than it was your friend."

"He's my captain."

"We both know he is more than that. But first. Let us have a proper look at you."

Surprisingly, the blind old woman walked straight up to Nyx and grasped her by the shoulders. Those milky white eyes looked her over as if they could see past skin, muscle, bone, and blood. To her very heart. To her very soul. Nyx fought hard not to flinch.

"Not the prettiest thing, am I?" the Seer said.

"I've seen worse."

At this, the old woman cackled. "And you shall again. Many times, before you die. You have a powerful aura. One I have not felt in a very long time. Pity you are so young."

"Does that mean you won't help me?"

"No. But you should know, all help comes at a cost. Life has more forks and branches than any can see. If just one of these paths is revealed to you, you might choose another out of fear or spite and then everything is thrown out of whack. You could suffer greatly for it. Or those you care about. You must be certain."

Considering the present circumstances, Nyx had to know. She nodded, but the Seer neither looked surprised nor happy.

"I must warn you. The Fates can be cruel and cunning. You must ask your questions wisely."

Nyx opened her mouth, but nothing came out. It was like her voice was trapped between two stones. The Seer shuffled slowly toward a small ledge in front of the window and waited. Nyx found her feet rooted to the floor. *Is this what Columbus went through?* She had seen his face when he returned. Gone was the sly smile, the easy quip. Whatever he'd been shown had shaken him to his core. Would he have warned her not to do this? Most likely he wouldn't have cared. But desperate times called for desperate measures, as

Mansa used to say. And no wisdom was gained without personal risk.

She walked forward as the Seer rolled what looked like an old rug across the floor. Nyx's first thought was she didn't want to get her clothes dirty.

"Step on the mat as Zeus once did and let the Threads of Fate reveal your destiny."

Nyx stepped tentatively on the fabric. She hadn't realized she was holding her breath until her chest started to burn.

"Three questions. Ask any more and you will suffer."

Nyx felt a terrible sense of foreboding as if something tragic was about to happen. And yet Princess Elara had spoken of her experience as if it was a blessing. The trick she understood was to ask the right question. And yet, she had a million questions, including the one most important to her. Where was her mother? Could she ask that, knowing she would be putting her desire above all else? Could she be that selfish? The Seer had spoken about paths. Nyx had a sense the questions she asked here could set her on the correct one or send her to oblivion.

"Of the past, what good and evil has the trident wrought?"

THE SEER HAD LOST her vision two centuries before, but that didn't mean she was blind. Her vision delved beyond the mortal senses, deep into the human psyche, allowing her to see all the strengths and fears of those who stood before her. She felt the child grow tense as she passed into the spirit world. She heard the Fates laugh as they danced in the mist. The child started to tremble, and her belly grew tight. Still, she stood her ground.

A question asked. A question answered. The girl flinched as if lashed, a single tear wetting her cheek. And yet she remained and asked another.

"For the future," Nyx said, her voice tremulous, "how can I retrieve the trident?"

This time the child's body bucked, and she held her breath. *Awe.* She was witnessing awe. The Seer felt something for the girl then. Compassion. Empathy. She remembered what it was like to be innocent and to have that innocence ripped away. Could she stop it? The Seer had no control over the Fates, the experience was far beyond her ken. To her surprise, she found herself wishing that was not the case. And for the first time since the Seer was a young woman herself, she offered a silent prayer to the Gods in the hopes they would leave some measure of the girl intact. *This one's fire should not be dimmed*, she prayed. *It should be stoked. For in her I see a spark that could one day light the world.*

* * *

Nyx unclenched her fists, though she never opened her eyes. She now understood the task in front of her, and as impossible as it seemed, she was willing to try.

But the third question loomed.

The present.

We were all hurtling toward it, but Nyx understood she was being given a chance to change hers with a single question. Was she strong enough to ask the right one? To do that, she had to believe in something larger than herself. She had to believe she was being guided by a purpose. But what was it? To find her mother? She wanted more than anything to believe that was true. And yet her heart told her it was something else.

"For the present..." she said, licking her lips—they'd become so dry—her voice hoarse, barely a whisper now. "Tell me, what does Columbus loves most?"

* * *

The Seer closed her eyes, hoping the answer didn't break the child. Then she heard her gasp and knew her prayers had failed.

* * *

P*AIN*. It was the one thing that let you know you were alive.

The thought didn't comfort Columbus because right now his was off the charts. First, he had hit his head when the trap door fell closed behind him. A short slide on a stone slab had also left his flesh bleeding and raw. Afterward, he fell. He wasn't sure how long. When he finally landed, the impact filled his vision with a wave of black stars.

His hand instinctively reached out for his sonstave. He couldn't find it.

The dark receded anyway. A gold halo lit by what few pyre worms hadn't been crushed by his fall. *Thank heavens for grubs*, he thought.

As his vision returned, Columbus found himself in a stone corridor with high walls but no roof. Only blackness above and in every direction. The warm air smelled of dust and dank earth. *Where the hell am I?*

Columbus tried to rise, only to feel a searing pain in his ribs. With each breath, it felt like he was swallowing fire. They were broken, no doubt. Each movement felt like a knife to his soul.

He finally struggled to his feet, trying to shake the clangor of battle from his ears. He assumed Elara, the king, and the others were still in the cavern above him, trying to find a safer way down. He hoped they did it quickly and without running into any more of those blasted demons. Though, if he was being perfectly honest, he'd rather they ran into them than him.

If the pain wasn't bad enough, he saw his sonstave, broken in the fall, lost beyond repair. He kicked the thing, wincing as the sound reverberated through the cavern. Great. He was alone, deep underground, unarmed, unprotected, wounded, and thoroughly exhausted. Despite this, he managed to cross himself and nod skyward. "Could have made the landing a little easier, Lord, but thank you anyway. Now, I don't suppose you can tell me which way to go?"

Almost as if in response, the pyre worms on his chest flared.

"I'll take that as a sign," he grunted, lurching forward.

The corridor was made of limestone, the slabs beneath his feet modest in size. The ones that made up the wall were larger. They must have been three feet by three feet each. Four stacked together meant the corridor was twelve feet high. Too high to climb, but with no roof, he wondered why. Despite this, the stone work looked impressive, nary a crack to be seen. *Say one thing about these slaves,* Columbus thought, *their devotion to their cause is impressive.*

Columbus considered shouting to let the others know he was still alive, but he quickly dismissed the idea. It was more likely to bring the serpents than his own people.

With no grasp of direction, Columbus started walking one way at random. After fifty paces or so, the path began to slant upward. After another twenty paces, he saw a columned archway above him. He was gasping when he passed through it, only to find the walls had fallen away, leaving him on a shelf of some sort, ten feet by ten feet. He walked to the edge. There was nothing beyond. He reached for a small rock and tossed it into the distance. He never heard it strike the bottom.

He was in another cavern, standing at the edge of a chasm. He felt the open air, its warm current, the propensity for every little sound to carry. There was also a smell he didn't recognize. It was foul, sour and pungent. There was an inherent wrongness to it that made him step back. Then it hit him.

He had reached the lair.

Even worse, he was lit up like a Christmas hearth and dangling like bait before the literal abyss. Was the trident really worth this?

He turned back the way he'd come when he spotted a staircase to his right. The steps were only a foot wide. No wonder he'd missed them. Stepping to the lip, he saw another trough carved on top of the wall, running down. He reached in and felt something wet. He smelled it and grimaced. That smell he recognized immediately.

Columbus slid his knife from his belt and carefully removed one of the pyre worms from his chest piece. The wriggling grub pulsed as Columbus lowered it and snapped it into the trough. A flash of flame sent him stumbling back before a trail of fire coursed down the wall through a hidden embankment where it branched into several different channels, lighting great pots of flame as it continued its path, revealing a vast underground maze.

The Labyrinth.

It was breathtaking.

The size and scope were beyond comprehension.

Rough hewn stones of unfathomable proportions stood end to end, twice as tall as a man; many feet thick. Each must have weighed more than the Santa Maria itself. And there were thousands, spread out as far as the eye could see. Its area was vaster than the Colosseum of Rome with a bewildering profusion of winding, twisting corridors that seemed to have no end; all cast in shadow with a gray fog hovering overhead. From on high, the sight made Columbus dizzy. He had to put a hand out to settle himself. How did the Athenians build all this? It must have taken them a hundred years. Or a thousand.

Finally, he located what he thought was the heart of the maze. A circular area, at the center of which stood a single tower or shaft rising above the maze, its precipice hidden in shadow. Was that his destination? Was that where he would find the second key? He had to reach it to find out and that would be no easy task. How many had entered this nightmare never to return? How many had stood where he stood now and turned back?

The thought was interrupted when that disembodied voice echoed through his head.

His strength is your weapon.

"His strength is my weapon?" Columbus repeated. "Any chance you can be more specific?"

His answer came as a jolt echoed through the cavern. The stones shook. Then a scraping noise reverberated from across the cavern. It sounded like something was *moving*.

Columbus was retreating when something clicked underneath his feet. A familiar grinding noise echoed loudly. Columbus ran for the archway, but his path was blocked when a massive stone slammed into place.

Instantly, his heart began to churn.

He heard another sound. More stones moving, followed by a familiar hissing noise. Realizing he was still vulnerable, he had no choice but to run down the stairs and enter the labyrinth.

Just within the towering entrance was a room with three more archways. Only the center one revealed a sloping path down into the heart of the maze.

"Left," Columbus said. "I've always been lucky going to my left. Except for that Austrian milkmaid's window I leaped out of. Who puts roses on the north side of the barn? Then again, right is my dominant side. Strong and sure. Though, the same could be said of most of the world, and no one's beaten this yet. So, it's the center, straight to the heart, which is crazy. But I've made a career out of crazy. Oh, Lord. I wish you would give me a sign."

At that very moment, two high-pitched hisses rang out over the labyrinth.

Serpents.

"Not exactly the response I was hoping for."

Columbus ran through the left archway.

The labyrinth was once a series of very tall corridors, but after only a few paces Columbus came across a fracture in the stone wall to his right. Rock and mortar were strewn about, as if some powerful force had torn through the wall with ease. Near the rift, Columbus saw flagstones stained black—blood, no doubt, from the poor soul who never saw their attacker coming.

The hisses carried overhead again, closer this time but from two different locations. Columbus understood this meant the serpents were scouring the maze looking for him. Were they hunting by scent? Perhaps. But when he looked down at his armor and saw the pyre worms, he cursed. He should have shed his armor much sooner. Of course, then he'd be left blind *and* defenseless. What he really needed was a weapon. His small knife would do nothing against these foes unless he wanted to slit his own wrists for an easy death.

Dismissing that option, Columbus rushed deeper into the labyrinth, twisting and turning his way through corridors that had been vacant for decades or longer. And, then he turned a corner and ran right into a serpent. It was perched on a crumbling wall, tendrils raised, mouth open with rows of razor-sharp teeth poised to attack.

Columbus wheeled back and tripped, his blade extended. To his surprise, the serpent didn't attack. It didn't even move. Confused, Columbus stood and warily stepped closer to the creature only to find it was incased in ice. Something—some magic—had frozen it mid-attack. What could do such a thing?

Following the path of the creature's eyes, Columbus saw a human skeleton a few feet away. A blackened halo surrounded the bones, suggesting it had been scorched by a searing blast of fire. What the hell had happened here?

A third hiss rang out, followed by a slithering sound that suggested the enemy was closing in. Columbus was about to move on when he noticed a shield in one of the skeleton's hands and a sword not far from the other. He scrambled and gathered them up. Both were rusty, but they would give him a fighting chance.

Almost immediately, something struck hard on the wall overhead. Columbus held his breath and leaned back into the shadows. Dust wafted down, coating his shoulder. He looked up to see the serpent just overhead. It hadn't seen Columbus because of the blazer that burned nearby, but that would change when its eyes adjusted.

The serpent sprang to the ground, its talon-lined appendages scuttling over the stones. Its head was conical, marked with two black eyes on either side with a parietal eye between them. The serpent halted when it saw its frozen brethren and hissed.

Columbus inched back as slowly as he could until he heard another thump behind him. He turned and came face-to-face with the second serpent. It bared its teeth and lunged. Columbus brought the shield up as that serrated appendage tore across it. The serpent hissed, drawing the attention of its companion, who quickly closed in from the other side. Columbus whipped the sword back and forth to keep them at bay, but he was stuck between a rock and hard place. And both had teeth.

Suddenly, a heavy boom sounded, and the labyrinth shook. Both serpents immediately raised their heads. One screeched, followed by the other. When a second boom resounded, both serpents sprang back atop the wall and fled.

Columbus was confused. Then a third boom shook the stones at his feet and he understood.

Something bigger was coming.

As those pounding footsteps drew closer, Columbus looked around for a place to hide. Unfortunately, this section of the maze was nothing but twists and turns, each corridor identical to the last. Soon, he was lost.

Finally, Columbus came to a confluence of corridors, across from which was a set of stairs that descended deeper into the labyrinth. Columbus was about to run for it when the rumbling stopped, and a shadow fell overhead. He held his breath and leaned back, hoping whatever it was wouldn't see him. An odor struck him then, a blend of dirt and something primal. He covered his mouth for fear he'd scream.

He was trying to talk himself into sprinting for the stairs when he heard something that chilled him to the bone.

The thing breathed in.

It was a great, raspy inhalation, the kind that preceded something. Columbus didn't hesitate. He sprinted across the open path just as a great blast of fire filled the corridor. He leaped down the steps, the heat scorching his back as a wave of fire rolled overhead.

Columbus tumbled to a stop, his uniform and hair smoking. Adrenaline pumped through his body so quickly that he had no idea if he'd been burned. His only thought was to continue running. He dashed down one of the lower corridors, the pounding steps hot on his tail. Whatever the thing was, it knew he was there, and it was after him.

Columbus had barely turned into another section of the maze

when the wall behind him exploded, showering him with debris. A gargantuan silhouette rose overhead, three shadows undulating. Whatever was behind him reared back and inhaled again. Columbus was too far from the next channel, so he dove into a small nook, ribs throbbing. He huddled down and raised the shield just as a second roar sent a shower of blistering ice all around him, coating the walls, sending plumes of supercool air upward.

Columbus kicked the shield free. As he rose, he glimpsed his adversary for the first time.

It was a towering monstrosity with an impenetrable calcified hide, a reptilian chest, and two small limbs for arms. Its most prominent feature, however, were its three identical heads atop three long necks, all of which were focused on Columbus.

A hydra.

Columbus's jaw nearly hit the floor.

Heracles had battled a hydra with nine heads, each growing back after it was cut off. Was this one of the same?

The thought was dashed when that third head opened its maw and sprayed a shower of green liquid that splashed the stones at Columbus's feet. It hissed as a blindingly acidic smell rolled over him.

Acid.

Acid, fire, and ice. What else could this thing do?

Columbus ran like he'd never ran before. He slammed into a wall as he turned a corridor, the ice and rust crumbling off his shield. The deeper he went, the more corpses he saw. Some were frozen in attack stances, others cowered in corners, their faces fixed with horror. The majority were bits of bone, scorch marks and acid trails having eaten their flesh away long ago.

Past them all, Columbus ran until his breath came so ragged, he thought his heart might seize. He stopped under a bridge and listened. The great booms had receded, the hydra's thunderous gait seemingly moving in the other direction. Had he lost the behemoth? For the moment, it appeared he had. Columbus took stock of his situation. His clothes were singed, part of his left boot eaten away, but save for a few bruises, he was still very much alive. But for how long? This was the hydra's territory. For all Columbus knew, that thing had lived here for eons, picking off any who dared enter its domain. Even if he could avoid its attention, he still had the key to think of. But where was it? Where did the labyrinth lead?

"Lord," he whispered. "I know I've made a mistake or two over the past couple days..." Three ear-piercing shrieks echoed across the labyrinth. "Fine, several. But if there's any way you could send me some guidance, I would really, truly try to change for the better. And I mean it this time."

Another rumble shook the labyrinth, and a small rock fell and struck Columbus on the head.

"You're really enjoying this, aren't you?"

He picked up the rock and looked skyward. *Hmm. Worth a try.* Setting the sword and shield down, Columbus step-kicked off the wall and climbed to the top.

From there, Columbus had a view of the entire labyrinth. The maze was circular with a byzantine set of corridors and channels that fed down to a smaller set of stones, this one in the shape of a snake eating its tail. Within that circle was a wooden platform holding a tall obelisk—at its peak, a glowing key.

There you are, Columbus thought.

He looked back over the labyrinth and saw a large shadow moving past the braziers, blasts of flame and ice exploding alternately. Whatever he was going to do, he needed to do it quick.

Scanning the maze, he thought he saw the proper path down to the floor. He slid down, picked up the sword and shield, and was off.

When Columbus arrived at the center ring, he found the stones smaller than the outer corridors, but still eight or nine feet high. To his surprise, the obelisk wasn't made of stone, but a type of wood. Was it petrified? No. It had been treated with something. The same substance also coated the boards of the deck at his feet. Even odder, a small pool of water sat outside the circle of stones. What could it be for?

Columbus was trying to make sense of it when the rumble of the hydra grew louder. He tried to scale the obelisk but found nothing to grab onto. Without a rope, how was he supposed to climb the thing? Even if he got on top of the inner ring stones, he still couldn't jump to the obelisk.

The stones shook again. The hydra was moving closer. Whatever Columbus was going to do, he needed to do it now. The Athenians had left the keys for a reason. They wanted a champion to retrieve them, but they weren't going to make it easy. If the trip to the tower taught him anything, it was that he was expected to use both his body and his mind. But how?

He remembered the voice. What had it said to him?

His strength is your weapon.

Columbus wracked his brain. What did that mean? The hydra was obviously powerful—it could crush massive stones with ease, and yet, the obelisk remained untouched. Was this area sacred to it? Was there something here it feared?

Columbus tried to remember the story of Heracles. The Goddess Hera had raised the hydra to kill Heracles, the son of Zeus. Heracles had managed to cut off several of its nine heads, but each time two grew back in their place. Heracles was only able to defeat the hydra by calling on his nephew to cauterize the stumps each time he cut one off. Was that what he was supposed to do here? Was that what the inner ring was for?

His strength is your weapon.

The solution came with the next effusion of fire. This one lit the top of the snake ring fifteen paces from where Columbus was standing. He dropped to the ground and rolled behind the obelisk, expecting another volley directed at him. It never came. Instead, the hydra's right head reared back, its mouth opened, and a jet of ice shot forth, dousing the flames atop the inner ring.

Columbus suddenly understood. He stepped out of the shadows and locked eyes with the monster. "Hey! Looking for me?"

The hydra's three heads reared back in unison and screeched.

Columbus ran.

At the end of the platform, Columbus leaped and latched onto the rim of the snake ring, pulling himself up. The hydra was already roaring toward him. Columbus ran in the opposite direction, timing the distance so the next spray of acid washed over the top of the stone a length behind him.

As the hydra rounded the outside of the snake circle, its three heads undulated, up and down, screeching and seething, as it bore down on its prize.

Columbus continued around the far side of the snake ring, legs churning, ribs screaming. Each breath was like breathing in fire. Each step, excruciating pain. When he finally rounded the front of the circle and closed in toward the pool, he saw a gap in the stone, right where the snake's head should be.

Columbus jumped off the ring and landed hard on the platform, nearly swooning from the pain. If his timing was right, the hydra's left head should be next. He rolled in front of the obelisk and whipped around just in time to see the hydra set itself, its teeth-filled maw opening, sucking in air. Against every instinct, Columbus waited. And just as the hydra head came forward and started to spew, he leaped out of the way.

Fire surged over the platform, engulfing it and the bottom half of the obelisk.

Columbus didn't wait. He sprinted toward the snake ring stones and climbed to the top again. This time, he led the hydra in the opposite direction.

The hydra roared with fury, shaking the entire cavern. As its legs hammered down, Columbus struggled to keep his balance and evade more volleys of ice, acid, and flame. Between barrages, Columbus looked down to see the fire had consumed the platform. Not only that, but the base of the obelisk had burned away, leaving only a thin stone column holding it aloft. Whatever element the Athenians had coated that wood with had preserved its flammable state for a long time.

When the hydra pulled up, Columbus turned to taunt it. "What's the matter, you giant polyp? You overgrown worm. You had enough?"

The hydra roared again and continued to chase Columbus. Every time the behemoth slowed, Columbus mocked it again. "I've seen some leviathans in my day, but you are a sad excuse for an oarfish!"

Acid.

"Marco!" Columbus shouted.

Fire.

"Polo!" Columbus howled.

Ice.

As Columbus had anticipated, the cavern was soon filled with smoke. It was like a fog of war had descended, obscuring the small man from the lumbering beast. Only then did Columbus toss the shield to ensure the hydra could see the pyre worms on his armor.

Encircling the snake ring a final time, a weary Columbus dove to the ground, grimacing as a surge of pain buckled his knees. He nearly passed out then but managed to stumble into the pool at the front of the ring just as the hydra stomped around.

This was the hard part. If he failed here, he would die. But if he succeeded? One step closer to the trident.

The hydra staggered through the smoke. When it saw Columbus thirty paces ahead, it stopped, likely wondering if this was some new trick. Columbus held his arms up, shouting, "Well? I'm here!"

As those three heads began undulating back and forth, a sliver of panic welled inside Columbus. Had he gotten the timing of the hydra's volleys correct? Was the last one fire or acid? He wasn't certain. He could only stand his ground. He waited until the right head of the hydra canted back and sucked in its biggest draw of air yet. Then the head shot forward, its great maw opening, and it spewed.

*　　　＊　＊　＊*

THE HYDRA SCANNED the smoke to see if it had finished the flesh thing. It couldn't see it. In all its time in the deep dark, no prey had ever made it work so hard, toil so long before surrendering its flesh. It knew the creature's way—to run, to hide. But he always found them in the end. So, when the hydra stepped upon the ice his previous attack had made of the pool, it never hesitated. It slid forward gleefully, ready to claim its prize. Only then, out of the corner of one eye, did it see him. Back in the forbidden place, beyond the fire and smoke. He saw them. The insects of flame that adorned its metal skin. It stood in the shadow of the great stone. *Safe*, it thought. It had hurt the stone, but it would hurt no more. The hydra drew in another draught and released hell.

* * *

THE ACID SPLASHED over Columbus's armor, which he'd removed and propped in front of the obelisk's base. He suspected the stone within was marble, not too fragile, but fragile enough. From behind the obelisk, Columbus watched the acid mix with the marble's calcite, the crystals started to break down. The obelisk wobbled. Only then did the hydra realize what it had done. Columbus watched the behemoth turn to flee, its legs skittering over the ice. It moved slowly, but so did the acid. Fearing the Hydra might escape, Columbus lifted the sword and charged. He swung the rusted blade with all his might. When it struck stone, the impact was so great Columbus's arm snapped at the wrist. And yet, it was enough.

A loud snap rang through the cavern. The obelisk jolted and then canted forward. The hydra tried to flee, but it had no traction on the ice. The great beast watched with dread as the obelisk fell through the gap in the snake ring, right on top of it, crushing the hydra under a mountain of stone.

The cavern shook. When the rumble ceased, and the smoke cleared, the hydra was dead. The head of the snake atop the obelisk completing a perfect ring as the Athenians had always intended it.

Columbus stumbled forward, broken and weary beyond belief. As he passed the great hydra's carcass, he wondered if he should feel guilt or relief. He had bested a pet of the Gods. Likely, there would never be another. He was proud to have faced the beast and won, but part of him lamented its death. One more mystery removed from the world only made it a bleaker, more mundane place.

Near the tip of the obelisk lay the second key. Columbus bent over and took it.

OUTSIDE THE LABYRINTH, King Atlas and the others continued searching for another way in. They had heard the battle raging within, knew Columbus was risking his life to save theirs, and yet they could do nothing to help him.

When the roars finally went silent, many assumed Columbus had failed. Only Elara knew otherwise. A few minutes later, a grinding noise echoed through the chamber, followed by the opening of another hidden door.

Through the smoke, a figure lumbered out, covered in soot, clutching a blackened sword and shield. Elara cried out. Fanucio called his name. But it was the king who caught Columbus as he fell.

The mariner looked close to death, but when he held up that gem-encrusted key, he managed something close to a smile.

"I've got you, boy," King Atlas said. "Well done."

CHAPTER EIGHTEEN

"Where is he?" Nyx gasped, out of breath.

She had waited atop the highest balcony for the king's vanguard to return, still distraught and confused after all the Fates had shown her, after what she'd read in the book Columbus asked her to steal. Her stomach had churned like a sea in tumult. And then, they appeared. Even from afar, she could see their numbers had dwindled significantly. Many Eldocks swam riderless behind the vanguard, a few pulling what Nyx assumed were bodies in their wake. She could hear the mournful bays across the water. It felt like nails on her skin. She waited as patiently as she could, hoping to see Columbus at the forefront, but there was only the king, his daughter, and their retinue, with Fanucio and the Pygmies behind them.

She didn't bother with the transportation tube, choosing to dash down the stairs instead. She had to press through the glut of tense faces outside the eldock pens as the casualties were named.

Columbus was nowhere to be found.

At last, she found Fanucio sitting alone in a corner of the eldock pens. He looked as if he'd aged a thousand years. World weary, uniform stained with blood. Still, his face warmed when he saw her.

"Where is he?" Nyx asked, her voice shaky. "What happened to Columbus?"

Fanucio held up a hand. "Easy, lass. The cap'n's alive. But he was injured, so the king sent him somewhere the healers could look after him. More'n that, I can't say. It was…" He shook his head. "We was lucky to have survived."

There was no bluster to his statement. He could barely look at the bodies of the dead as they were carried past. Nyx couldn't look away. She was no wallflower. She had grown up on an island after all and had seen her share of injuries, even deaths, but this was something else entirely. Limbs shorn off, flesh gnawed away. Her stomach churned. Fanucio must have seen her discomfort because he stood, taking her by the hand, walking her up to the next floor to a balcony where they could take in the fresh air in the afternoon sun. When he sighed, it was with that easy peacefulness he reserved for the company of his captain.

"He's somethin', that man," Fanucio said at last. "Battled another sea serpent, all by his self. And damned if he didn't slay it too."

"Sea serpent? Like the one before?"

"Well, I can't speak to its parts and such. I was on one side of a wall, and it was on another. But I heard it—tromping around like a heard of lions, blustering. Must've been a goliath too the way it nearly brought the damned mountain down around us."

"Why was he alone? Where were the others?"

"It was the labyrinth. Once he got in, the doors closed, and the rest of us was left to spectatin'. Say what you want about them slaves, they know drama. When the cap'n finally reappeared, he was in a state, talking about ice, fire, and demons. Woulda thought he was drunk except by the state of him."

"I want to see him," she said.

"Soon, lass. Do you want to hear the good news? He got the second key."

"I don't care about the keys, Fanucio. I need to see Columbus now."

"Easy, lass," Fanucio said, looking around. "Those keys are why we done this. They're the one thing can get us home. Not to mention, save these folks' bacon."

"That's the thing. I'm not so sure it can."

Fanucio's eyes narrowed. "What do you mean?"

Only then did he really look at her. The realization that she'd been through something terrible spreading across his face. He reached out and clamped his two meaty hands on her shoulders.

"What is it, pea? Did something happen?"

Nyx's lip trembled. For the first time, she looked like a little girl.

"I didn't want to say anything until I spoke to Columbus, but...I saw the Seer."

Fanucio's face grew grave. "You saw her or you *saw* her?"

"Before he left, the captain asked me to retrieve something for him. I did, but what I found...it wasn't what I expected. I went for a walk to clear my head. And somehow it led me to her. I can't explain it any better."

"She took you to her lair?"

"It's not a lair—"

"Did she put you under her spell?"

"Fanucio! Focus. She's not a witch. At least, I don't think she is. My point is, I visited the Fates. I saw the past, present, and future. Fanucio, *Columbus lied.*"

Fanucio looked around nervously before pulling Nyx closer. "Tell me everything, lass. From the beginning."

As Nyx spoke, a figure stood silently in the shadows, listening.

* * *

WHEN COLUMBUS FIRST WOKE, he had no idea where he was or how he'd gotten there. Last thing he could remember, he had just defeated the hydra and had exited the labyrinth to find the king and the others waiting. Now here he was, lying in an enormous bed with sheets softer than silk, blinded by the sun that was pouring in from a window that must have been three stories high. It hurt his eyes.

"He's awake," a husky voice said. "Draw the curtains."

A blurred figure crossed to the windows and touched the wall. A tone resonated, and the glass magically darkened.

As Columbus's vision returned, he found he was in a grand bedroom with opulent furnishings. A tapestry showcasing some bloody battle hung on the opposite wall, surrounded by statues of warriors in various states of repose. Though the walls and ceiling were gilded, something about the room felt cold.

"How fare you, adventurer?" the voice said.

Columbus turned to find King Atlas sitting by his bedside. Dion and a healer stood a few feet behind him.

"Well enough, Your Grace," Columbus responded. "I don't recognize this place. Where are we?"

The king looked around briefly. "These were my son's chambers. The healer's ward was full."

The healer's ward? Why did he need...? And then Columbus remembered. He'd been injured badly in the labyrinth. A broken arm. Broken ribs. Burns by acid, fire, and ice. He lifted the sheet to check his body. His skin was pink as if rubbed raw, but his wounds were gone. His head snapped to the table where he saw it. A broken vial. He snatched it up.

"You used another heart on me."

The king nodded. "Your injuries warranted it, and I approved it."

"Thank you."

The king nodded. That's when Columbus got a good look at him. He was still dressed in half his armor, riddled with claw marks and dried blood. He looked weary, had scores of Gadeir wounded and dead, and yet he was here.

"I would hear the tale of the labyrinth if you can recount it."

An image of the hydra flashed through Columbus's mind. He closed his eyes.

"It's still a bit of a blur, I'm afraid."

The king nodded. "Later then. For now, let me offer my sincerest gratitude for your actions of this day. In my worst nightmare, I could not have foreseen the horrors that lay beneath that mountain. To overcome such evil—and to defeat one greater on your own—it showed courage I did not believe men possessed."

"Maybe we're not that different after all."

King Atlas grinned softly.

"The princess!" Columbus said, suddenly sitting up. "And my crew..."

The king raised a hand. "Safe, all. Even now, my daughter examines the second key in hopes it will lead to the third. She waits for you to join her. *After* you have recovered, that is."

Just then, another quake shook the city. It was a slow rumble, likely to do little harm, but it drew Columbus's eyes to the bedside table. The broken vial jounced toward the edge. Columbus reached out and snatched it just before it fell.

Columbus weighed the vial as the rumbling stopped. "Do you ever regret it, sire? Letting go of your ancestor's advances? I would think they could make life so much easier."

"Easy isn't always better, mariner. No matter how much wisdom and experience we accrue, we only truly learn through pain. And no lesson is ever complete. For times change and we must change with them. My father taught me this, though I never really understood it until now. Yes, I suppose it's easy for you to marvel at our advances and applaud our feats, but I tell you this, the beauty of this realm lies not in its cities or its riches, but in its people. They are the measure of our worth just as your friends are the measure of you."

Columbus thought of Fanucio and Nyx. Were they better for knowing him or worse?

"Now, I have a question," King Atlas continued. "It is important, so spare me the witty japes and tell me, how did you come by these?"

The king gave a signal and Dion handed him a gleaming shield and sword. Columbus didn't recognize them at first. And then he saw the graven images on the shield's face and the lettering on the sword. Someone had cleaned the rust from them, revealing both as true treasures.

"I found them down there," Columbus said. "I thought they were junk. Clearly, I was wrong. Are they valuable?"

"In your world, I suspect they would fetch quite a price, but to me, they are priceless."

Columbus understood. "They belonged to your son."

King Atlas nodded. "He was a brave boy, but foolhardy and rash as most youths are. I think he disliked being a prince. Or at least he hated the notion that his achievements might be something other than earned. Can't say I blame him. Sovereignty is a burden few appreciate and many scorn. Can you tell me how they were found?"

"When I first entered the labyrinth, I saw the signs of many a battle. Toppled walls, scorched stones at my feet. And in every nook and corner lay rusted armor and discarded weapons like these. As all else had turned to dust, these were the only way to mark the fallen. The labyrinth was true to its name. It is a maze of such dizzying complexity, I feared I might never escape. Then *it* came. I will spare you the hollow embellishments, Highness, and say only when I looked upon the hydra, I knew Satan and all his works to be true. How I survived where so many others had failed? It was luck. Blind luck."

"I don't believe in luck. Neither do you. You say you found these there? That my Atreal made it to the labyrinth?"

In the low light, Columbus saw the man's face had changed. Gone was the monarch who could shoulder any burden. In his place, sat only a desperate father who wanted nothing more than to save some piece of his lost son. Had Columbus's dad done the same? In that moment, he felt deeply for the man, and wished he had the courage to remind him he still had one living child who would give anything for a fraction of the love he held for the dead.

"I found many weapons there, sire. But these were not among them." The king's shoulders started to sag. "These I found at the heart of the labyrinth, closer to the prize than any other."

King Atlas's chest swelled as Columbus spoke.

"And when I took them up—I don't know how else to say it—I felt spurred by something in that dark place. I wonder now if it was your son's light that carried me to the end."

The king's eyes grew moist. He swallowed before he spoke again. "You would have liked him, adventurer. Like you, he was flawed, but you could see glimpses of the who he would become. A man among men." Then, to Columbus's surprise, he held the shield out.

Columbus eyed the shield, the artistry of its construction. No doubt the king was right. It would be worth a fortune in Columbus's world. But right then, he didn't feel worthy of it.

"I can't accept that, Your Grace. It is too great a gift."

"You've earned it."

The whooshing sound of the door closing prompted both men to turn. Dion had left the room.

"Poseidon's breath," King Atlas sighed, "even my attempts to do the right thing fail me. Will I never learn?"

"Elara told me about his vow."

"And did she tell you how I condemned it immediately? Dion has as much responsibility for my son's death as you do, but the Gadeir hold themselves to a different standard. In all my kingdom, none has reaped greater honor than this loyal servant, and yet the boon he most needs, I cannot give him."

"And what's that?"

"Forgiveness."

"And now I've taken that from him too. Maybe I will take that shield."

"Ah, mariner," King Atlas said with a shake of his head. "He's already given you much more than that."

Columbus looked down at the heart in his hands, eyes widening.

THE MUSIC SWELLED in the grand room, though less discordant and more somber than the night before. A bevy of pale-colored globes floated in the air, casting the room in glittering shadows that lit the glass above like the heavens that even the occasional quake couldn't dim.

On this night, each Atlantean wore a mask of a thousand different styles, some ornately painted and bejeweled, others sterile and cold. These were the death masks, worn to honor those that had fallen in battle. At the far end of the room was a long table where the widows and orphans of the dead accepted condolences. They bowed with honor when approached and were given small flowers picked from the garden, setting them in woven baskets on the table in front of them.

Through the throng slipped a short, lithe figure, head turning on a stick until it zeroed in on a bumbling oaf seated between three maidens. The small figure made her way over.

"Fanucio," Nyx said. "Have you seen Columbus?"

"Oy!" Fanucio exclaimed. "I'm wearing a mask. How did you know it was me?"

"I could smell you from across the room."

Fanucio's misshapen teeth shone as if this was the best compliment he could be given.

"Now, can you please tell me where Columbus is?"

"He's coming! They needed to fit him for some proper clothes. At least, that's what the handlers told me. Didn't you see him in the healer's ward?"

"I tried, but they'd moved him somewhere else. Fanucio, we need to tell him."

Fanucio excused himself from the maidens and pulled Nyx toward the banquet table. "Now, don't be getting your britches into a tizzy. The captain's been through a lot. What say we let him enjoy the party?"

"I told you what the Fates showed me."

"Aye. But wasn't you also warned them nymphs might lie? Rather'n get all in a frump over it, I say enjoy some food and spirits, maybe find some more lads to dance with. Let the cap'n worry about these things when he needs to. Ooh, have you tried these?"

Fanucio scooped up a handful of something that looked like eyeballs before funneling them into his mouth. With a grunt, Nyx turned and walked away.

IT WAS an hour into the service when a stately figure made her entrance through a side door. She had hoped to go unnoticed, a task made all but impossible when one took in the red dress she wore, its chiffon and silk fabric perfectly matching her sculpted locks and the surfeit of gems that winked from behind her golden mask. As a murmur ran through the room, she rubbed her pale, naked arms impatiently, hoping to see *him* before he saw *her*. It was not meant to be.

"Every time I think you can't look any more beautiful, Princess, you make a fool out of me."

Elara turned. Columbus was clad in dark green, his golden hair piling over the black mask he wore.

"And every time you open your mouth," she replied, "I grow keener of fools."

Columbus laughed, and Elara felt her nervousness ebb away. They both raised their masks, eyes twinkling in the light. "Maybe I should become a jester then, just to be near you."

"You need no appointment for either."

They stood silent, not knowing what to say. Then Elara turned to look out over the crowd. Despite the losses to the Gadeir, the success of their mission had raised the people's spirits. While no one was outwardly celebrating, there was a tranquility to the room she would have thought impossible a few days before. It was as if everyone there had taken a large collective breath and exhaled. Even her father, so notoriously gruff and withdrawn, appeared to be of lighter spirits. He was seated at a table in the mezzanine, the two gem-encrusted keys within his reach. When he smiled at some random comment, Elara thought he looked like the kings of old.

"This is the Atlantis of my dreams," Elara said. "And it's all because of you." Columbus looked down at his feet. "What? You solicit compliments with ease, but the moment one is offered freely, it makes you uncomfortable?"

"Compliments are one thing. Expectations are another. I'd hate to disappoint you."

"As if you could. To think of all the stories I've heard about men from the upper realm. If you are what they have to offer, then we are a poorer race for having spurned your friendship for so long."

His eyes searched hers. Something about that look troubled her.

"Elara," he said. "There's something I should tell you." Before he could finish his thought, a clanging sound stole across the air. Everyone turned to see the king striking his golden cup with a knife. The music died. The room grew still.

"Citizens of Atlantis and venerable guests," King Atlas began. "Tonight, we honor those brave Atlanteans who gave their lives so that our realm might endure. There is no greater sacrifice—no higher calling—than this. In my lifetime, I have seen many battles, defeated many foes. They all pale in comparison to what awaited us in that abyss. *Evil.* There is no other word for it. And yet despite these foul abominations, we persevered. No. We did more than that. We triumphed. And our triumph is a stark reflection of the courage shown by your mothers and brothers, your fathers and sisters. It is by their hand that Atlantis lives!"

The crowd roared with approval. King Atlas waited for the cheers to die down before addressing those at the mourning table.

"I salute them as I salute you. But there is still much work to do. With help from our northern brethren, we have recovered the second key." All eyes turned to Columbus, who looked uncomfortable with the attention. "That's right. Who would have thought it possible? That our enemies should become allies? And yet, my own daughter foretold of his arrival. The *Anak-Ta Eleece*. A new age is surely upon us."

"Lies," a voice in the room said.

The crowd startled, whispers rising as heads jockeyed to see whom had spoken. King Atlas shot to his feet and slammed a heavy fist onto the table. "Who said that? Reveal yourself!"

Through the crowded room strode a man in black, his bearing rigid, his identity hidden behind a white mask. Columbus craned his head, hoping for an early glimpse. He'd had an ill feeling since he woke to find the king by his bedside. Things had been going a little too well for his taste. Now, this stranger looked to upend everything. Columbus had a good idea who he was and why he'd only uttered a single word.

The man stopped at the foot of the mezzanine. "I beg forgiveness,

Your Grace, but this man," he pointed to Columbus, "is no more your ally than your savior."

The king stomped forward. "If you would make accusations, reveal yourself!"

The man stripped the mask away. The room gasped.

"Vespucci?" Columbus whispered. He had expected Dion. Instead, the Italian explorer stood firmly in the face of the indignation leveled at him. That alone filled Columbus with a heavy dread. His instinct told him to flee, but there was no place to go.

"Eel-tongue," King Atlas hissed as he tromped down the stairs. "You have provoked my ire for the last time. Guards!"

As the Gadeir closed in on Vespucci, he raised a hand. "Before you condemn me, Great King, won't you at least allow me to explain how my kinsman deceives you?"

King Atlas held up his hand, and the Gadeir halted. "Speak quickly. These words will be your last."

At the front entrance, Nyx appeared, harried. Columbus saw her take in the scene in an instant before realizing she was too late. It's never easy to see those close to you suffer. But the fact that she was hurting for him was almost too much to bear.

Vespucci continued. "Two days ago, our intrepid captain admitted, however reluctantly, that he had come here in the pursuit of treasure. What he failed to explain was that he had only a single object in mind. The Trident of Poseidon." Gasps spilled across the room. Even the king was momentarily taken aback. "I submit that even the accord reached between you was made with the sole intention of recovering this object."

Elara looked at Columbus. He refused to meet her eyes. He knew what he would find there. From the moment he arrived in Atlantis, all its citizens had questioned his intentions. All but one. The worst part of his betrayal wasn't knowing how she would now question others, but how she would question herself.

"The trident hasn't been seen in Atlantis in over two thousand years," the king said. "Even if it still exists, I've seen no evidence it is hidden here."

"Allow me to present it, sire." Vespucci held up the red leather book for everyone to see. "This was taken from your private library, stolen by one of my companions at the behest of our captain."

Columbus locked eyes with Nyx, who shook her head, perplexed.

Vespucci continued. "It is an account of the creation of your realm, written by the very slaves who constructed the quest Columbus now leads for you. It details with stunning clarity how the trident was stored within the Temple of Poseidon and how its pommel can transmute anything it touches to gold. And as anyone from our world can tell you, Columbus desires for nothing more than gold."

King Atlas turned to Columbus, but the mariner couldn't hold his gaze. He recognized the look of disappointment. He remembered it on his own father's face as he set out from the family home, in defiance of the man whose name he bore. He wanted to stop this, to speak his truth. But Vespucci wasn't done.

"His deceit delves much deeper, my lord. The keys on which he's pinned the hope of your people lead to the trident itself. Don't believe me? See for yourself! The trident symbol not only adorns this book, but the keys themselves."

King Atlas didn't have to look. He'd seen the symbol with his own eyes.

"This proves nothing," Elara said. "The *Anak-Ta Eleece* was sent here to save us."

Vespucci shook his head indignantly. "How can he save you when it is these very actions that will seal your fate? You don't have to take my word for it. Ask the girl. She's read the book. She's also visited the Seer." He turned to Nyx. "Tell them. Tell them what awaits the people of Atlantis when the keys are used."

All eyes turned toward Nyx, who paled.

"Tell us, child," King Atlas said softly.

Nyx looked to Columbus, only to find his eyes downcast. "Using the keys will awaken Poseidon's immortal guards—" The room erupted. "But that doesn't mean they can't be defeated! The Fates told me only one true of heart can claim the trident and use it to save Atlantis!"

Vespucci chuckled with derision. "*One true of heart?* And where is this person to be found? Surely not this man, who has lied to you all at every turn. Who has stolen from the kings of our realm and seduced their queens. No, he is not the one."

Elara turned to Columbus again, her heart breaking. "What he says...is it true?"

"I tried to tell you."

"But your promise?" Her lip quivered. "The question of the future you asked the Fates? Was it not how Atlantis might be saved?"

The look on her face was too much to bear. Columbus knew he had to tell the truth. "I asked only after the trident."

A pitiable moan escaped Elara's throat as she stumbled back. Immediately, citizens stood and jeered angrily. At a table, Fanucio stuffed food into his shirt as fast as he could.

Finally, the King seemed to come to his senses. He roared, "Guards! Seize him!"

Several Gadeir pushed through the crowd and took Columbus by the arms. He looked back at Elara, tears streaming down her cheeks.

"I'm sorry, Elara," he said. "I never meant to hurt you. I—"

Before he could finish, a powerful quake rocked the city, sending shockwaves through his bones. The alchemical lights flickered and dimmed. A second more powerful jolt brought the glass ceiling down as people screamed and clamored for the exits.

Columbus bolted through the crowd. King Atlas saw him fleeing and shouted, "After him!"

The Gadeir grabbed Fanucio and hauled him away. He left a trail of food in his wake.

Nyx pushed her way through the crowd to plead with the king. "Please, King Atlas. Columbus is a good man. I know he can still help you!"

King Atlas said nothing as she was dragged away.

Across the room, the Pygmies were corralled by guards.

"*They love us, they hate us,*" Monday said. "*I wish they'd make up their minds!*"

* * *

Through the chaos, Elara made her way to the king. "Father, I beg you. Spare him. He doesn't know any better."

When he looked down at her, she was stunned by the revulsion in his face. "No, but you did. This is your fault. I knew it was wrong to trust them. Just as I knew it was wrong to trust you. I won't make that mistake again."

His words cut like daggers. Elara turned and rushed away. King Atlas rubbed his eyes before he realized there was one person still near him.

"Such fortitude in the face of misery, my lord. I commend you," Vespucci said, tapping the red book in his hands. "Now, would you like to hear how your city can truly be saved?"

King Atlas sighed, seeing what he was reduced to.

Columbus pulled his mask down to hide among the revelers rushing through the city's dim central colonnade. Then he spotted a group of Gadeir who had set up a perimeter ahead. They were removing the masks of the people who passed. With more guards behind him, Columbus cursed and lowered his head, stepping behind a taller man and his family. He was about to skirt past when one Gadeir caught his eye. Before he could utter a word, Columbus ripped the sonstave from his hand and fired a blast into the air. The crowd instantly panicked, overwhelming the guards and allowing Columbus to run ahead.

A larger crowd had amassed outside the transport tubes. It appeared the earthquake had stopped them from working.

As Columbus turned for the stairs that led to the eldock pens, someone shouted and pointed to him. A hand latched onto Columbus's coat, pulling it off as he hurdled over the glass walkway to the floor below.

Alarm klaxons rang through the city, the lights flickering in time with Columbus's heart. He heard more guards approaching ahead and turned down another corridor, narrowly dodging a patrol of Gadeir hustling past.

He was gathering his breath when he felt a familiar flutter in his chest. And the voice spoke.

Come to me.

Columbus looked around, but he knew the voice hadn't been spoken aloud.

Come to me, the voice said again. *It is time.*

Columbus still didn't know who the voice belonged to, but he was desperate to leave, to be anywhere else.

"Where?" he asked.

Look beyond the light.

A SONSTAVE BLAST struck above Columbus's head as three Gadeir closed in. Columbus fired a blast in return and fled in the opposite direction.

Aftershocks continued to hit the city as Columbus sprinted through the smoky corridors, the air thick with sulfur and ash.

Finally, Columbus burst outside and ran toward the Garden of the Blest. He hoped he might be able to hide in there until daybreak and possibly escape to one of the other islands. The feeling in his chest had changed. It was tight, like he was being gripped in a vice. How had things gone so wrong? Was he really the devil Vespucci made him out to be? Yes, he came here for the trident, but in two short days, he'd grown to care for the princess, her father, and their people. Could he really sacrifice them for his gain?

And what of his crew? Fanucio and the Pygmies had fought valiantly by his side. They didn't deserve to be left behind in chains. A real captain would have taken responsibility for his actions and done everything in his power to see his people spared. Well, short of dying, of course.

Nyx had turned on him. If not, how had the book found its way into Vespucci's hands? Had she given it to him out of guilt? Columbus doubted it. She would have confronted him first. Maybe she would have given it to Elara, but even then, she would have pleaded for him to be spared. Why? What did he mean to her? He had treated her poorly, convinced himself it was the law of the sea. Crew always paid their dues. But this had gone beyond that. Columbus knew why. She resembled Lizete in too many ways, but she couldn't be his. As much as he loathed the idea, as much as he wanted it to be true, there was no way in the world she could be his. The timeline simply didn't add up.

The thought disappeared as Columbus came to a halt. The night was cold, the garden full of mist. Columbus looked back at the city, heard people headed in his direction. He wasn't even sure where he was until he felt that pull once again, stronger than it had ever been before. He raised a hand to his chest, trying to will it away, but it only throbbed harder. Then he turned and saw it.

The bridge.

He was being pulled toward it, toward the Void. What had the voice said? "Look beyond the light." He stared at that dark roiling storm twenty paces away. Was that what the voice had meant? Was that the dark beyond the light? Elara had told him death waited on the other side. She should know. Over the years, her people had sent hundreds, if not thousands, into the Void and none had returned. Even now, he could feel its power coursing through him, the thrum inviting him into its warm embrace. Did he have the courage to find out what waited on the other side? Even if it was oblivion?

Before he could choose, a large silhouette moved into his path.

Dion.

He held his sonstave, grim as ever. Had the giant followed him? He couldn't have known where he was going, and yet here he was, ready for a confrontation that had been long coming.

"I don't want to fight you," Columbus said.

More shouts behind him. Columbus looked back and saw lights headed in their direction. He faced Dion again, expecting the familiar sneer. To his surprise, the giant looked almost sad.

Columbus tossed his sonstave into the grass. "Move aside."

The giant hesitated. Then, to Columbus's surprise, he stepped from the path. Columbus inhaled and walked forward. He had just set foot on the bridge when Elara cried out behind him. He turned to see her and a glut of Gadeir behind him.

"Columbus," she said, "don't do this."

But they both knew he didn't have a choice. One direction lay a quick death, the other an execution. The bridge remained here for a reason. It gave the guilty and the condemned a chance to save their honor and to choose their own fate. The thrumming in his chest told him what was right. The pulsing Void called him. How could he refuse?

"I'm sorry," he said.

Tears spilled from Elara's eyes as Columbus turned. He heard her run for him and then shout as Dion took hold of her with his mighty arms. She continued to cry out as Columbus turned for the Void. All sound faded away, leaving only the throbbing of the storm and what awaited beyond.

Without another word, Columbus stepped through the barrier and disappeared.

CHAPTER NINETEEN

Fanucio had seen the inside of more brigs than he could remember. Brigs in ships, brigs in castles, brigs on battlefields, even one in a cave. All had been bad. But the worst of them fared a far sight better than being dead.

Not that you didn't suffer while imprisoned. Suffering was always the soup du jour for those in fetters. In one prison, he had been beaten 'til he couldn't walk. In another, walked 'til he couldn't stand, starved 'til he couldn't sleep, talked to 'til he couldn't listen. The list ran on. Of course, all those paled in comparison to solitary confinement. There was no enemy more dangerous than a man left alone with only his mind. Fanucio had chartered a million courses in his day, but he knew sure enough that one led straight to madness.

Another thing all brigs had in common—the smell. Each and every one stank of shit, sweat, and desperation. The nice ones offered a bucket or at least a hole for your duties. The others left you to deal with it yourself. Fanucio had seen men do creative things with shit, but no matter how it was disposed of, the smell always remained.

The Atlantean brig was the exception to the rule. For starters, it had its own shitter—one Fanucio giggled at after using, so productive it was at funneling the fruit of his labors onto unknown waters. Also, it smelled nice. The cell, not the shit. Apparently, those eyeballs had a way of mucking up his plumbing something fierce.

Despite these new accommodations, Fanucio still fell into a funk because any hardscrabble man worth his salt knew two things lay on the other side of a cage: death or freedom. To him, death was irrelevant, since men of his station rarely had a say in it. When God drew your lot, it was time to pack your ruck, put a lick in your hair, and hope St. Peter had a few pints waiting as you put to quay.

The harder part was freedom, since those in irons found it more elusive than the alternative. Here at last, Fanucio had to face facts. Columbus was dead. He was on his own. Well, not entirely on his own. The others were with him here too—for what that was worth. And though he'd been wracking his brain all night, he couldn't think of a single move that would help them.

According to Nyx, it was still possible to save Atlantis by tracking down the third key and recovering the trident, but without a doubt that cur Vespucci had already pledged himself to that task. Should he succeed, and Atlantis be saved, the princess might be of a mind to set them free, but even then, she'd still have to convince her dad and that didn't look promising at this juncture. But say it did. Say everything went perfect, the skies opened, and they found another leviathan to ferry them up, Fanucio had no ship to speak of. And he was no captain. Even if the four of them could crew a vessel, where would they go? They were wanted in Spain. Wanted in Portugal. Hell, half the countries in Europe wanted Columbus dead, and hearing how they'd been cheated out of his hide likely wouldn't endear them to his.

For the first time in his life, Fanucio felt truly lost.

What made matters worse was the girl. In the short time he'd known Nyx, she had proven herself tough as nails. And yet from the minute she'd entered the brig, she'd done nothing but sob. No doubt she blamed herself for the captain's death, but hadn't she only told the truth? At twelve, she hadn't accrued the experience to know being an adult was all about lying. Why, without lies there would be no order, no civilization, and a hell of a lot fewer bastards.

Could she have really believed Columbus was her dad? It made no sense to Fanucio, but the girl seemed convinced. Even in the face of Columbus's details; even after what Fanucio had told her. Odder still, Columbus—may he rest in peace—had been incredibly cold to the child, almost to the point of reviling her. That wasn't the man he knew. In private, Columbus doted on his own children and enjoyed being around others as long as he wasn't on the deck of a ship. So why had he ridden this one so hard?

Fanucio decided to push it from his mind. With the captain gone, it would do no good to dwell in the past. He was alive, as was the girl, as were the wee ones. He should know. He'd listened to them cut logs the entire night. Maybe isolation wasn't such a bad idea after all.

Another hour passed before the barrier outside their cell dimmed and the princess appeared. She was back in uniform, and yet Fanucio noticed her eyes were red. He imagined she'd slept as poorly as they had.

When Nyx saw the princess, she took to her feet and rushed into the older woman's arms. Not surprisingly, the princess held her tight, running her fingers through the child's hair, whispering comfort she herself likely needed.

"I never meant for any of this to happen," Nyx said, her voice shaky and raw.

"I know, dear," Elara said.

"Vespucci must have been eavesdropping when I mentioned my visit to the Seer. But your father didn't hear everything."

Elara stepped back, tipping her head to hold Nyx's gaze. "It doesn't matter now. All that matters is you not blaming yourself."

"But I'm responsible. If I had done what he said—if I'd stayed in my room and translated the book—none of this would have happened."

"And you would have withheld information that might have cost all my people their lives. We all make choices, Nyx. Columbus made his. Now, you must do the same."

Nyx wiped her tears and stepped back. "But we're your prisoners."

"Temporarily. My father was very angry last night, but he has changed much in the past few days. He is more apt to reason than I have seen him in years. In time, he will see how you and your friends were also lied to. I believe he will set you free."

"Lot o'good that'll do us," Fanucio said. "I counted thirteen quakes last night, Highness, and many more this morning. Columbus was right about one thing: this ship of yours is set to sail."

Elara took a heavy breath and nodded. "We are working diligently to ensure otherwise."

"You can't trust Vespucci," Nyx said. "The man is a snake."

"In my experience, snakes have a way of drawing attention to themselves. It's more important for you to tell me everything you know—including your visit to the Seer—about this book you took from my library."

"I'm sorry for that," Nyx said, her head lowering with shame.

Elara lifted her chin. "You believed you were doing the right thing. I cannot fault you for that. But know this: there is nothing I have, nothing in this world I would not give you. All you have to do is ask."

Nyx nodded, her eyes brimming again. Her next question was so soft, it was almost impossible to hear.

"Do you really think he's dead?"

Elara's gaze shifted to Fanucio and back. "I believe there are many mysteries in this world, and the only truths are the ones we find settled in our own hearts. Now, tell me of your visit to the Seer."

Nyx wiped her nose. "It was after I read the book on Poseidon. I was troubled, so I decided to take a walk. I hadn't even realized I'd gone there until she opened her door."

"This is how I found my way to her too. What did the Fates reveal?"

Nyx took a deep breath. "I started with the past. Because of what I'd read, I wanted to know more about the trident. I saw it forged in the depths of an ocean greater than our own. I saw Poseidon take it and use it to do amazing things. Amazing and terrible. But *this* was his attempt to make something perfect. And then war came, and he was forced to separate the realms, but in doing so, he tied the power of the trident to this realm. That's why the trident was left behind. Without it, Atlantis would be gone. Even then, I think he knew it might not last. That's why he ordered the Athenians to do what they did. They knew if they succeeded at the tasks he'd given them, they could earn their freedom and their place at his table again."

"The quest?"

Nyx nodded. "It's still there, in the temple, waiting to be used."

"By whom?"

"That's just it. I don't know. The Fates—"

"Are cunning and cruel."

Nyx nodded again. "I can tell you this, the only way to save your people is by using the trident. That's what I asked of the future. How to save Atlantis."

Elara felt a swelling in her heart. She had asked the same of Columbus and yet it was this girl who'd done it instead.

"Nyx, is it true claiming the trident will awaken Poseidon's immortal guards?"

"Yes. But in my vision, they were called something else. Something really bad. I don't know why I can't remember the word, but even thinking about it…"

She shivered. Elara laid a hand on her shoulder.

"And you can't remember how the trident is to be used?"

"No. I thought Columbus would, but with him gone…"

"The *Anak-Ta Eleece* did what he was supposed to do. He revealed the path and now we must see it through."

Nyx's chin trembled. Tears coursed down her cheeks. "He would have done it, you know. He would've saved your people in the end. You might not believe that. He might not have either. But I do. I know it in my heart."

Elara nodded and exhaled. Fanucio thought she did a remarkable job holding her composure. At last, she smiled.

"You didn't tell me what you asked of the present. Sometimes we're so eager to know what came before and what looms ahead that we forget to take in the world around us. So, what did you ask?"

"I asked to see what Columbus loved most."

Fanucio watched as Elara's smile disappeared.

"And? What did you see?"

Nyx looked at the floor and shrugged. It was a small gesture, but one that betrayed her youth.

"His face. Nothing more."

Elara did her best to hide her disappointment. "Well, it's not a complete surprise. It *is* a handsome face."

Nyx put on a brave smile. "Yes, it is."

* * *

The water enveloped him, infinitely cold, darker than any abyss. He hovered there, unable to move or breathe, knowing at any moment the veil would be torn away and the weight of leagues would crush him in an instant. Each cell in his body screamed for life as the darkness threatened to devour him from within.

He expected his consciousness to dim at any moment. A prayer cut through the pain. *Take me into your bosom, oh, Lord. Let me pass in your all-encompassing embrace.*

But the dark wasn't through with him yet.

The pounding in his ears was unremitting. That thrumming that had filled his chest now pulsed beyond just his physical form. He felt the temperature of the sea change, the eddies near him shift. His hand reached out and touched something firm. It filled his spirit. He tried and failed to open his eyes. His hand coursed along that smooth surface until it found purchase.

And then it began to draw him down.

Down through more depths, though Columbus would have sworn it wasn't possible. Down where the water grew still colder and where he thought his head might explode.

And then he felt the tug of another barrier. An instant later, the pressure evaporated, and he was overcome with a blissful silence. The water was still cold, but at least now, he could feel the chattering of his teeth and knew he was still alive.

Whatever pulled him had mass. He felt his legs bump against it as they glided downward, moving across the distance now until the water changed again, much warmer now. Columbus thought he saw flashes of light. He tried to steal a glimpse at his guide but saw only blotches. The water grew hot. Columbus's lungs started to burn. He needed air. His guide seemed to sense it. They picked up speed, turning this way and that until Columbus feared he would black out. Then all at once, they rose and broke the surface of the water.

Columbus gasped, taking in an equal measure of water and air. He retched again and again. Somewhere in the darkness, he saw an orange glow, though his eyes were still too blinded by tears to see it clearly. Spinning around, he realized his guide had left him. He swam forward until his hand hit stone. He pulled himself over the edge before collapsing, utterly exhausted.

Columbus lay there panting as the water trickled off him. He tried to clench his hands, but they were numb. As his pain slowly receded, he looked around. He was in another cavern of some kind. The air was stale and thick with sulfur. And he felt heat. Real heat. Where was he?

Columbus sat up and looked around.

He was in a subterranean cavity, held up by a procession of vaulted arches that seemingly had no end. In the distance, pools of molten lava bubbled up. No wonder he was hot.

Working gingerly to his feet, Columbus looked back at the water. The surface had nearly grown slack. There was no sign of whatever had brought him here. He looked over the series of endless canals that bisected most of the cavern. He wondered what their purpose was. Columbus couldn't guess. His mind was still muddled with all that had happened. Even the events that transpired in the city were a daze. He remembered the king ordering his arrest. He remembered running through the city as the walls shook around. Then Dion at the bridge. Why had the giant moved from his path? Had he wanted Columbus to end his own life? To die in shame? Or had the man spared him an even more ignominious one? And then there was the princess. She'd begged him to step back from the Void. The look of pain on her face—it resembled the one Nyx had made when she announced his betrayal. To know he was the cause of both nearly buckled his knees. But he couldn't dwell on those things now. He had been spared, though he didn't know why or by what. *The voice.* Was it Poseidon? Was it something else? He had to find out.

Across broken flagstones, Columbus saw several shelters huddled together like aged shanties, though it was obvious no one had lived in them for a very long time. He walked to the nearest of them and pushed the wooden door. It broke apart like kindling. Inside, a bed, an earthen hearth, and clay cups overturned. The next shelter was the same.

"These are the slave quarters," Columbus said.

Yes.

Columbus spun around. "Who said that? Where are you?"

Here.

The water rippled. Columbus thought he saw a large form beneath the water. "Where is here?"

Safe.

Columbus moved closer. Only then did he see the patchy hide, its true bulk. The dorsal he'd clung to. The spotted eldock had saved him.

"*You're* the one that's been inside my head all this time?"

Yes.

It made sense. He was there when they headed for the tower and later on in the eldock dens.

"Only eldocks can survive outside the Void."

Yes.

"Thank you," Columbus said.

The spotted eldock didn't reply.

Columbus wiped the sweat from his brow. The heat was already getting to him. In no time, he'd need water, and he doubted he'd find any here. He headed back to the shelters and saw a stone bench with several wooden sticks beside it. Two dusty old vases sat beneath an open window. He opened them and looked inside.

Sulfur and lime.

Columbus tore a strip of fabric from his shirt and wrapped it around one of the sticks before dunking it in both minerals. Then he jogged to the nearest magma rent and lit it on fire. The heat was scorching.

When he was finished, he returned to the canals and the spotted eldock.

"Do the Atlanteans know about this place?"

Once.

"Elara said they were flooded. Is this where you've been hiding? You and your kind?"

At first the eldock didn't answer. And then it maneuvered up the canal.

Come.

"Where to?"

To see.

The path was dark, the broken cobbles hard on Columbus's feet. He passed through a grove of crumbling columns, all the while taking in the final residue of slave life. A rusted kiln. A broken spinning wheel. A dry cistern. An old box held a bevy of scavenged tools, mostly broken and lost to time. There were more poignant signs of life. Dusty plates that once fed the hungry. Children's toys shrouded in dust. Columbus tried to imagine what life here had been like. Exiled for a century or two in the abyss, attempting to help those who hated your very existence. *How did they stop themselves from going mad?*

The spotted eldock continued slowly down the canal, his occasional breaching and pulse of air the surest way to follow. Columbus knew unequivocally that if the creature abandoned him, he would die here. One day, should Atlantis survive, someone might stumble upon his bones. Likely they would mistake him for an Athenian. Would they wonder what events shaped his life? What led to his death? No. They would never know he was an adventurer from the above realm, who risked all to be the first to visit Atlantis in two thousand years. They would never know he'd been named the Star Rider and that an entire nation state had pinned their hopes on him. Or how, in the end, he'd failed them.

After walking a considerable distance, Columbus passed through the last series of columns and stumbled to a halt. There, in front of him was a temple carved from stone. At the edge of what looked like marble floors, the canal ended. The spotted eldock could go no farther.

Enter.

Columbus felt that old dread prickling his senses, but the spotted eldock had already saved him once. He didn't think it would endanger him now.

As he scaled the steps, the sound of his footfalls echoed loudly through the building. There, in the dark, something loomed. Or the absence of something, for the closer he crept, the more apparent it became that the statue that once resided here had been toppled, felled by stones from above. The marble limbs and torso were fragmented across the floor, leaving only two legs shorn at the knees and a trident thrust into the ground, a hand still wrapped around its shaft. *Poseidon.* Here in the depths, he had fallen. Was it a portent of things to come?

Moving past the shattered remains, Columbus came to another room, two vaulted braziers on either side. He lifted his torch to the first, surprised when it came to life. The chamber was oval with a vaulted ceiling swept with stars. No, not stars. Gems. Enough treasure to make him a king many times over.

Near the back of the room Columbus found a trough like the one he'd discovered in the labyrinth. Once again, he lowered his torch to it. This time, the fire spread across both sides of the room, revealing an intricately designed mosaic that spanned fifty paces or more. Each section showed an image. Each tableau showed one part of a larger story.

The first panel displayed a startling truth. The Athenians were not the aggressors Columbus was led to believe. In stark detail the mural revealed the Atlanteans were the aggressors, looking to extend their dominance beyond the seas. War ensued. Only when Atlantis was attacked did Poseidon raise his leviathans, not to destroy the enemy, but to protect both sides from the destruction of another jealous God.

"This is it, isn't it?" Columbus whispered. "The true history of Atlantis."

More, the voice insisted.

Columbus continued.

After Atlantis had been claimed by the sea, Poseidon sought to make his own Elysium by endowing it with all the wonder and functionality of the higher world. Glorious winged creatures with brightly colored feathers patrolled the skies above, endowed with the voices of angels. Beneath the sea, his famed water horses, which would come to be known as eldocks, kept everything in balance.

Paradise was complete but for one thing.

The Atlanteans. They refused to share their birthright.

Columbus moved on, seeing with his own eyes the manifestation of corruption. The images grew darker.

The Athenians forced into bondage, consigned to the depths of the city.

The eldocks taken captive and enslaved with the bridle.

The sirens shot from the sky, retreating to the caves.

War ensued.

Bloodshed.

Atlantis fell into darkness.

The penultimate image, a devastating revelation. This one showing a single ray of light shining down on penitent figures kneeling in this very room. At the foot of Poseidon.

"So, it wasn't the Atlanteans whose prayers were answered. It was the Athenians."

Yes.

"But if Poseidon knew the Atlanteans were the problem, why didn't he enact his justice on them?"

The flames near the second image flared. *Paradise.* Columbus thought he understood.

"If one is unworthy, all are unworthy?"

Yes.

"That's why the slaves engineered the quest."

Yes.

"And why your kind stayed behind. You could have left for the surface anytime, but you didn't. Instead, you remained here in bondage, as your children were feasted on in the labyrinth; all so the quest would endure."

The eldock said nothing. It didn't have to.

"And the sirens?"

Innocent.

Columbus groaned. He felt sick to his stomach. It was too much. Too painful to contemplate. He'd never felt more insignificant in his life. He'd come here expecting adventure, but had found only pain, some of which he'd brought on himself. If only he had his ship. He could slip aboard and set sail for some corner of the world where the names Poseidon and Atlantis meant nothing. He knew who he was. He was a mariner. A loner. He belonged to the sea and nothing else. So, why did this hurt so bad?

"No one can accomplish what you're asking."

The final image was illuminated. A small figure riding atop a star. The Star Rider.

The Anak-Ta Eleece.

"I can't," Columbus said. "I'm not who you think I am."

It is in your blood.

"I'm not *worthy*."

For her.

Did he mean Elara? He saw her again, standing in the garden, pleading with him not to enter the Void. He knew then he didn't deserve her pity. Or her love. He shook his head, about to refuse this final plea when the entire cavern lurched, throwing him from his feet. The quake split the earth, opening a chasm that lit with magma below. Columbus scrambled across the broken marble, diving to avoid the rocks that fell from above. The rumbling grew to a deafening roar. The murals cracked and toppled. The raised statue split and fell into fire. He shot out of the temple doors as the entire building crumbled behind him.

Across the subterranean floor, the columns snapped like twigs, giving rise to gouts of lava that threatened to bring the entire city down on top of him.

Just when Columbus thought the cataclysm would go on forever, it stopped.

Smoke billowed through the cavern, the heat nearing unbearable levels. Coughing, covered in soot, dust, and ash, Columbus stumbled to the canal. The spotted eldock was nowhere to be seen. Somehow, Columbus knew it was still there. And he knew what he had to do.

"Fine. If I'm going to die, it won't be down here. Take me to Gaia's Craw."

CHAPTER TWENTY

"Gadeir! Quell that fire!" King Atlas bellowed through the smoke, pointing to the flames that had broken out near the central colonnade. "And someone turn those damned horns off! I can't hear myself think!"

The sirens that flooded the city mercifully went silent, giving way to the wails of the injured and dying.

King Atlas had been conferring with Vespucci and his senior staff in the Nave when the quake first struck. It felt like the entire city had been shorn off its foundation. People were tossed violently from their feet. Half the alchemical lights blew in an instant. Walls crumbled. Support beams groaned as the towers bucked and swayed. Many of the glass walkways shattered and collapsed, raining down shards on the unprotected, leaving them gashed and bleeding. Many citizens fled for the transport tubes only to find them flooding with actual water, drowning those unlucky enough to find themselves caught in transit.

If there was any bright side, it was in how quickly citizens responded to help the wounded. King Atlas felt a sliver of pride that none of his people panicked. The true measure of a civilization came when times were at their worst, his father used to say. If that was true, this was an elevated realm, indeed.

The king was helping a bloodied woman to her feet when Elara appeared through the smoke.

"Father!" she cried, rushing to his side. "You're bleeding."

The king was surprised how much relief he felt at seeing her. Then he noticed the worry on her face and felt ashamed. He knew his earlier words had wounded her. Later, when they had the time—if they had the time—he would need to make amends.

"His Grace was injured by falling debris, Princess," Vespucci said. "But to our good fortune, he remains in full command of his faculties."

"Which include speaking for myself," the king growled. He turned back to Elara. "I sent Dion to prepare an emergency meeting in the Command Tower to assess the damage."

"But the Command Tower is lost. I thought you would have heard."

"Lost? How?"

"It toppled after being struck by the Void."

The king grew wan. "It has fallen that far? Poseidon help us."

"That's not the worst news, I'm afraid. More fissures have broken out across the seabed. Currently, the number stands at thirteen, though there may be more. Even at full strength with every resource at our disposal…"

She didn't have to finish. He understood the implication.

"I'll order a full evacuation. Send the citizens to the Isle of Arcadia. As it's the closest to the center of the Void, and it will be the last to fall."

"If I may interject, Your Grace," Vespucci said. "While an evacuation of your city is certainly a sound plan, it doesn't address our most paramount concern. The retrieval of the third key."

King Atlas grabbed Vespucci by the lapels and lifted him into the air. "My people are my paramount concern, you worm!"

"I-I did not mean to suggest otherwise, only that the time for retrieving the key is fleeting. It was estimated we have less than thirty-six hours to stop the Void's collapse. After this, I would wager that window is much smaller. Please, sire. I can't breathe."

"He's right," Elara said.

"What?" both King Atlas and Vespucci said, surprised.

"He's right. Finding the third key is our only hope."

King Atlas released Vespucci, who stumbled back, gasping.

"But you haven't even deciphered the third symbol."

"I don't need to. It's an egg. I saw its twin in Gaia's Craw."

"Preposterous," the king said. "The sirens are not birds."

"Not now, but I believe they were once. We've all seen the stunted appendages on their backs, the smattering of feathers. And it feels right, Father."

"*Feels?* Since when do you act on feelings?"

"Since others suggested I do so and were proven right."

King Atlas knew who she was thinking of by "others." "It is my sincere belief that we will find the key in the siren's den or not at all."

"I concur with the princess, Your Highness," Vespucci said, rubbing his sore throat. "In the book I deciphered, your slaves wrote at great length about the sirens and how they would play a central part in this narrative. And while there's no telling how this most recent quake has affected them, it could provide just the distraction we need to launch an attack."

King Atlas mulled over the point. "My father's father once tried to root the sirens from their hovel and nearly lost his entire army in the process. The Craw cannot be taken by force. Not by a thousand, not by ten thousand."

"Agreed," Elara said. "Which is why you should send just one."

"One?"

"The sirens appeared *en masse* to defend the Isle of Illumination. I don't know whether it was to protect their flank or simply to engage us on open ground. But if you were to stage a similar landing on the same beach..."

The king saw where his daughter was going. "It would draw a significant portion of their army away from the Craw. It makes sense —from our perspective. Whether they follow through is another matter."

"The diversion need not descend into full-fledged warfare, sire,"

Vespucci said. "We simply need to turn their eyes away from the prize long enough for one to sneak in and claim it."

"And who would this prize-claimer be? You?"

"Me," Elara said.

King Atlas balked. "Don't be ridiculous."

"I'm the only person who's been to the heart of their lair. I made it out once. I can do it again."

Realizing she was serious, King Atlas grew incensed. "I forbid it. The cost is too great."

"Not for Atlantis. Not for *you*."

King Atlas locked eyes with Elara and understood she'd thought this through. What made matters worse was that he knew she was right. This was their only chance. He looked at her again with fresh eyes, for once not seeing her as the shy little girl who used to climb onto his lap during meetings or cry when her brother's wooden sword stung her fingers. She was a woman, capable and judicious, noble and honest. What a fool he'd been. So blinded by pride and tradition, he'd failed to see her as she truly was: the best parts of him. It made him think of his actions of the past few days. He felt more than a little shame. Elara must have sensed it. She reached out and touched his arm.

"Father, you've prepared me for this since the day I was born. You would give up your own life a thousand times over if it meant the survival of our people. Who would I be if I didn't offer the same?"

King Atlas looked down and shook his head. For the first time in his life, he wished he'd never been crowned King. Better to be a simple man with a simple life than carry the burden of so many others. So many deaths. Yet, this was his lot. And it was hers too. Finally, he nodded. "But I will not send you into the heart of evil alone. You will take another with you." He nodded to Vespucci. "Him."

The Italian startled. "Me? B-but Your Grace, I am no warrior."

"A warrior cannot serve this mission. But an expert in Athenian lore can." Vespucci opened his mouth again, but King Atlas waved him off. "Spare me your humility, *Ambassador*. You read the book, claimed to know it better than any other. Now is your chance to prove it.

Unless you're not the *Anak-Ta Eleece,* as you suggested? If that were the case, I would have no need of you."

"But once you reach the upper realm—"

"Scores of countries you said. A procession of kings you said. I imagine one or two beyond your monarch might find allying with Atlantis favorable." Vespucci looked to Elara and back. "Did you not claim to be an adventurer like Columbus?"

"Better, he said," Elara added.

Vespucci looked as if he wanted nothing more than to flee. "I prefer *explorer,* actually."

"Then go explore. You've been inside once too. It is decided. Go make yourselves ready. You will depart within the hour."

"Yes, Your Grace," Vespucci said numbly. He turned, but hesitated, unsure where he was supposed to go.

"Oh, and explorer?" the king said. Vespucci turned back. "You will return with my daughter alive or not at all. Understand?"

"Yes, Your Grace," Vespucci said before walking away.

When the king looked back at Elara, he winked. She nearly laughed.

"Thank you, Father."

"Don't thank me yet. When Dion learns of this, he will do everything in his power to stop you."

"Dion will stand by his king's side as he always has. And he will lead your vanguard to the Isle of Illumination with dignity and honor."

"So, you're saying I should withhold the truth from him?"

Elara shrugged. "Sometimes it is better to ask for forgiveness than permission."

"Did your mariner teach you that?"

Elara nodded.

"Why am I not surprised?"

With nothing more to say, Elara turned for the stairs. After a few seconds, the king called out. "There are words that need to be said between us."

Elara replied over her shoulder. "Then we will say them upon my return."

King Atlas smiled before returning to the aid of his people.

It was dusk when King Atlas, Dion, and the Gadeir arrived at the Isle of Illumination. Their eldocks bayed as they breached the waters near the southern beachhead. Even here, the smoke from the rent sea clouded the air and left the moon glowing blood red.

A cry went up in the distance. Dion looked over their forces. Even with several hundred, they would be outmanned. He signaled the king. *They know we're here.*

"Aye," the king replied. Then he addressed the Gadeir. "Remember your orders. We are to hold the beach here. Front lines stand your ground. Back lines, alternate fire, but only after the sirens breach the trees."

Three hundred voices shouted in response.

Only then did Dion realize the princess wasn't with them. He signaled the king.

"Doing her duty," the king responded aloud. "As you will do yours."

Dion nodded grimly, joining the ranks on the beach. In the distance, a score of inhuman shrieks filled the night.

A half mile away, Elara and Vespucci bobbed in the water just off the shore where the cave entrance loomed. They heard the cry go up and saw shadows filtering past in vast numbers, all headed south to the army of humans that awaited. One group of sirens appeared to scout the beach. When they saw no one, they joined the others, leaving only two sirens to guard the entrance.

"Please, Princess," Vespucci whispered. "I beg you to reconsider this course. The only thing that awaits us within that mountain is death."

"Look up, signore. Death has already laid claim to this realm and all in it. At least this way, we get to choose the means of our exit. And perhaps earn us some honor in the eyes of Poseidon with what little time remains."

In a flash, Vespucci pointed his sonstave at Elara. "Poseidon is your God, not mine. So maybe your blood should be enough to sate him, eh?" He depressed the gem, but nothing happened.

"Did you really think I would arm you? The man that betrayed his own captain?"

"Columbus was not my captain," Vespucci spat as he tossed the sonstave.

"No, but he was a man, whereas you are not." A sword emerged out of the water, its tip kissing Vespucci's chest. "Which is why *you* will lead."

The pair slipped quietly out of the water, the high cliffs obscuring the moonlight from the beach. They quickly found the stone steps cut in the sheer rock face. Once in position, Elara handed Vespucci a smaller sword. "You see that inlet?" she whispered. Vespucci looked up to see a narrow fissure at the top of the stairs that separated the path from the shelf where the siren guards stood. "Make your way there. When you hear me loose the arrows, I want you to take and hold that position."

"What if you miss?"

"Then you'll be the first eaten."

Elara watched with disgust as Vespucci scampered off. The man was a coward. Had she her druthers, she would have slain him or left him behind, but her father was right. She might need his help. And if all else failed, at least she would die knowing the snake that drove Columbus to his death would face an even worse fate.

When Elara finally saw Vespucci reach the inlet, she pulled two arrows from her quiver, sinking one into the soft sand. The second she nocked against her bow. On this side of the rock face, the wind was light. She looked up at the two shadows standing outside the cavern entrance, a single torch marking their presence.

With a firm hand, she drew the bowstring taut, took aim, exhaled, and released. Before the hiss of the arrow was gone, the second was already slipping into place. A thud echoed as the first arrow struck.

Before the second siren could react, Elara loosed arrow number two. It must have flown true. Elara heard another thud and nothing after.

At the tunnel entrance, Elara and Vespucci pushed the siren cadavers over the cliff and covered their blood with dirt. At the same time, a barrage of sonstave fire erupted on the far side of the isle. Elara felt her stomach tightening and thought of her father and fellow Gadeir. Knowing she needed to focus on the task at hand, she tucked her fear away.

Vespucci watched as Elara uncovered a map she'd sketched before their departure. "This is the path I followed before. It led me deep into the mountain. I was within sight of the queen's nest before I was captured. Anything we encounter between here and there will be random patrols. Do not hesitate. If they are within your sight, attack. If you can hide, do so."

"And if they sing?"

Elara retrieved two circular buds and handed them to Vespucci.

"Place these in your ears. They will block out all sound, so keep your eyes open."

Vespucci nodded. Elara hated to think so much was relying on this man, but she had no choice but to work with him now.

At length they crept through the winding tunnels, staying mute as they stole past archways that forked in untold directions, into untold gloom. The torches that lit the way were few and far between, making the passageways even more treacherous.

After several dizzying turns, the roughly trodden path began to slope downward so steeply that Vespucci nearly stumbled off a crag before Elara grabbed him by the scruff and pulled him back. He nodded in thanks before continuing.

Thrice they managed to avoid patrols hastening by. Once a siren paused a dozen feet from the bolder they were hiding behind. It raised its snout, and its large, porous nostrils sniffed the air. Elara tightened her grip on her sword as the creature's black eyes scanned the cavern. Mercifully, a call beckoned, and the siren trudged on. Once it was gone, Elara put a hand on Vespucci's back and felt it wet with sweat. She might have felt pity for him then, but she kept remembering the look in Columbus's eyes right before he stepped into the Void. Regret. Yes, he had betrayed her. He had failed to ask the Fates how to save her people. But with that one look, she knew he would have done it differently a second time around. What she wouldn't give to have him by her side to find out.

At last, they came to a crossroads where four tunnels branched off in opposite directions. The most foreboding of them bore a set of narrow stairs descending deeper into the mountain. Vespucci stopped when he heard a sound coming from a tunnel. It sounded like moaning, though it was most likely the wind. Elara pushed him down the passageway until it opened into a cavern with a vast gorge. The source of the noise turned out to be a towering underground waterfall that cascaded from unseen heights down to a rock-filled river far below. In the middle of the gorge was a rope bridge. Two sirens stood guard on both sides.

Elara pulled Vespucci into a narrow fissure before pointing to the ornate archway on the opposite side of the bridge. He removed one earbud, and she whispered, "The nest lies just beyond."

"Four guards, maybe more. How do we get past them?"

Elara looked around. Outside of the rope bridge, there was only one area where the two sides came close enough to cross. An outcropping just in front of the waterfalls.

"There," she said.

Vespucci's eyes ballooned. "Are you mad? We can't—"

Elara wrapped a hand over his mouth and pulled him down as a patrol of sirens passed overhead. They were so close Vespucci could hear their razor-sharp talons scratching the rocks at their feet. The blood drained from his face.

Once clear, Elara crept along the outer rocks, closing in on the waterfall as its spray wet her face. When they reached the precipice's edge, Elara determined the distance was farther than she'd judged. She strapped the sword to her back, steadied herself, and leaped. She landed hard on the other side, feeling the sting of rock bite into her chest, hips, and legs. Still, she made no sound. Once secure, she waved Vespucci across.

Vespucci stepped to the edge and looked down. A mistake. The cavity pulled him like a magnet, and he lurched back. He was about to slink away when he noticed the princess had nocked an arrow. It was turned to the side, but she was looking at him. Taking several deep breaths, he readied himself, closed his eyes, and jumped.

Vespucci landed hard just where Elara had, but his foot slipped on the wet rocks, and he started to fall. Elara grabbed him, his body twisted and the belt holding his sword fell. It slid through his fingers, clamoring loudly as it bounced off rocks until it mercifully splashed into the water below.

Elara winced as the sound echoed through the cavern. She knew Vespucci was in a precarious position, but she waited before pulling him up. A few seconds later, a flicker of light glowed above. Elara squatted down, forcing Vespucci to hold on for dear life as water sprayed over him.

When the torchbearer neared, Elara released Vespucci's hand and quietly drew her sword. The waterfall grew brighter as the torchbearer reached the edge of the cavern. Elara could see the creature's shadow stretching over the rock, its head craning in both directions before it turned back. Then Vespucci's foot slipped, and he let out a huff as he struggled to hold on. The light above Elara swung around and she thrust her sword up as hard as she could. She felt it slide into flesh, the body go ridged. Then she pulled and flung the creature over the rock and down into the depths.

Once in the passageway, Elara wiped the black blood from her sword. Vespucci plopped down behind her, ghostly white, shivering, less from the water than adrenaline.

"It won't be long before others come looking," Vespucci said. "Perhaps we should—"

He never finished the thought. A thud preceded his eyes rolling back. He fell, revealing a siren with a gnarled club behind him. The creature opened its mouth to release a warning. Elara was too far away to stop it, but she charged anyway. She'd taken two steps when something whistled past her ear. An arrow pierced the siren's throat.

As it gurgled, Elara cut its head off with her sword. Only then did she spin to see a silhouette step into the passageway.

"Why, Princess," a familiar voice said. "We keep meeting in the oddest of places."

Columbus stepped into the light. Elara was too stunned to move.

"How?" she gasped. "I saw—"

"In a realm of magic, anything is possible."

She ran into his arms. She thought it might be some cruel joke of the Gods. And yet he felt real. His arms felt real. He definitely smelled real. *Real bad.*

"I thought you had died," she whispered into his ear.

"I might still…can't breathe."

She released him and stepped back awkwardly.

"Better," Columbus said, his familiar grin returning. "Logistically speaking. There are some scenarios in which a royal confluence can be quite welcoming."

She nearly laughed. Even here in the depths of foulness, looking as if the Gods themselves had trampled him, he still made jokes. He would never change.

"Royal confluence? That's a rather unsavory description. And, inaccurate, considering only one of us is royal."

"A royal pain in the derriere, you mean."

"Don't take it personally. You have your charms."

"Well, as much as I would love to continue *this*, my duplicitous colleague was right about one thing. We need to keep moving. Give me a hand."

Together, Elara and Columbus lifted the dead siren and rolled her over the edge.

"What do we do with him?" Elara said of Vespucci. Columbus looked back to the edge, hopeful. Elara shook her head.

"Fine," Columbus said. "I suspect the underside of a dark rock would be a comfort to him right about now."

Together, they picked up Vespucci and carried him to a dark crevice. Before leaving, Elara retrieved the sound-defeating buds from Vespucci's ears and offered them to Columbus.

"What are these?" he asked.

"They shield the wearer against sound. Even the sirens' song can't penetrate."

"These are worth their weight in gold."

"I wouldn't go that far—"

"In Europe alone, there must be tens of thousands of fathers and husbands who would pay any price for these."

"May we?" she hissed, pulling him down the passageway. "There is still a checkpoint to get through."

"Actually, I found another way."

He led her to a ridge, fifteen or twenty feet above the archway where a series of shield-sized holes vented smoke. Columbus clasped his hands and boosted Elara up, following close behind. The shaft sloped downward a spell before it began to narrow, forcing the pair to shimmy the rest of the way on their bellies. Eventually, Elara spilled into a narrow cleft behind a steep embankment. The air was stifling. A warbling chant echoed from the other side.

As cautiously as they could, Columbus and Elara crept up the embankment and looked to see what was on the other side.

Through a smoky pall they found the siren kingdom, laid out chaotically with no discernible order. To the right, a sweltering forge belched fire and smoke as a half-dozen sirens worked their metal offerings with hammer and anvil, crafting weapons Elara found all too recognizable.

In the center of the cavern was a web of thatched roosts where the elder sirens doted over the fledgling newborns, each trilling away, maws opened as worms, grubs, larvae, and other things of disgust slid down their gullets. Their constant, high-pitched chittering was like a sword to the brain.

Elara couldn't pull her eyes away until Columbus nudged her and nodded to their left. There, atop a series of jagged stone steps sat a throne made of roots and bones. And on that throne sat the Siren Queen. She was larger than any of her brood, with a long torso and saggy white breasts, sporadic tufts of unruly feathers, and talons that glistened in the torchlight. Worst of all were the queen's large black eyes that scrutinized everything in her dominion.

Elara counted enemies holding weapons. Bows. Cudgels. Swords. A dozen at least. And those were the ones she could see. Too many for a surprise attack.

On the ground to the queen's left sat an octet of colorfully feathered sirens chanting outside a stone archway, seemingly lost in trance. Those guttural tones filled the cavern, pulsing as the volume increased and receded. It was hypnotic. Elara hadn't even realized her eyes were glazing over until Columbus shook her. It seemed women were not totally immune to the siren song. Columbus held her attention by pointing out the familiar symbols graved into both sides of the archway, leading to a single symbol on top—*the egg*.

That was their destination.

Suddenly, Columbus put a hand to his chest and looked around nervously. At the same time, Elara heard something and her head snapped to the right. A fledgling siren had waddled up through some unseen pass. It was small, less than half the height of the adults, but when its small black eyes locked onto the strangers, it staggered to a halt, and both Columbus and Elara knew they were in trouble. The creature's head canted, a thin chirrup issuing from its beak.

Elara glanced to the bow and then to Columbus. He nodded ever so slightly. The small siren chirruped again. Elara's hand inched back and carefully drew an arrow from her quiver. She nocked it, took aim, and drew the string back. She didn't fire.

"Do it," Columbus hissed.

Elara knew what hinged on this moment. She understood the stakes. But for some reason her grip on the string remained taut. She had never seen a young siren before. She looked into its black eyes, expecting to find hate and fury, only to see herself instead. *Is this what the enemy looks like? Is this what it takes to win? Butchering their young?* Any other day of her life, she would have slain the creature without hesitation, but something in her refused to follow through. She heard Columbus's plea; she knew the chant was playing with her mind, but in her heart, she knew this was wrong. She lowered her bow.

Maybe it was the movement that did it or the eventual realization that there was a threat in its midst, but all at once the fledgling siren began its retreat, issuing a series of shrieks that filled the cavern. Columbus looked over the rise. The chanting stopped, replaced by more shrieks. The sirens were on the move.

Elara turned, finding no recrimination in Columbus's eyes. "What now?"

Columbus plucked one of the earbuds out. "Be ready," he said, scrambling to figure out a method of escape. "We can hold here, but not for long. How many arrows—"

He never finished his sentence. The siren song flooded the cavern in unison. Columbus's eyes glazed over. Elara caught him as he fell, the ear bud falling from his hand. She slapped a hand over his naked ear while searching for the sound suppressor with her other.

For Columbus, everything took on a dreamlike quality. He tried to imagine his consciousness as a fixed state—something he could grab on to—but he was rapidly being pulled into a tidal wave that threatened to consume him.

That's when the spotted eldock's voice sounded in his head.

Call to them, children of Poseidon.

Columbus's mind felt like it was mired in treacle. What did the voice mean? He ground his teeth, tasted a splash of copper in his mouth. The pain brought him out of the fog, but only barely. Looking to his right, Columbus saw torchlight growing behind the rocks. He tried to stand, but his legs wouldn't obey. When the first shadow appeared, Elara fired an arrow. A screech issued in response. Elara grabbed him and turned for the ventilation holes, only to see shadows moving within them too. They were trapped.

Summon them, as you once did.

The voice was weaker than Columbus remembered. Was it because they were underground? Far away from the sea? What did it mean? Columbus had never summoned the sirens, had he? Why would he want to? They'd been intent on killing him since he entered Atlantis. First, under this very mountain. Then again... *Wait*, Columbus thought. The second time was at the Isle of Illumination. But the sirens weren't summoned there. They had attacked on their own. Or did they? The truth was that they only responded when their space had been violated.

Columbus opened his eyes. Elara was shouting at him, firing a steady stream of arrows. He felt the sword in his hand—the urge to take it up. Instead, he dropped it, put both hands over his ears, and opened his mouth. The first note came out thin, shaky. Could he even recall the rest? Desperate, on the edge of blacking out, Columbus concentrated and tried again. The fog in his head receded momentarily, allowing him to whistle a second note and then a third. All at once, they began to flow, the whistling replicating the organ notes Elara and Nyx had played in the Tower of Illumination.

Elara continued firing arrows until the sirens halted, their eyes on this strange, blond-haired human male whistling the melody of the slaves over and over. He stood, those seven notes now filling the cavern until a blood-curdling screech echoed from down below. Columbus looked over the rise, right into the gaze of the Siren Queen. It waited as her warriors retreated, taking their place at her side. When Columbus stopped whistling, the nest was silent.

The Siren Queen looked abruptly to the Athenian archway, and the octet of sirens began chanting the same seven tones. The Siren Queen looked back up at Columbus.

"Come on," he said to Elara.

They descended to the cavern floor through the hidden fissure. Elara kept her blade poised low, not that it would do much good here. A few of the sirens chittered as they passed. Most remained silent. All were ready to attack should their queen give the command.

Approaching the queen, both Columbus and Elara noticed her distended belly.

"She's with child," Elara whispered.

Columbus said nothing. When he reached the foot of the archway, the Siren Queen snapped her beak, and the chanting stopped. Those black eyes burrowed into Columbus, talons at her feet tickling the stones. She was waiting for something. For a reason Columbus could not quite understand, he dropped to a knee and lowered his head.

In response, the Siren Queen shrieked, snatched a torch from a sconce and passed through the archway. Columbus followed. When Elara moved to join them, the other sirens shrieked. Elara held up her hands.

"Looks like she wants you all to herself," Elara said.

"Can you blame her?" Columbus smiled. Elara rolled her eyes.

Inside the archway, Columbus followed the hulking Siren Queen through a winding, rocky path to a second cavern. A cool current of air brought the smell of moisture and a series of popping sounds beyond.

The Siren Queen halted before lifting her beak and releasing a singular, hypnotic note that reverberated through the cavern. Columbus's knees felt momentarily weak. Then, blazers around the cavern sprang to life, illuminating not one, but three separate areas.

The first area featured a series of small columns that led to the second area, popping geysers. The third area was a rectangular pool of dark water at the foot of a giant nest made of roots and sticks.

"I take it I'm supposed to reach the nest?" Columbus asked. "Doesn't appear too difficult."

The Siren Queen shrieked before stepping to an ornately crafted chest, Poseidon's Trident glimmering atop it. It opened with a creak, revealing a golden egg the size of a cannonball inside. The Siren Queen stepped back.

"Seems straightforward enough," Columbus said before lifting the egg. It felt delicate in his hands. "When do we begin?"

The Siren Queen shrieked again. This one resembled a laugh. Then she turned the torch toward a hole in the rock wall. A flash of smoke preceded the line of fire that quickly began to run through another vast trough, moving hastily for the three tests.

A timed event. So be it.

Columbus hurtled down the stone steps toward the first obstacle, passing the flame that trilled along through a series of gates. With each step, the brittle egg shook in his hands. He would need to tread very carefully.

Arriving at the first obstacle, Columbus found the series of columns descended deep into a chasm, lost in mist some twenty or thirty feet below. He kicked a rock over the edge and waited to hear it land. It never did. With fifty columns placed at random intervals, Columbus would need to choose his path carefully. And keep his balance, of course. By no means a simple task, nor the most demanding.

He stepped onto the top of the first column only to feel a jolt and hear something crack far below him. The column started to topple, forcing him to leap back to the start as it plummeted into the mist.

"Should have known that was too easy," Columbus said.

He turned to see the line of fire drawing near. He was about to step again when he noticed lettering on the stones at his feet. He knelt and wiped away the dirt.

"Where the father leads, the son shall follow," Columbus read. "Easy enough. Poseidon is the father, and I'm the son. In old Ionic, Poseidon starts with the Greek letter, Pi."

Looking down at the columns, Columbus saw they too were marked with letters. 'Pi' was etched on the center left column. He leaped onto it, only to hear a second crack. He leaped back again as it tumbled downward.

What the hell? This needed more analysis, but the line of fire was already moving past him. Columbus looked down again, this time noticing a symbol etched below the words. It was a *harpe*—a sword with a sickle protrusion along one edge near the tip of the blade. It was one of the symbols for Cronos, Poseidon's father! Damn, he'd taken the slaves' words figuratively instead of literally.

Columbus identified the pillar bearing the first letter of Cronos's name, *Kappa*. He jumped on it and it stood firm. Finally! He followed the progression. *Rho. Omicron. Nu. Omicron.* But where was *Sigma*? He'd reached the penultimate row, but there were no columns marked *Sigma*, only a Void where it should have stood. With the fire moving past the first obstacle and onto the second, Columbus didn't have time to wait. He leaped for the pillar closest to the end of the chasm. It broke and canted forward. Columbus fought the instinct to jump right away, instead letting the column's momentum carry him forward. At the last moment, he jumped and hit the ground on the far side hard, rolling to protect the egg. When he scrambled to his feet, he looked down at the egg and saw a thin crack in its shell.

"The yolk was almost on me," he exhaled and quickly moved for the second task.

The flame was halfway through the second obstacle—a section of volcanic rock that spewed sporadic gouts of superheated gas into the air. Stalactites and stalagmites filled the low channel, more obstructions to evade. Still, Columbus saw little trouble ahead. And that's what worried him. These Athenians were clever—and perverse. They wanted to make any challenger work for the prize. So what was the catch?

The answer came quickly. Two steps into the grotto and a geyser popped twice in front of him. He dodged to his left just before it blew, blistering gas roaring over him. A few drops sprayed his cheek and hissed as it burned his skin, the rest struck against the rock ceiling and dispersed.

If that wasn't bad enough, something tittered behind Columbus. He spun but saw nothing. As the line of fire was moving quicker than he was, Columbus stepped forward tentatively and felt something brush his ear as he rounded a stalagmite. When his head turned, something grabbed the egg and tried to rip it from his hands. Columbus reared back, catching only a glimpse of something long and slimy slipping into a dark cleft above. A second and third titter echoed close by.

Columbus moved quickly as more geysers erupted. He nearly heard one too late and was forced to launch himself forward as a spray of hot gas mushroomed overhead, this time burning his shoulder. His cry elicited more titters. Columbus felt a sinking feeling in the pit of his stomach. This was not going to turn out well at all.

Columbus ran hard to his right. In response, a quartet of erupting geysers blocked his path. The instant their heat dispelled, three long appendages slithered down, black and slick as eels. Mouths appeared at the ends of those appendages, revealing pink mouths full of teeth. The nearest creature snapped at him, ripping the fabric of his suit while a second wrapped around the egg and pulled. Columbus shouted as the egg was nearly snatched from his hands.

He was halfway through the obstacle when a geyser forced him behind a stalagmite. Just after it popped, the egg was ripped from his hands. The slithering creature had it in its mouth and was rising to steal it away, but the egg was too big for the aperture. The lanky appendage tossed the egg before Columbus could snatch it back. Columbus ran through a glut of those hanging eels as they passed the egg across the room. A loud hiss announced a geyser about to pop just under the creature currently holding the egg. In response, it dropped it and slithered upward. Columbus dove, catching the egg just before it struck the ground, before twirling away to avoid the hot gas that spewed up behind him.

Sweating and bloody, Columbus tucked the egg and ran, hunkering down to avoid the strikes from above while spinning and leaping over the hissing geysers. A bite struck his arm, another, his leg. A hiss sounded directly in front of him and as it erupted, he instinctually held up the egg to protect his face. The egg was struck by the gas. To Columbus's surprise, it felt cool to the touch. *Interesting.*

More of those eelish things appeared, snapping and tittering as the path ahead of him closed. Columbus saw a buildup in a geyser in front of him. Thinking fast, he shouted, "You fellas hungry? Here!" He rolled the egg onto the top of the geyser. A herd of hungry slithering eel things swarmed down for the egg. Just as one wrapped around it, the geyser blew, sending hot gas spraying over all of them. They screeched in pain and retreated.

Columbus shot forward, scooped up the egg as he dashed pell-mell through the fray, geysers blasting him from all sides, the eel-like projections snapping and biting until finally he broke free of the second obstacle, bloodied, but alive. He looked down at the egg and winced. More cracks tattooed its shell. He didn't think it would survive a third obstacle.

That's when Columbus remembered the line of fire. It had already reached the third obstacle and was headed straight for the thatch nest where the egg was supposed to go. Columbus knew if the nest caught fire, his quest was over, and the Siren Queen would likely feast on him herself.

But as he moved up to the third obstacle, Columbus had no clue how it worked. The pool was thirty feet long, rectangular, with water black as pitch. Along the sides were two sloped walls dotted with a thousand circular holes. He picked a rock up and tossed it onto the wall. Instantly, a thousand razor-sharp barbs shot up on both sides.

"Someone really wants us to swim," Columbus muttered to the egg.

The fire line was halfway across the pool. He was running out of time. And yet every instinct he had told him not to go near that water. Nothing good would come of it. His stomach churned. He was tired beyond belief. The nest was too far to throw the egg without cracking it. The only option left was to swim.

He stepped up to the pool and took three quick breaths. As he leaned forward, a drop of blood fell from his chin and splashed the surface of the water. Instantly, the water churned with a bubbling frenzy.

"Mother Mary," Columbus whispered. What the hell was in there?

Columbus dipped a toe of his boot into the water. Again, the water percolated. He pulled his boot out to find the tip had been eaten away. His head snapped up. The line of fire was three quarters of the way past the pool, almost to the nest. If he couldn't swim and he couldn't go around, what was he supposed to do? He looked up. The ceiling was too high to reach. Even if he had a rope, there was nothing to tie it to. Columbus looked back to the Siren Queen, who watched silently from her ledge.

"What am I supposed to do?" he shouted.

There was no answer. The fire line continued to run. Columbus gauged he had less than thirty seconds to get the egg to the nest. That's when an odd thought struck him. Why did the slaves build a nest here when the sirens birthed their young? He'd seen the Siren

Queen's distended belly with his own eyes, as well as the fledgling young. What he hadn't seen was a single egg of any kind.

Was it possible?

Columbus looked at the Siren Queen again. "If the egg isn't yours, maybe it doesn't belong in the nest. And if that's the case..."

Columbus knelt and cracked the egg on the edge of the pool. He held it over the lip and let the viscera inside spill into the black water. In an instant, the entire pool exploded in a frenzy. The water bubbled and churned as the occupants beneath swarmed the gooey contents of the egg.

In the same instant, Columbus dove as far forward as he could. As he hit the water, he felt thousands of fish swarming past him. He swung his arms and kicked his legs as fast as he could, keeping his eyes shut and his mouth closed until he reached the end of the pool and scrambled up onto the stones. The fire line broke the last gate and was spreading to the oils beneath the nest as Columbus scaled the thatch and looked in. There, sat the third gem-encrusted key. He grabbed it and leaped down as the nest burst into flames.

"Yes!" he roared. "Yes!" He looked around. "Now someone get me out of here!"

THEY STOOD at the exterior bridge outside the siren lair. Elara bowed to the Siren Queen.

"This will not be forgotten," she said.

The Siren Queen tipped her head before she and her brood funneled back into their lair. Columbus and Elara headed in the opposite direction.

"You look terrible," Elara said.

"Gee, thanks, Columbus," Columbus replied. "You really saved my bacon back there. Thanks for being the man of my dreams."

"You mock me. I deserve this."

"No. I..." He stopped to face her. "I want to say I'm sorry for what happened before. Nyx was right. I came here seeking only the trident. But somewhere along the way, you became important to me."

"Me or Atlantis?"

"Both. But mostly you."

To his surprise, she stepped close and put a hand on his cheek. "It is a sweet irony that one who ventured here purely in the pursuit of treasure should find the most valuable one within himself."

"Does that mean our deal's off?"

Elara laughed out loud and resumed walking. "You are truly a hero of the ages."

"Ooh, I like that. *Christopher Columbus, Hero of the Ages.* Now, that's a catchphrase I can get behind."

At that moment, another quake shook the cavern. Both smiles died.

"The *Anak-Ta Eleece* is not through just yet. We have retrieved the three keys. What's next?"

"We take them to the Hall of Poseidon."

"But the Hall is outside the Void. How do we pass it?"

"The same way I did. With the eldocks."

"So, they *can* survive outside."

"While protecting us in the process."

Columbus ducked through the final stone archway out into the night. The cool air hit him, followed by the gentle sound of water lapping on the shore. Even with the smoke from the seabed billowing in, it was a welcome sight.

"First, we need to get back to your father. Convincing him won't be…" Columbus turned, but Elara wasn't behind him.

"Princess?" He saw a shadow lying on the ground near the cave entrance. "Elara!" He rushed to her side. "What happened?"

Before he could rouse her, a club struck Columbus across the back of his head. The last thing he remembered seeing was a hand picking the gem-encrusted key out of the dirt.

"God's will happened, Columbus," Vespucci said with a grin. "And one must never go against a God."

Vespucci turned and hustled off into the night.

CHAPTER TWENTY-ONE

"She's dead?" King Atlas repeated, his husky voice given way to breathlessness. Though he held the third gem-encrusted key in his hand, it might as well have been air. At his behest, the king's daughter had gone into the devil's den and retrieved what no one else could. She had paid her life for it. Now, both his children were gone, and he didn't even have their bodies to mourn. He was truly alone.

"I am terribly sorry, your Highness," Vespucci said. "If it makes any difference, her sacrifice was quite valiant. Without it, I would not have been able to acquire the third key and escape."

The king's eyes snapped up Vespucci, as if he'd forgotten the man was even there. Three days ago, the king would have drawn his sword and cut the man down where he stood. Now, he wasn't sure he could even pull the blade from its scabbard. As he fell back into his chair, several of his coterie moved to comfort him. He waved them all back, eyes returning to the foreigner.

"I will require a full accounting of what transpired in the Craw," King Atlas said.

"Of course, Your Grace," Vespucci answered.

"And when this is done, I give my solemn oath, not a rock will stand unturned in my efforts to hunt these creatures down and scratch their very essence from the earth."

"No more fitting end could be warranted. But now, it is my painful duty to remind you that time is of the essence. You have the three keys in your possession. Let us not hesitate. We must head to the Temple of Poseidon and recover the trident. Only then will your kingdom finally be secure."

"But the Hall passed outside the Void long ago. It's impossible to reach."

At that, Vespucci leaned in. "Not so, my lord. In fact, I have learned how a small party of men might pass between the two boundaries unscathed. But only if *I* lead them."

"You?" King Atlas said.

"It appears my predecessor was correct about one thing. The long-rumored savior of your kingdom did come from the realm above. What he got incorrect was his identity."

"You?" the king asked again.

Vespucci shrugged. "I am as surprised as you are, my liege, but I understand the gravity of my role and assure you I am up to the task."

The king was far less confident. In his heart, he knew this man was craven, and yet hadn't he returned with the third key?

Behind him, Dion glowered, his own face reflecting the torment and loss the king himself felt. Should he give the order, Dion would rip the man limb from limb. But where would that leave them? They knew too few details of the slaves' quest. They couldn't even read their words. Their ancestors had robbed them of that. Now, they were beholden to this interloper, and unlike Columbus, the king had no idea what price he would command.

"The ancients warned any who dared violate Poseidon's Temple would wake the Immortal Guards," King Atlas said.

"All but one," Vespucci replied.

Dion motioned to King Atlas, his hands moving sharp and concise. *This man speaks heresy. We have always known not to meddle with the Gods.*

"That was before the Gods took half my kingdom!" King Atlas

bellowed as he stood. "Look out there and tell me what you see! The ocean's afire. The heavens crashing down. The mountains to the east have already been swallowed by the Void. What would you have me do? Sit on my throne while our world whittles away to nothing?"

But to join leagues with them? It is a devil's bargain.

"He offers sanctuary," the king said.

It is not his to give. Nor the trident. My King, you executed the adventurer for pursuing this very prize. Even his girl-child admits it is a weapon. Should we risk our realm and the one above on the word of an interloper?

King Atlas grit his teeth in turmoil. "What should I care for other realms if it means sitting by while mine is destroyed? I have already lost my wife and children protecting Atlantis. I will not lose it too." He looked to Vespucci. "You will have your party." The king snapped his finger toward a runner. "Have six eldocks readied, mine among them."

Dion turned for the door. King Atlas held a hand up.

"Not this time, my friend," he said. "Our city needs one of strength to remain behind, and there is no one I trust more in my stead than you. Should we fail in this task—or should I fall—it will be up to you to decide Atlantis's future, however short that future might be. Do you understand?"

Dion nodded gravely. King Atlas's anger faded, allowing his sorrow to slip through. He clutched the giant's thick arm. "But know this. No matter the outcome, the old debt is paid. Though my children might have passed the gates of Elysium, their city—our city—still stands. It would bring me comfort knowing your booming laugh might once again fill these halls tomorrow and many more days to come."

Dion's eyes welled as he nodded.

King Atlas looked over his remaining Gadeir. "To the Temple of Poseidon." He strode for the door, Vespucci, and the others falling in behind him. As he turned the corner, the king glanced back at Dion, knowing in his heart it was the last time he would ever see him.

* * *

ON THE SHORE outside the Craw's entrance, Columbus looked out over the sea. The molten glow beneath the waters meant the fabric of this world was unravelling. With every minor rumble, Atlantis ushered closer to oblivion.

"Where are you?" Columbus whispered.

"Most likely he's returned to the city by now," Elara answered. She sat in the sand and rubbed her head where Vespucci had struck her. "Probably trying to convince my father to set out for the temple."

Vespucci had taken both eldocks from the beach. Or maybe he'd removed the bridle from Elara's, allowing it to swim free. Either way, they were stuck and had no way to get word to her people. Still, that wasn't what Columbus had been asking. He was thinking about the spotted eldock. The creature had communicated with him since the moment he'd arrived, aided him through every danger. But now, when he needed him most, that voice and presence were absent. It frightened Columbus.

"There has to be another way off this island. Maybe if we asked the sirens—"

"Did you not see the look in their eyes when we left? They aided us because Poseidon willed it, but if this quest fails, I don't believe for a second they won't kill us if freed to do their own bidding."

Columbus plopped down next to her in the sand.

"I suppose there is one small comfort to having a front seat to the end of the world – I get to share it with the prettiest girl here."

Slowly, she laid her head upon his shoulder. "You know, that's the nicest thing you've ever said to me. When you weren't trying to get me in your bed, that is."

"Princess, I would have gladly settled for your bed. Or any bed for that matter."

"Too bad we have no bed here."

"Actually, we do," he said, looking up. "Maybe we can't see it right now, but it's up there, beyond the Void and the oceans, beyond the clouds and the sky. And every evening when the sun slips beneath the waters, the heavens give rise to a bed of stars. They shine so bright in their multitude. I wish you could see them. They're deafening in their silence. But sometimes, if you watch closely, you can see them flying overhead. When they do, people make wishes on them."

"And what do they wish for?"

"Anything. Everything. Love. Riches. Peace."

"And do they ever come true?"

"All the time, I expect."

She nudged him. "Have they ever come true for you?"

Columbus shrugged. "Not yet. But I have hope."

Elara smiled. Even in the half-light, it was radiant. "Close your eyes, mariner, and make a wish."

With a smile, Columbus did. That's when Elara leaned over and kissed him. He looked at her in surprise.

"Was your wish answered?" she asked. He nodded. "Good. Then let's see to mine."

She kissed him again and pulled him back into the sand.

* * *

"What is it?" Nyx asked. "What's happening?"

"Another party is heading out," Fanucio answered. The first mate was standing on his tip toes looking through the cell's small window out to sea. "I count six, and the king is with 'em."

Nyx vaulted from her seat. "Do you see Elara?"

"No. But Vespucci is there."

Nyx cursed. She knew Vespucci had read the book, which meant he understood the trident's potential as a weapon. Columbus's fascination with gold was one thing, but if a man like Vespucci gained the trident and returned with it to their world, he might upend the balance of power in Europe and beyond.

"This is bad, Fanucio. Really bad. We have to get out of here," Nyx said, kicking the invisible barrier that kept them locked inside the brig. Once again, it shot a wave of energy though her boot that shocked her foot. "Earthquakes, shrinking voids. This city's coming apart, and this damn invisible wall won't give an inch! Do something!"

"Me? What can I do?"

"Anything! You're Columbus's first mate. What would he do in a situation like this?"

Fanucio thought about it. "Seduce the warden's daughter? I don't know! Start a riot. Or a fire."

Nyx looked down at his wooden foot.

"Don't even think about it," Fanucio warned.

"We have to do something." She looked at the Pygmies, asleep on their beds. "These two are useless. Why does the captain even keep them around?"

Fanucio slipped his hand inside one of their coats and pulled out a hidden flask, offering a toothless smile only a bat would love.

"Figures," Nyx said. "This is what he leaves me with."

"What are you doing here?" Fanucio asked.

Nyx was confused. Then she realized, he wasn't talking to her. She whirled to see Dion standing outside the barrier door, his face wan and brow furrowed.

"Come to gloat like some damn ghost?" Fanucio continued. "Or do you plan to murder us now—"

"Shut up," Nyx said before stepping closer to the barrier. Something about the giant was different. "Something's happened, hasn't it? What is it?"

Dion said nothing, but his eyes darted between the four prisoners.

Nyx pressed on. "We saw the king leave, which means the third key was found. Was it you?"

Dion's eyes narrowed.

"No, Elara won it. She solved the final challenge!" Her smile quickly faded. "So, why didn't we see her come back? Did something happen to her?"

Dion looked down. The man was wracked with pain. Even Nyx, so unversed in love, could see how deeply the man felt for his princess, but the depth of his suffering hinted at something worse.

"Is she *dead*?"

The giant held Nyx's gaze. It was answer enough. Fanucio muttered softly before tossing the flask aside.

Nyx put a hand to her belly to fight the sickness blooming.

"How?" she whispered.

Dion turned to go.

"Wait!" Nyx said. When the giant looked back, Nyx stepped as close to the barrier as she could. "I'm sorry. I know what she meant to you." Dion snorted, about to turn again. "I mean, I don't know exactly. But I understand your loss. I feel it too. For my mother. Even Columbus. I'm not sure why. The man was never nice to me. Some people, you have an idea who they are, of how they'll see you, but it never quite works out the way you think it will. People invariably let you down. Why do we stay loyal when all they do is hurt us? I'll tell you why. Because when we look at them—when we really look at them—the parts we see missing are the ones we fill ourselves. The best we can hope for is to be there when we're needed."

To Nyx's surprise, Dion appeared moved. Fanucio was too. He muttered, "Well said."

Nyx realized something else. "You didn't go with her. Who did?"

Dion's eyes narrowed again. He pointed at them before raising a hand with five fingers.

"Vespucci?" Nyx said. "Impossible. The man is a coward. There's no way he could have retrieved the key unless…"

Dion stepped forward, sensing something.

"Unless what, lass?" Fanucio asked.

To their surprise, the Pygmies had also been roused.

"I have to tell you all something. I didn't want to say it for fear everyone would think I was going crazy. Hell, I thought I was going crazy, but…I've been hearing voices."

"Voices?" Fanucio said.

"*One* voice. It's spoken to me since we first arrived here. In my dreams too. For what purpose, I can't say, but when Columbus stepped into the Void, the voice disappeared. And then it returned, fainter, as if it was a long way away. Fanucio, I know this is going to sound nuts, but I think Columbus is alive."

"Alive?" Fanucio stood. "But they said he passed through that wall. And no one's ever come back."

"True. But no one's ever recovered the keys before either. And they're supposed to open the Temple of Poseidon. Elara said the temple rests outside the Void, correct?"

Dion nodded.

"But we saw the king headed there himself. So, there must be a way through. And if you can pass to one side?"

"The cap'n can come back from the other," Fanucio finished. "So, where's he now?"

Nyx looked back to Dion. "If I had my guess, with the princess. That's why you're here isn't it? You think she might still be alive too, but you can't go after her. The king ordered you to remain behind. Why?"

Another quake rattled the city. Dion held a fist to his chest. Nyx understood what it meant. *Orders.*

"And you always follow orders," she said. "So, if you can't go in search of her, maybe someone less scrupulous can."

The Pygmies sat up. All eyes turned to Dion.

"Well, big fella?" Fanucio asked. "What's it gonna be?"

Dion took a heavy breath. And then the barrier came down.

THE VOID LOOMED JUST beyond the tip of the northern isle. King Atlas knew it had been shrinking fast, but even he was surprised to see how far it had come. The nearer they drew, the more it pulsed, as if it might collapse at any time, taking them with it in a sea of storm. To his surprise, the eldocks remained calm.

King Atlas turned to Vespucci. In the Nave, he'd seemed so sure of himself. Out here, however, he looked paralyzed with fear.

"Well?" King Atlas said into his mask. "I won't waste my breath threatening you. I'll merely allow you to go first."

Vespucci held out a shaky hand. "The keys, sire?"

King Atlas shook his head. "Pass and return. Do that, and I'll accompany you to the temple. Don't and..."

Vespucci understood. Looking back at the Void, the man almost lost his will. Then without another word, he spurred his eldock forward and entered the Void.

"Now, we see," King Atlas said.

The seconds stretched. The king felt the others growing tense. Nearly a minute had passed when a shadow appeared, and Vespucci returned.

"Shall we?" he said.

King Atlas nodded, and the entire party entered the Void.

* * *

"Oh, my god!" Nyx shrieked. "What are you doing?"

Columbus saw Nyx avert her gaze, but by then it was too late. She'd already seen him and Elara, naked as babies, rolling in the grass.

Columbus and Elara fumbled for their clothes. *What irony,* Columbus thought. *One minute they were the last two people on earth and now they were surrounded by his entire crew.*

"Nyx, it's not how it looked," Elara said, as she dressed quickly.

"It looked like you two were having *relations*."

"Then, it's exactly how it looked," Columbus grinned. "Albeit at a very high level." Elara glowered at him. "What? Could any less be expected from *the Hero of the Ages*?"

"Hey!" Fanucio said, pointing.

"I know!" Columbus responded.

Suddenly, Nyx rushed into his arms. The move surprised him. What surprised him more was how good it felt. When she looked up at last, she had tears in her eyes.

"You have to believe me," she said. "I never meant—"

"I know, Brommet," He knelt to her. "You were only doing what your heart told you. And that is never a bad thing. But promise me something. When we make it out of here, we must work on your aptitude for prevarication. Honesty might be the best policy to some, but for adventurers like us, it's a terrible burden."

Nyx hugged him even tighter.

"Vespucci?" Columbus asked.

"Headed to the temple with the king," Fanucio replied.

"Then we must hurry. If he claims the trident from his resting place, it will awaken Poseidon's guards. If that happens, the Void will be the least of our worries."

"Follow me," Elara said as she hopped atop the nearest eldock. "The path is north. Let us pray we reach the temple in time."

After Fanucio distributed the breathing masks, everyone mounted their eldocks and submerged. Once under water, Elara cut a course for the temple at breakneck speed, only pausing when they approached the Void. Columbus knew she had been afraid of it all her life. And even though he'd successfully passed through it, the thought of doing the same must have terrified her.

"If you're scared, Princess," Columbus said. "You can always wait here."

With a huff, Elara charged her eldock into the barrier and beyond. The others followed. Monday and Tuesday drew up at the last.

"*Are we really going in there?*" Monday asked.

"*Of course,*" Tuesday answered. "*We need a cliffhanger for the final chapter of our biography. I'll call it, 'Into the Great Beyond.'*"

"*Wasn't that chapter six's title too?*"

"*Indeed!*"

The laughed as they prompted their eldock forward and passed into the inky night.

CHAPTER TWENTY-TWO

*P*assing through the barrier the second time was no less terrifying than the first. Only when Columbus crossed the bridge, he felt drawn by something on the other side. This time, he was alone. Of course, he understood it was the eldocks who safeguarded the transition. And yet the spotted eldock had gone silent. He took it as a bad omen. If something had silenced that ancient voice, what could it do to his?

The passage was the same. Disorientation, nausea, followed by a kind of vertigo that felt as if one had been turned inside out. Then all at once, they were through. Elara activated the light on her staff, followed by the others. The water was much darker and colder on this side.

"He's not here," Nyx said.

"Who?" Elara asked.

"The owner of the voice I told you about."

"You heard it too?" Columbus asked.

"Since we arrived. I thought it was a dream."

"It's not a dream. The voice belongs to the spotted eldock, the oldest of its kind. It aided me when I crossed the first time. Has anyone else heard him?"

"I often hear voices," Fanucio said, "though it's usually when the rum's run low. And then, the advice is almost always shit."

Columbus kept his eyes on Nyx. "He'll be back. For now, we're on our own."

They moved forward at a brisk pace. After a few hundred yards forms appeared out of the dark, a mixture of Greek and Atlantean architecture. While inside the Void, these works of art remained pristine. Down here though, time and the depths had eaten away at them, leaving scattered ruins that looked truly haunting.

"Which way?" Columbus asked.

Elara pointed toward a set of stone caryatids, sculpted in the forms of female bodies. They formed a path that led deeper into the dark. Some were toppled. A few towered into the fathoms above.

As they continued, the ocean floor gave rise to more ancient buildings, covered with sand and age. Stoas. A great stone amphitheater. Various temples, through which their path cut.

"This road had a name once," Elara said. "I'm embarrassed to say I've forgotten it. I certainly never thought I'd see it with my own eyes. The colonnade above us once supported an entablature made from gold and precious stones. Presumably it was vast enough for Poseidon's chariot to pass through."

"I've seen the ruins of his temple in the Aegean," Columbus said. "The Cape of Columns it's called, though it holds no candle to the spectacle before us."

Their eldocks pushed forward, passing through the debris until a colossal building materialized. It was Greek in nature with columns ten feet in diameter, vaulting a thousand feet into the sky.

"Do you feel it?" Elara whispered breathlessly. "*This* is the home of a God."

Mighty steps led from the ocean floor to a set of towering golden gates. Those gates were slightly parted. Something shimmered in the lock.

"The first key," Fanucio said as he pulled it out and handed it to Columbus. "They come this way, all right."

Columbus pocketed the key before pushing through the gates.

That's when he saw two unfathomably large doors at the temple's entrance. These were not opened, nor did he see any key. "They must've found some other way inside."

"There," Elara said, nodding to the right. She led them to the base of the temple where a cleft in the wall led inside. Once through, the group rose until they saw the silhouettes of six eldocks waiting above.

They broke the surface of water to find themselves in a marble room lit by two braziers. Six masks laid strewn, and wet footprints led to an archway at the end of the room and a set of stairs beyond.

"Looks like they went this way," Columbus said as he set his mask down. He headed for the stairs, surprised to find them pristine.

"I don't get it," Fanucio said. "This place's as tidy as a priest's frock. And we're moving without the sea horses protecting us."

"Poseidon's house," Columbus said. "Poseidon's rules."

Fanucio swallowed as they continued to rise.

Eventually, the stairwell led to an immense room filled with a glowing light. The party before them had lit several braziers, revealing a host of towering statues of the Greek Gods. Far above, the ceiling glimmered with dazzling frescos of the Gods at play and at war.

Nyx turned her sonstave light on each of the statues as they passed. Elara named them one by one.

"Hera. Chiron. Demeter. Hestia. Hades. Zeus. Poseidon's brothers and sisters."

"And this one?" Nyx asked, illuminating a statue of a scantily clad woman bearing a crown, water at her feet.

"Amphitrite," Elara said. "Poseidon's wife. It is said the other Gods reduced her title to consort to punish Poseidon."

"She doesn't look reduced to me," Columbus said of her ample bosom. Elara pushed him forward.

The group continued up another set of steps into a second, massive room. Once again, they were awed by what they found. On one side was a chariot made of wood and gold. It was adorned with seashells, glimmering gems, and engraved with Greek lettering that looked like waves.

"Poseidon's chariot," Nyx said. "And look there!"

On the opposite side of the room was a long, narrow wooden ship with three masts and a bevy of sails. Columbus gaped, having never seen anything like it.

"What is it?" Columbus asked. "A galley?"

"A trireme," Fanucio answered. "I believe the Athenians used 'em during the Peloponnesian War."

"It's huge."

"If that impresses you," Nyx said. "Wait until you see this."

At the far end of the room, a final statue stood alone. Poseidon. He sat atop a seat of waves, holding his trident in one hand and the world in the other.

"That is more gold than I have seen in my lifetime," Columbus said. "Enough to make kings of us all."

He bent over and sunk a tooth into one of Poseidon's golden toes. Elara struck him, glaring. He shrugged as she passed. Columbus glanced back at the Pygmies, both of whom had removed knives. He motioned for them to wait until they were gone.

"We have a problem," Nyx said. "The rooms end here."

"But we followed my father's tracks," Elara said. "They must have come this way."

Everyone shone their lights around, but there were no other doors.

"Maybe they went to Elysium," Fanucio said.

"They didn't go up," Columbus said. "They went down."

At the back of Poseidon's statue, the second gem-encrusted key twinkled from a hidden keyhole. Columbus turned it. A rumble shook the floor as a secret staircase appeared. One by one, the group descended. Columbus took up the rear, pocketing the key before the darkness swallowed him.

* * *

"WHAT TRICKERY IS THIS?" The king's voice echoed in the cavernous room. They had managed to enter the Temple of Poseidon and pass through its halls. They'd even found the secret keyhole and staircase that allowed them to reach the underground sepulcher. Now, they stood two dozen feet away from a room that glowed, presumably from the trident. It was within their sight, but not their reach. After all their work, they were stymied, stuck behind a twenty-pace pool of spring water that looked as placid as ice until one of the king's men tried to cross it. Only then did the water rise in an instant like a giant wave, propelling the man against the far cavern wall and smashing him against rocks until he ceased to move.

"Is this another test, Star Rider?" King Atlas spat toward Vespucci. "And if so, how do we pass?"

"We use the t-third key," Vespucci stuttered.

"I know that, you fool! But where do I put it?"

They stood before a pedestal with three keyholes, each showing the corresponding images of a *book, a snake eating its tail, and an egg.* Vespucci looked like a half-wit trying to decide which keyhole to use. He knew the king would probably kill him if he didn't act fast, but he knew he'd also be killed if he chose incorrectly. He was sweating, stymied. The trident was mere feet away. He could feel the power rippling off it, enough to make him a god himself. All he needed to do was solve this final riddle. He held the third key over the central keyhole, about to slide it in when a voice spoke behind him.

"I wouldn't do that if I were you."

King Atlas and his party whistled around as Columbus appeared out of the dark.

"Columbus?" King Atlas gaped. "But I saw you die."

"We saw him pass through the Void, Father," Elara said as she appeared. "And now we all have."

"Elara," the king uttered, crossing the room in an instant and pulling her into his arms. "I thought I lost you. I was told…"

"Let me guess," Columbus said. "Vespucci said he retrieved the third key from the sirens but watched Elara die in the process?"

Everyone turned to glare at Vespucci, who shrugged meekly.

"Columbus won the key," Elara said. "This man took it from us and left us for dead."

The ring of King Atlas's sword being drawn from its scabbard filled the chamber.

"His lies end here."

"Wait!" Vespucci said. He held up the third key, poised to throw it into the pool. "Come a step closer and the quest ends here."

"The key will dry," Columbus said, stepping forward. "Your blood, however—"

"Stop," King Atlas said, arm extended. "The water is enchanted. Phemaph tried to cross it and was crushed as the water engulfed him."

Vespucci grinned. "Just like your city will be crushed unless Columbus solves the last riddle."

"What riddle?" Nyx said.

"Three keyholes, three symbols. Unfortunately, I have but one key left. I would try them all, but you see these words here? *Of three, only one may pass.* Do you know the answer?"

"Give me the key, Vespucci," Columbus said. "Let's end this."

"Do you know what it means?" he shrieked.

"Yes."

Vespucci scoffed. "No, I see the gears working. And I know your methods. Make a few quips, stall for time, and you'll distract your target long enough to make a move. But you won't fool me this time. I hold all the cards. Now, tell me the answer to the riddle, and I give you my word, all of you will live. With some luck, Atlantis will survive, and you and your friends can rot down here for another two thousand years."

"Fine," Columbus said. "'Of three, only one may pass' might be written in Greek, but the original version was first seen in Egyptian hieroglyphics, a subset of pre-African proto-literate recovered at Abydos."

Nyx's face twisted in confusion.

"Go on," Vespucci snarled.

"Well, loosely translated it means..." What followed were a series of grunts and clicks that troubled Vespucci, though he wasn't sure why.

Vespucci said. "What? What is that?"

"Pygmy. The language, anyway. As for specifics, it means, 'Aim for the foot.'"

Vespucci's brow furrowed, but just as he grasped the meaning, two thin spears flew in from the dark, skewering his foot to the floor. Before he could scream, Columbus bounded forward and ripped the key from his hand.

Monday and Tuesday appeared from behind.

"*Did you see my throw?*" Monday asked. "*A perfect strike.*"

"*I hit his little toe,*" Tuesday mused. "*A much smaller target.*"

"What about me?" Columbus prompted. "as if anyone could decipher hieroglyphics!"

King Atlas strode up to the whimpering Vespucci, lifting his sword into the air. Columbus grabbed his arm.

"As much as I appreciate the immediacy of Atlantean justice, I will need every available seaman if I'm to make it home. Even this one. But I promise, Your Highness, a sword is no match for the shame this one will suffer when news of his failures reaches our king's ears."

King Atlas re-sheathed his sword. "He's yours, then."

Elara appeared next to Columbus. "Quick thinking. But I assume you have a real translation?"

"Actually no. Afraid I'm rather riddled out. The obvious choice between the three is the book since it represents you, his children. But suffice to say, you've been a bit of a disappointment. Enslaving his favorite water horses and driving the sirens from the sky."

"So, one of those is more fitting?" Elara asked.

"Well, the eldocks have been more helpful, but I don't think that's the point." And to everyone's surprise, he turned to Nyx. "Do you?"

"No," she said. The answer was so unlike her. Columbus could see she'd thought of something.

"It's seems I've been remiss in recognizing your many talents, Nyx. And I feel like you might have an idea brewing in the little peanut of yours. Care to enlighten us?"

"Well, Vespucci translated this as of three, only *one* may pass, but this doesn't mean 'one.' It can mean single, but in this case, I think it means 'unified.'"

Columbus nodded. Of course. "Of three, only *together* may they pass."

"The other keys!" Elara said. "We have to go back for them."

"Don't bother," Nyx said. "Columbus has them."

Elara looked at Columbus askew.

Columbus looked at Nyx the same way. "How'd you see that? You were ahead of me."

"I didn't see it. I just know you."

With a smirk, Columbus pulled the two gem-encrusted keys from his shirt. Elara took one and handed a second to her father, leaving Columbus with the third.

"We turn together," Elara said.

They inserted the keys. Elara gave a countdown and they turned the keys simultaneously. For a second, nothing happened. And then the floor began to shake. The keys glowed hot. The water of the pool began to rise, moving up into a curtain of water, almost as terrifying as the Void itself. Everyone stumbled back, expecting the water to release on top of them at any time. And then all at once it disappeared, leaving a path forward.

"After you," Columbus said.

King Atlas and Elara led the way. Once they were gone, Columbus tried to remove the keys for a second time. They didn't give. He cursed. It was a shame. They would have been worth a fortune.

The tunnel continued for another twenty feet until it opened into a modest, circular room whose stones glowed with a magical light. Looking up, Elara gaped in wonder. The oval ceiling high above shone down like a window to the heavens.

"You wanted to see the stars," Columbus said.

Elara giggled into her hand as her eyes welled.

As they pushed deeper into the room, more statues emerged. These were smaller than those in the first few chambers, but they were still larger than the living. The silhouettes were human with individual characteristics and weapons. Even the faces were distinct. The women ranged from stately to beautiful. The men from handsome to imposing. They all shared one distinct characteristic: they were crafted from solid gold.

"Poseidon's immortals," Elara said.

"They're so lifelike," Nyx said. "It's almost as if—"

Columbus finished her thought. "Something turned them to gold."

A limping Vespucci watched, mesmerized.

"Is it possible?" King Atlas asked. He stood near a towering male statue, inspecting the two golden orbs in its hand. "Do you know whose likeness this is?"

"He holds the world in his hands," Elara said. "It must be Atlas, our ancestor!"

"No, dear daughter. These aren't the earth. They are the sun and moon, which makes this fellow far older than the ruler of Gaia. This is Hyperion, one of the original Titans."

"Who?" Fanucio asked.

"The Titans were the second generation of Greek deities," Nyx answered. "They ruled the Golden Age before being overthrown by the Olympians in the Titanomachy. That's what they called the war of the Titans."

King Atlas moved onto a second statue. "Legend told of them being imprisoned in Tartarus for all eternity. What are they doing here?"

"What's Tartarus?" Columbus asked.

"The deepest, darkest part of the underworld. Where evil suffers. Could this really be them?"

"There are twelve," Elara said. "And this one has the winged brow of Tethys. And here. Her mount is a lion, as Rhea is known for."

King Atlas walked through their ranks. "Oceanus, Theia, Phoebe, Cronos...They're all here. Poseidon's immortals are his greatest enemies."

"And his family," Elara said pointedly.

"A testament to giving one's children too much free rein."

Elara looked askew at her father. Only then did she notice Columbus moving past the Titans.

"Columbus?"

The others took notice and followed. Still, none could be ready for what waited ahead.

On a raised dais sat a golden ark with red satin bedding. Nestled within lay the golden trident of Poseidon. Six feet long with three barbed tines and a shimmering round pommel that glowed with the energy of the Gods.

"I can feel it," Columbus said, "pulsing in time with my heart."

He didn't realize he was reaching for it until Elara stopped him.

"Remember, this is a tool of the Gods. The Athenians warned that claiming it would awaken the guardians."

"For all but one. *The Anak-Ta Eleece*. Which you've kindly pointed out many times is *moi*."

"Please," King Atlas said, stepping forward. "If any should claim it, it should be me. It is my legacy."

"Here we go," Fanucio muttered.

The pair continued to argue, their voices growing louder in the stone sepulcher. They were so preoccupied that no one noticed Vespucci rush past them.

"Look out!" Nyx said.

Vespucci launched himself for the trident, but Elara tripped him at the last moment. Two Gadeir corralled him.

"It's mine," Vespucci moaned. "It was meant to be mine."

"I'm sure we can find a set of irons to your liking," Fanucio said.

Pulling Vespucci back, only Columbus, Elara, King Atlas, and Nyx were left at the foot of the trident, each within reach.

"The draw is strong," King Atlas said.

"It is a test of will," Elara added. "Poseidon's final act to prove our worthiness."

"I can feel it too," Nyx said. "Calling me."

"It calls to us all," Elara said before turning to Columbus. "But only one may lay claim to it."

Columbus stared at that golden pommel. The power to transmute anything into gold.

"The eldock said only one true of heart could take it."

"Which should rule you out," Nyx said.

"Hey. I was surprised myself."

His hand reached out, stopping a few inches away. Why was he hesitating? This was what he always wanted. The power to decide his own fate. Enough wealth to make him a king himself. So, why couldn't he take it? It wasn't fear—though there was surely a modicum of that. He kept thinking about the Atlanteans. Their kingdom was in ruins. Would taking the trident make him responsible for them?

"Take it," Vespucci growled from the floor behind him. "Only a fool would stare fate in the face and hesitate. You can feel the power! Take it!"

"Only a king should wield such a gift," Atlas said.

Elara saw the look of desire in her father's face. She'd seen it before, but in this golden light, it looked twisted, pained. His chest was heaving, perspiration wetting his pate.

"Father don't—"

"If Atlantis can be saved by this, it is my right."

She was about to warn him again. Then King Atlas's hand reached out and picked up the trident. The room instantly filled with a blinding light. Elara shouted as her father stumbled back, his body glowing as power coursed through him. His arm rippled as it grew distended, larger.

The walls shook. Plaster crumbled down from above.

When the King spoke again, his voice was deeper, foreign. "The fire surges within me! The power of a God beckons!"

King Atlas's shoulders began to widen, his compact frame expanding, growing taller, muscles stretching. His shadow rose as the lamps flickered.

"Get it away from him!" Nyx shouted.

One of the Atlantean guards ran toward the king. The trident swung around, the pommel slammed into the man's gut. He flew across the room and struck the wall, screaming as a shimmer ran up his body. Within a few seconds, he had turned to gold.

"The transmutation," Columbus whispered, "it's real."

Another female guard fired a stun blow at the king. It bounced off him. He turned, snarling, and aimed the tines of the trident toward the woman, unleashing a blast of holy fire that instantly incinerated her in a wisp of smoke. Elara screamed. Columbus dragged Nyx back as the king blasted two more of his guards, tearing the stones of the floor as if they were paper.

The king's armor split and fell off his body as he continued to expand, until he towered over them all.

"Father!" Elara screamed. "You put Atlantis in peril!"

"Only I can save my kingdom!"

The king bounded over the Titans, his massive feet crushing the stones where he landed. He shouldered through the pathway, crushing it open as he ran from the room and disappeared.

Columbus helped Elara to her feet. "Are you all right?"

She shook her head. "We have to go after him. Find a way to reason with him."

"I'm afraid we've got bigger problems," Fanucio said.

He was looking behind them. The nearest Titan's golden skin was cracking and shedding, revealing a paler hue beneath. Everyone in the room watched with dread, realizing the worst of the Fates' prophecies was about to come true.

The Titans were waking.

CHAPTER TWENTY-THREE

"We need to go," Columbus said, backing for the stairs. "Now!"

As the Titans stirred from their endless slumber, a surge of energy filled the room. Nyx felt the hairs on her arms stand up, and her teeth rattled. She felt nauseous. She heard a crack and glanced back just as she was exiting the room. One of the Titan's mighty arms had broken free and was stretching out, the gold flaking off it like dust.

The group ran through the debris left in the tunnel in King Atlas's wake, working together to shove one giant slab from their path. When they reached the shelf with the three keys, Elara tugged at each of them, hoping it might restart the water barrier. Her efforts proved futile.

Just then a piercing wail resounded from the sepulcher, freezing Elara mid-step. Columbus grabbed her and pulled her after the others as more unearthly cries joined in.

King Atlas had crushed his way up the hidden stairwell, toppling the statue of Poseidon. As each of the survivors emerged, they saw the mad king had also broken open the two mighty doors at the temple's entrance. Only the magic preserving it prevented the ocean from storming in.

As the group sped through the Hall of Elders, the entire building shook violently. This was no earthquake. Two pillars cracked and toppled over. Half the ancient fresco fell, nearly crushing Vespucci as he limped behind the others.

"Once the Titans are free of the sepulcher, they'll head for Atlantis," Columbus said.

"How do you know?" Elara asked.

"Poseidon put them here for a reason. They're his final proclamation. His promise of doom. I'm sorry I failed you, Princess."

"You didn't fail me. And this isn't over yet."

In the pool room, the eldocks bucked furiously in the water, held from retreat by the thin bridle that covered their heads. Stones splashed in the water as the group mounted their eldocks and secured their masks as quickly as possible.

"We have to find my father," Elara said. "Try reasoning with him."

"Reason with a mad king?" Fanucio said. "I'm no history expert, but even I know that never ends well."

"For once, I agree with the fool," Vespucci said. "Your father has been corrupted by the trident's power. Even if you were able to wrest it from him, you would still have the Titans to deal with."

"If you believe I will abandon my people now, you are the fool!"

"Atlantis is gone, Highness. Our only chance at survival is to ride these beasts to the surface. With luck, one of our ships might remain."

"You are such a coward! If I had the time, I would cut you down without a single—"

"He's right," Columbus said.

Elara turned in shock. "What?"

"I said, he's right. I'm sorry, Princess, but there's nothing more that can be done. If the Void doesn't destroy Atlantis, your father or the Titans surely will."

Elara's face twisted with pain. "You would leave me? After all that's happened?"

"We've done all we can. It's time to face facts. Atlantis is doomed, but we don't have to die with it. Come with me and I'll show you a realm filled with more beauty than you can imagine. We could find a small corner of the world where there are no wars, no Gods to appease, where the stars come out every night to fill you with hope."

She shook her head, tears filling her eyes. She held a hand to her chest as if to will away the pain. When she finally spoke, her voice trembled.

"What use are stars, adventurer, if they defy your deepest wishes? Go. I will stay and rally my people. Atlantis might fall, but perhaps we can find an ending worthy of its beginning."

"I'm staying too," Nyx blurted out. "You told me once that adventure is born of risk and great peril. Seems like there's enough of that down here for a girl to make a name for herself."

Columbus smiled, though inside, her words hurt him more than he cared to show. He looked to the Pygmies. "And you, my friends?"

Monday shrugged sheepishly. Tuesday spoke in clicks and whistles. *"He wants to fight a God. I want to see who wins."*

"You have my blessing," Columbus said, before leaning over and whispering in Pygmy. "Watch over the girl."

They nodded. And then to Columbus's surprise, Monday extended a hand and Columbus shook it.

Vespucci groaned. "Can we leave before *we* become the artifacts?"

The eldocks sank beneath the water and exited out of the building through the cleft. Once free, the two parties halted.

"I'll send the eldocks back when we reach the surface," Columbus said into his mask. "That's *if* a ship is waiting."

"And if it's not?" Elara asked.

"Then I guess we'll find out if we can swim to Spain. Good luck, Princess."

"And to you, *adventurer.*"

Elara turned and headed off for Atlantis with the other three following. Columbus sat there a moment, watching their lights fade, his gaze locked solely on the girl. He still didn't understand why she rankled him so. Then, to his surprise, she paused, and his heart skipped a beat. He could barely make her form out. When she spoke, he struggled to hear her voice.

"Farewell, Captain," she said. "May we meet again one day under a full sail and a warm sun."

Columbus felt as if he'd been punched. "What did you say? Nyx? Nyx!"

He shouted her name several times, but she never replied, vanishing instead into the dark.

"Captain?" Fanucio asked.

"That phrase... I knew someone once who used to say it."

Vespucci scoffed "I'll whisper it in your ear every night if we depart now. I don't want to be here when those *things* escape."

Neither did Columbus. After one last glance in the dark, he directed his eldock upward, and the others followed.

The instant Elara and the others passed back through the Void, they knew things had only gotten worse. The seabed continued to shake, and it looked like even more fiery vents had broken out.

"Where would he go?" Nyx asked. "Back to the city?"

"I don't think so," Elara answered. "There's nothing for him there. I can still see that look in his eyes. He didn't recognize me."

"Well, at ten feet tall, he shouldn't be too hard to find."

A man's voice cut in their headsets, husky and raw. "Your father attempts to mend the ocean floor."

"Who....?" Elara asked.

And then a single rider approached through the cloudy waters.

Dion.

"Dion? You *spoke?*"

"My penance ended when your brother's killer was vanquished."

"Why didn't you speak then?"

"I wasn't sure I could."

"You picked a hell of a time," Nyx said. "The king stole Poseidon's Trident and the Titans are coming to finish off what's left of your kingdom."

"The Titans?" Dion asked, unable to keep the dread from his voice.

"Poseidon's immortals," Elara clarified. "It's quite a story."

"I hope to hear it one day." Dion looked around. "Where is the mariner?"

"Gone. Back to his world."

Dion took a moment then nodded. "It is as it should be. What orders, my liege?"

"Gather the people. We need to set up one last defense. Here."

"It won't be enough," Nyx said.

"No. We most likely will fail, but we will do it with our heads held high, knowing we did everything we could. And who knows? Perhaps we can earn back some good will from Poseidon. Some parents are quick to forgive their children. And some children should do the same."

Nyx swallowed. Then, her head turned unexpectedly, as if she'd heard a ghost.

"I-I have to go," Nyx said. Elara's eyes narrowed. "I'm not leaving you. But I need to see if I can find a friend. I wish I had time to explain."

"I trust in your heart, Nyx. Gods willing, we will see each other again."

Nyx reined her eldock around to face the Pygmies. "Protect her. I'll be back."

The Pygmies nodded as if they understood. Nyx sped off into the dark. Elara turned back to Dion. "To Atlantis!"

Together with the Pygmies, they set their course across the sea.

A LIGHT WIND was blowing across the ocean when three forms broke its surface beneath a crystal blue sky and a golden sun.

"We done it!" Fanucio said, laughing. "We're back! And, look, the sun! I never been so happy to see that beautiful ball of flame in all me life!"

"There!" Vespucci shouted.

A league away, a vessel sat still in the water, its sails furled. Columbus thought it was the *Pinta*.

"I was right," Columbus said.

"First time for everything," Fanucio said. Both men laughed, but Columbus's smile faded when he thought he heard a voice. His hand went to his chest, troubled. Fanucio noticed.

"You all right, Cap'n?"

"Yes," Columbus said. "Let's go."

ELARA PUSHED her eldock through the ashy waters when she came upon an open patch and reeled to a stop. She couldn't believe her eyes. Where the seabed had once been filled with rents, there was now only scorched earth. Her father had managed to seal the ocean floor, but in the process, he'd destroyed everything. The coral. Plankton. Even the fish. Life would never flourish here again.

"The trident did this," Elara said. "We must hurry."

* * *

MARTIN PINZON HAD BEEN MANAGING the quadrant with a critical eye. He had given his word he would wait four days before departing, and that time was almost up. Then a shout rang down from above. All eyes turned to the starboard side.

"I don't believe it," Pinzon said. "That's Christopher Columbus. But what is he riding?"

A rope was lowered as the trio reached the ship. Vespucci and Fanucio were the first drawn up. As Columbus secured the rope around his chest, he patted his eldock and thanked him. The gray eyes stared back at him a moment before disappearing beneath the waters.

Once the trio was on deck, the *Pinta*'s crew gathered around to look over Columbus's suit and the survivors' conditions.

"Thanks be to God, you're alive," Pinzon said, touching the fabric of Columbus's suit. "I expect you have quite the story."

Fanucio locked eyes with Columbus. "One for the ages."

Before they could talk further, Vespucci pulled a sword from the master-at-arms and aimed it at Columbus.

"Captain Pinzon," Vespucci said, "under orders of his royal Highness and as envoy of your vessel, I order you take these men into custody immediately."

"Now, wait a damn minute, Vespucci," Fanucio said. "The cap'n saved your life!"

"That's not how I remember it. Nor how the king will hear it. But I promise, when he learns what transpired here, I will return with his entire navy to sift through the rubble and—"

A blast echoed, and Vespucci flew across the deck. The startled seamen turned to Columbus, who held a humming sonstave in his hand.

"Apologies, Captain," Columbus said. "I'm afraid Signore Vespucci suffered a little heatstroke while we were adrift. Perhaps if you took us to the Canaries, he could seek proper attention for his malady."

"I'm sorry, Columbus, but I have strict orders to return to Spain with you in shackles. And his majesty will want a full reporting of what I've seen."

Columbus reached into his pocket. "Maybe this will change your mind." He opened his hand to reveal the shimmering gems he'd taken from the slave quarters. The crew gasped.

"Well, we do need repairs," Pinzon said. "And after all we've endured, my memory seems a bit fuzzy."

Columbus smiled as he handed the gems over. Pinzon stuffed them in his pocket and called out to his crew. "To your stations. We set sail for the Canaries."

The crew cheered as they rushed across the deck. As the sails unfurled, men began to sing. One of the sailors played a flute, a spirited tune that Fanucio sang to.

Columbus leaned against the gunwale, looking back over the ocean. He'd done what he'd set out to do. So why did he feel so low?

"Well done, Cap'n," Fanucio said. "I hope you saved some of them rocks for us. First thing I'm going to buy when we reach the Canaries is a big, juicy steak and a big juicy woman to go with it, eh?"

Columbus was in the process of smiling when he heard a faint voice.

Only united can the children save their world.

"The voice," Columbus whispered. "I can still hear it. Why can I still hear it?" The eldock had to know he was gone. His children had left them. Likely they'd already passed back through the Void. Did the damned creature think he would change his mind?

Yes, come.

Columbus gasped in pain, a hand going to his head. An image penetrating his mind. It was Nyx. She was riding an eldock alone and approaching Ophidian's Mouth. What the hell was she doing?

We are ready.

It made no sense. And then Columbus remembered. The night he'd slept in the tower. He'd heard the voice then too. *Only one true of heart can save a people*, it had said. He'd bolted out of bed. At the same time, he'd heard Nyx scream from the adjoining room. He thought it was because of the earthquake, but later in Poseidon's Temple, she revealed that she'd been hearing the voice too.

"Only one true of heart can save a people," Columbus muttered to himself.

"Come again, sir?" Fanucio said.

"One true of heart." Suddenly, Columbus felt the sky falling around him. "We have to go back."

"We *are* going back. Straight to blessed civilization."

"No, we need to go back down there."

"Atlantis?! Now, see here—"

"I know what it means by one true of heart. I was never true of heart, but I know someone who is."

"I'm confused. We talking about the princess again?"

Columbus looked around for Pinzon but didn't see him. The man with the flute was walking past. Columbus grabbed it and stuffed it into his pocket before he climbed on top of the gunwale.

"Are you coming?"

"But they have rum," Fanucio said plaintively.

Columbus leaped overboard. Fanucio grudgingly followed.

"Well, what now?" Fanucio said. "The water horsies is gone."

Just then, they reemerged. Columbus grinned. Fanucio growled as they mounted the eldocks.

Atop the ship, Pinzon appeared. "Columbus?"

"Captain, I've just remembered where I stashed a fortune in treasure. If you'd like a bigger share, you might consider sticking around a bit longer."

Pinzon mulled the idea. "How big a share are we talking about?"

"Enough to make us both kings."

"You have twenty-four hours."

Columbus slipped his mask over his face. Fanucio did the same.

"If we're looking for the princess," Fanucio said, "I think she went back to the city."

"I have another destination in mind."

* * *

THEY HAD REACHED the Isle of Arcadia, the central most isle in all of Atlantis, and the only one with enough resources for her people. They were still funneling in, but already a thousand had gathered. Elara climbed to the nearest rock and raised her hands. The crowd fell silent. Elara took in the faces of her people. Among them, Dion, the Pygmies, and even the Seer.

"I know these past days have been hard. Can any of us remember a time that wasn't? Today we grieve for our king as we grieve for all our fallen. But Atlantis can still survive if we stand together. Our ancestors did this long ago, and Poseidon honored them with this realm for it. Today, it is our turn. Today, we will send him a message that the same blood runs through our veins, undiminished and unbowed. And no matter what forces align against us, we will remain Atlantean until the end."

"But the eldocks have shed the bridles and fled," someone said.

"Do not fault them. The truth is we have bound them to our service for too long. We will meet the Titans alone using the boats that carried us here. And when they are filled, we will swim. I know the future looks bleak. I know I am not the leader you asked for, but I promise to be one you can be proud of. I call upon you now, my brothers and sisters, if you can carry a sonstave and wish to fight for our homeland, follow me. Together we will win this day or win the honor that will carry us into Elysium!"

The crowd roared as they ran for the beach.

* * *

THE WAY WAS BLACK, the water cold. Nyx knew she could activate the light on her sonstave at any time, but what was the point? Her eldock knew where it was going. It ran through a series of dizzying tunnels that filled the subterranean depths beneath the Isle of Oblivion. Finally, they exited into a vast cavern with a honeycomb of tunnels.

The spotted eldock was waiting.

It is time.

"Are you ready?" Nyx asked.

We have always been ready.

And from the honeycomb, a thousand faces appeared, more eldocks than Nyx could have imagined. She had come for an army. Now, she had one. She prayed it would be enough.

* * *

UNLIKE COLUMBUS'S FIRST DESCENT, he was completely aware this time around, which to him, made it even more harrowing. For he knew what he was going back to. Poseidon's immortal guards were actually the Titans, imprisoned by the children who had overthrown them many millennia before. They were primordial, capable of what, Columbus couldn't imagine. Yes, the Olympians had defeated them, but at what cost? History was vague on the subject, which made the hope of the Atlanteans repeating it seem more impossible.

Thankfully, the eldocks understood Columbus's intention. When they finally arrived at Gaia's Craw, Fanucio was aghast to see Columbus scramble from the surf and run up the beach, halting in front of the entrance to the siren cave. He paused long enough to gather his breath before he raised the flute to his lips, blowing out several notes that sounded like a cat whose tail was lit on fire.

"Bit out of practice," Columbus shrugged. He tried a second time. This go around, he blew the melody from the Tower of Illumination—the same one he'd whistled in their nest. He knew he was taking a big risk. The sirens had already helped them once. But if he was right, this was the moment they'd been waiting for.

He watched the mountain passage carefully, expecting to see those malformed creatures brave the sun to answer. The tunnel remained empty. Instead, a thousand silhouettes appeared along the mountainside, near the beachhead, and in the waters behind him.

Fanucio gulped, his voice suddenly lost.

Columbus lowered the flute. "It's time," he said.

The Siren Queen tromped from the grass, her dark, avian eyes locked onto him, her cadre of warriors ranked behind her. As she passed Columbus, she let out a slow hiss before slipping into the water. Her legions followed, as did the mariners.

* * *

ELARA STOOD, feet planted atop the bow of a fishing boat as it rocked just off the edge of the northern part of the Void. The Pygmies sat behind her, honing their spear tips to razors. They had made good time. The boats had settled. Her Gadeir had prepared their masks and their sonstaves. Hundreds more civilians had done the same. She looked over those in boats and in the water.

They were ready.

A moment later, Dion emerged. He pushed up his mask before giving Elara a single nod. She turned back to her people.

"The Titans have breached the Void. We will meet them here. Be ready, be resilient, and have no fear. Together—"

"Look!" someone shouted.

Elara turned to see two riders approaching from the west, both on eldocks. She couldn't make either out at first. Then, as they drew closer, she recognized the lead one's fair locks and his bearing. A wave of emotion threatened to overcome her. She couldn't have her people see that. Instead, she waited until he drew to a stop and offered a single curt nod.

"Sorry we're late," Columbus said.

"You are here as I expected you," Elara said.

The Pygmies yipped.

Columbus winked at them and smiled, looking back to Elara. "Hope you don't mind, but I brought some friends."

A thousand sirens emerged from the waters, startling the Atlanteans, many who reached for their weapons. Elara held up her hand. "Fear not," she shouted. "*This* is Poseidon's will."

The Siren Queen made her way toward Elara's boat, hissing low as she came face-to-face with her mortal enemy again. To the surprise of all, Elara didn't flinch. She bowed instead. "Thank you for coming, great Queen."

The Siren Queen tipped her head just as Dion emerged from the water once again.

"They approach," he said.

"He speaks!" Fanucio said. "I knew he could talk. I knew it."

Elara addressed her people once more. "It is time. In the water now. We descend together."

As the splashes echoed around them, Columbus pulled near. "The prophecy said all of Poseidon's children had to come together. Where are the eldocks?"

Elara shook her head. "They have done their part. We must do ours. I've ordered our ranks to form three lines, at depths of twenty-five-foot intervals. At these numbers, communication will be difficult."

Columbus patted his eldock. "I've always wanted to be a runner."

Elara couldn't manage a smile. Neither could she manage to turn away. She opened her mouth to speak. Columbus beat her to it.

"There'll be plenty of time for sweet words after, Princess. To the task at hand."

She nodded, grateful, before they slipped their masks over their heads and dove under water.

The ranks were already forming when they arrived, the lights of the sonstaves creating one massive underwater wall that illuminated everything down to the ocean floor and several hundred feet in front of them. Already the sirens had integrated themselves in the formation. Enemies standing together.

Columbus and Fanucio took position near the back where they could get a view of everything below them. The lines settled. Now, it was time to wait.

Columbus heard Fanucio grumble over his headset.

"Hungry, my friend?"

"Thirsty. I keep picturing Vespucci up there, toasting our demise with my rum."

"Let him make toasts. We'll make history."

"Sure. If anyone's around to record it."

Elara settled in at the center of the wall, issuing orders calmly through her headset. The lines drew still, leaving the undersea current to carry ash past them.

Then all at once, silt billowed out of the dark in front of them, coming in time with the deep base of what sounded like the world's largest drum. Only it wasn't a drum. It was footsteps. Even high above the seabed, wearing their masks, they could all hear it.

One step. Two. More. Many more.

Columbus felt his chest tighten and took several deep breaths to loosen it.

"Steady," Elara called. "Ensure sonstaves are at full strength. And no matter what emerges, give no quarter."

The thundering steps continued. And then the first form appeared. It had grown larger than Columbus could have thought possible. Twenty-five feet tall at least, its mighty legs pounding the earth. It looked female, something held in her hand. Columbus recognized them.

Scales.

The first Titan was Themis.

When she saw the ranks allayed before her, the Titan-Goddess began to swing the scales in an arc. As they spun, they began to glow hot until she snapped them forward and a terrible blast of light shot forward, striking a siren and a human. They exploded in a cloud of flesh and blood.

"Release!" Elara screamed.

A barrage of smaller, sonstave fire lit up the waters of the sea. A thousand points of light accompanied by the sirens, who opened their mouths, issuing harmonic salvos that buzzed the brains of the humans. The first bombardment struck Themis, pushing her momentarily back.

And then the rest of the Titans appeared.

The mighty Hyperion carried a burning flame in his hand, which he threw at the opposing forces, charring the flesh from their bodies in an instant.

Theia came next, her eyes glowing magically, blinding any that looked in her direction.

Crius. He used a ram's horn to fire kinetic blasts of energy that took the shape of a ram, bludgeoning its victims and propelling them violently into the darkness.

Iapetus. He threw a giant spear that skewered victims only to return magically to his hand.

"Elara," Columbus shouted into his mask. "Your people are bunching together. They need to make smaller targets!"

Elara relayed the order. Columbus watched as the army spread out to attack the Titans from different levels and vantages.

At the same time, the sirens coordinated their attack, aiming for the Titans' ears. It must have worked. Several of the behemoths covered their ears and roared with pain. Two of the closest sirens were caught in violent streams of energy coming from the mammoth mouths of Coeus and Phoebe.

Columbus and Fanucio pushed into the fray, firing off sonstave blasts at the Titans' feet, their throats, trying anything and everything. For a moment, it looked as if the army would hold the Titans back. Then a line opened and the last two forms appeared. These were larger than any other, mountainous.

Cronos, father to all.

He carried his sickle in his hand, slashing it back with unfathomable speed, separating torsos and limbs.

The second figure, Rhea.

Her shimmering crown glowed brightly, putting multitudes to sleep with the wave of her hand.

The attack grew more frantic, the Titans assailed from all sides, but they continued to push closer.

Columbus saw one swimmer speed to the front. Dion. He raised his sonstave and fired a blast directly into Crius's eyes. The Titan roared in response. Columbus wanted to cheer. Then he saw the Titan grow bigger.

"The blasts aren't hurting them," Columbus said.

"They're only making them stronger," Elara replied.

Only then did Columbus realize the Titans weren't even close to full force. Their long slumber had robbed them of their power. But that time was quickly coming to an end. If they didn't stop them now, the Titans would soon be invincible.

"What can we do?" Elara shouted.

Columbus was about to shout back that they needed to retreat when one of the Titan Goddesses locked him in her sights. Even in the dark, he could see her physical form, curvaceous and alluring. He felt a burning in his loins, flooding him with a desire unlike any he had ever felt before. The Titan giggled as she closed in on him. He was caught in her trance. And then, out of nowhere, a Gadeir fired at her from the side. She turned and pulled back her hair to reveal a naked breast. The Atlantean immediately went still, eyes glazing over. Columbus realized the Goddess was Mnemosyne. Her beauty had erased the man's memory.

He hid his own eyes as he fired blast after blast toward her, his eldock bucking as another Titan flew past him. The figure's torso was sculpted and mighty, but the lower half of its body looked like that of a snake.

Oceanus.

He carried an oar, which bloomed radiant fire that eviscerated more Atlanteans. A gang of sirens swarmed him, sinking their claws and teeth into his neck. Before they could do much harm, the last Goddess, *Tethys*, appeared, her bracelet gleaming hot before a whirlpool of water hurled them away.

"Our weapons are having no effect!" Elara shouted. "We need to pull back!"

Atlanteans and sirens continued to fall, their numbers already reduced by half. They had won nothing. The Titans pushed on, claiming more victims, growing in strength, their diverse powers leaving the combatants blinded and confused.

Columbus surged back to take in the battlefield, hoping for sight of anything that might turn the tide. There was nothing. The Titans were too powerful, their weapons too deadly. He clenched his fists in rage. What did it mean to be the one spoken of in prophecy if he could do nothing to help these people? How could the slaves have written lore to give a kingdom hope if it all amounted to nothing in the end? If he'd only claimed Poseidon's Trident, maybe he would have stood a chance, but King Atlas had claimed it first. Even if he could find him now and take it from him, it was already too late.

Columbus despaired. He was about to tell Elara she needed to sound a full retreat when Fanucio shouted, "Look!"

Columbus turned. It took a moment for his brain to register what he was seeing. Elara grasped it instantly.

"The eldocks," she uttered. Then she shouted for all to hear. "The eldocks have come!"

From the southeast, an army of eldocks surged in. A cheer went up as they swept past at breathtaking speed.

Now, this is a spearhead, Columbus thought. Poseidon's army was complete. He looked for it then, through the darkened depths. Until its silhouette appeared. The spotted eldock. Even from afar, that mottled skin shone brightly. And as it neared, Columbus saw its pattern had changed to resemble the one from his vision. The one with a small form riding on its back, the dark smear of the rider's leg turning the pattern into the perfect star.

Destiny had arrived.

The Athenians had foretold of the *Anak-Ta Eleece*, the one who would bring hope to a realm in ruin. Columbus had thought all along that he was the one. But now he knew the truth. And it came back to those words that had filled his mind again and again.

One true of heart.

Of course, it was Nyx. It had always been Nyx. Who else could have been the Star Rider?

When the front of the eldock line slammed into the Titans, the Gods stumbled under their charge. Wave after wave rammed the enemy, forcing them back, striking with such strength they howled with rage. The people cheered as the onslaught continued. The Titans were too slow to counter their much faster enemy. But even this attack failed to fell them. And with each strike, the Titans continued to grow. The sickle slashed. The spear launched. The scales of justice spun. How could mortal creatures defeat Gods? Columbus understood the answer had been with him all along.

Only united can the children save their world.

"We have to work together!" he shouted. "Man, eldock, and siren! Target the magical items. It's the only way!"

Despite the barriers of language and communication, all three species seemed to understand. The Atlanteans mounted the unshackled eldocks as the sirens swam alongside of them. Dion emerged at the front of the pack, directing a group of one hundred at Rhea. Her crown glowed hot as she waved her enemies to sleep. The numbers were too many, however, for her to stop them all. The sirens came first, issuing their harmonic song to daze her. The eldocks followed, striking her from all angles until her crown fell askew. Only then did Dion ride in and blast the crown from her head. As it fell to the seabed, Rhea's mouth opened in an abominable scream, only to watch as her body turned to stone before Nyx and the spotted eldock rammed her, and she exploded into dust.

A cheer rang out as Elara ordered the others to follow suit. The Pygmies led an attack on Hyperion, ducking beneath his fire as the sirens' song froze him. As the eldocks slammed into him, Monday and Tuesday used their spears to stab at the God's hand. His powerful flame fell, and Hyperion turned to dust.

The other Gods roared at the loss of their kin. Tethys sent spinning vortices of water at all those approaching, but soon her bracelet had been stripped away, and she too died.

Coeus and Phoebe found themselves surrounded, torn fabric wrapped around their mouths until they imploded, their dust mingling as it had first formed epochs before.

Oceanus's oar was broken, and he fell. Iapetus's spear was caught mid-flight upon return, and he passed too. Mnemosyne was driven into the silt, her beauty hidden, her magic fire extinguished. Crius's horn was broken. The scales of justice lost. In the end, only one Titan remained standing.

Cronos.

Surrounded by impossible numbers, his fellow Gods all fallen, he raised his arms open wide and released his sickle. And the last God of his age crumbled to dust.

The Titans had been vanquished.

Poseidon's children stood victorious.

During the celebration, Columbus looked for Nyx. He eventually saw her at the far end of the battlefield, apart from the others. He locked eyes with her as he closed in, only to see her turn away. She was hurt. He understood. She had every right. He would need to find the right words this time. Before he could even begin to form them, the earth shook, and another volcanic rent appeared.

"The Titans' death hasn't stopped the Void's collapse," Elara said.

"This was never about them," Columbus said. "We need the trident. We—"

Suddenly, Nyx and the spotted eldock sped off to the south. He called after her, but to no avail.

Elara pulled up beside him. "Where's she going?"

"After the king. We have to stop her."

Just when Columbus thought it was over, he realized the worst had yet to come.

CHAPTER TWENTY-FOUR

Before departing for Atlantis, Elara rose to the surface to meet the Siren Queen. She was surrounded by her remaining sisters. Many bore wounds, including the queen herself. Despite this, Columbus thought she looked almost regal in the moonlight.

"This was my brother's sword," Elara said, holding the shimmering blade out. "I offer it to you in the hopes our kinds might find peace once more."

The Siren Queen hesitated only a moment before taking the sword and tipping her head. Elara bowed again, and the Siren Queen and her legion turned for the long swim back to the Craw.

Columbus waited as Fanucio and the Pygmies approached. His crew had only suffered minor injuries. He said a prayer to thank God, though his answer came in the form of another rumble, this one reaching far enough to send a ripple of energy wafting over the firmament above.

Just my luck, he thought. *Save a world and be rewarded with the roof caving in overhead.*

By the look on Elara's face, she was thinking along the same lines. She turned to Dion. "Load the wounded into the boats. We'll return for the dead when we can. I need you to escort the survivors back to the Isle of Arcadia. I'll be there when I can."

"You cannot face your father alone, my Queen," Dion said.

Elara looked to Columbus and his crew. "I won't have to."

Dion nodded, accepting his orders, and set out to aid his people.

Columbus helped Elara onto the back of his eldock while Fanucio took on the Pygmies.

As they set back off across the sea, Columbus saw the smoke and ash had dissipated. The trident had fused much of the seabed, leaving it a lifeless husk. He wondered if it would heal with time and decided it probably wouldn't. Even if they found a way to save Atlantis, it would bear the scars long after they were gone.

When they came in sight of Atlantis, they saw two more towers had fallen. The city that once shone as a beacon of enlightenment was now in utter ruin. The wall leading to the eldock pens had collapsed, leaving no passage inside. Only as they drew near the rocks did Columbus see the spotted eldock floating near the reef.

Columbus bounded off the eldock into knee-high water, drawing as near to the ancient eldock as he could.

"She went inside?" he asked.

Yes, the voice answered.

"Back in the slave dens, you said the Star Rider was *in my blood*. But you didn't mean me."

No.

"But Nyx can't be my daughter. It doesn't add up."

There are more mysteries to your world than you understand. The truth you will find in time.

"Is she my daughter?"

You know the answer. You have always known.

Columbus turned and ran inside. Elara called out, pausing long enough to address the spotted eldock.

"I thank you for your courage, noble one, and ask for your forgiveness. No words can justify what we put you through or the sacrifice you made on our behalf. I can only give my word that you and our siren sisters will be hunted no more."

The spotted eldock took one last look toward the city before it sank beneath the waters and disappeared.

Elara and the Pygmies rushed for the city.

"Wait for me!" Fanucio shouted, limping along behind them.

MORE QUAKES RATTLED THE CITY, toppling columns and sending glass raining down. Most of the alchemical lights had burned out or been destroyed, leaving the halls in shadow.

Columbus saw Nyx under an awning near the central colonnade. She was peering around the corner when he huddled in behind her.

"Where is he?" Columbus asked moments before Elara and Fanucio joined them.

Nyx nodded to the transportation tubes, one of which looked as if it had been torn open.

"He went up to the royal suites," she answered, "but I don't think he found what he was looking for."

"How do you know?" Elara asked.

An inhuman roar echoed through the city, followed by the sound of more breaking glass. Through the exterior window, the king's bed plummeted to the sea.

"He already has the trident," Columbus said. "What else could he be looking for?"

A set of titters sounded behind him. Everyone turned to see the Pygmies grinning wildly.

"What did you two do?" Columbus asked.

Monday pulled a large sack from behind him. He opened it to reveal the bronze disk that appeared identical to the one that led them to Atlantis. Where the hell had it come from?

"Well, if the eldocks truly leave," Fanucio said. "At least we have another way home."

"If we survive," Columbus reminded him.

The city shook again. Scrap cascaded down the transportation tube.

"He's coming back," Nyx said. "We need to find a place to distract him long enough to take the trident."

"How about the Nave?" Elara asked.

Columbus nodded, and the group ran for the Nave. Once inside, they found the auditorium half covered in rubble, the sky roof above shattered, the stones beneath their feet smoking.

"How do we get him in here?" Nyx asked.

"I have an idea," Columbus answered. He pointed to the bronze disk. "Give me that thing."

Outside, an enormous form burst from the transportation tube, ready to stalk outside when it saw a beam of light coming from the Nave. It lumbered in that direction.

The walls shook as Columbus and his crew spread out in the auditorium, taking up hiding places behind seats and columns. They all watched the doorway grow dark as King Atlas approached. Then an immense hand reached up under the lip of the doors and took hold of it. With a single wrench, the wall crumbled, and the king slipped inside.

He had grown huge. Fifteen feet tall, rippling with distended muscles, his eyes blazed with dark power. He held the trident—also more than twice as tall as a man.

Chest heaving, the demigod scanned the room. Then his booming voice filled the auditorium.

"WHO DARES ENTER MY COURT UNINVITED?"

Everyone was frozen. No one knew what to do next. In the sea, they fought the Titans with three species numbering in the thousands. Here, they had six with few weapons to speak of and little room to hide.

Then, Elara called out from behind the throne.

"It's me, Father," she said. "I've come to help you in your time of need."

The king laughed, his voice so loud it shook the walls and sent more debris plummeting down.

"NEED? I AM A DEMIGOD. I HAVE NO NEEDS, ONLY POWER!"

He raised the trident and a blast of blinding holy fire broke open the rest of the sky window.

Elara covered her head until the danger passed.

"Yes, you have power, Father. Power unrivaled, as one of your station should. But our city needs that power now. And you. Can't you see how Atlantis fares?"

The king's eyes glazed a moment. He looked around, as if trying to wake from a dream. Then he shook his head, those dark eyes falling to his daughter again.

"ATLANTIS IS A DYING SEED. A PRISON. I SEE IT CLEARLY NOW. WHY SHOULD I CARE FOR A CAGE WHEN THE WORLD ABOVE AWAITS MY RULE?"

King Atlas turned to leave when Elara shouted out.

"Father!" Elara stood, revealing herself. "You forget yourself."

The demigod turned back with a willful sneer.

"DO I NOW?"

The king aimed the trident at Elara. She stood her ground. There was nothing to protect her now. But before King Atlas fired, a kinetic blast shot from the seats, striking the demigod in the back of the head. King Atlas turned to see Fanucio, wide-eyed, halfway up the auditorium, smiling meekly, a glowing sonstave in his hand.

"Apologies, your massiveness," Fanucio stuttered. "Misfire. Totally my fault."

The trident spun, and holy fire ripped through the seats. Fanucio dove out of the way as several rows were instantly destroyed.

"Do something!" Nyx shouted.

Columbus stepped from behind one of the columns. "Fire at his eyes! He can't hit what he can't see!"

A series of sonstave blasts struck the king in the face and head. He responded with a roar, sending more holy fire across the Nave, blasting through columns, and eviscerating more seats. Columbus dashed across the aisles, grabbing Elara as the throne was obliterated.

Smoke filled the room as the trident fell silent. King Atlas stalked to the side of the room, searching for the interlopers.

In one of the narrow alcoves, Columbus and Elara huddled together.

"What can we do?" Elara whispered. "His mind is gone."

"Keep trying," Columbus answered. "You can get through to him. I know it."

"Look," Elara said.

In the rafters, a large section of metal and glass hung perilously over the room. At the top of the seats, Monday and Tuesday took aim with their spears. They tossed them both, striking the target dead on. The metal cracked, and the entire section fell, striking King Atlas across the back and sending him tumbling to a knee. Monday and Tuesday let out a cheer and touched heads. Then, King Atlas's eyes locked onto them and he snarled.

"Oh, shit," Tuesday muttered in Spanish.

Holy fire ripped across the balcony, chasing the Pygmies as they ran for their lives. More columns fell, the walls of the great amphitheater threatening to come down around them.

King Atlas's chest heaved as he stood, spinning around to look for more targets. Elara remained hidden but called out again.

"Even now your city crumbles around you. The city you gave an oath to protect."

"OATH?" the demigod echoed as he searched for her.

"To save our people. They live still. And they need you more than ever."

King Atlas bellowed. "NO. I COMMAND THE SKIES AND THE SEA. I RULE THE ANIMALS OF EVERY KINGDOM. I ALONE CAN RESHAPE THE VERY EARTH. BEHOLD!"

King Atlas slammed the pommel of the trident down into the cobbled floor. Instantly, a shimmering wave swelled out, turning everything within a ten-foot radius into solid gold.

Columbus's eyes narrowed. Then he noticed the transmutation

had stopped at the center of the Nave where that familiar pale rock with three holes still sat. It hit him at once. His trip to the Fates.

"Elara look at your father's feet. The stone. The Fates revealed that stone to me. It's the one from which the trident gave birth to Atlantis. We need to get him to strike it again before the floor collapses."

King Atlas stormed around, peeling stones away with his hands, hunting for any sign of the humans.

Columbus looked for another route to the floor. Only then did he notice Elara had gone. He looked, horrified to see her stepping out on the floor, approaching the monster without a shred of cover. Her voice stopped everything.

"King Atlas, protector of Atlantis, thirty-second son of your line. Do you not know me?"

King Atlas turned. Elara was ten feet away, well within his reach. Despite this, he didn't move, even as she tread closer.

"I am your daughter and your most devoted servant. Can you not hear my plea through this veil of madness?"

The king blinked, as if trying to see through a fog. "I KNOW YOU."

Seeing the demigod was distracted, Columbus slipped from the alcove to the balcony and crept along the bannister behind him.

At the same time, Elara made her way to the center of the floor, stopping only when the three-holed rock was beneath her feet.

"Yes," Elara said. "All my life I have watched you from the shadows, marveling at your strength and courage, wanting nothing more than to earn your respect and love as the people loved and respected you. Do you not know me?"

King Atlas grimaced, fighting against the storm that raged in his mind. Then it came to him. "ELARA?"

"Yes," Elara cried. "It's me. Put down the trident, Father. It was never meant for us. If you put it down, we can rebuild Atlantis together."

Behind them, Columbus slipped over the bannister, tip-toeing his way toward the trident, still clenched tightly in the king's hand.

"I CANNOT. THE DRAW IS TOO POWERFUL. EVEN NOW, I FEEL IT BENDING MY MIND TO ITS WILL. HELP ME."

"Strike me down, then! Do it now, with all your strength. Strike me down and your torment will end!"

The demigod's body shook, the struggle within him building with rage until it was too much.

"NO. I CANNOT—"

It was all Columbus needed to hear. He ran and latched onto the trident with both hands, ripping it from the king's grasp before running off.

King Atlas's head spun back to Elara, his eyes filling with rage. His mighty hand struck her, flinging her across the room as he yelled, "DECEIVER!"

Elara struck the wall and lay motionless.

King Atlas charged after Columbus, watching as he whirled the trident around and pointed it at him. He squeezed it, expecting to unleash holy fire. Nothing happened.

"What...?" he asked.

"FOOL!" King Atlas bellowed. "NONE BUT A GOD MAY WIELD IT!"

King Atlas stomped his foot down. The cobbles of the floor split. Columbus tumbled to the ground. As the glow of lava burned below, the trident shot from his hands and slid across the floor. The pommel struck the bannister, turning a long section of it to gold.

King Atlas lumbered for the trident, leaning to pick it up when Nyx fired a blast from her sonstave, striking him in the eyes. He reached out and grabbed her with his hand, ready to squeeze the life out of her when a streak of red whipped by overhead. It was the Pygmies, flying on the ends of two banners. When they wrapped around the king's eyes, Fanucio fired his sonstave and hit the king's forearm. Nyx fell to the floor.

"The trident," Nyx screamed. "Put it in the rock!"

Columbus scampered across the stones and through the king's legs. He scooped up the trident, twirling it in his hand as he closed in on the center rock. With careful aim he lined the tines with the three holes and heaved downward with all his might.

A blast shook the room and Columbus was sent sprawling. When he looked up, the trident lay broken in two pieces. The top half by the demigod, the bottom half by Elara, who looked up, woozy.

"WHAT HAVE YOU DONE?" King Atlas roared.

Elara whispered, "He is not the *Anak-Ta Eleece*."

The walls shook again, this quake bigger than any other. The city was coming down around them.

"We're out of time!" Fanucio shouted.

Elara watched as her father closed in on the top half of the trident, those tines glowing with power "Father!" she screamed as her hand wrapped around the bottom half of the trident. "Forgive me."

She flung the broken trident as hard as she could. It skittered across the floor, spinning until it struck his foot. King Atlas looked down. The pommel was touching him. The golden wave already rising up his legs. He looked back at Elara and saw only sorrow in her eyes. In those final seconds, he looked like himself again.

"No," he said. "The injury is mine. Forgive—"

As the transmutation concluded, Elara turned away.

Columbus rose to his feet as the floor shook. It felt like another quake, but Columbus knew differently. "He's too heavy! Nyx!"

Nyx sprinted across the floor. Columbus grabbed the top half of the trident and threw it toward the center of the room. Nyx caught it and slid to a halt over the rock, hefting the trident up with both hands. She looked to Elara.

"Do it," Elara said.

Nyx slammed the trident into the rock.

The voice spoke a final time.

It is done.

A wave of power radiated out from the rock, blowing past Columbus and the others. It passed through the remaining walls of the city, extending out over the water, healing the seabed as it continued to expand. As it bubbled outward, it reached the Void. A blinding light broke over the realm as the two barriers became one.

Instantly the volcanic rifts disappeared, the sea grew calm. The trees and foliage grew more vibrant, and the animals came out of their dens.

Outside Gaia's Craw, the sirens waited, watching as the light approached. They held their heads high, lilting a simple song as the energy washed over them. Instantly their sickly bodies shed away. Their stunted appendages grew longer, feathering with brilliant plumes as they took to flight, their song becoming clear and beautiful as if it had been born of the angels themselves.

On the Isle of Arcadia, the people of Atlantis cheered. Mothers and fathers cradled their children as they cried. Many ran into the water, singing their own prayers of hope in honor of Poseidon.

Back in the Nave, Elara cried. A weary Columbus nodded to her, and she nodded back. Then his gaze turned to Nyx. She shrugged as if embarrassed by what she'd done. He laughed softly, but inside he hurt for the pain he'd caused her. *His daughter.* He would need to make amends.

From high above, more cheers resounded. The Pygmies had found a bottle of Atlantean wine and were toasting with it. Even Fanucio laughed.

Then the remaining half of the cobbled floor began to shake. Nyx was still in the center.

"Nyx!" Columbus shouted. "Get out of there!"

Nyx tried to run just as the floor collapsed, toppling into the inferno below. She was hanging from a stone a foot beneath the surface. She tried to pull herself up but didn't have the strength. That's when she saw the bottom half of the trident on a small shelf to her right. It had already turned the rock to gold and was dangling over the abyss.

Elara screamed.

Columbus slid up to the edge and extended his hand. "Give me your hand!"

Nyx looked at him and back to the treasure. She watched his eyes turn toward it, saw him register what it was. *It was so close.*

"The treasure," she groaned.

Columbus hesitated only a moment before he moved.

As he passed to her right, she felt something leave her, as if a knife had been lodged in her heart and now it had been pulled out, leaving a vacuum that hurt worse than the blade itself. She shouldn't have been surprised. *This is who he is.* She had known that all along. Her only mistake was believing he could change.

Just as she began to accept her fate, Columbus leaped down on that rock, his boot kicking the trident, sending it plummeting over the edge. Nyx looked up, tears spilling over her cheeks as he latched onto her arm.

"The only treasure I need is right here."

He lifted her up and pulled her into his arms. She sobbed in relief as she collapsed into him, hoping beyond anything he would never let her go.

Up above, Elara and Fanucio cried too.

At the top of the Nave, Tuesday sniffled. Monday stared at him.

"What?" Tuesday asked. "*All this smoke is hell on my allergies.*"

Monday wrapped his arm around his friend.

CHAPTER TWENTY-FIVE

They gathered in the Garden of the Blest. The Void had been pushed back by several miles, leaving a meadow of such overwhelming beauty Columbus wanted to get lost in it. The citizens of Atlantis lingered there, unwilling to celebrate in the face of so many losses but relieved the worst was behind them. Though their kingdom lay in ruins, work had already begun on a new one on the Island of Arcadia. This city they would name after their king.

As Elara spoke, she told her people some of the ancient crafts might be necessary to rebuild their kingdom, but that they were only tools. The true worth of a kingdom came from its people and their character could only be forged by hard work. The people embraced the idea. Poseidon must have too. When she was done, the old bridge finally crumbled and fell. No longer would any be separated by difference or station. Each man, woman, and child would thrive on their own merits.

Finally, the moment everyone had been waiting for arrived. The honoring of champions. First, Elara bestowed gifts and praise upon her own people, including her father and those who had given their lives. An eternal flame would burn so all could come and honor the sacrifices of the dead.

Next, she honored those who had fought or served bravely. Some were Gadeir. Others were simple citizens. The healers that tended to wounds. The fishermen who swept people to safety. All were humbled in their queen's presence.

At last, she turned to Columbus and his crew.

"And to our friends from the dark continent," Elara said, handing two beautifully crafted spears to Monday and Tuesday. "These are given to replace the ones you lost. May they guide you in the light and dark and only serve your hand."

Monday and Tuesday bowed before taking the spears and slipping them into sleeves that had been crafted from Gadeir fabric.

"And to the most loyal first mate of this realm or any other. I present you with this." She held out a golden foot. "May it always keep you fleet of foot."

"My golden foot!" Fanucio shouted as he replaced his peg leg with it. "And it fits! Thank you, Princess. I mean, my Queen. I'll treasure it always."

Elara smiled as she stepped forward and kissed him on the cheek, whispering into his ear, "Just don't let your captain sell it." Fanucio blushed and turned away.

Dion was next, looking as uncomfortable as a warrior standing in a field of flowers could.

"And to our kingdom's most faithful son. Without your fealty and strength, all would be lost. This belongs to you." She held out her father's sword. Dion's eyes grew wide, and his lip trembled. Then he shook his head.

"No gift could be greater, my lady, but I must refuse. All I have known is a life of bloodshed, though I see from these strangers there is far more to it. No longer will I take up weapons. From now on, I pledge to live a life of peace."

Elara was moved. "If that is your wish."

"If you would allow me one request? Allow me to accompany the mariner. A strange world awaits above. If there are more people like him, I would like to meet them before I return."

"Atlantis has need of leaders."

"I beg pardon, my Queen, but they have all they need in you."

Elara took a heavy breath before nodding. Dion bowed, and she moved on.

Next, she came to Nyx. The girl stood straight and stiff, fighting with everything she had to keep the smile off her face. At this, she failed miraculously.

"Nyx, you hold a special place in my heart. Throughout your journey, you have maintained the light from which all good things flow. For that, I give you this." A woman handed Elara a beautiful cape, which she gave to Nyx. "It belonged to my mother. It is called the Cape of Royals and allowed me to move freely about the city as a child. It will not make you invisible, but those not looking will be hard pressed to see you."

"Thank you, Queen Elara," Nyx said. "I already love it because it's from you."

Elara kissed her on the cheek and moved on to Columbus.

"Christopher Columbus. Walk with me."

He nodded and held his arm out. She took it and together they headed deeper into the garden, passing over the brook that ran with fresh water again. They stopped where it forked and listened as it ran over the rocks. They stood there in silence for a time, both unsure what to say. Eventually, Elara spoke.

"The gift I chose for you, I know you will not take. But I offer it anyway. Stay. Share my kingdom with me."

Columbus gazed into the eyes of this stunning, regal woman and knew any man in his right mind would be a fool to say no. But in his heart, he knew his destiny lay elsewhere.

"As much as I would love to, Princess, my place is on the sea. But you could always come with us."

"See the sun rise every morning?"

"And the stars shine every night. No allegiances but to each other."

"A tempting proposal. But you have your world to rule, and I have mine."

"Since Dion will not take my father's sword, I'd like you to have it. It will pair well with my brother's shield. Neither will fail you."

Columbus bowed. "Oh. And I have something else. To start you on your new journey."

She drew a rolled-up parchment from her pocket and handed it to him. He nodded again and slipped it away.

"May I ask one last thing before we part?" Elara said.

"Don't worry, Princess. I will keep the location of Atlantis secret."

"Thank you, but I actually had something different in mind."

Columbus smiled. He took her in his arms and kissed her deeply.

COLUMBUS JOINED Dion and his crew at the front of the city.

"Are we ready?" he asked.

"Wee problem," Fanucio said. He was holding the bronze disk in his hand. "The first time we used this, we had a ship."

Columbus grinned. "Leave that to me."

VESPUCCI STARED OVER THE WATER, still bewildered by how he'd gotten into this predicament. After Columbus's second departure, Vespucci had begun whispering in Pinzon's ear, telling him his position would improve greatly if they left the troubled mariner behind. After all, Pinzon had a pocket full of gems, which to his mind was far superior than having to deal with a meddlesome prisoner like Columbus for the next four weeks. Unfortunately, Captain Pinzon had taken his opinion to heart, tossing him in a dinghy with two weeks' provisions before setting course for home.

In the oppressive heat, Vespucci was certain he was going to die. Then bubbles started roiling up around him. All at once, a massive tentacle broke the surface, in its grip a ship with a large mast and a full set of sails. The Athenian vessel from the Temple of Poseidon! Somehow, Columbus had retrieved it.

Once atop the waters, the leviathan released the ship, and Columbus yelled over the side, "Again, sorry about the eye!"

As Columbus's crew cheered and hugged, Vespucci waved both his arms.

"Columbus," he shouted. "Over here!"

Vespucci rowed like mad. As he approached the boat, he saw the Atlantean giant had joined Columbus's crew.

"Vespucci," Columbus said. "Where's Pinzon and the *Pinta*?"

"Headed back to Spain. I decided to remain behind to ensure your safe return."

Columbus smirked. "How chivalrous of you."

"Should I assume that you saved Atlantis?"

"Indeed."

"I even got me golden foot!" Fanucio shouted, plopping the glowing prosthetic atop the gunwale. With a laugh, he pulled his leg back and the foot flew off and plunged into the sea.

"No!" the first mate shouted.

"Well?" Vespucci asked. "What are you waiting for? Help me aboard. That ship and my word should be enough to return you to the good graces of Spain."

"Afraid we're not going back to Spain just yet. You see, the princess gave me a map. Apparently, some leagues due west is a whole new continent, yet unnamed. You know what? I'm going to name it after you."

"Truly? Why, I-I'm flattered—"

"Of course, continents are like women, full of beauty, deep, and undiscovered. So, I think I'll go with the feminine version. *America*."

"You, cur! You—"

Columbus gave the orders to set sail.

Vespucci panicked. "You can't leave me out here! I'll die!"

"A league or two for an explorer like you shouldn't be too much ground to cover. As long as you mind the head wind."

As the ship started to pull away, Vespucci shook his fist.

"You'll pay for this, Columbus. I swear on my life, you'll pay!"

THEY WERE SHORTLY underway when Columbus found his first mate hobbling around on a new wooden peg leg. This one had seven toes.

"Don't look so glum, my friend. We'll have you walking in style again, but next time it'll be more than a golden foot. It'll be two golden boots."

"Pah. We don't even know if this new world exists. And if it does, what's to say there's gold there?"

Columbus unfolded the map, revealing the vague shape of two continents, the lower of which showed a Mesoamerican pyramid colored in gold and the words, *El Dorado* scrawled beneath.

"Call it instinct," Columbus said with a wink. He turned to Nyx behind the wheel.

"Ready, Nyx?"

"Aye, Dad," she replied.

Columbus huffed. "On the ship or when anyone else is around, it's Captain. Unless we're in the presence of royalty. Then, it's *Christopher Columbus, Hero of the Ages*. It's my new catchphrase."

"That's not a catchphrase, it's a title. And a laughable one at that."

"*Hero of the Ages* is laughable?"

"It is for you. Everyone knows I'm the real hero."

"Just because you slammed the trident into that rock doesn't mean you're the hero. I rallied the sirens."

"And I rallied the eldocks."

"But I recovered the keys!"

"With the help of the *Anak-Ta Eleece*."

Fanucio laughed. "She's got you there, Cap'n."

"Don't you have work to do?"

As THE ARGUMENT RESUMED, Dion shook his head, wondering what he'd gotten himself into. Still, it was beautiful up here. The wind in his hair, the water spraying his face. Yes, he could get used to this.

He really could.

DEAR READER

Although Christopher Columbus is a historical figure, I took a lot of liberties in developing his character as well as the world around him. Errors, inaccuracies, infeasibilities, and the occasional *whoopsadaisy* were done in service of keeping the story moving and entertaining. I hope you understand.

Despite this—and some excellent editorial help—grammatical and typographical errors always slip through the cracks. If you notice one (or more), please let me know, and I'll thank you in future updates of the book.

If you're new to my work, I invite you to check out my first trilogy, *the New Chronicles of Robinson Crusoe*, available at Amazon in Kindle and paperback.

Also, please consider signing up for my spam-free "Newsletter"—an email alert you will <u>only</u> receive when I have something new in the works. Your email and personal info will remain completely confidential.

DEAR READER

Click Here to Sign Up
(Link also available at: http://erikjamesrobinson.com)

ACKNOWLEDGMENTS

First and foremost, I'd like to thank the readers that waited patiently for this, my fourth novel. I hope you enjoyed reading it as much as I did writing it. With *the New Chronicles of Robinson Crusoe*, I rarely had the opportunity to to inject humor onto the page, something that's a big part of my life in the real world. I hope the snarky japes and sardonic puns kept most of you smiling.

This time around I relied far more heavily on my beta readers. Phil McGregor, Matt Erwin, Diane Epstein, Jason Templeton, Erik Palma, Fred Shahadi, and Ric Morelli, your advice was invaluable. I'd also like to thank Stacey Broadbent, Petrina Jenkins, Linda Robinson, Matthew FitzSimmons, Stephen Mack Jones, John L. Monk, Sloane Howell, Celia Aaron, Nannette Halliwell, Colt Crawford, Lynn Jorgenson, Vic Bonds, Jai Khanna, Charlie Vignola, and Malk Williams for their continued support.

Lastly, thanks to my family and friends for always keeping my honest and pushing me to be my best. Despite what the experts say, there are still undiscovered places in the world where magic flourishes. It's inside of us. And you keep mine burning brighter and brighter.

Made in the USA
San Bernardino, CA
12 December 2018